FIRE DRAGON

M. KEI

KEIBOOKS
PERRYVILLE, MARYLAND, USA
2012

ISBN 978-0615597706

KEIBOOKS
P O Box 516
Perryville, MD 21903

All poems attributed to the 'ancient poets' are classic Japanese tanka poems. 'Master Kung' is the Chinese name for Confucius.

OTHER BOOKS BY M. KEI

PIRATES OF THE NARROW SEAS

BOOK ONE: THE SALLEE ROVERS
BOOK TWO: MEN OF HONOR
BOOK THREE: IRON MEN
BOOK FOUR: HEART OF OAK

POETRY BY M. KEI

Slow Motion: The Log of a Chesapeake Bay Skipjack
Catzilla: Tanka, Kyoka and Gogyoshi about Cats (editor)
Fire Pearls: Short Masterpieces of the Human Heart (editor)

TABLE OF CONTENTS

Chapter 1: The Untouchable Trade

A haze lay over the town of Low Marsh. It was an early autumn morning and the ground was cracked and hard because it had not rained in several weeks. The haloed moon was particularly bright. Marshes along the river gave off a wet fog that lay in the streets and chilled the early risers as they went to work or market. Farmers pulled heavy carts laden with the year's last harvest into the cities by hand because horses were forbidden to all but the *taran* warriors, or to those special few who had permits. Shuibai hurried along, stepping over the streams of blood that flowed from the butcher shops into the open gutter. Already the flies were gathering, big black flies as long as a man's knuckle that bit and stung when swatted. The acrid smell of charred wood was in the air as charcoal makers fired up their ovens in the nearby woods while darker lines of heavy soot stained the sky as the ironmongers fired their forges. The sound of hammers rang loud as he turned down the Narrow Way with blacksmiths on one side and tanners on the other.

Had he been an educated man he might have been put in mind of the ancient poem, "In the eighth month and the ninth month when the nights are growing long, a thousand times, ten thousand times the fuller's stick beats." But he was not educated; he had grown up in squalor, and squalor was where he continued to live. Dogs and rats scurried beneath the shops in the crawl space between the floor and the ground. In wet weather the raised floors stayed dry while vermin roamed and bred in the filth that accumulated underneath. At such times overflowing privies added their pungent aroma to the ordure of industry and slaughter. Shuibai was glad of the dry weather; when the fall rains finally came the stench would be unbearable.

Unfortunately, fair weather had a price: the neighborhood well was running low. Shuibai hoped it would not give out completely before the rains came. Otherwise he would have to resort to carrying his own scummy water from the river or else buy it from the waterseller. It was bad enough that he had to tip the 'helpers' at the well to draw his own water; in Low Marsh there was no law but the dovetailed corruption of gangsters and Councilwomen. It was just the way things were. The glorious victory of the young Golden Emperor over the Pangu hordes had not changed things one jot. He did not complain, although he often sighed.

He arrived at his shop which was little more than a shed attached to the side of a taller wooden building. It had a thatch roof, a wooden chimney lined with mud, a low hearth and a plain plank floor. He dropped the front panel of the shop to make a counter top, supported by a chain and hook hanging from the eaves. Thus was his shop (little more than a booth) opened for business. He hung a row of buckets across the top of the opening. Buckets were not hard to make, but his were better than the usual homemade buckets; he had riveted them with copper rivets to make them sturdy and almost leak proof. They were brown leather but he had stamped them with his own symbol, a swan carrying a bucket in its beak. It was a pun on the name 'Shuibai,' which his mother had given him in a fit of pretension.

"Good morning, neighbor!" he called as he saw the tanner unlocking her shop across the way. "Buy a bucket?" he called, tying up his green sleeves with an orange cord. Later when it got hot he'd strip to his loincloth, revealing a thin, muscular frame, but for now the morning was chilly.

The tanner shook her head. "I'll make my own if I want one."

"A busy woman like you? Save yourself the time. Only three bronze pennies."

"No need, young man."

"Didn't you hear? The Fire Lord says all houses or shops must have at least three buckets hung on the front gate to be used in case of fire."

She snorted in derision. "The Fire Lord doesn't know that buckets grow legs and wander off on their own. I've seen the bucket gremlins and they do no end of mischief."

Shuibai was taken aback. He didn't know whether she was being sarcastic or superstitious. "I assure you, none of my buckets harbor gremlins," he answered cautiously.

She just laughed and shook her head, a few grey hairs escaping from their pins. "It's another fad from the Capital. It'll blow over like all the others." She waved a tan sleeve at him in parody of courtly manners. "You'll see, young man. There's been at least three Fire Lords in my life, and none of them ever did one jot of good. It's the *taran* way, you know. Put on a mask and play at being important. But down here none of that matters. We're a Free Town. The *taran* have no right to plague us."

Shuibai watched her shut the door. He looked at the hides he'd bought on credit from his sister and thought about the money he owed her. She'd given him a low rate of interest, seeing as how he was her brother, but if nobody bought his buckets he had no way to repay her. He had staked his fortune on the recent decree but nobody in Low Marsh seemed to care. He feared would have to plead with his mother to make good his debt. More than anything in the world he wanted to avoid that. He sat down on the cold hearth and put his head in his hands. Each day he came to his little shop full of hopes, but each day he sold no more than one or two things, and he was rapidly running out of what little money he had. What he was going to do he didn't know.

It occurred to him that perhaps his sister would take buckets or other leather goods in payment or partial payment for his debt. That seemed a hopeful approach, so with his confidence shored up for the moment, he got to work. Musing in his mind he decided to make a couple of leather aprons—that was something that a butcher like his sister would need and might take as payment. If somebody else wanted to buy a leather apron before his debt was due, well, that would be good, too. He unrolled a hide of leather on his low wooden table and laid the muslin pattern on it. He was cutting out the needed pieces when a sharp rapping caught his attention.

He looked up, surprised to see a *taran* official in a richly embroidered coat. The coat was dark purple and grey in a pattern of bricks with a magnificent orange and gold dragon embroidered over the back. The lord wore an orange Dragon mask with gilded features and his long black braid was wrapped once around his neck and hung down the front of his coat. He wore a black cap that peaked high over his forehead and had a long tail covering the back of his neck. His valet held a large lacquered umbrella to protect him from the sun. The lord was accompanied by a staff of two *taran* officers in the same uniform, but with plain orange half masks, and an entourage of eight or so commoners with short hair and no masks, their heads protected from the sun by straw coolie hats. The peasants wore short practical cotton coats in the same uniform as their superiors. Shuibai gaped in astonishment, then realized he must be face to face with the Fire Lord of Alla Far, the man who had been appointed by the Golden Emperor Himself to protect the Capital from the scourge of the Fire Dragon. Shuibai dropped instantly to his knees and kowtowed, putting his face to the floor.

"Get up, I can't see you down there," the Fire Lord snapped. Even when irritated his voice had the cultured tones of high society. Shuibai, accustomed to the coarse dialect of Low Marsh, could barely understand him. The leatherworker remained kneeling on the floor, but lifted his head cautiously.

"Stand up, man. I have business with you."

Shuibai got cautiously to his feet, but stood with shoulders stooped so he did not inadvertently put his head higher than the *taran*. It was difficult because the shop was one step above street level. He crouched awkwardly. He had never been spoken to by a *taran* before; they were rarely seen in the filthy streets of Low Marsh. He said nothing and kept his eyes down.

"Are you the proprietor of this shop?" the Fire Lord demanded.

"Yes, Noble Lord," Shuibai replied, hoping he hadn't done anything wrong.

The *taran* looked Shuibai up and down, noted the simple green willow shirt and knee pants, stooped posture typical of the lowest class, the round head topped with dark brown hair cut just above the collar, and the face with its almond eyes, small nose, and thin mouth, which were pleasant enough features inasmuch as they had not yet been pinched and tanned by years of penury and overwork. Then he surveyed the displayed wares, most of which were buckets, but with a few boxes, purses and other such items. "You are a bucket-maker by trade?"

"Yes, Noble Lord. A leatherworker, actually. I can make many useful things." Shuibai was hedging his bets, uncertain whether it was good or bad to be a bucket-maker at that moment.

Waving a gloved hand, the Fire Lord gestured for one of his commoners to fetch him a bucket. A middle-aged man in a coolie hat handed it to him, and the Fire Lord took it and turned it over, inspecting it carefully. He yanked on the handle, but the handle did not come off. Then he punched the bottom with his fist, but the bottom did not tear out. He twisted and pulled the thing between his silk-gloved hands, but it held together. "Good enough," he judged.

Shuibai gathered that he had just passed some sort of inspection. He didn't dare ask any questions. The unpredictable *taran* were authorized to execute male commoners for their offenses. Women had more rights; an offense that would get a man killed would only get a woman whipped. Shuibai held his tongue and waited. Either the *taran* would make things clear to him or he would not. In either event, he would go away and never come back — if he was to believe the tanner's wisdom. And yet, although Shuibai was startled by the arrival of the Fire Lord, he was not stupid. He knew that simply walking through a vile neighborhood like Low Marsh would require the aristocrat to undergo ritual purification before returning to his usual haunts; something powerful had motivated him to come down on a personal tour of inspection of what was generally regarded as the bunghole of the Two Queendoms.

The Fire Lord chose to enlighten him. "It has been a very dry autumn and many accidental fires have been occurring in the Capital District. Many shops and houses have been lost due to inadequate care on the part of householders. Therefore His Majesty the Golden Emperor has decreed that the Capital's fire laws shall be extended to all of the Capital District. As His Fire Lord, I am charged to enforce His laws. You are aware that the fire code requires each home and shop to keep three buckets readily accessible at all times?"

Shuibai nodded; he had heard the announcement read at the public well. Hence his decision that now was a good time to go into business for himself. Bucket brigades were the only way to fight a fire. That required a lot of buckets.

"In addition, the suburbs are now required to establish fire wards just like the Capital, and Fire Wardens are being selected." The Fire Lord pointed a purple gloved finger at him. "I'm appointing you Fire Warden for Low Marsh."

Shuibai's jaw dropped. "I am not worthy of your attention, Noble Lord," he quickly recited the commoner's stock courtesy whenever addressed by a *taran*. He bowed very deeply and took a step back.

The Fire Lord's mouth smiled grimly beneath the mask. "I have no doubt of that. But you are new in the bucket business, are you not? As Fire Warden it will be within your power to levy fines against property owners who fail to provide the requisite number of buckets. You will profit financially by making certain that all homes and shops have the required number of buckets, and for that reason I expect you will be diligent in the enforcement of the edict. The fines are yours to keep. Use them to defray the cost of carrying out your duties."

The opportunity was quickly apparent to Shuibai's eyes. "Yes, Noble Lord. I understand. I will be zealous in the enforcement of the fire law."

The Fire Lord fished his seal out of his sleeve and one of his retainers opened up a portable writing desk and set it on the counter. The lord quickly wrote out an elegant piece of calligraphy, stamped it with his seal, then nodded. "Present yourself in one month to make a report on conditions in Low Marsh." His nostrils flared. "And make sure you bathe first."

"Yes, Noble Lord."

The Fire Lord mounted up and rode away with his escort, but a tall fireman with a stooped shoulder stayed behind. He waited quietly until the Fire Lord was out of ear shot before speaking to Shuibai. "I'm Mizaka, a fire watchman from Alla Far. That was Captain Chuja Harada, our Fire Lord, and the stout fellow was Fire Chief Byan of Alla Far, in case you didn't know." His voice was mellifluous as if he habitually spent time around *taran* and had picked up their accent. But it was underscored with a note of humor as if he found the whole thing faintly amusing.

Shuibai regarded him carefully. The young man was well dressed in the uptown fashion; he wore a slimmed down version of the divided skirts that the *taran* affected. His pant legs were gathered and tucked into ankle high boots. His uniform jacket was the dusty purple color of the Alla Far uniforms with the orange dragon on his back. His jacket wrapped left over right and was belted in place. He wore a conical straw hat to protect his head from the weather. His nose was long and straight and his eyes were large and almond-shaped. His complexion was olive and his brown hair was cut short and barely visible underneath the hat. His mouth was small and would be the envy of many of women with its perfectly arched upper lip. But he was lame on the left side with a stiff leg and a drawn up arm. The Spirits had made him beautiful, then twisted his frame as if They were jealous of what They had wrought. Shuibai, impressed by the dress and manners that were much more sophisticated than even the prosperous merchant women of his town, thought Mizaka was the most handsome man he had ever met. He avoided looking at the stooped shoulder.

"I'm Shuibai," he said, mesmerized by eyes that regarded the world with a secret humor instead of the coarseness, anger, fear, contempt or weariness that characterized the expressions of most people he knew.

"Yes, I caught that," the fellow replied dryly. Shuibai flushed and felt foolish. Mizaka continued speaking, "The fire code is very simple. Each householder must display three buckets upon the front of the building. Each house of two stories or higher must have a ladder high enough to reach the roof. Chimneys must be cleaned monthly. Hearths must be surrounded by a stone, tile or dirt floor. Fires cannot be left untended. No smoking out of doors." He spoke as if delivering a familiar lecture.

"No smoking outside? Why?"

"Because people are careless when disposing of their pipe embers and the city is made of wood, thatch, and paper."

"Ah."

Mizaka continued, "You are allowed to assess fines of five to fifty pennies for each offense, but you have to allow the householder ten days to correct the problem before collecting. You have the authority to collect fines by force if necessary, and to seize any money or goods equal to the value of the fine if necessary. You should hire a couple of firemen of your own—big brawny fellows —to assist you with the collection of the fines. You'll have to pay their wages out of your own pocket or the revenues you make from your position. You are permitted to wear the uniform of the fire service, but you must purchase it yourself. It is capital offense for any person to interfere with a fireman carrying out his duties—the penalty is death for any man or a whipping for any woman who so interferes, but only a *taran* may administer the penalty. You will deliver a written report once a month to the Fire Lord's office, and you will stay to hear any announcements the Fire Lord has to make and to answer any questions put to you. Do you understand?"

"Yes," said Shuibai. He was a peasant, and an untouchable one at that. But he had just become a man of power in his own neighborhood.

"Good luck. You're going to need it."

"Why?"

A shadow crossed Mizaka's face. "Shuibai, Fire Wardens put their noses into other people's business and assess them fines. People don't like that. Not only that, but sometimes you stumble onto things that people don't want you to see. In the old days if you found anything like that, you were supposed to report it to the Secret Police. But now that the new Black Prince has disbanded the Secret Police, things are not in good order. If it constitutes a fire hazard you can report it to the Fire Lord. Other than that," he shrugged. "Do whatever seems best. But remember, it is always better to err on the side of saving your skin." He drew his crippled arm deeper into the boxy sleeve of the fire coat.

"I can't do this work!" Shuibai wailed plaintively.

Mizaka shrugged his good shoulder. "It doesn't really matter. It's one of those modern ideas from the new Imperial Court. Just go through the motions and they'll be happy. Nobody expects anything more than that."

"If I have any questions, how will I find you?"

Mizaka hesitated, then admitted, "I'm Chief Byan's son. Come up to our house. It's near the Fire Court."

Shuibai immediately bowed deeply. "Please forgive me for my ignorance. I didn't realize you were important."

Mizaka laughed merrily. "Me? I'm just a crippled ex-firefighter and a watchman. I'm not important at all!"

Shuibai straightened up and smiled at the sound of his laughter. "Oh, I'm not important either. My mother was a butcher."

"An honest trade. Why didn't you follow it?"

Shuibai shrugged. "I can't stand blood. Besides, I like making things instead of carving them up."

Mizaka was smiling at him. He raised his right hand to give Shuibai a comradely touch, but Shuibai stepped back. "I'm sorry, I'm untouchable." He did not raise his own hand to meet the other's. He bowed his head.

Mizaka lowered his hand. "Oh. I'm sorry."

"There are lots of untouchables down here in Low Marsh. We work in all the dirty trades. You should be careful who you talk to."

Mizaka answered soberly, "Thank you for warning me."

"Thank you for your help. You have been too kind to me." The words were the rote courtesy people of Shuibai's class always accorded their superiors, but to his surprise, he realized the words were true. He did not like to dwell on why that might be so.

"Think nothing of it," Mizaka replied. "Goodbye and good luck. I mean it." With that he turned and limped away.

Shuibai watched him go. He assumed he would never see the lame firefighter again. There was no reason why somebody of good family with a respectable trade should ever associate with a person of his class. But perhaps when he went up to the Fire Court he would catch a glimpse of him there. The thought made his heart lurch. He had no other friends. He told himself that Mizaka was only doing his job and that if he had known from the start that Shuibai was part of the pariah class, he would not have been so helpful, nor spoken with him for so long. To be a leatherworker was marginally better than being a butcher, but he still traded in the skin of dead animals. The taint would never leave him. He put his head down and went back to work.

CHAPTER 2: HARRIDAN ON THE HOME FRONT

Shuibai closed the shop and hurried home to his mother. His route led up the Narrow Way, across Broad Street, and down the Wet Lane, so called because even in dry weather it was wet due to the bogs. It ran from Low Marsh into the Iris Bottom where the flower growers lived. Cattails stood in many places and circles of cut logs had been laid down to make stepping stones through the worst mud. Carts routinely bogged down. The houses were close together, but not cheek by jowl as in the business district. They had small yards with brush fences, frequently planted with irises or day lilies or other bog plants, alternating with the many compact gardens where herbalists and florists grew plants for market. The Iris Bottom fell just outside of the Low Marsh town limits and still maintained an illusion of rural charm, even as prosperous tradeswomen moved out of the squalor of Low Marsh and built or rented homes in the area. Shuibai's mother, matriarch and tyrant, had bought an old house there; a project enabled by being the mother of four daughters, three of whom were successfully established in some aspect of the meat trade, and each of whom was obliged to surrender half their income to their mother for as long as she lived. Several ex-husbands were unaccounted for, although Shuibai had heard a rumor that his father had joined a construction gang building a highway west to Ton Far during the recent war.

Shuibai removed his muddy wooden sandals before climbing up onto the veranda of his mother's house. He rapped on the door frame and his youngest sister promptly answered. She wore her hair pinned up in a bun; common women were obliged to cut their hair short or pin it up. Pony tails and braids were the *taran* prerogative; loose hair was a sign of mourning. She was dressed in a pale blue robe that reached to her calves with white stockings beneath. A peach-blossom sash finished her ensemble. Her garb was practical, feminine, and modest.

"Elder Brother!" she greeted him. "What brings you home so soon?"

"News. The Fire Lord is making a tour of inspection in Low Marsh."

The shocked look on her face was immediately replaced by panic. "A member of the Celestial Court in our town? What does he want? What is happening?" The arrival of *taran* aristocrats boded no good for the common folk.

"Shush. It is all to my good fortune. Tell our mother I have news for her."

She let him in. Shuibai bowed as he entered his mother's house and resentment flared up in him. He did not have to bow when entering his own shop. He quickly squelched such thoughts. Things were the way they were. There was nothing he could do about it. The rebel's life was not for him.

His mother was sitting and smoking her morning pipe. Her home smelled of the sweet blend of tobacco she preferred. She ascribed to the common belief that tobacco instilled vigor and that smoking the aromatic herb was a sure way to drive away contagion and vermin. At least it masked the stench of the town. Aside from the lingering haze of tobacco smoke, her house was small and neat, kept that way by her youngest daughter, who by tradition would not marry but would care for her mother into her old age, serving as her mother's voice and legs when she was no longer able to terrorize her offspring in person.

Mother was dressed in a dark blue robe with long sleeves. She was sitting cross-legged, the grey stuff of her divided skirt arranged neatly around her. The dark blue robe was patterned with clouds and cranes which combined with the divided skirt patterned with wheels made a literary allusion that was lost on Shuibai. Like most boys he was equipped with only a rudimentary education. The finer arts were thought to be beyond the limited intellectual capabilities of boys. Not that Mother had thought of the allusion herself; the salesgirl had told it to her as a selling point.

He knelt before her and said, "Reverend Mother, I have important news. I have been appointed Fire Warden for Low Marsh by the Fire Lord himself."

"What, when? Preposterous! What nonsense is this?"

"Mother, I assure you it is true. It happened today."

"No one discussed this with me! I am the head of the household; they have no right to make decisions about my family without me!"

Shuibai schooled himself to patience and a bland expression while he explained, "They told me that the capital city's fire code is being extended to all the towns of the Capital District. The Fire Lord will be lord of all the fire companies, not just Alla Far."

"He can't do that. Low Marsh is a Free Town. He has no right to meddle in our affairs. It's against our Charter! This is what happens when a man takes the throne. All the other men get uppity and think they can do as they please!" She glared at him. "You had no right to accept an offer of employment without my permission!"

"I also get to keep all the fines I collect." Shuibai did not even attempt to appeal to her better nature; long experience had taught him that appealing to her avarice was a more effective course of action.

"What?"

He shrugged. "All I have to do is make sure every house and business in Low Marsh has the right number of buckets. I'm sure that when they realize being fined is the penalty, they will happily buy my buckets."

"Yes, well, it appears that bucket-making will prove to be a profitable trade after all. I expect half the profits, just the same as if you were a daughter of mine."

Shuibai didn't remark that he was used to be ignored as a worthless son and would prefer to continue that way. He just sighed and said, "Yes, Mother." Then he asked hopefully, "Reverend Mother, acquiring my uniform and hiring a fireman are going to be expensive, and it will be at least ten days before I can collect any fines to pay for my expenses. Would you be kind enough to assist me?"

She laid her pipe on the four-legged tray at her elbow. She withdrew a bright pink fan from her sash and snapped it open with one sharp motion of her wrist. She fanned herself and stared at the wall behind him while she considered his request. He waited in suspense, a little surprised that he had had the temerity to ask, and even more surprised that she seemed to be considering it. At last she said, "Allow me to make you a gift. I have several old dresses which are too frivolous for a woman of my years."

Shuibai's heart fell. He had hoped for something more substantive than his mother's old clothes. She shouted for her daughter, then gave instructions and the girl went into her mother's room. Shuibai watched the coal in the bowl of the pipe burn itself out. A short while later his younger sister returned with a stack of items in her arms. Mother started pawing through it, tossing garments this way and that. She made her selections and her daughter neatly picked up the discarded items and folded them. His mother stacked things in front of him. "One yellow jacket with camellia blossoms. One ruby brocade divided skirt. One green robe in the willow leaf pattern. One divided skirt in the wheel and spoke pattern. A night quilt in the valley pattern. A pair of wooden sandals, lacquered green. One pink robe in a cherry blossom pattern. One white divided skirt. One white under robe."

He looked at the clothes. The willow leaf robe and wheel patterned thing he could wear and the sleeping quilt was useful. The sandals were quite nice, but the floral robes made his face burn. He and many other poor boys had often worn their sisters' hand-me-down clothes and had taunted one another mercilessly when it happened. *"Choli, choli!"* Male harlot, male harlot.

"Mother, I am a man with my own shop now. It would not be proper for me to wear your clothes any longer. People will think I'm somebody's apprentice instead of a shopkeeper in my own right." He tried to salvage his manly dignity.

She frowned at him. "You're still a boy. You're not even gainfully employed. You owe your sister money. You can't afford to be putting on airs like a swashbuckling gambler. You need to mind your manners and be grateful to your old mother. These are fine gifts!"

He was twenty-three years old and she treated him like he was twelve. He bowed lowly. "Thank you, Reverend Mother. I shall cherish your gift always."

She smiled benevolently at him and waved her hand. "I'll write you a letter of introduction. That will enable you to establish a working relationship with anybody in town. I'll send it over later."

The letter would prove useful; it would certify that he was an honest laborer and not some riffraff or con artist. It would have been more useful if she had done it in the beginning when he was trying to set up shop. His heart burned with resentment, so just for spite he reached into his sleeve and withdrew the Fire Lord's letter of appointment. It had been written with careless haste but the letters were beautifully formed in a running script that he himself could not read. He handed it over to his mother and she took it, laboriously reading the letter silently to herself. Her jaw set and he knew he had wounded her vanity—it took her numerous rewrites to produce a passable hand. She would make him pay for it later, but for the moment it felt good.

She handed it back to him. "You shall erect a prayer stone for the Fire Lord and pray for his wellbeing because of the favor he has shown you," she commented coldly. The stone, the carver, the priestess to consecrate it . . . It all cost money. Money he didn't have. Her revenge had been swift.

"Yes, Reverend Mother," he replied. He said nothing more and took his leave. He did not want to rebel, and yet, whenever she spoke to him like that he was filled with the urge to do the opposite of what she counseled, even though it was a reasonable suggestion. He told himself that if he had been less selfish he would have thought of it himself. The lower classes depended upon the favor and good will of the upper classes, so it was only fitting he should recognize the Fire Lord's generosity. Even so, he did not feel blessed to be noticed in this manner. On the contrary, he felt frightened and worried that it would quickly run him to disaster. When one is a mouse it is better not to be noticed by owls.

CHAPTER 3: FORMAL REALITIES

Shuibai needed money. He walked over to Iron Street and called upon Essen, a blacksmith with whom he was acquainted. He spoke politely to the man, showed him the letter of appointment which the blacksmith couldn't read, and told him that he was in charge of enforcing the fire code in Low Marsh. Essen's face went bland when he heard about the appointment and Shuibai felt a shiver work up his spine. He had become a representative of the Fire Lord and hence the whole *taran* elite. He wasn't sure he liked it.

"Congratulations," Essen replied, his bald pate gleaming in the sunlight. They stood upon the dirt floor in the front room of his shop. It was lit only by the sunlight leaking in from the outside and the glow of the embers within his forge.

Shuibai said, "I wanted to let you know that I have many good buckets for sale, and that if you are in need, you can have them this morning."

Essen's expression hardened, but he nodded politely. "I will buy three new buckets, of course," the blacksmith replied with a small, stiff bow. Always before it had been the young leatherworker who had bowed and agreed politely.

Shuibai was slightly surprised, but pleased, although Essen's manner made him uncomfortable. "I'll bring them over immediately."

"You are too kind," Essen replied, using rote courtesy. "I'll send a boy over with the money and he can bring them back. How much are your buckets?"

"Four pennies each. That would be twelve pennies."

Essen nodded. "A fair price." He seemed relieved. He wiped his hands on his leather apron, then said, "Excuse me. I'll send the boy immediately."

Shuibai walked quickly back to his shop. A boy too young to be an apprentice arrived only moments later with twelve bronze pennies in a small leather purse. He handed the coin purse to Shuibai and said, "Master Essen sends his compliments and begs you keep the purse as a gift."

Shuibai accepted it. "Give him my thanks." He removed three brown buckets from their hooks and gave them to the boy who hung them on his arms. He was an urchin lad, running barefoot, with his shoulder length hair all tangled. His shirt was a tattered bit of cotton that had once been red but had now faded to a faint hazy rose tint. He had no shorts and his legs were skinny. Shuibai said, "Wait a minute."

He went to the stack of clothes his mother had given him. He selected the pink robe and gave it to the boy. "This is for you. You can sleep under it this winter if you're too proud to wear it."

The boy gaped at him, then bobbed up and down rapidly. "Thank you, Master Fire Warden sir, thank you so much!"

Shuibai shooed him away. The boy ran down the street with the buckets dangling from his arms and the robe fluttering over his shoulders. The young Fire Warden was relieved to see the garment disappear; had he worn such a thing in public he could have been mistaken for a prostitute. That would have elevated his status, but he didn't care. He preferred to be the master of his own modest destiny. A successful courtesan might live a life of luxury but was little better than a slave to the one who owned his contract. Shuibai stood a long time watching young men and boys passing by with their heads and backs bowed from weary hours of labor. He vowed silently that he would never, ever, surrender to the will of another. He would starve to death rather than be beholden to a tyrant mistress. He managed to conveniently put his obligations to his mother and sister out of his head.

The novice Fire Warden squared his shoulders, screwed his courage to the sticking point, and set out upon his next errand. He called upon a tinsmith whom he had briefly met but did not know. He politely introduced himself, showed his letter, and told her that she needed to display at least three buckets on her front wall. It took some not so gentle hinting, but she also purchased three new buckets. She did not send a gift, merely handed over the money with a frown upon her brow. Shuibai had to deliver the buckets himself. He visited a few more shops and managed to sell some more buckets.

With more than sixty bronze pennies in a new leather purse Shuibai felt wealthy and decided to hike up to the Fire Court to see about his uniform. It took him several hours of getting lost and pestering people for directions, but at last he found his way. The

Fire Court was a magnificent large compound located a few blocks inside of the Eastern Gate of Alla Far on the Capital Highway. A wall ran around it with a gate large enough to admit four soldiers abreast. The heavy doors with massive iron hinges stood open to reveal a neatly graveled courtyard. The mansion house was two stories tall with a broad veranda running across the front and both wings. A stable was on one side and a barracks on the other. A small gate between the house and stable was topped by the green branches of maple trees, their leaves turning scarlet, indicating the private garden of the master of the house. The Fire Court was more magnificent than anything he had ever seen, and yet, more ordinary. It was a place where men lived and worked, not a palace in a fairy tale.

Well dressed *taran* were going in and out the front gate or lounging on the veranda. Some of the younger *taran* were playing battledore, the colored paddles flashing through the air as the soft cloth ball bounced back and forth among them. They laughed as they ran after the ball and batted it high in the air. Shuibai stood in the street a long time looking in; men at leisure in Low Marsh were rare. They tended to play rougher games, such as a ball game in which the ball carrier was tackled by the other players while he tried to dodge them. Shuibai was afraid to go in. The two *taran* at the gate regarded him askance as he stood there. They wore fire uniform coats over divided skirts of bright colors and the long and short swords of their *taran* rank were in the ready position. Each warrior held a staff topped with a steel hook in their hands, a hook he would later learn was used in tearing down walls while fire fighting. The *taran* themselves did not do any such work but used the hooks as a symbol of their office. They could be used equally well to motivate civilians who were reluctant to volunteer. Shuibai removed his commission paper from his sleeve and approached, extending it before him like a shield, bowing and scraping at every step.

One of the guards took it from him and the gloved hand brushed his fingers by accident. He almost fainted; touching a *taran* without permission was an offense punishable by death. The guard didn't seem to notice and his racing heart slowed. The guard read the letter, showed it to the other guard, then handed it back to him. "What do you want?" The guard's voice was level and flat.

"Please sir, I have been instructed to wear the uniform. Where do I obtain my uniform?"

The guard looked bored. "The establishment of Warani sells them. It's on Cloth Sellers Street."

"I have to buy it?" Shuibai asked, his face falling.

The guard snorted. "Did you think we were going to give it to you?"

"Thank you, sir. I'm sorry to bother you." Shuibai bowed and retreated, then practically ran from the Fire Court without actually entering it. In thirty days he would have to enter and make his report, and if the Fire Lord was unsatisfied with a bumpkin like him, he would be executed and someone else appointed. His stomach tied in knots. He was a fool to have taken the assignment. He had been greedy and short-sighted to see only the profit to himself.

Yet he wouldn't quit. There was something stubborn and angry and hot inside him, no matter how often he shoved it down and bent his head in submission to others.

It took him another hour to find the Street of the Cloth Sellers. It was lined by drygoods merchants and heavily thronged with shoppers, mostly upper class women accompanied by their guards and servants. The women shopped at their leisure while shop girls waited on them. Male porters squatted in the street, content to have a little rest before they were laden down like the beasts of burden they were to carry their mistresses' packages home. The richest women had the handsomest guards and ordered them about as if the warriors were little better than servants themselves. The men bore it patiently; it was the nature of men to be placid in temper while women were fiery. Women ruled; men served. It was the proper way. Shuibai kept his head down as he passed but he felt a rebel to his sex and a traitor to his culture. Or maybe it was just his low birth that made him behave so. In Low Marsh women dominated men, but there were not so many differences between them. Men owned and operated their own workshops and nobody had servants who could stand idly in the street doing nothing. In Low Marsh everybody worked and they worked hard.

The Warani store was huge. It was three stories tall and as wide as three shops. It was bigger than any store in Low Marsh and it was not the largest store on the street. They sold all manner of cloth goods but specialized in fire uniforms. The shop employed half a dozen young women who waited on customers. They greeted him courteously, apparently assuming he was the servant of an important woman. He told them he wanted to buy a fire uniform. A tall willowy woman with her ponytail tied in loop, (thereby skirting the restrictions on commoners wearing their hair down) showed him a fine hemp jacket in the brick pattern, lined in orange cotton, and decorated on the back with a fire dragon in shades of orange and amber, smoke belching from its nostrils. "Will this suit your master?" she asked.

Shuibai's eyes ran over the fine garment. "It is very nice," he replied. "How much is it?"

"Two pieces of silver."

Thirty bronze pennies made up a piece of silver. He had just enough money to make the purchase with a little left over. "Yes, that will be fine," he agreed, trying not to show his shock.

She draped it over her arm and moved to the sashes which were displayed by hooking them to the ceiling beams and letting them hang down like ribbons. "And the sash?"

"He already has a sash he desires to use," Shuibai equivocated. He regretted his extravagance, but was unwilling to lose face by backing out of the sale.

"Very well. Hood? Trousers? Boots?" she asked, looking for more business.

"I was sent only to obtain a jacket," he hastily replied. "But I will tell him that you purvey such wares."

She accepted his bronze pennies and if she thought it strange that his 'master' paid in bronze instead of silver she did not show it by her expression. She wrapped the purchase in a bit of plain gauze to keep it from the dust and tied it with a string. He took his bundle and fled.

Shuibai's mother might have sturdy enough nerves to ape the upper classes, but he was exhausted by the time he reached his shop. He could not even bring himself to open the expensive bundle. He set it aside and laid out a piece of leather to make more buckets. Someone rapped on the shutter while he was putting the handle on a bucket. He unfastened the counter top and lowered it slowly so that he didn't accidentally hit whoever was out there. A young woman dressed in two cotton robes, a pink floral over primrose yellow, was waiting for him. He wondered what her work was. "I have come to buy two buckets," she said haughtily. "Are you the new Fire Warden?"

"I am," he replied. He took down two buckets. He didn't like her attitude, so he told her, "Six pennies each. Twelve pennies total." She paid without comment and took them in her hands. She did not wear gloves, so he knew she was of low birth. He stuck his tongue out at her back as she walked away. He didn't like common folk who put on airs, even though it was a common failing. Many women and even a few men got themselves deeply into debt for clothes and other fashionable items. He promised himself to be frugal and temperate in his taste. The expensive fire coat sat on its shelf and mocked him with his hypocrisy.

He closed the shutter again and finally untied the string and opened up the coat. It was a beautiful heavy thing with boxy long sleeves that came down to his wrists. One of the sleeves was lumpy and he discovered a pair of quilted cotton gauntlets with leather backs inside it. The gauntlets had very long cuffs that ran up his forearms, meaning that his arms were completely protected while fighting a fire. That sent a chill up his spine. He'd served in bucket brigades on several occasions but had never been close enough to a fire to need hand and arm protection.

While he studied the jacket somebody else rapped on the shutter. He let it down again and sold another bucket. Then someone else approached and he sold two. By the end of the day he had sold every bucket he had but one, and it was filled with bronze pennies. He had never seen so much money together in one place. He was afraid to take it with him for fear of being mugged, but likewise, he was afraid to leave it in the shop unattended. There was also the thought that if his mother saw how much money he had, she would take half for herself. It was impious of him to cheat his mother out of her share of his earnings, but all the same, he did not want his mother to know about his small fortune just yet. He closed the shop and sat counting his money. He had over a hundred bronze pennies!

Shuibai wrapped half the coins in a handkerchief that he tucked into his shirt, then hid the bucket under the floorboards and went out. He stopped by a moneychanger and converted the oval bronze pennies into the less bulky silver pennies at a rate of thirty to one, minus the moneychanger's fee. Next he stopped by a noodle shop and splurged by buying himself a carton of hot noodles and vegetables with a little chicken on top. Home again, he hastily checked his money bucket and was relieved that nothing had happened to it while he was out. He ate his dinner and slept in his shop with his arm around the bucket of money and his mother's old quilt wrapped completely around them both. He was discovering that being rich was far more nerve wracking than being poor.

CHAPTER 4: UNWELCOME RECEPTION

Shuibai worked hard for two days, making inspections and selling buckets until he had enough money that he felt he could afford to take half a day off to go up to the city and buy the rest of his uniform. He hiked up to the Warani establishment again where he picked out dark grey-purple trousers, orange lacquered wooden sandals, orange socks, and an orange sash to complete his uniform. They were made out of sturdy hemp fabric. An orange cloth could be tied over his nose and mouth to filter out the smoke. Very practical, as compared to the ornate and precious *taran* masks that covered the upper part of the face and were meant to conceal the wearer's emotions. The *taran* took great pride in stoicism. Shuibai's mother, with her slavish aping of everything that outranked her, had carped on him about the necessity for self-control, although in his case it more often resembled unhappy resignation rather than noble fortitude. Now he appreciated her schooling. Surely if he had been as bad mannered as so many others of his class, he would have offended the Fire Lord and had his head lopped off. Maybe the oppressive way his mother had raised him was right after all.

Clad in his full regalia, he made a self-conscious circuit of the town to post the flyers he'd had printed up by a professional scribe. His first stop was the post station on the Southern Highway where the Imperial Gazette was pasted on the front wall of the compound. The Gazette was another innovation from the Capital; it published the Imperial edicts and other items of note. In this way the people knew what was expected of them and could hope to order their behavior so as to avoid the chastisement of the *taran*. Very sensible, and yet, disquieting. In previous reigns the Sovereign had seemed very far away, irrelevant even. Life in Low Marsh had followed its own seasons and was rarely disturbed by affairs in the Capital.

Shuibai couldn't read the formal script of the *Imperial Gazette*, but if he had, he would have seen that the *Gazette* had duly published his appointment along with the appointments of more than a dozen other fire wardens in suburbs surrounding the capital of Alla Far. He pasted up his flyer among the various notices and advertisements that covered the wall on either side of the gate. His posters were printed in simple block script, "Notice. Shuibai the bucket maker has been appointed Fire Warden for the town of Low Marsh. All persons not displaying three buckets upon their gate or shop front are ordered to report immediately and purchase the requisite number of buckets. Inspections will be held and violators will be fined ten bronze pennies for each omission, as per order of the Fire Lord." It was sealed with Shuibai's own bucket and swan seal stamped in red ink.

His presence on the Southern Highway did not attract much attention, but by the time he reached the well in the Broadway Market, he was in his own neighborhood where he was recognized. It was warm weather and he was overheated in his uniform, but he thought it would be undignified to hike up his skirts the way the working women did, or worse, to strip to his loincloth like a common laborer. There were some young hoodlums on the street. They were dressed in bright colors with the tails of their robes tucked up into their sashes and their arms out of their sleeves so that their clothes were nothing more than a bright wrap of color twisted around their waists. Tattoos patterned their arms and backs so that even stripped to the waist they had an illusion of apparel. They idled in the open facade of a shop, smoking pipes of tobacco or something stronger. They had no visible means of employment.

"Hey Shui-girl, that's a fine set of clothes you've got!" one of them howled. Nervous laughter tittered along the side of the street.

"Hey, gorgeous! Are you the new girl at the whorehouse?" another one called. "I sure do like that fancy dress!"

Shuibai's face burned. He kept walking, face fixed forward, and pretended he didn't hear. Women laughed at him and men grinned at him. Some of the more roisterous young men laughed out loud. Shuibai felt the color mount to his face and for the moment he hated his uniform, hated his job, hated the Fire Lord, and most of all, hated the whole stinking town of Low Marsh that dragged down everything that tried to rise above it.

A sudden burst of laughter broke his composure and he whirled, discovering that a young man dressed in red had stepped into the street and was following along behind him, parodying his stiff-necked posture and making effeminate gestures with his hands. "Stop it!" he snapped. "I was appointed by the Fire Lord himself!"

The young man rolled his eyes and said, "I'm soooo impressed. Did you have tea with the Emperor this morning? Did you kiss His butt before you came down here to grace us with your high and mighty presence?"

The sacrilege shocked him even more than the insult to his own person. "Don't you people care if the city burns?" he demanded. "Don't you understand how important this is?"

The young man snarled, "You're so stuck up. You think a piece of paper makes you better than us? I know you. You're a *butcher's* brat."

Butchers, tanners, garbage collectors, rag pickers, sewer cleaners, and others who dealt with dead or decaying materials were the lowest of the low, the untouchables.

Shuibai reached out and put his hand right in the young man's face, saying, "Now you'll have to be purified before you go home to mother."

The young man punched him in the stomach and the fight was on. Four more ruffians in gaudy clothes swarmed to the aide of their friend, fists and feet flying. He struck back, landing a few solid blows, but received more than he gave. They hit him in the stomach, the face, the back and the groin. They knocked him to the ground and stomped on him and kicked him in the ribs so he rolled to the side, trying to get clear of the flailing feet. They followed him, knocking him down again as he tried to get up, then he cut his hand on a rough hewn foundation stone, and rolled under the floorboards of a shop to escape. He crawled into the dim filthy space with its trash and rat burrows.

"Hey! The rat's crawled into a hole!" They got down on their hands and knees and peered into the crawlspace. He wriggled on his belly, dragging his fancy uniform in the dirt and animal droppings as he crawled frantically through to the other side.

"Go after him," one of the young men urged the others.

"No way I'm going in there. You go in if you want him."

"Hey, let's take a shortcut through Karira's place and catch him on the next street." In a moment they ran off and Shuibai heard the reverberation of their sandaled feet on wooden floors as they rudely ran through the building without removing their shoes. He didn't dare come out on the next street, so he crawled the length of the block and came out on the cross street. Down here some of the shops had shoved trunks and baskets underneath the floor for storage and he was able to slide amid the carelessly stored parcels to escape detection.

He pulled himself out from under the boards and lurched to his feet and held his aching ribs. People passing in the street gave him strange looks. He walked rapidly toward the intersection, only to hear, "There he is! Down this way!" He turned the other way and broke into a run.

The five ruffians took a moment to counsel among themselves. Several of them were satisfied to have put their quarry to ignominious flight, but two of them, including the young man who had accosted Shuibai in the first place and his companion in a yellow shirt, decreed that the matter had to be brought to a more definitive conclusion. They ran after him.

Shuibai reached his shop safely ahead of his hunters, let himself in, and locked it tight. Peeking out the shuttered window he didn't see them and heaved a great sigh of relief. He hoped they had given up the chase. He used the water which he kept by the hearth to wash his face and hands then tried to clean some of the mess from his uniform. Two silver pennies was a dear price to pay for a coat to be worn while crawling through garbage.

A sharp whistle sounded in the street. "Hey, Fire Chief Shuibai!" somebody shouted in a mocking tone. He peered through a crack in the shutters and saw Red Shirt and Yellow Shirt in the street. He kept quiet and hoped they would think he wasn't there.

"Hey! I'm talking to you!" Yellow Shirt yelled.

Shuibai armed himself with a wooden mallet in case they came to the door. Yellow Shirt reached into his sash and took out a pistol that had been hidden by the carelessly worn shirt. He held it in the air beside his head. "Come out, come out, wherever you are!"

At the sight of the gun Shuibai knew he was deep trouble. Gangsters carried guns, newfangled flintlocks made in secret smithies by gunsmiths reputed to be genies, assassins, or outlaws. Guns were everything the *taran* hated about the rebellious and indecorous underclass; *taran* armor was not proof against a bullet. Possession of a gun was punished by death in a particularly hideous fashion. The felon was stripped naked and tied to an X-shaped frame. The barrel was introduced into the vagina if female, or anus if male, and the trigger pulled. The lucky ones bled to death within a matter of minutes; others lingered longer and died of infection after several days. The *taran* hated guns more than they hated anything. Accordingly, the ownership and display of guns was very rare and highly prized among the criminal elements.

Yellow Shirt fired. Shuibai had never heard a gunshot before, but he was certain to never forget the sound. The noise made him jump. Fortunately, the bullet passed harmlessly through the wall near the eaves. The shop was a small space; he didn't know where to hide. But he was certain that if he tried to run they would shoot him. He stayed inside and stayed quiet.

The gangster fired again without taking time to reload and Shuibai flinched badly. He was confused. He had thought the man had only one gun, but perhaps they each had one? Four more shots were fired in rapid succession and he dropped to the floor and put his hands over his ears, certain the end had come. In the hollow silence following the shooting he lay quivering on the floor, wondering why the gangster had stopped. He put his eye to a low knothole and peeked out.

The two men were annoying each other as they tried to open the breech and insert more bullets into the chambers. Red Shirt dropped a bullet and stooped to pick it up. Shuibai had half a chance and he took it. He bolted from the shop and leaped across the Narrow Way into the tanner's shop.

"There he goes!" the gangsters shouted.

The tanner and her apprentices were clustered together watching from behind closed shutters; they were not happy when he tore through their shop and leaped out the back door. He jumped over the fence into the next yard where another tanner would have been at work if she too had not been busy peeking out her shutters at the commotion. Shuibai leaped more fences, glancing over his shoulder to see if he was pursued, but he was not. He came out on Iron Street, and continuing to watch over his shoulder, ran up to the well at the corner of Broadway and Narrow Way where he stopped to catch his breath. He was shaking in terror; he had seen men quarrel and kill each other for reasons as trivial as this, but he had thought his mild temperament would make him an uninteresting target to anyone with a combative personality. Unfortunately, a bully wanting to show off his new weapon needed no provocation. Perhaps the uniform had been provocation enough.

Suddenly the ratcheting clatter of a noise-maker echoed up the narrow street. *Fire.* He turned and saw a trail of smoke etching across the afternoon sky where there had not been one before. The forges and the cook fires marked their own trails; this was one more amongst them. Sick suspicion filled him—they had fired his shop. He didn't dare go down in case they were waiting for him, but if he didn't then his shop would burn and he would lose everything he owned. The dragon on his uniform mocked him; truly it was an all devouring beast that ate up men with fire and fear. He had made a promise and accepted a responsibility he was powerless to fulfill; in a crisis he was a failure, driven from his own shop by hoodlums. He tore his hair and wailed in frustration, wanting to surrender to the hysteria that was the only socially acceptable demonstration of excessive emotion. When the world unraveled, and it often did for people who lived such tightly constrained lives, the mad oblivion of the dervish was the only relief. As Master Kung had said, "In the rites of mourning heart-felt distress is better than observance of detail."

He began to whirl, wailing out his grief and frustration, the sound ripping from his lungs. Passersby avoided him and paid no attention, although some sent him pitying glances. He was oblivious; the hopes and fears of the last few days had succeeded in cracking a constitution inured to hardship. He wailed and whirled; nothing mattered any more. Not the social order, not his own dignity, not his property, not the opinion of his neighbors, not the safety of the town; all was lost in the jumbled maelstrom of misery.

CHAPTER 5: A NARROW FIRE

The alarm was taken up by new voices. People poked their heads into the street and asked, "What's going on?" An apprentice boy ran up the lane crying, "Throw out your buckets! Fire!"

"What, where?" they asked. The gunshots had been heard and general uncertainty reigned. Nobody wanted to venture outside if the gangsters were still about. Invisibility was a survival trait.

The apprentice spotted Shuibai's orange and dusky purple uniform. "Fireman, come quick!" he cried. The boy was a lad of no more than fourteen years dressed in a threadbare floral robe that must be his elder sister's castoff. Shuibai spun to a dizzy stop. He was disoriented and did not answer.

The apprentice ran up to him and bowed. "Mister Firefighter, please come quick! My mother's shop is going to burn!"

"There's nothing I can do," Shuibai said.

"But the buckets," the boy replied.

Shuibai shook himself. He could organize a bucket brigade and pump the well, that would not require him to go near where the brigands might still be lurking. He started down the lane with a fair amount of trepidation. He was dizzy and his head was throbbing. "Throw out your buckets! Form a bucket brigade!" he called. No one paid any attention to him.

He reached the crossing of Iron Street and Narrow Way and halted, peering nervously down the narrow street. Two men with outstretched arms could span it from shop front to shop front. He met the tanner with her apprentices carrying two old wooden buckets they'd had in the shop. "Do something, you useless Fire Warden!" the tanner screamed at him. "My shop will go up too!"

"Stand your ground," he barked at her. "I'm forming a bucket brigade. Form up. Send your apprentices to find more buckets."

At her command the girls started banging on the shutters. "Throw out your buckets!" they cried in their piping, panic-stricken voices. Housekeepers and shopkeepers tossed their buckets out the windows, and about a third of the buckets bore Shuibai's swan and bucket seal. "You men, form a line and pass the water. Women and children form another line, pass the empty buckets up to the well." He shoved buckets towards a tradeswoman dressed in a long navy blue. "My shop," she said. "I have to save my shop!"

"Dammit!" Shuibai swore. "We have to stop it now before it gets a hold!"

"Buckets are useless! The whole block will go! I have to rescue my goods!"

"So help me, I'll slap you if you step out of line!" Shuibai was about to lose his mind with fear and frustration.

She stared at him in shock. "Don't you speak to me that way!"

"It's the Fire Warden," another woman interrupted her.

"I don't care who he is! No man has the right to speak to me like that!"

"Carry the water!" Shuibai begged her. "Please Reverend Mother, carry the goddamn water before the whole block goes up!"

Another shopkeeper was bundling bales onto the backs of her apprentice girls and sending them up the road.

"Everyone has to help!" Shuibai shouted. "If you think only of yourselves, the whole street will go! Work together and we can save all the shops!" The women ignored him and ran into their own shops. They grabbed their tools and goods and flung them into baskets and boxes.

It was several minutes before a bucket full of water was finally passed down the line. Properly there should have been two lines, the men passing the full buckets to the fire while the women and children passed the empty buckets to the well, but there weren't enough people and there weren't enough buckets. They formed a single line, hopping back and forth to pass the full buckets one direction and the empty buckets the other direction. A lot of water was spilled. Shuibai found himself at the foot of the lane, staring at the flaming structure of his shop. The fire had already run across his thatch roof and up the wall of the building to which it was attached. The buildings on this side of the street were tightly clustered two story edifices with shared walls. Shuibai's shop had been a shed added in the corner formed by the imperfect alignment of buildings who shared a back wall. It protruded partway into Crane Street. There were no yards. Crane Street was wide enough to serve as a fire break, but Narrow Way was not; the signs from the shops on both sides practically met in the middle.

Fire consumed the front wall of the shop, burning merrily. The leather hinges that held the shutter closed disintegrated and the shutter fell open, revealing the interior. He had not a moment to lose so he rushed through the door and swept his clothes off the shelf in one lunging grab. Smoke filled the interior and the ceiling dropped fiery brands on his head and shoulders. He grabbed his toolbox and ran out again, clothes trailing and falling on the ground. Somebody hit him in the head and he kicked them, afraid the gangsters had caught him again.

"Your hair's on fire!" a woman yelled at him and hit him again, trying to beat out the fire in his hair with her canvas apron. Burning brands charred his clothes, then suddenly he was drenched with a bucket of cold water. He was intoxicated with terror, but he felt no pain. The whole horrible day was too much. He was standing closest to the fire so the man at the end of the bucket brigade handed him a wooden bucket full of water. He dropped the clothes and toolbox and took the bucket.

He turned and saw the fire was eating into the front facade of the building beside his shop while a light breeze was picking up sparks and sprinkling them across the wooden roofs. The whole block was going to go. There was nothing he could do. But he heaved the water onto the flames anyhow. To his horror, the flames licked over the bucket and scorched his fingers. He yanked away and discovered that a spark had lodged in the tarred rope used to bind the wooden bucket. He spit on it to extinguish it and passed the bucket back again. A leather bucket was handed to him and he tossed the water, feeling like he was shoving his hands into a furnace. He was that close to the flames. The wet leather was more resistant to fire than the old wooden bucket had been and did not catch any sparks. He kept tossing buckets of water as they were handed to him, managing to get his gauntlets onto his hands in between buckets. The heat was getting to him and he started coughing. His eyes and nose ran. He quickly pulled up his hood and covered his face but while it helped, it did not help much. His gauntlets caught fire and he shoved them into the next bucket.

"Dump it on me!" Shuibai told the man. The man, a short old man in a tan shirt, soaked the front of his uniform coat with water. "My sleeves too," Shuibai added in a voice that had been reduced to gravel by the heat he was breathing. A second bucket of water was applied.

The heat was intense. It drove them away, too far away to be able to toss the water on the flames. The brigade broke up as people left to salvage the valuables from their homes and shops. Nobody thought the block could be saved; initial efforts had been too slow and poorly organized. Shuibai saw one woman standing in the street, pointing and ordering the evacuation of her shop. Suddenly the paper cap she wore as part of her coiffure combusted and she shrieked, slapping her head with her hands. More shrieks echoed up the street as her panic caught and people dropped their property and ran headlong. Abandoned furniture and barrels, buckets and bundles remained as obstacles to trip the runners.

"Come back! Come back!" Shuibai shouted.

The women cried, "Dragon! Dragon!" They tore their hair, chignons coming unraveled and streaming over their shoulders, they tore their sleeves and their skin, and when they spilled out into the Broadway they whirled recklessly, crashing into one another, overturning vegetable stands, surrendering to the madness of terror. Shuibai didn't know what to do, but he had to do something. His personal panic had given way to a feeling of desperate urgency; he felt that if only he were smart enough he should be able to think of something to do that would matter.

The smell of burning flesh tainted the air. The butcher shops had caught fire. Shuibai slipped in a bloody runnel in the street and fell, but nobody paid him any attention. Nobody gave him a hand up. The crowd was melting away; each to do whatever she thought best for her own salvation. Gawkers whose property was not threatened stood at the street corner and made bets on how quickly it would jump the street and how far it would run.

Flames leaped three times as high as the roofs of the building, tongues of fire shooting straight up into the still air. Smoke billowed up in a huge column, and sparks and smoke drifted in the tight space. A light breeze carried a few brands across the street where women like insane monkeys wielded buckets and swabs to mop out the landing sparks. The heat was blistering the paint on the facades opposite; if they could be wetted down they would not ignite, but no one could get close enough to do so. The Narrow Way had become an oven.

Shuibai turned and walked up the street. Much to his amazement he found some of his clothes and his toolbox strewn along the way. Some person had scooped up his things, carried them up the block, then dropped them again. He had been lucky;

only his money was lost in the fire. That bucket had been too far away to snatch when he'd jumped into the burning building.

At the intersection he turned and watched the fire leisurely eat its way through the block. It was like watching a gourmet devour his dinner, first tentatively tasting a new dish, then tearing into it and disposing of it in a matter of moments. Sparks popped and brands fell against the facades of the shops. Fire flamed in the cloth curtains hanging in a shop door; the dragon had a toe-hold in new territory. Meanwhile the dervishes whirled and wailed on Broadway.

Shuibai dropped his property on the far side of Broadway, then began gathering up buckets and hanging them over his arm. While the buildings on his side of the Narrow Way were packed close together, the shops on the other side had backyards and a little more space around them. There was even an alley down the middle of the block. "Maybe we can keep it from crossing the alley," he called, but nobody paid any attention to him. A stream of refugees was pouring out of Strait Place, the next street over, pushing or pulling handcarts piled high with property. Women carried children and men staggered under immense bags of household items.

"We have to do something or it'll run all the way to the highway!" he called to them.

Nobody responded. They trudged away, doing what human beings had always done in the face of fire: retreating.

"You can't fight the dragon," somebody told him.

The well in Broadway was a stone construction, about head high, with a stout wooden handle sticking out of one side and a bamboo spigot on the other. A bushel-sized stone trough caught the spillage from the spigot and was used for watering livestock. The buckets could be dipped into the trough to be filled. He was there, all alone, pumping the well when the mounted *taran* officers arrived on the scene.

The Fire Lord was at the head. He kicked his fine white horse around as he surveyed the scene with his curved sword in his hand. He pointed his blade at a man and snapped, "You! Grab that bucket." The man stood gaping. Perhaps he had never seen a live *taran* before. The sword flashed and his head departed his shoulders. "Now!" bellowed the Fire Lord.

People scrambled. They collided with one another and fought over buckets. The mounted *taran* enforced cooperation with the points of their swords as the Fire Lord directed the formation of a new bucket brigade. He didn't even try to save the Narrow Way; he formed the line down the alley. Buckets were dipped and Shuibai pumped as hard as he could.

The Fire Lord pointed his sword at a woman. "You, get a broom." He selected another citizen. "You, get a swab." While he was passing out assignments the regular firemen arrived on foot. They had come at a run but had not been able to keep up with the mounted *taran*. Commoners were forbidden to own horses or even to ride, even if they were firemen on duty. Shuibai recognized Chief Byan, the short burly commoner who had accompanied the Fire Lord the day he had appointed Shuibai as Fire Warden for Low Marsh. It seemed a lifetime ago. The Chief was leading men who carried hooks and ropes over their shoulders; teams of men carried ladders of various lengths. Shuibai had no idea what they intended to do with their tools, but he thought he had better find out.

"I need a break," he gasped, stepping away from the pump. His stomach hurt and he braced his hands on his knees and blew like a spent horse. Another man took his place and pumped violently. He lasted even less time than Shuibai, then he too was swallowing bile to try and keep himself from puking.

Shuibai didn't wait to see who filled in at the pump next; he ran after Chief Byan. The firefighters from the Capital worked with well organized efficiency. They began by soaking each other with water, then went down Narrow Way right into the teeth of the dragon. They threw their ladders against a house two doors down from the fire. They climbed up to toss their hooks over the ridge pole of the house, then a team of men gave a wrenching yank to the rope, and the ridge pole broke, dropping the roof into the house. They tossed their heavy iron hooks into the second floor windows and yanked again, ripping the front off the house. The other three walls sagged in toward the middle, and the hook was once again thrown. More yanking brought down a second wall, bringing a rain of burning embers with it. The other two walls fell like a box folding in on itself and smothered the sparks.

The firemen climbed over the debris to the house behind the demolished house and set their hooks again. They were working in scorching heat and Chief Byan pointed at Shuibai and ordered, "Get us more water! We're burning up down here!"

Shuibai ran up the street, snatched two buckets of water away from the bucket brigade servicing Strait Place, and said, "We need more water down Narrow Lane!"

He ran the water back to the Fire Chief, who soaked two of his men and called for more water. Shuibai ran up the Narrow Way, paused to soak himself at the well, then ran buckets down again, cold water slopping against his legs. Shuibai ran an endless path back and forth to keep the firemen wet down. He had thought pumping was hard work, but forcing himself into the blast furnace heat where the firemen worked was even worse. The heat sucked all the water from his body, leaving him dry and exhausted. It was like a wall he had to push into and the buckets were dead weights dangling at the bottom of his arms. He got blisters on his hands in spite of the gauntlets and his shoulders were wrenched by the constant weight.

As he passed close to a front facade of a shop a rain of embers poured down on him. He cursed and danced, slapping at embers lodging in his coat with wet gloves, extinguishing them with a sizzle. He felt no pain and hoped he was unhurt rather than numb. The embers continued to fall from the eaves in a hellish rain, and looking up, he saw the tall, stooped figure of Mizaka moving across the shingles, wielding a broom to sweep the burning brands from the wooden roof. As long as he kept the sparks moving they didn't catch, but if he didn't move quickly enough, they lodged and kindled the roof, and he had to extinguish the tongues of flames by stomping on them with his boots. If Shuibai looked up he got cinders in his eyes, if he looked down he ran under falling debris, which was usually on fire. But he couldn't stop, he was the only person providing water to the firemen. He kept going. The firemen worked swiftly but never in haste, pacing themselves, knowing they could not overpower the fire dragon. They could only circumvent and confine it.

Finally, many hours later, the fire had burned to smoldering wreckage. Three quarters of the block between Iron Street and Crane Street had burned, and half of the buildings on the opposite side of Narrow Way had been burnt or demolished. Shuibai was utterly exhausted. He walked down the street, red-rimmed eyes glaring at the smoking ruins in stupefaction. When he reached the spot where his shop had stood, nothing remained. Even the roof beams had been consumed. He sifted through the debris with a hook and found it still hot. His arms ached miserably, his neck ached, his lungs ached and he coughed repeatedly. Night had fallen, but he was not chilled, the ruins were hot and kept him warm. He sorted through the ash and charred lumps until he found a cache of round objects. He pulled them out of the debris and into the filthy street. The bronze and silver coins were indistinguishable from one another on account of the soot, but they had survived the heat and not melted into slag. He tossed a little water from a puddle over them and they sizzled. It was like a serpent hissing, or maybe a dragon, though he was not one to indulge in superstitious thoughts.

A clatter of hooves and a shout interrupted him. "You there! No looting!"

Shuibai looked up to see the silver point of the Fire Lord's sword looking him in the eye. "With all due respect, sir, you might as well kill me because I've lost everything. This is all I've got left. This was my shop. Now it's nothing but smoking ruins."

The Fire Lord lowered the blade. "You look familiar. Do I know you?"

"Yes," Shuibai replied with uncharacteristic bluntness. "I'm Shuibai. You appointed me Fire Warden for Low Marsh."

The orange dragon mask hid the Captain's features as he studied Shuibai. "And the fire started here?"

"Yes, Noble Lord. Two men chased me with a gun. When I got away they set fire to my shop. The tanner might know who they were; she was watching through the shutters."

"Guns?" the Captain asked. "Guns are illegal. What kind of guns?"

"A pistol that opened up and had a lot of bullets in it. I never saw anything like it before. They shot my shop and I ran. I'm sorry for being a coward, sir, but I didn't know what else to do."

"How many guns?" The Fire Lord was sheathing his sword.

"I only saw one."

"Who had it?"

"Two men, gangsters by the looks of them. I don't know them."

The Fire Lord gave him a searching look. "Why were they chasing you?"

"Because of the uniform, Noble Lord. They didn't have much respect for the fire service."

The Fire Lord's mouth quirked in twisted smile beneath his mask. "That's an understatement. I haven't been getting the cooperation I would like. In fact—" He broke off before he became too informative. "I expect you to make a full report at the Fire Court tomorrow at noon. This incident must be investigated."

"Yes, Noble Lord. I'm sorry I'm not a very good Fire Warden. I tried to get people to fight the fire, but I was afraid of the gangsters. I didn't know what to do."

"You did as much as could be done, considering the circumstances. You might have done something very important. That revolver you saw—the pistol that opened up and had many bullets inside—is a piece of a dangerous foreign contraband. If you learn anything more about it, let me know. But don't let anyone know you've seen it. Somebody has been a fool, and somebody will pay dearly for it. Keep your mouth shut."

Shuibai was too terrorized to realize the Fire Lord was not threatening him, but merely thinking out loud about the enemy—whomever that might prove to be. Shuibai nodded dumbly, too stunned with weariness to think any further about it. The *taran* wheeled his horse up the lane and Shuibai staggered home to his mother's house.

CHAPTER 6: THE PENALTY FOR ARSON

Shuibai was an hour late to his appointment with the Fire Lord. When he had awakened, his eyes and lungs had hurt and his feet and hands were burned, but he hadn't really noticed until then. Youngest Sister had cleaned his uniform and patched the holes. It was still damp, but it was his only uniform, so he dressed and limped to his appointment. It was mostly dry by the time he got there. He expected to be executed for failure of duty over the burning of the block, so before he left he packaged his blackened coins in a ceramic jar and gave his sister instructions about what to do with the jar in case he didn't return.

The Fire Court was buzzing when he arrived. Many *taran* had come to quiz the firemen and officers who had fought the fire the night before. Wild stories were told; the residents of Low Marsh were castigated for their knavery, the fire was attributed to malicious demons, to a chimney fire, to a drunken revel. Nobody said anything about guns. The Fire Lord was managing to keep that quiet.

Shuibai presented himself at the gate. When the guards realized he was the Fire Warden for the burned district he was suddenly swamped with *taran* who wanted to know how the blaze had started, why didn't he stop it, and was anyone killed. Shuibai was appalled. He had no idea if anyone had been killed. "I am making my report to the Fire Lord," he answered. That was as much as they could get him to say.

He removed his shoes and a female retainer dressed in the uniform of the Fire Guard admitted him to the mansion house. Inside, the house was made of polished wood in the modern fashion, with ceiling beams joined in aesthetically pleasing geometric shapes, rather than in the more functional straight-beamed style which derived its aesthetic value from the way in which the beams were ornamented. The modern style was a mastery of the joiner's art, illustrating the different ways wood could be puzzled together; the artisanship itself was the ornament.

Heavy paper screens of plain white marked off most of the rooms, but in other places, painted screens and even the walls were decorated, usually with landscape scenes. He was taken to an antechamber where brightly garbed warriors waited for their masters. A pair of *taran* Fire Guards stood beside a wall that was a rack for an extensive collection of weapons. Gentlemen did not carry long arms inside, but neither did they leave them unattended. His guide bowed to the weapons rack as did Shuibai; the swords of the *taran* were shown as much respect as the *taran* themselves. Near the swords a small black lacquered table supported an ornate gold incensor made in the shape of a reclining dragon. The incense was placed between its jaws so that it appeared to be breathing smoke. His escort bowed to the woman that was kneeling beside a great double screen, saying, "Here is the Fire Warden from Low Marsh at last."

The waiting woman bowed and slid the screen open so slowly and smoothly it did not even squeak. "Take your place with the other firemen," she instructed him in a low voice.

Shuibai bowed low and stayed hunched, trying to not attract attention as he joined the small crowd in the very large room. He crabbed sideways, trying not to show his back to any of the *taran*, and took his place at the end of the line farthest from the dais of polished wood where the Fire Lord sat. The Fire Lord himself was dressed in formal divided skirts of an iridescent moire silk composed of purple-grey, an orange silk shirt with box kite sleeves, covered over by a long vest in the brick and dragon pattern of the Alla Far fire uniform. He was a mountain of color in a sea of polished wood. His queue was neatly braided and tied at the bottom with an orange silk cord, but his hair was still damp; the Lord had been late to his own audience. Unfortunately, Shuibai had arrived later still, and his tardiness was been noticed.

"Good. Fire Warden Shuibai has joined us at last. He will give his testimony about the fire in his district last night." The rolling syllables of the upper class accent were almost a foreign language to Shuibai's tired mind. The young Fire Warden gulped and knelt at the foot of the aisle formed by the two ranks. He didn't know what else to do; he had never been in a formal audience with anyone higher ranking than his mother. He bowed his face to the floor and waited.

"Get up. We want to hear about the fire." There was a trace of irritation in the Lord's voice. Shuibai lifted his face but remained hunched into as small a bundle as he could manage. "It started when some men mocked the uniform of the fire service," he began.

44

Everyone was staring at him and he wished he could melt through the floor and disappear. He kept his eyes fixed on the floor in front of him. It was easier to speak if he didn't have to look at them.

Gradually, as he told them about the attack in the street and the confrontation at the shop, his words came more easily and he dared to look up. The *taran* wore masks so he couldn't see their expressions, but he felt the atmosphere growing grimmer as he spoke. This did not reassure him and his voice grew fainter.

He said in conclusion, "I don't know if anyone died. I didn't know what to do when the fire started except to make a bucket brigade. The street didn't have enough buckets, even though I've been enforcing the fire laws. People panicked. I didn't know how to make them work. I failed my duty. I'm sorry." He bowed deeply and remained bent over. He wondered if the *taran* would execute him on the spot.

There was a little silence, then the Fire Lord spoke. "On the contrary, I think you performed your duty with more diligence than the average citizen. However, I am concerned about the resistance to my authority."

Shuibai bowed deeply. "Low Marsh is a Free Town. People think you don't have the right to enforce fire laws on them."

The Fire Lord's lips pursed. "The Free Towns are chartered to the Will of the Sovereign. Their recusance is noted, but their rebellion against the law will do them no good."

Chief Byan sat at the head of the line of firemen. While he was neatly dressed, his muscular body was tending to portly and he was a bit rumpled. With his short balding haircut and round features he looked like a bumpkin and not at all like a Chief. Lifting his hand he addressed his lord. "The fact of arson is more important than any grumbling the people of Low Marsh might do. People always grumble. Pay them no mind."

"Did you see them actually set the fire?" The Fire Lord asked.

Shuibai answered,"No, I didn't. But yes, I believe the gangsters did it. They were the only ones there."

The Fire Lord looked around his court. "Chief Byan is correct to point out that arson is the most serious crime a city can suffer. It is the same as attempted murder. Most of a block has been burned out, property lost, livelihoods lost, taxes lost. The offenders will be found and boiled in oil. The punishment must fit the crime. But as heinous a crime as arson is, this crime goes one step further:

45

sedition. It was a deliberate insult to the authority of this office and I will not tolerate it."

It was a fine speech, but Shuibai wondered how the Fire Lord was going to do anything about it. He refrained from voicing his doubts, though. He did not think they would be well-received.

The Fire Lord pointed at one of his *taran*. "You, Tazura-don, take four men and go with him. If the rebels were gangsters you ought to find them roistering in a tavern somewhere." When the man didn't move, he clapped his silk-gloved hands. *"Now, Tazura-don."*

The *taran* bowed low and said, "As you command, My Lord," and scooted back from the line of *taran*. Only then did he rise, back away from the dais, and exit the room.

The Fire Lord pointed at Shuibai. "Go with him. Identify the culprits."

"Yes, Noble Lord." Shuibai backed to the door, slipped on the wooden floor as he turned, and fell out into the antechamber, face burning with embarrassment over his graceless exit. Nobody snickered. He picked himself up and hurried along the hall. He overtook the *taran* Tazura who was pausing in the entrance to don short leather boots with upturned toes.

"You there," the lieutenant said brusquely. "How are you called?"

"Fire Warden Shuibai," he replied.

The man snorted derisively. "Wait here. I'm going to get my armor." Shuibai sat shivering on the front step for thirty minutes before Tazura returned.

When the retainer returned he was well dressed in dark purple armor with orange laces and the jacket of the fire service over it. His flared helmet was dark purple, adorned with the golden horns that were a common form of ornament for the *taran*. His arms and legs were wrapped with studded leather vambraces and cuisses mostly concealed beneath the volume of his clothes. Since he was not wearing the arm panels that gave the *taran* their distinctive winged 'butterfly of war' silhouette, he could almost pass for being unarmored, other than the helmet. But he rotated the sword in his sash from the peaceable position to the ready position. With the curved blade uppermost it could be drawn and extended in one smooth motion that would decapitate his opponent. Shuibai stayed well away from the man. Hot tempered *taran* had been known to cut down a man for no greater insult than that someone had accidentally bumped into them. Striding authoritatively into the yard, Tazura-don started calling names, and in a few minutes had a crew of four men assembled, each armed and armored like himself in the livery of the Fire Court. They mounted up and Shuibai was forced to run alongside their horses as they descended on Low Marsh.

Shuibai started in the neighborhood where he had first been accosted. Looking around, he spotted the teahouse with its open shutters and lolling patrons where the gangsters had been hanging out before pursuing the Fire Warden. The sound of horses' hooves, so rarely heard in Low Marsh, turned people's heads. They clustered near the front of the shops and pretended to window shop while craning their necks under their straw hats to get a better look.

"This place stinks," one of the *taran* muttered, holding his sleeve over his nose. "Don't these people ever wash?"

Shuibai was immured to the smell of slaughter and sweat so that he never noticed them, but coming from the fresh air of the highway and the perfumed enclosure of the Fire Lord's mansion, the stench of poverty hit him like a collapsing house. The clothes on the people were cheap and tawdry compared to the fine clothes of the *taran*. The shops and houses were narrow, dark, and mean. The street was filthy and the dust blew in small whirlwinds, only to be broken up by the trudging crowds in the street. Trash lodged in the crannies along the edge of the road. Shuibai had thought himself poor before, but the disdain of the *taran* let him know he was only quasi-human.

Shuibai walked up to the teahouse. The screens were open to admit the warm sunshine into the front of the room, illuminating cheaply dressed men and women who were lounging about smoking and drinking tea or stronger stuff. Teenage servants, male and female, waited on them, and the patrons fondled or swatted them as the mood struck them. The servants gave no indication that they noticed either. They did their duties with a sullen expression. The teahouse was two storefronts wide and the walls were decorated with posters of famous wrestlers, actors, and beauties. In the back corner a lively dice game was in action. The gamblers, stripped to the waist, were kneeling on the floor, tossing the ivories and betting vigorously, oblivious to the change in the mood of the establishment. Shuibai pointed at the man with his bright blue robe wrapped around his waist who had a courtesan tattooed on his back. "That's one of them. I recognize his tattoo."

The *taran* dismounted in a rush and stormed into the teahouse, overturning the tables and scattering the patrons. Nobody fought back; they all fled. The *taran* cut down several for the simple reason that they didn't get out of the way fast enough. The gamblers jumped up and leaped for the back door. The man in the blue robe, recognizing Shuibai, kicked over a folding screen and ran through the kitchen. He made it into the alley, but the *taran* were after him like hounds after a rabbit, and one *taran*, drawing a small knife from his sash, threw it and it stuck in the gangster's lower back. He stumbled and they pounced on him, rapidly hamstringing him across the back of both thighs so he couldn't run any more, then proceeded to stomp and kick him. He curled up, but they grabbed his legs and spread them, and Lieutenant Tazura stood between his legs and kicked him in the crotch with his pointy-toed boots until the man's loincloth was stained red and he fainted.

Shuibai turned his face aside. The violence numbed him, even though the arsonist deserved it. No one showed themselves as the *taran* dragged the unconscious body back through the teahouse to the main street, though Shuibai felt the weight of watching eyes. In the street Tazura-don tied a rope around the gangster and the body was dragged at his horse's heels.

"Now where?" Lt. Tazura asked, mounting up. His boots were bloody, a fact which Shuibai noticed, but the *taran* apparently did not.

"I don't know," Shuibai replied. "If the other one was here he's sure to have run away. We won't be able to find him."

"Eh? Why didn't you point him out to us?"

"I didn't see him," Shuibai responded, quickly backing out of sword range. "I said that was *one* of them."

"Don't split hairs with me," snapped Tazura-don.

"Perhaps this one will tell us how to find the other one when he wakes up," Shuibai suggested.

Tazura-don's mouth underneath the purple mask was angry. "You better hope he does and right quick, too."

"I will continue looking for the other one," Shuibai promised.

Lt. Tazura whistled to his detail. "Let's take this scum up to the Fire Court." He trotted off, the gangster's limp form dragging and bouncing in the dirt behind him.

When they had gone nobody dared approach Shuibai. He had brought the *taran* to Low Marsh and they in turn had delivered a casually vicious death to several innocent persons as well as the arsonist. He walked home with a heavy heart. All manner of thoughts and emotions troubled him, not the least of which was that the *taran* seemed to have little grasp of the fire service they were supposed to administer. If he was to win the cooperation of the people of Low Marsh, he had to show them that the fire service was a good thing, something that would benefit them all, not just another arbitrary method for the *taran* to abuse the common people.

He turned down the road to his mother's house. The Wet Lane was beautiful. Chrysanthemums and anemones were in bloom, all white and yellow and orange under a brilliant blue sky. The day was crisp, but exercise made his clothes stick to the sweat under his arms and across his back. He stopped to refresh himself at the well. It was a small wooden structure about waist high. It had a bamboo handle and a bamboo spigot. There was no horse trough because horses never came down this way. None of the residents could afford them, even if they could have gotten a permit. He pumped, washed his face and hands, and suddenly stared. Tentatively he took the handle in his hand and pumped it.

The well was a bamboo pipe stuck deep into the ground, pumping the handle caused it to suck up water. Why not pump the water into a gutter to run through the street so the buckets could be filled from the gutter instead of having to be carried for blocks? he wondered. Gravity would carry water downhill from the well. But if pumping sucked the water *up* from the bowels of the earth, wouldn't it be possible to pump the water up a hill? A gutter wouldn't work, but an enclosed bamboo pipe would. What if there were pumps on every corner? Then water could be pumped from place to place as needed by a small crew of men instead of the horde needed to form a bucket brigade. The pipes lying in the street would be a nuisance, but fires were a worse nuisance. When the alarm was sounded he could send men to pump the well, which would fill the pipes, which would pour out the end to fill the buckets to fling on the fire. It could work!

CHAPTER 7: ODD LOTS

Shuibai did not want to live with his mother anymore. He rented a new shop composed of two rooms in a narrow lane off the Low Road. The new shop was entered by a small dirt-floored vestibule containing rickety steps leading up to the apartments overhead, the entrance to the shop next to his, and his own door. During good weather most of the front wall of his shop could be slid back on runners to open the interior to the street. The floor was of wood worn gray with age, as was all the woodwork in the place, although in places traces of white paint lingered. Once it had had a fresh and tidy appearance, but now it had the patina of age that some aesthetes found quaintly rustic, although others found it grimy.

The kitchen in the rear was very modern much to Shuibai's delight. It was floored with dirt and contained a simple brick hearth with a mud-lined chimney. The chimney occupied the middle of the room and the brick hearth extended to the side to provide a work space. Vegetables could be chopped right there and slid into a cooking pot on the fire. It was very convenient. The kitchen also had a built-in wooden cupboard whose broken hinges he fixed, a wooden sink with a drain that ran through the wall into the gutter in the backyard, and a wooden counter top with pot storage underneath. The back door opened into a rather wide alley almost big enough to be called a street. The alley provided space for the residents of the many little shops and apartments to do their laundry in tubs in the yard and hang their cheap cotton garments on crisscrossing clotheslines. A privy at the bottom of the alley dumped its effluvia directly into the river. The ground sloped downward and rain had eroded a gash down the middle of the alley which served as a gutter, although it was now choked by debris of various sorts. Shuibai did not look too closely to identify either the objects or the stinks emanating from it. Tendrils of ghostly mist rose from the marsh, bringing with it the dead, damp smell of vegetation surrendering to autumn, and the cries of loons whose manic calls disturbed the people's sleep. Dampness crept through everything and made the bones of old people ache.

Shuibai thought it was paradise.

He scavenged his tool box, clothes, and quilt from the Narrow Way. They were filthy with soot and mud which explained why nobody had bothered to steal them. He hired a laundress to clean them. He bought a thin mattress and dishes from a second hand dealer. While the clerk was rolling up the mattress and tying it with a string, he browsed the rest of the store. One curious item caught his attention: it was a trunk of foreign manufacture. Opening it up he found part of a green and purple uniform, some tent stakes, a beaded vest, and narrow pair of trousers that would have indecently hugged the legs of anyone who wore them. The trunk was a real oddity.

"What is all this stuff?" he asked the dealer.

The proprietress was a tall thin woman with her hair pinned up at the back of her head. Her temples were going grey, which gave her a distinguished look. Her clothes were dark and sober, brown and rust in color, old and neat, formerly of respectable quality. Her face was as worn as her clothes and her whole person had an aura of genteel poverty. There were several customers in the shop, picking through neat stacks of used clothing, shelves of housewares, and other items.

"Junk left from the campaign in the Barren Lands. Military salvage. The *taran* were cleaning out a storehouse and gave the junk to anyone who wanted to haul it away. I took as much as I could carry. I've sold most of the good stuff out of it already."

He picked through the junk with a fair amount of curiosity. The gaudy bits of old uniforms and mixed up pieces of foreign clothes gave the whole chest a distinctly romantic appeal. Heroes had worn these clothes, heroes and exotic foreign spies perhaps. Stale incense wafted up from the items and he fancied he could smell blood and brimstone. "How much for the lot?" he asked impulsively.

The dealer ran her hands through the debris. "The uniforms aren't worth anything, but maybe you can use them as rags," she said. "There's not more than two or three decent pieces in here, and a few useful accessories." She picked out a large paper fan and tried to snap it open, but it was stuck closed. It was light grey with a silver foil edge. She tossed it back down into the trunk. "The trunk alone is worth forty bronze pennies," she announced.

"Ah, I don't want the trunk. I'm just curious about the stuff in it."

She overturned the trunk spilling the garments and a few other objects onto the floor. Setting the trunk aside she sorted through the little stuff that had been in the bottom. It consisted of worn down wooden sandals with purple thongs, a battered metal canteen, a dented green half mask, and a few other nearly useless items. "Twenty-five pennies for the lot."

Shuibai looked through his purse. "I've only got eighteen left. Will you take it? I've already bought the dishes and mattress from you, after all. It didn't cost you anything, so it's all profit for you."

She held out her hand. "I'll take it."

He poured the coins into her palm and then used a dirty lavender under-robe that was in the mess to bundle them all together. The pieces of uniform were green with large violet irises, faded and stained. Since the uniform was made of sturdy hemp cloth, he used it to wrap his dishes against breakage. He did not stop to ponder the irony of a once glorious uniform being used as nothing more than packaging for second hand dishes for an untouchable in a slum. Neither did it occur to him to wonder how the garments of a Pangu soldier had wound up mixed together with the old uniform of a soldier of the Iris Battalion. The stuff was salvage. After a battle whatever might be useful had been picked off the field, dumped together, put in storage, and two years later, since it hadn't been wanted, dumped. Had he been of a philosophical turn of mind, he might have marveled how once a man or woman had worn the beaded vest, a foreigner to be sure, but somebody who had once loved and struggled, then died far from home, only to be stripped by the conquerors and left naked on the field of battle, eventually to be reduced to bones by the buzzards and small creeping things. Such things never entered Shuibai's mind; no, not even when he accidentally stepped upon some loose glass beads, crushing them under his foot.

He lugged his purchases home. He could patch the uniform bits together to make a crazy quilt. He'd have to cut up the pieces so it wasn't obvious it was Iris Battalion fabric, but that was all right. He'd have to mix it with some other old fabric to get a piece big enough for a coverlet anyhow. A worn out blanket would serve as the batting and the lavender robe could be pulled apart and restitched flat for a lining once it was cleaned. If the stains wouldn't come out, it didn't matter. They'd be on the underside where they weren't seen. The lavender robe was silk and would feel nice to sleep with. He didn't own anything made of silk. He poked his hand into the bundle and felt the soft, supple cloth. Oh yes, a man could get used to luxury like that!

At home he opened his package, folded and stacked the uniform bits with the beaded vest on top. The foreign garment was composed of black fabric supporting white, orange and black beads in geometric patterns that were alien to his eye, but interesting to look at nonetheless. He wasn't sure what to do with it. Maybe he'd turn it into a trivet. The canteen was a useful thing. He checked to make certain it didn't leak. He had to clean it out by boiling vinegar in it, but once he did, he could make a leather cover for it to hide its dented and scratched sides. It would have cost him eight or ten pennies to buy a new canteen. After his experience fighting a fire, he thought it would be handy to carry his own drinking water.

He held the stuck fan in the steam over his tea kettle and gradually was able to loosen it without damaging it. It was quite elegant and made of a paper of such high quality that it almost appeared to be made of a heavy silk fabric. It was dirty with old mud and there was a footprint on the lacquer as if it had been stepped on, but he was able to clean it up. The smell of a good grade of sandalwood still clung to the fan. He opened it carefully. It was stiff with disuse but had remained tightly shut all this time, protecting the decorated surface. It had calligraphy in black ink on one side and a crescent moon, which was the symbol of the Silver Princess, on the other side. Considering that She had not been born until after the war, it could not possibly have belonged to the infant princess. Still, it was a fine thing. He fancied that perhaps a lady of the Court had noticed a dashing young soldier of the Iris Battalion and sent it to him as a gift. Such gestures were an accepted part of upper class flirting rituals, or so the stories said. Now it belonged to an untouchable. If Shuibai got desperate he might be able to sell the fan for money. He set it aside in a safe place.

Shuibai bought more hides on credit from his elder sister and begged her not to tell their mother that he had done so. She agreed, provided he made payment in a month. Over the next several days he thought hard while he made buckets. He had not levied any fines, so he did not see why he was unpopular. He thought about his plan for pumps on every corner and wondered if the people would laugh at him. Tucked down there on the side street he didn't sell many buckets, though he dutifully called upon his neighbors and exhorted them in the name of the law. He made some other things, such as little boxes, purses, snuff and tobacco pouches. A week whiled itself away in this unsatisfying manner, and he realized that like it or not, he was going to have to levy some fines on his uncooperative neighbors—a deed that would serve to make him only more unpopular. Yet if he didn't levy any fines, what would he report to the Fire Lord at the end of the month?

He sat with his mother's painstaking written letter of introduction and read it over and over again, but it did not hearten him any. It was traditional for mothers to make disparaging remarks about their sons when trying to obtain employment for them; really it was a great favor for a shopkeeper or tradeswoman to take on somebody who would require a great deal of effort to train in a trade when the apprentice or employee might never amount to anything. All the same, Shuibai wondered if other mothers were quite so harsh on their sons.

He thought about going to the crime boss of Low Marsh without a letter and simply introducing himself as the Fire Warden to ask for his help and protection. Jozatha, who reputedly knew everything about everyone, would most likely view that as a surrender. And in fact, it would be. Asking the gangster for help or protection would require giving him a gift, say, a portion of the proceeds of his office. Graft was a fact of life.

Shuibai sat a long time weighing the possibilities and concluded that his life was equally at risk no matter who was his master. Yet the Fire Lord's ambition seemed to Shuibai plain and laudable, whereas the ambition of the gangster boss was unknown but shady. The virtue of the law did not weigh much into his considerations; it was as arbitrary and abstract as the *taran* concept of justice—a thing to be endured rather than understood.

CHAPTER 8: LESSONS

Shuibai inquired at the Fire Court and was given directions that led down a nearby side street to Chief Byan's home. The neighborhood was much nicer than Low Marsh, though not so elegant as the handsome houses that lined the highway where the Fire Lord lived. The barracks housed the families of employees and servants that worked in the big mansion houses; in addition there were apartment houses and townhouses with gardens where low level *taran* retainers resided. Chief Byan lived in a modest, well-kept rowhouse at the end of a street with a small garden surrounded by a rustic fence. A gate opened into the garden, where vegetables, flowers, herbs, and shrubs were mixed together in a garden that was more useful than attractive. Shuibai preferred it to the sculpted perfection of the gardens of the *taran*, which he had glimpsed as he traveled through the better neighborhoods. The spindly pot of ginseng on the doorstep let him know he was among people of his own class.

A medium size tan dog with bristly hair jumped up on him as he let himself in the gate. The dog barked joyfully and was duly ignored by a large cat with white ears on a black body who was sunning herself near the gate. Shuibai paused to offer his hand to the cat, and she sniffed it delicately. He stroked her back and scratched her behind the ears in the spot that made her twist her head as far around as it would go. A little pink tongue protruded between her white fangs in a happy cat smile. The dog kept barking and children ran to the door and peeked out from under the curtain, then ran crying, "Gramma Gramma Gramma! Somebody's here!"

He walked up to the door and rapped politely on the doorframe. A minute later the curtain was drawn aside by a grey haired woman with limp breasts and bony, precise hands. She was dressed in a tasteful dark grey robe with the sleeves tied up with a black string. Her face was lined and she wore her hair cut shoulder length with bangs across her forehead. She held aside the curtain while she surveyed Shuibai from head to footg. "Yes?" she asked.

He bowed politely. "I'm looking for Chief Byan. Is this his house?"

"It is. I'm Miryem, his future widow," she replied humorously. "Are you a firefighter?"

"Yes. I'm Fire Warden Shuibai from Low Marsh."

"Please come in, Fire Warden."

He left his sandals in the vestibule and stepped up onto the wooden floor. Balls and dolls and battledores were strewn across the floor. The black and white cat wended her way through the mess to sniff his socks contemplatively. Deciding that he was an unowned human, she rubbed her head against his ankle to mark him as part of her property.

"Please watch your step," Miryem said needlessly. "The grandchildren are everywhere."

Inside the house was well worn and comfy; the main room's floor was supposed to be covered with thick straw mats and provided with bright cushions for sitting on and elbow rests for leaning on, but the children had assembled them into something resembling a fort. The walls of the room were lined with many woodblock prints featuring actors and courtesans. Shuibai noticed they were from one publishing house. "Is that your shop?" he asked.

"No, but I work there. I'm the principal block carver, as Chief Byan can attest." Again the good natured jest. Shuibai smiled in spite of himself, though he wasn't sure what the joke was. She continued speaking, "Please be seated. I'll send Mizaka-don to see you, maybe he can help. Chief Byan won't be home for a while yet. I'll fix some tea."

"Thank you." He selected a bright orange cushion from the pile and sat on it, only to hear a wail from the kitchen, "Gramma, he broke my fort!" He stood up hastily. The old woman entered the kitchen with dignified haste, hushing whoever it was that had complained. A moment later he heard her singing up the stairs, "Zashi-lan, a fireman has come to see the Chief. Will you come down, please?"

At that moment Shuibai would have given everything he owned to have traded places with the Chief's son. The home was comfortable and happy and he never wanted to leave.

Mizaka descended the steps. He was, or had been at one time, a tall handsome young man with a supple frame and an intelligent face. He wore his hair cut short just above his shoulders. It was a glossy dark brown with auburn highlights and thick bangs which covered his eyebrows. His grey eyes were surrounded by lines of strain, and he walked with his left shoulder hunched up and his left hand pulled up inside the sleeve of his grey star-flecked shirt. He wore dark grey trousers in the new style that was more economical of fabric than the usual divided skirt. A scar marred the left side of his face along the jaw, extending up in front of his ear. He cocked his head to the left so that Shuibai could not see the scar. He limped across the floor and stood with his left side turned partly away. He was the fireman who had recited the law to him the day he was appointed Fire Warden and who had swept the roofs during the Narrow Way fire, but without his uniform Shuibai realized how extensive his crippling and disfigurement were.

"Fire Warden Shuibai," Mizaka said in a strained voice. "What brings you here?"

Shuibai swallowed. He tried not to stare. "I needed to ask some questions about the fire service. The Old Woman said you might could help me." 'Old Woman' was a respectful title; it would have been forward of him to call her by name when she was so much older than he.

Mizaka looked him up and down, then nodded. "What did you want to know?"

"Everything," Shuibai blurted out honestly enough.

Mizaka almost smiled, an expression Shuibai thought was probably foreign to the scarred face. "That will take a while," he commented. "Why don't we sit down?"

They sat down. Mizaka pushed away the toys and pillows to make a space for men to talk of manly things. He retrieved a small wooden table that the children had hijacked and put it between them. Miryem entered with a ceramic teapot painted all over with flowers and birds. She knelt and poured tea with dexterous hands. The old woman and her youngest son looked a lot alike, but where her motions were deft, her son's movements were carefully controlled. Her expression was grave, his was melancholy, and where light twinkled in her eyes as if she had just thought of something funny, his were etched with suffering. They both had lines on their foreheads, even though he was half her age. His youth had been stolen from him while she was settling into a contented old age.

"I'll leave the pot for your conversation," she said. She rose and glided away with a rustle of skirts. The smell of ink remained when she had gone.

"So, you want to know everything I know? I've been raised to it ever since I was little. Chief Byan has been a firefighter for all the years I've been alive, and so are each of his sons."

"Please, I know it's a lot to ask, but I don't know anything. I wonder if the Fire Lord knows how little I know, or if he cares."

"Oh, he knows you don't know anything. He doesn't expect anything of you, either. He handed you a sinecure. It's all politics. He's just trying to curry favor at the Imperial Court; he doesn't have to actually accomplish anything. The Black Prince backs him, but the prince is a foreigner from Pangu and has crazy ideas. They say He's even trying to convince the Golden Emperor to put a tile roof on the palace when everybody knows that the palace has always had a bark roof. Lady Nayabashi is arguing for *sanaka*, tradition. It would be impious and bad luck if they changed the old ways of doing things. Nayabashi is a lady of the old school, a very staunch supporter of the former Empress.

"But the Golden Empress has been dead for three years," Shuibai replied in bewilderment.

"Which must be terribly inconvenient for Lady Nayabashi," Mizaka said humorously.

"But what's that got to do with fire fighting?"

"Not a blessed thing, which is precisely my point."

Shuibai was learning his lessons all right, and he didn't like it. "Doesn't anybody care if the city burns down? I was there! I could have stopped it if I'd known what to do!"

"Don't tell me you take this seriously?"

"But of course I do! It's important!"

Mizaka got a bemused look on his face. "Heaven help us, we have an idealist on our hands."

Shuibai was so frustrated he didn't know what to say or do. "You're a firefighter, so you have to take it seriously, don't you?"

Mizaka stared back at him for a long moment, then he lowered his eyes. After a moment he said, "Yes, I do, but I don't expect anyone else to. I have my own reasons for doing what I do." Then he extended his left hand.

The hand was burned and healed. The scars bound the fingers together like a mitten. He opened and closed his hand a few times, showing that the fingers could not move independently of one another. His hand remained in a perpetually cupped position. Then he lifted his sleeve and showed Shuibai the mass of scars running up his arm. With a gesture he pointed up his arm to his neck, and turned his head to show the scar on his left cheek, then gestured over his back and along his left ribs and leg.

"The Dragon got me," he said simply. "I lost my regular job because it took me so long to recuperate. My mother tried to get it back for me, but they'd replaced me. And then there is my melancholy and sarcastic nature which does not endear me to potential employers. So my father got me a job as a fire watchman, which pays poorly enough, but it pays. So I spend my nights freezing in the winter and boiling in the summer, stuck up in the watchtower, ringing out the alarms."

Mizaka pulled his sleeve down and covered his arm again, tucking the maimed hand back inside the voluminous sleeve. "I've seen the Dragon gloating overhead as I overhauled debris and found the bones of children. I've seen neighbors fling a man into the flames because he had a box of those new sulfur matches and they blamed him for arson." He was rocking back and forth, soothing himself with a motion remembered from childhood. "Oh, I take it seriously all right. But that's not the way the *taran* see it and you must never fool yourself into believing that Fire Lord Chuja cares about anything more than his own advancement at court."

"I understand," Shuibai whispered. "But what can I do? Tell me how to make it stop."

Mizaka talked at length. Simply put, watchmen like Mizaka watched at night because chimney and roof fires were the most common cause of fire. Such fires could spread easily before the sleeping inhabitants were ever aware of the dragon stalking across their roofs. They might never waken and their charred bones would be found amid the ashes of their beds. Upon spotting a fire, the watchman hammered an alarm code on the bell which told the volunteers where the fire was. They turned out with axes and ladders and other implements of destruction because demolishing the burning structures was the only way they had to prevent the fire from spreading. There was rarely any chance of saving a structure once it had caught; extinguishing implements were simply too primitive. A bucket brigade would be formed by civilians who would provide the water necessary to wet down the debris and prevent it from sparking. Firefighters would climb up on roofs to sweep away the embers and watch for fires in case the flames leaped.

Firemen were also responsible for policing their neighborhood with respect to the fire code. The fire watchmen and firefighters were under the Fire Warden for the district. Byan was the Chief Fire Warden of Alla Far, generally just called, 'The Chief,' and the Fire Lord normally left the firefighting to him and his men. The Fire Lord's job was to prevent looting which was the usual consequence of a major fire, to force reluctant citizens to participate in the bucket brigades, to punish arsonists and those judged negligent, to perform traffic control and so forth. Irate property owners sometimes tried to prevent firefighters from demolishing their property; such resistance was ended on the point of a *taran* sword.

Firefighters were volunteers who worked a regular job and reported when the alarm sounded; they were fined or whipped if they missed a fire. The watchmen were paid to watch every night, no matter how foul the weather, but in point of practice a good many kept their watches in a nearby tavern or teahouse. The watchman's job, being sedentary, usually went to injured or disabled firefighters. It didn't pay much, but it was the closest they had to a pension.

"If that isn't enough," Mizaka said, "You'll find only the lowest of the low—" he paused a moment as he realized his guest was a member of the class to whom he referred, "That is to say, the work is hard and dirty, so you'll find no reputable men willing to do the work. Firemen are almost always drawn from the laboring class, and are generally men who are used to getting dirty and wet and working outdoors in all kinds of weather. They tend to be rowdy, but if you can win their respect they are diligent and loyal, although they do need supervision."

"How do I win their respect?"

"Set a good example. Shirk nothing. They won't do what you won't do, not in the teeth of the dragon they won't. It's like going into battle. The brave lead and the foolish follow."

The front gate banged open and the dog started barking and the children pelted out the door and into the garden. A booming laugh rang through the yard and the dog yipped frantically. The children shrieked in delight and a faint smile came over Mizaka's face. "Chief Byan is home."

A savory smell floated in from the kitchen and Shuibai's mouth watered. Chicken, he thought, glad to discover the Old Woman kept a pagan household. He wondered if he lingered long enough would he be invited to dinner? But that would be intruding, so he rose and said, "Well, I don't want to be underfoot when the family comes home."

Mizaka got to his feet awkwardly as if his side pained him. "Be careful you don't get run over on the way out," he said lightly, showing a trace of his mother's sense of humor.

Shuibai liked it when Mizaka's face eased and he was not being cynical or guarded. He looked at Mizaka, really looked at him, and memorized the details. Mizaka had a thin nose, sensuous lips and fine almond eyes. His jaw was strong and cleanly shaved. He was trim in body, and would have had a stately presence like his mother if he had been allowed to grow old gracefully. Shuibai didn't notice the scar anymore. He thought Mizaka very handsome.

"Perhaps I can call on you again. You have been very helpful to me."

Mizaka seemed pleased at the remark. "It's little enough I can do." He shifted the injured shoulder unconsciously. "I'm glad somebody has a use for me."

Chief Byan pushed through the curtain into the room. He was shorter, fatter, and crasser than his son, which all added up to him being a burly, good-natured peasant completely different from his much older wife. "Zashi-lan, I see we have company," he addressed his grown son by his childhood nickname. "Good day to you, Fire Warden Shuibai. What brings you uptown?"

"The simpleton has been touched in the head. He wants to be a firefighter," Mizaka joked.

Byan laughed. "Does he?" He eyed Shuibai. "That would be unusual in a political appointee."

Shuibai's face burned. "I admit I'm not experienced in the job, but I think it's important. I've seen the devastation of fire first hand, and—"

"Peace." The Chief patted him on the shoulder. "We're teasing you. You have to be a little crazy to do this kind of work."

"I don't see what's crazy about trying to keep the city from burning down," Shuibai grumbled.

Mizaka said, "Only a crazy man would run into a burning building when everybody else is running out."

Shuibai wasn't certain if Mizaka was joking with him or not.

"Where's my pipe?" Chief Byan asked his son. Mizaka lifted it down from the shelf. Byan settled down amid the cushions and toys and packed the bowl with loose tobacco, then took one of the expensive sulfur-tipped matches that had recently become available and held it in his fingers. "Where does fire come from, Fire Warden Shuibai?"

"I don't know. Some people say dragons."

Mizaka and Shuibai settled down across from him. Chief Byan flicked the match with his thumbnail. The match flared and hissed, then settled into a steady burning flame. "Humans." They waited while he touched the flame to the tobacco. "Why do humans make fire?"

"Because it's useful?" Shuibai answered.

"Because it's beautiful," Mizaka answered almost at the same instant.

Chief Byan puffed on his pipe until it was burning well, then he held the dwindling match before their faces. "Fire is many things. If you let your attention wander for one instant," the match burned to within a hair's breadth of his fingertip before he shook it out. "It turns on you. Like an unfaithful woman or a treacherous employer, but we never want to believe the bad along with the good. We think our own fire will not sting us. But we are fools."

He laid the burnt match in the ceramic ashtray. "There is no man or woman who will tolerate being told that they are idiots. Hence, they hate the fire service. We check their chimneys to make sure they keep them clean and fine them when they do not. We count their buckets and ladders and make them change the way they live. We make them haul water until they drop, but we still can't save their homes and shops. We can't win. The fire is always first, and it always destroys something before we get it under control. The people never count what we have saved and always weep for what is lost. That's the way it is and always has been, Fire Warden Shuibai."

Silence fell. A tendril of blue smoke spiraled up from Byan's pipe. He waved his hand through it. "Look at this. How many fires are started by smokers? As many as are started by chimney sparks. But still I smoke. I know I'm going to burn myself out of house and home some day, but I can't stay away from the stuff. A few weeks, maybe a month or two, then I reach for the tobacco. Do you smoke, Fire Warden Shuibai?"

"No."

"Good. Don't start."

That was the sum total of Byan's advice. Shuibai wasn't sure it was helpful. He mulled over the many things that had been said to him as he took his leave. Mizaka walked him to the gate. Children were running down the street, rolling hoops ahead of them, their short robes flapping around their skinny legs and their long ponytails flying in disarray. Strict rules were not applied to children. In fact, very few rules applied to children. They were simply let run until it was time to be adults. It was a pleasant scene, but lifting his eyes Shuibai saw the tall wooden skeleton of a fire watchtower behind the row of houses. Seeing the direction of his gaze, Mizaka said, "I'll have to get my supper and go to work. It'll be another dry night, I imagine, which is comfortable from my point of view, but bad for fires."

"Does your wife mind you being gone all night?"

"I'm not married," Mizaka replied, suddenly distant.

"Oh, I thought those were your children."

"No, they're my brother's. I'm the last one, the unmarried one, so it looks like I'll be looking after our Reverend Mother in the last years of her life. Which is not a bad fate for a crippled man."

"Oh." Shuibai didn't know what to say to that, but he was relieved that Mizaka wasn't married. "Would you like to come watch birds at the Lantern Bridge?" he asked. It unnerved him almost as much to ask as it had unnerved him to be called before the Fire Lord. Fortunately, Mizaka was a commoner and therefore would not kill him if he made a mistake. Laugh at him, perhaps, but having been humiliated and beaten in the street, Shuibai was not afraid of little things anymore. Short of dying, he didn't think anything worse could happen to him. He was mistaken, but it would be a while before he learned that.

Mizaka looked vaguely surprised. He considered the idea. "There's a poem about viewing cranes from the Lantern Bridge, isn't there?"

"I don't know, I suppose there is." Shuibai's ears burned. He didn't want to appear the bumpkin before a man who was even better educated than his mother. "The view is very nice at sunset," he added enticingly.

"I'd like to see it," Mizaka said, surprising him.

"You would?"

Mizaka smiled and nodded. "Yes, I'll come."

"When?"

"This weekend?"

Shuibai's heart was beating like a drum. He was sure Mizaka could hear it. He nodded. "I'll see you there."

"Goodbye until then, Fire Warden Shuibai."

"Goodbye, Fire Watchman Mizaka."

They bowed to each other and went their separate ways.

CHAPTER 9: FAMILY RELATIONS

When Shuibai got home his mother was waiting for him. His landlady had let her in, and his younger sister was tending the hearth, keeping a kettle of water hot so that his mother might have tea. His mother was sitting cross-legged on the floor with Shuibai's night quilt folded up as cushion beneath her. She was smoking and the sickly sweet smell of her tobacco was perfuming the room. She was dressed in a cinnamon brown robe, green-brown divided skirt, and an orange sash. Shuibai had gotten used to the brilliant but tasteful plumage of the *taran*; he was shocked to discover that his Reverend Mother, whom he had always thought of as so tasteful and worldly, was in fact a crass imitator of that which she did not understand and could never obtain.

Today, since she was making a public appearance, she had shaved her eyebrows and painted them higher on her forehead, an affectation that had made its way down from the high city to the lower districts. Her hair was bound up on her head and she was wearing ornaments of the 'waterfall' style, which dangled from a comb inserted in the chignon at the back of her head, and trailed down her back as if she had a pony tail. They jingled as she moved, an enticement that might have been attractive on a younger, more elegant woman, but only churned his stomach. Once again he was forced to face the fact: he did not like his mother. A pilgrimage to the Shrine of Filial Devotion was definitely not in his plans. He kowtowed in front of her, dipping his face low to hide his expression because he was sure his revulsion must show in his features. He longed for a *taran* mask that would allow him to hide his feelings.

"Get up. I didn't give you permission to move out." Her anger sparked from her eyes as she spoke. She didn't remove the pipe from her mouth and her teeth gnashed upon the clay pipestem. "You're disrespectful and disobedient. I never know what you're up to! I have to find out through gossip. Do you know how that humiliates me, that people tell me things I don't even know about my own son?"

"Reverend Mother," he began in a placating voice. "My shop was burned, I had to . . ."

"It's your fault!" she screeched. "You and your foolish ways. Your rudeness, your folly, your vain social climbing, your complete and utter ignorance of all things civilized—" she gulped for breath continued "—I am a laughingstock! My son is a fool! How people pity me!"

His face burned. He turned scarlet from his neck to his eyebrows.

"You are utterly inept! You offend people. You anger the Council. It's your fault! If you had behaved yourself, this never would have happened!" He opened his mouth, but she rolled right over him. "Think of your Eldest Sister! What if her shop had burned? Think of the misery, the poverty! Our family would have been destitute. Everything I worked so hard for, up in smoke! Because I have a fool for a son!" She jabbed the handle of the pipe at him.

"But Mother—"

"Don't take that tone with me, young man!" Her left hand swept out and cracked him across the face.

"The Fire Lord appointed me, I had no choice!" He hated the way his voice rose and cracked. He felt like a child again, always too young and stupid to amount to anything.

"He had no right. The Council appoints wardens. You could have played both sides for profit, but you bungled it."

"I didn't—"

She smacked him again. "Don't interrupt me."

"I wasn't—"

Her hand cracked yet again and he shut up.

"Pay your Eldest Sister what you owe her. Never darken my door again. I'm taking back what I gave you."

She stood up and gestured to his youngest sister, who hastily gathered up the old quilt and went to the cupboard and took out the green clothes and the camellia robe. "Where are the others?" his mother demanded.

"They were burned in the fire," he lied, judging it better to not admit to giving away the pink robe.

"You owe me. That robe cost me thirty-seven pennies! The skirt was another fifteen!"

All together his mother's old outfit had cost less than the price of his uniform coat, and her clothes had been considered the height of fashion for her neighborhood. The gulf between the upper and the lower classes yawned wide and he was surprised to find himself on the opposite side from where he had always been. He didn't know how that had happened. He had never desired it while his mother, who craved it, had never achieved it. He bowed and said, "Yes, Revered Mother."

"This weekend. Don't make me send a collection agent," she said. She swept regally out the door. His youngest sister, dressed in her usual pale blue, looked sorry for him, but she followed her mother out without speaking to him.

The rank smell of tobacco smoke lingered long after she was gone, so he threw open the shutters. Air and light streamed through the house from front to back. It brought with it the pungent smell of the marsh, which was the smell of things dead and rotting, mixed with the smell of wood and coal burning. Carts clattered in the street. Somewhere children were screaming or laughing, he wasn't sure which. As he stood at his back door soaking up the clean sunlight, an old man dressed in a ragged shirt and shorts came down the lane, his knobby bare legs bending stiffly, straw sandals scuffing across the rutted tracks. He had a big barrel in the cart he was pulling, and he stopped at the back door of each house, emptied a jug into the barrel, and put the jug back, laying a single oval penny on the doorstep. When the man arrived at his house Shuibai asked him, "What are you doing?"

"Collecting urine. I pay a penny a jug for it. But only if the jug is full."

Shuibai made a moue of distaste. "And what do you do with it?"

"The fullers buy it and use it in the making of cloth."

"I had no idea."

"Leave me a full jug and I'll leave you a penny. Not bad, eh, getting paid for something other people throw away?"

A penny a day meant ten pennies a week, not much, but not a sum to be ignored. "I'll have to buy a jug first," Shuibai said.

The man shrugged. He was old and thin and his head was mostly bald. "No matter to me. I've been doing this thirty years. Make sure it's a big one." He rolled on, collecting the jug from the next door. His leather pouch of pennies hung low on his sash. The sash itself was so grimy and worn that it had rolled itself into a rope. Shuibai stared in dread fascination, watching him make his way down the rutted alley, and swore to himself that he would never ever wind up in such an awful occupation. Not for anything in the world. He'd throw himself to the trolls under the Lantern Bridge first.

Shuibai made buckets. He bent his head to his task for the next several days, emerging only to buy vegetables and noodles or rice at the shop up the street. It was meager fare and he was hungry, but his money rescued from the fire had dwindled rapidly acquiring his new shop and materials. He trekked to the well to fill his buckets and saw that the fire notice had been torn down. He hiked by his old neighborhood and saw men working. They were stripped to their loincloths, legs and arms and faces smudged with soot, raking out the debris. Their backs were bent and none of them were fat. Some of them were tattooed and many of them had shaved their skulls. They were human animals. They worked too hard for too little pay for too many hours. Shuibai went home and worked from dawn into the dusk until he could no longer see, then he slept wrapped in second hand clothes for blankets. Next day he hiked around, found a few buyers for his buckets, and memorized places that had none so that he could come back in a week and fine them. He warned them first as required by the code, then went on. After a few days of this he was having trouble keeping track, so he bought a scroll and a pencil and began taking notes. The week flew past.

Quietude intruded on his awareness. He was in his shop, pounding copper rivets to make the buckets that were more durable than the usual stitched leather buckets. Looking out the front door he saw that many shops had closed up and he was puzzled until he realized it must be the weekend. He had an appointment! The agreement seemed long ago and in another life, but the memory of the young fireman with the burned hand sent a sudden surge of life through him.

He finished the bucket, put away his tools, put away the hides, and closed up the shop and locked it. He hurried to the public bath where he happily gave over his clothes to be laundered and accepted the offer of a bathboy to scrub him. The place had a tearoom in the front, the middle room was the washing room, and the rear room was the bath. The place was warm and steamy and many people were chatting and relaxing. The weekend was the one day in ten that most tradeswomen took off, and therefore most employees had the day off.

Shuibai lazed under the bathboy's ministrations; it was delicious to let somebody pamper his body. It was a terrific luxury, and he enjoyed every moment of it. The bathboy chatted as he rubbed, saying flattering things like, "You're very muscular," which he ignored, because he knew the boy was cadging for a tip. He gave the boy a bronze penny, then moved to the bath.

He paused a moment on the threshold and looked down at himself. It was true, he was lean and muscular with a wiry frame and soft dark hair on his chest and legs. It hadn't really occurred to him to notice before. It embarrassed him, but at the same time it pleased him. Did Mizaka think he was attractive? He banished the thought because he had no idea where it would lead, or rather, was afraid it would lead to disappointment. He steeled himself to expect nothing. It was better that way. Hardship was easier to bear if he expected nothing else.

There were three large tubs, each of them occupied. Several women were soaking together in one, smoking pipes and drinking tea, while naked children were horsing around in one tub, splashing each other with the water and throwing it, so he settled in a tub with several older men. They were all wallowing in the hot water, letting it soak the aches from their bones. Shuibai slid down until his chin touched the surface. One of the men, who was bald in the middle of his head with a tonsure of black hair around the sides, said, "You're the new Fire Warden, aren't you?"

Shuibai froze in position. He opened his eyes warily and sat up cautiously, prepared to leap out of the tub, his good mood extinguished.

"How many fines have you collected?" the man asked. He seemed polite, but it was a loaded question and he was a large fleshy man well supplied with both muscle and fat. He was twice Shuibai's size.

"I haven't collected any. I would rather people display their buckets as required by law." His anxiety showed in his voice.

"No fines?" the man asked in surprise.

"No, none."

The men looked at each other in consternation. "Then how did you pay for that fine courtesan at Ryoichi's place the other night?" a skinny fellow with tattooed arms and short dark brown hair asked.

"I've never been to Ryoichi's. I make buckets all day and I sleep all night."

"It wasn't you? But she said it was you."

"She said so?" Shuibai asked.

"No, but my sister works at the tea house next door, and she heard it from one of the porters who works at Ryoichi's, and he said her maid told him. You must be making a lot of money if you can afford Ryoichi's place." His voice was tart.

"It wasn't me," Shuibai insisted. "You can come home with me. You'll see how modestly I live. I don't have much money. It couldn't have been me." He climbed out of the tub in agitation. "I haven't levied any fines at all. It's a lie, someone is trying to hurt my reputation just like they burned my shop."

"Ah, that was arson? Somebody told me you fell asleep with your pipe lit," the third man said, his eyes pinched to slits, the heavy lids giving him a sinister look.

"I don't smoke!"

The bald fellow nudged the man next to him with his elbow. "He doesn't smoke and he doesn't visit courtesans. He doesn't levy fines. Know what I think? He's soft in the head."

The others nodded and hissed with laughter.

"Why do you scorn me for living a virtuous life? Why do you make fun of my misfortunes? Do I ridicule you because you're old and your dicks have gone limp? Do I laugh at the way your bald heads shine in the light? Do I—" They were glaring at him and starting to rise, so he beat a hasty retreat.

"Impudent young whippersnapper, isn't he?" one of them remarked as they resettled in the tub.

"If it weren't for impudence he wouldn't have any personality at all," the bald one replied.

The tattooed one said, "You can't trust a man with no vices. His only entertainment is badgering other people about theirs." They all nodded and sank down in the hot water, content to have asserted their authority and vanquished the upstart so easily.

Shuibai donned his wet clothes and sulked all the way home. If he had been *taran* he could have killed them on the spot, but then, if he had been *taran* they would not have dared to speak to him like that. Even Chief Byan had teased him. He wondered if there was something about himself that invited attack, or if it was the nature of human beings to pick on everyone. He was not like other people, that was for sure. He didn't like the rowdyism of other boys, but he wasn't smart like girls. He was obedient, or he had been up until recently, but he was not a loving son. The prospect of marriage appalled him and he worked too much to make any friends. There were no answers to his personal dilemmas, so he put them out of his mind and got ready to meet Mizaka.

He had never paid attention to himself before, but he badly wanted to make a good impression upon Mizaka. It was dreadfully important that the crippled firefighter find him pleasant company. If he did, perhaps they could be friends. Shuibai had had playmates when he was little; but no boy he'd ever known was as elegant and accomplished as the retired firefighter. Making friends seemed a reasonable ambition, something he might be lucky enough to accomplish if he didn't make a foolish mistake. He would think no further than that. His mother's words burned in him and he put his face in his hands. He tried not to think about it, he tried not to think about anything. He swallowed hard and rubbed his eyes, refusing to give in to the despair that was always at his heels. He was living the best life he had ever lived. He had his own shop, his own apartment, and an important job. Why wasn't he happy?

He brushed his hair back from his forehead. It was getting long; he had usually worn it down to his collar and now it was past that. He had a broad forehead, with finely arched brows that hinted at a more delicate ancestry than four generations in the meat and leather trades. His brown eyes were deep set and his cheekbones prominent. His nose was strong, but not large, as were his ears. He had thick lips, and he wondered if he were good looking. He had never been complimented upon his appearance, but neither had he been subjected to ridicule on account of his face. He supposed that meant he was plain, neither handsome nor ugly. Unremarkable. He shrugged in disappointment. He had never thought much about his clothes either, and he was acutely self-conscious that whatever he wore would appear cheap and tawdry to Mizaka, who was accustomed to the Fire Court and the fine houses of the capital city. Finally he settled for his old willow leaf shirt and a pair of short pants. They were the most ordinary sort of clothes, worn by people of many classes and many trades. He could have worn his uniform, but he was afraid of attracting attention. He dreaded the possibility of being insulted and assaulted in front of Mizaka. By the time he finally dragged himself forth his stomach was in a knot.

CHAPTER 10: THE LANTERN BRIDGE

Shuibai arrived at the Lantern Gate extremely early. Yet he was afraid if Mizaka saw him waiting he might think Shuibai was desperate to see him—which he was. So he paused to blankly study the contents of a riceball stand. He thought perhaps he should go away and come back later, so as to arrive late and appear nonchalant, but he was afraid that if he came too late, Mizaka might give up and go home again. He decided to take refuge in a tea shop along the road. He sat against the wall, trying to be invisible while he watched the traffic in the street. Not many people came to view the Lantern Bridge at sunset. The travelers were farmers streaming back into the countryside after a day selling in the markets or tradesmen trudging their weary way home after a hard day of labor. A horsewoman dressed in the yellow panoply of the Imperial Post passed over the bridge, but that was the only noteworthy traveler.

The bridge itself was a remarkable piece of work on account of the gatehouse that straddled its near end. High up in the gate hung a giant red paper lantern. The roof of the gate sheltered it from rain and the lantern burned during the hours of darkness. The lantern was extinguished only in times of war, at which time the gate would be closed and manned by soldiers. No one could pass through without an inspection and written permit.

The last time the gate had been shut was a couple years ago, during the succession troubles in the wake of the death of the Golden Empress and the installation of the new Golden Emperor. He took heart from that. A man was on the throne for the first time since the Warrior Sun had reigned two centuries ago. Perhaps that would bode well for his own personal fortunes. And yet, the Golden Emperor Himself was plagued by rebels and intriguers. It was a time of disorder. The reign of a male sovereign could never be peaceful, that was what the sages said. Such a disruption in the normal order of things could only bring chaos in its wake. It was no coincidence that both the Warrior Sun and the current Golden Emperor had gained their thrones through force of arms. They called the new emperor the 'Hero of the West,' because of His triumph over the Pangu hordes and their foreign allies. Only in a time of war could such a thing occur.

Maybe things needed to change, he thought, but he didn't dare say the words out loud, not even to himself. Lost in his reverie he almost missed Mizaka passing by. Mizaka was wearing a conical straw hat, a maroon jacket over charcoal grey trousers, and tall wooden sandals. He cut a dashing figure amid the lower class workmen who went bare legged or in short pants. Shuibai jumped up and ran after him, then thought better of it. He schooled himself to walk with dignity so that when Mizaka saw him coming, he would see a man and not a fool. He tugged at his sleeves trying to get them to hang better, but his second hand clothes were paltry things compared to the elegant townsman. He had even forgotten a hat and the breeze was flipping locks of hair about his face.

Mizaka stopped at the top of the bridge. It was a long arch that stretched high above the Crane River. The far end anchored to a hill above the edge of the marsh, while the near end anchored to a low embankment that had been built when parts of the marsh had been drained and filled. Boggy hollows still remained within the district known as Low Marsh, but as the city encroached and the population escalated, those spots were being filled in. Such were the unromantic thoughts running through Shuibai's mind. He was feeling embarrassed for himself, for his town, for his clothes, for everything. Mizaka's greeting took him by surprise.

"The crane on one leg at the water side—how still it stands! But in the ripples its reflection sways."

Shuibai gawked in blank incomprehension.

Mizaka smiled. "You are not a connoisseur of the classics, I see."

"No," Shuibai admitted. "But I can read simple script."

"It comes from the time of the Green Mountain Prince."

"Oh, I see," Shuibai said, although he did not. He had heard stories about the doings of the Green Mountain Prince who had founded the new country of Hu Shen after a sandstorm wiped out the old queendom of Ton Shen, but the poet was beyond his ken. "Have there been many male sovereigns? I thought they were always supposed to be female."

Mizaka tilted his head as he considered. "I can think of three. The Green Mountain Prince, the Warrior Sun, and our Golden

Emperor. All of them warriors who saved their people in time of trouble. I like reading about them. Do you like to read?"

"Can you read the high script?" Shuibai asked, dreading the answer.

"Yes, I can! Can you?" Mizaka looked hopeful.

Shuibai shook his head.

Seeing his discomfort Mizaka turned to view the marsh. Low Marsh on the right bank was crowded close with lumberyards and tenements, and Shuibai could even pick out the shack that was the privy at the foot of his alley. The left bank was far away and crowned with trees like golden lamps. Water lay dark in winding streams while tufts of marsh grass were turning a shade of yellow that almost seemed to glow in the rays of the fading sun. The sky was occluded with stripes of purple cloud, and the sun itself was a fiery orange ball falling toward the horizon to quench itself in the waters of Crescent Moon Lake. Wild geese honked and a great flock of them leaped into the sky and wheeled uncertainly before settling back again. "It's a magnificent landscape," Mizaka said.

"If you ignore the town," Shuibai could not help adding.

Mizaka tipped his head to listen. He leaned his forearms on the railing of the bridge while a cart rumbled behind them, pulled by a team of oxen lead by a wealthy farmer and her husband. Horses were forbidden to commoners. Human beasts of burden provided most of the motive power. To have oxen was a great luxury. Next a long cavalcade of porters balancing poles over their shoulders passed over the bridge, each pole supporting a large bundle at either end. Shuibai wanted to step closer to Mizaka, but the townsman smelled clean and fresh while Shuibai was afraid his clothes were tainted with the stench of Low Marsh.

"What work did you do before you became a fire watchman?" Shuibai asked.

"I was a woodblock carver in the same shop where my mother works. I was quite good at it."

"It takes two hands?"

"Yes."

"I'm sorry for you. It must have been good work."

"I liked it. I even carved and printed some of my own designs. I thought I might become an artist even."

"I would like to see your prints."

Mizaka shrugged. "There won't be anymore prints."

Shuibai slid a little closer. His sleeve was almost touching Mizaka's sleeve. Closer than that he dared not come. They stood side by side, staring out over the mud flats and hillocks of marsh weed. Ducks swam towards them with their necks craned up and quacked. Mizaka smiled. "We should have brought rice for them."

Shuibai answered, "There's a tea shop at the end of the bridge. We can buy some rice."

They trotted down to the shop, bought a heap of rice in a paper box and went back to the bridge. They picked the sticky rice out with their fingers and dropped it to the birds below. They grinned as the ducks bobbed and squabbled for the morsels, then threw rice in a broad sweep so that the whole flock boiled into action as they darted after the flying bits of white. Green-headed, brown-headed, and blue-headed ducks bobbed together in a mixed flock, then Mizaka pointed. Herons were walking along the edge of the stream. They were as tall as a man with blue-grey feathers. They were so thin as to be almost invisible against the background of weeds and shrubbery. Then Shuibai pointed out a nest on top of a thatch-roofed house that was the last or first building of Low Marsh, depending on which way you were traveling. Shuibai had not gone down to the river since he was a child; he had forgotten that right at his own doorstep was a different world. He wanted the evening to last forever.

Their eyes met and Mizaka smiled. "Thank you for inviting me. We don't have anything like this where I live."

Shuibai was lost in those strange grey eyes and he managed only to make the standard polite reply, "The pleasure is all mine, Mizaka-don."

"Call me Zashi. Everyone does."

Shuibai swallowed hard. "If you wish, Zashi-don." It was hard for him to say it like that—he wanted to tack on the affectionate term -lan which threatened to roll off his tongue like the name of a lover.

Zashi turned to look across the marsh again. "I would like a house on those hills," he said. "Where I can look at the city but be apart from it." He strolled slowly along the bridge, running his good hand lightly along the rail. The burned hand remained hidden in his sleeve. The sun was dipping its lower edge in the waters and a path of orange light lay across the marsh, leading from the Lantern Bridge into the sunset. "They say that the Spirits dwell upon the far shore of the lake, and that the Fire Dragon enters the world of men along roads of skyfire. Like this one, I imagine. I wonder if we will see a dragon tonight?"

"I hope not. I'd be upset if dragons turned out to be real."

"They're real, all right," Zashi remarked. He was not looking at Shuibai. "I've seen the Fire Dragon many times."

Shuibai was not certain whether he believed him or not. He had never see a spirit, dragon, gremlin, or troll, although he had heard plenty of stories about them. Like the other excuses peasants offered up to the *taran*, he thought the fire dragon was yet another way of avoiding responsibility. Who would admit to burning down his own house? It must have been a dragon.

Zashi was speaking. "It rose up out of the house, its great tail curled in a double curve, its spiked and horny head erect. It was made of fire and brass and it was wreathed in clouds of smoke. I only saw it for an instant, but it looked right at me. Then the house collapsed, and the wall fell on me. I was burned all across my left side, my left arm especially, and I lost part of my hair. I can't bend my arm like I used to. I always know when the weather is going to turn because my shoulder aches."

"You're lucky to be alive."

"I have always wondered why I survived. I don't know if the dragon dropped the wall on me because I saw it, or if because I saw it, it saved me from dying."

"The minds of men are mysterious to me. I couldn't presume to know the mind of a dragon."

Zashi laughed. "Shui-lan, you just said something profound."

"I did?"

Zashi smiled and looked at him. "You did."

"I've never been profound before," Shuibai responded, flushed to be called by the friendly nickname. He was smiling because Zashi was smiling, and he thought he would do anything at all for that smile.

Zashi caught hold of his sleeve and pulled him along the bridge. "Let's go walking."

They descended the far side of the bridge and Shuibai grew excited. He had never gone beyond the Lantern Bridge before, never gone into the countryside at all. They found a footpath worn along the crest of the hills that marked the far edge of the marsh. Zashi walked briskly and Shuibai struggled to keep up. The happy glow inside him was replaced by the glow of exertion, and he hoped they would not go too far. He was afraid of getting lost, or getting into trouble for trespassing. Or meeting thieves. Or ghosts.

They rounded bends, traveled through a copse of trees, and stepped over tiny streams. They met no one. They came out on a sandy spit of land with marsh on three sides and looked across to the city. Lines of smoke from a thousand chimneys smudged the sky and a cool breeze flitted through the grasses. "It doesn't look so ugly from here," Shuibai said.

Zashi turned suddenly dark. "Doesn't it? I have to live with it," he said, deliberately misconstruing Shuibai's words. He cradled his burned arm against his chest.

"I didn't mean that," Shuibai tried to explain, taken aback by the sudden change in mood.

"I did," Zashi snapped.

"It doesn't matter—"

"It matters to me! Look at it." He slipped his jacket and shirt off his shoulder, revealing scarred and lumpen flesh. He turned so that Shuibai could see the great purple-brown scars covering his left arm and shoulder, running down his ribs to disappear under the fabric at his waist. He pulled the shirt back on. "I take my baths at home now. People draw away when they see the way the dragon has marked me. Now that you know, you won't want to get close either."

Zashi turned and walked rapidly back the way they had come. He kept a bitter silence. Shuibai trailed in his wake. He didn't know what to do. His heart ached because he didn't mind the scars, but he didn't know how to say it in a way that wouldn't sound like he didn't care. But he was also afraid to sound like he cared too much. Zashi recrossed the Lantern Bridge without speaking and Shuibai trudged miserably a step behind him.

"Would you like some tea?" Shuibai asked hopefully.

"No, I need to go home. I have my pass, but the watchmen will be annoyed if they have to unlock the gates for me."

"Did I do something wrong?"

Zashi finally looked at him. He relented. "No, Shui-lan. I just . . . I don't know. You've been nice to me. I shouldn't have snapped at you." He folded his arms, cradling the scarred arm against his chest. "I'm sorry. I'm not very good company. I thought I was going to have an ordinary life, work an ordinary job, get married, all that. But the Fire Dragon changed everything. Now I'm a freak. It's been so long I can't remember what it's like to be normal. I envy you."

"Oh," Shuibai said. He thought about it, then said, "I thought I was going to have an ordinary life too."

Zashi smiled ruefully. "Yes, firefighting certainly disrupts your life if you aren't raised to it."

Shuibai was glad Zashi seemed to be coming out of his dark mood, and he cast about for something to carry the conversation forward. "Can I see you again?"

"Do you want to?" Zashi seemed genuinely surprised.

"Yes." Shuibai bowed his head shyly. "I like you."

"You do? Me, a bitter old cripple? Why?" His voice was light and mocking.

Shuibai hung his head. "Please don't talk that way."

"I'm sorry, Shui-lan. It's just that, well. I'm used to people either pitying me or being shocked. It makes me say rude things. You didn't deserve that. You've really been quite nice. I'm sorry."

"It's all right. I understand. I just want you to know that I think you're a fine man. I appreciate you taking time to help me. You've been very nice to me."

Zashi's expression softened. "If you say so." He was struggling to accept the compliment. "I guess there's a use for me after all."

Shuibai wanted to keep talking, but he was afraid he was going to say something wrong, so he just said, "Well, good night, then, Zashi-lan."

Zashi's eyebrow quirked at the nickname -lan; he seemed to have forgotten that he had used it first. "Good night then, Fire Warden Shuibai," he said lightly, and started walking briskly along the Southern Highway, limping on his left leg.

Shuibai called after him, "If you turn down Broadway and take the Wet Lane, it's a shortcut,"

"Show me?" Zashi asked, pausing.

Shuibai hung back. "I can't."

"Why not?"

"My mother lives on that street. I don't want to take a chance running into her."

Zashi laughed and waved. "I wouldn't want to get you in trouble with your mother. I'll stick to the road I know. Good night, Shui-lan."

"Good night." Shuibai stood grinning goofily as he watched Zashi's form disappear along the dusky highway. He didn't know what to make of Zashi's sudden mood swings, but it didn't matter. All in all it had gone well. He stood a long time staring along the highway before practically skipping back to his own home.

CHAPTER 11: THE FULLER'S LANE INCIDENT

A penny left every other day on his back step and an occasional bucket sale were Shuibai's only income. He was losing weight and his ribs were becoming prominent beneath his shirt. Accordingly he decided that since someone was giving him a bad reputation he might as well live up to it. He worked his way along the block, found several shops with less than the proper number of buckets hung on the wall, and coerced the sale of a dozen buckets. He found the task repugnant, but not nearly as repugnant as it had seemed back when he was adequately fed. He spent three days selling buckets and collecting fines. He made a note on his scroll about each place visited. Then he put his mother's money in a leather purse and dropped it off at his sister's butcher shop.

His sister was about average height which made her a couple of inches shorter than Shuibai. She had muscular arms and kept her brown hair cut short with bangs across the front. Her eyes were hazel, her skin was a parchment color, and her features fine, all of which would have made her a modest beauty if she had been employed in a more graceful profession. She was dressed in a ratty brown robe that reached to her knees, the soiled white collar of her under robe showing around her neck. She wore a blood-stained canvas apron over it. Her hands were bloody as well, and she had to hunt to find a clean corner of her apron to wipe them off before accepting the purse from Shuibai.

He bowed. "Would you be kind enough to convey this to our Reverend Mother? It is the repayment of the loan she made me."

The smell of meat made his mouth water. The shop was clean; an apprentice girl mopped the floors and walls several times a day to remove the blood before it crusted. An odor of strong soap mixed with the smell of meat and blood.

"Where's my money?" she demanded.

"Mother comes first," he rebuked her. "You'll have to wait."

"You know, Little Brother, you are growing up to be a real pain in my ass." Her hazel eyes flashed.

He gritted his teeth. "By the way, Eldest Sister, I notice you are not displaying three buckets on your front wall as required by law.

I'm fining you thirty pennies for each omission. You owe me ninety pennies." He decided to omit the ten day grace period in her case.

Her jaw dropped. "What?"

He pulled out his paper appointing him as Fire Warden and held it up in front of her.

"You can't fine me, you're just a brat!"

He folded the letter of appointment carefully. "You owe me ninety pennies. I'll come back in a week and see if you've provided the buckets or not. If you haven't, I'll fine you again. In the meantime, I owe you sixty pennies. Put that against the fine, and you only owe me thirty pennies. You can send your apprentice with the money this evening and that will be fine."

"I should slap you silly, the disrespect you show me!"

"Interfering with a firefighter while he's carrying out his duties is grounds for summary execution, Eldest Sister. Do not make me report you to the Fire Court."

She looked as if he had spit on her. "You wouldn't dare."

He bared his teeth. "Try me, Eldest Sister. One man has already been beaten bloody on my testimony."

"I always said you'd come to no good. You'd better sleep with one eye open, Little Brother!"

Shuibai stared at her. She was angry—angry enough, he suspected, to carry out her threat. He was angry, too, and not happy over the fact that simply talking to his relatives made him act like a lunatic. The thought sobered him. He turned on his heel and stalked away. Had he always hated them? Perhaps he had. They treated a dog better than they treated him. They would rather turn on him when he found a little bit of success than wish him well and support him. He no longer felt any obligation, financial or otherwise, to his blood kin.

He renewed his inspections, carrying out his task with grim determination. He was sometimes chased off with blows and curses, but usually he collected a fine or sold a bucket. Once in a while he even discovered households properly displaying the buckets. Word began to get around that he meant business. However, when he turned down Fuller's Lane he noted that none of the shops displayed buckets upon their fronts. He stopped at the first one and identified himself.

"I'm Fire Warden Shuibai, here to inspect your property. I notice that you are not displaying the proper number of buckets as required by law."

The fuller was a plump little woman with long black hair going grey pinned up on her head in a disarrayed chignon. A silver comb was slipping from her hair. Her brown eyes were made small by the fleshiness of her face.

"Oh my goodness, those good for nothing apprentices, they never put things back where they belong. Hold on a minute." She ducked under the curtain and back into her shop, from which the strong stench of urine emanated. The whole lane was foul with the smell and it nauseated him. He didn't know what they did with it, only that it was somehow involved in the making of felt. Hammers were pounding in shops all along the lane and the noise made his head ring. A minute later he noticed that the shopkeeper next door had brought a stool out front and was standing on it while an apprentice boy was handing buckets up to her, which she hung from hooks in her eaves, making them high enough not to be easily stolen. The first fuller came back with buckets in hand, and she chatted away at him, trying to engage him in conversation while one after another the shops on Fuller's Lane suddenly had apprentices lugging out buckets or pails or tubs or kettles or any other item that could be used to haul water and setting them up in front of the shop or stacking them in the tiny yards no bigger than a grave plot. The woman had sent her apprentice running down the back way to warn her neighbors that he had arrived. While he watched a young woman darted across the street, stuck her head in the shop opposite, then ran along the street, rapping and calling, glancing back at him to see what he would do. He did nothing. The street was short, but everyone displayed three items intended to hold liquids, ranging from chamber pots to washtubs in front of their stores, so he levied no fines and sold no buckets. The first woman was grinning broadly at him, white teeth shining in a berry brown face, pleased that she had bested him.

"Thank you for your cooperation," he told her politely and walked down the block.

He turned the corner and waited a few minutes. He heard laughter drifting down the lane but he kept quiet. After a few minutes when everything had quieted, he turned back into Fuller's Lane. As expected, they had taken their things inside as soon as they thought the coast was clear. He rapped politely on the first doorframe, and when the shopkeeper appeared, he smiled politely and said, "I notice you seem to have put your buckets to other use. You can buy my buckets for five pennies each. Or I can collect a fine of thirty pennies right now for failing to display your buckets as required by law." Crestfallen, she handed over fifteen pennies. "I'll bring your buckets by tonight," he told her with a small bow.

The same scene was repeated at each shop. The shopkeepers he had caught were too embarrassed to go to their neighbors about it. In that way Shuibai was able to sell buckets all along the block. He went home and gathered up the buckets, stacking them together and making a sack out of the old clothes he had bought. All in all he had sold close to thirty buckets, so his load was large and bulky. He returned to the Fuller's Lane, opened his package and set three on each step as he went up the lane, and then as he came back down the lane, rapped at the doors, and called out, "Your buckets are here!" Not waiting for an answer he moved to the next shop and did the same. He walked away, leaving the street chastened, not realizing that he had won their respect by outsmarting them in a sharp deal.

Shuibai did wonder what he was going to do once his district was completely inspected and supplied with buckets, but that was going to take him a long, long time—all winter at this rate—so he decided not to worry about it. He made his notes on his scroll, and kept plugging away, head down as he walked, reciting his notice by rote at each stop. Sometimes people were cooperative, offering to trade him goods of theirs in exchange for his buckets; he generally agreed to the barter. He had so little that almost everything they offered him was useful. He even acquired an apprentice.

Kanko was a thin, wiry boy with a mop of black hair and brown eyes. He lived with Shuibai, cooking and cleaning and doing all the things Shuibai didn't feel like doing for himself. The boy worked hard and never got to play with the other lads who kicked their balls in the lane. He was a quiet and withdrawn person, for which Shuibai was grateful. The boy reminded him of himself at that age, so he tried to show him a little kindness, but the work was too hard and the pay too little to allow much in the way of niceties.

CHAPTER 12: POETS AND REBELS

One morning Shuibai awoke to find snow upon the ground. It was light and fluffy and would melt by noon, but opening his shutter to the chill air revealed Low Marsh in a way he had rarely seen: pristine and clean. It was early and few householders had risen to light their cook fires or forges, so the sky was a brilliant cerulean blue. White softened everything, hid the garbage, smoothed over the rutted roads, rounded the forms of buildings. The world was new and beautiful and clean. For one morning he was not ashamed to live in Low Marsh.

He was unschooled in the finer arts and had no command of calligraphy; his knowledge of poetry was limited to such poetic lines as had become proverbs. Yet the weather and his feelings both seemed to require a poetic expression, so he sat and shivered on his front step, wrapped up in his blanket while Kanko lit the kitchen fire and boiled the rice and tea. Finally, he shut the shutter, ate his breakfast, and set the boy to work. Then he huddled over the fire and wrote, "The snow on the ground made the world look like it was new again, and it reminded me of the way I felt when I was with you." He set the paper aside and wondered if he had been too forward, too subtle, or totally wrong. He had not heard from Zashi for over two weeks. Having written the poem he had no idea what to do with it. Finally he folded the note inside his sleeve and called to Kanko to get ready to go out.

He donned his fire uniform. Since he was going to the Fire Court, he rather self-consciously tucked the silver fan from the second hand shop in his sleeve. He had never carried one before, but if he were to carry one anywhere, the Fire Court was the place to do it. It was past time to deliver his monthly report to the Fire Lord. He had delayed, feeling like he had accomplished very little that would make the aristocrat happy and hoping something might turn up. But nothing special happened, so at last with a heavy heart, he resigned himself to make his report. Fearing displeasure, he selected a scroll case to give as a gift. It wasn't much, but it was all he could do. He didn't know how to make a saddle, and he doubted the Fire Lord needed any buckets, but maybe a scroll case would be useful. He tucked it inside his shirt.

Next he tucked the inspection scroll in its leather case inside his shirt against his heart; he felt he was staking his life on it. Yet surely if the Fire Lord saw how hard he had been working he would stay his hand and Shuibai's head would not part company with his shoulders. In a moment of madness he even allowed himself to hope the Fire Lord would approve his work, but then he disciplined himself to expect nothing but ridicule. He was not an experienced fireman like Chief Byan, so of course his work would be inferior. All he could hope was that Zashi was right that it didn't matter what he did. It burned him to remember Zashi's cynical assessment. Surely the Fire Lord expected something, or why had he bothered to make the appointment? Thinking about such things only depressed him.

The master and apprentice (how strange to think of himself as the 'master' of anything!) set off through the wet snow, making fresh tracks. The smell of breakfast was in the air, and the snow was rapidly being churned to mud by workmen on their way to work. Snow or no snow, they must work. Shuibai and Kanko took the shortcut through the Iris Bottom where the gardens were blighted by the weather, dry brown spokes of stems sticking up from clumps of snow-covered shrubbery. Some big black chickens wandered in the lane and pecked at the pebbles churned up by passersby. Shuibai and his apprentice skirted them and kept going. He passed his mother's house, but all was quiet and nobody hailed him. His mother was still in bed. There was only one person in the whole town who went about dressed in the uniform of the fire service, so perhaps her neighbors would tell her that they had seen him and she would know he had not stopped. It jangled him to think she might show up unannounced again with yet another tirade—but he still didn't stop.

They climbed the rutted track to the Capital Road and went up to the city, only to meet a cavalcade coming out the Eastern Gate. Green and purple banners waved and deep voiced drums sounded the cadence. First came the heralds in their uniforms of brilliant green with purple iris blossoms, crying, "Make way for the Iris Lord! Make way for Lord Tellani!" They were followed by two ranks of honor guards on white horses that completely filled the road from side to side, followed by the Iris Lord himself and his closest retainers, then a troop of horsemen, then a rank of drummers, then a troop of foot soldiers. Gold glinted from the finials atop the guidons and the pennants were held out stiffly by a rod through their upper edge making it seem as if a stiff breeze was blowing the flags. The soldiers each had vertical banners on their backs made of green fabric with a white circle and a purple iris on the circle; the horsemen were outfitted with uniform jackets over their armor.

The Iris Lord was one of the great aristocrats of the land, so Shuibai and Kanko hastened to step off the road and kowtowed, pressing their faces into the cold snow until the lord passed. When the foot soldiers drew abreast they cautiously raised their faces, but did not get up from a kneeling position, even though the frozen ground was cold and uncomfortable beneath them. When the last rank passed, they got up stiffly and dusted off their knees.

"Who was that?" the boy asked. His brown eyes were wide.

"The Iris Lord, I guess," Shuibai replied. Now he felt guilty about using the old Iris uniform shirt as a rag for cleaning his house. Up until that point the Iris Lord had been an abstraction, just as the Golden Emperor was an abstraction. He had never expected to see either one.

"I wonder where he's going. Do you think he has to fight some brigands?" the boy asked.

"Possibly. But the Tellani lands are over the Lantern Bridge and down the Southern Highway, very far away, so I guess he's going home after serving at court."

"Is he important?"

Shuibai laughed. "I guess so. He's the leader of the Neutrals, they say. He didn't get involved in the succession fight."

Kanko pondered, his thin tan face flexing as he struggled with his thoughts. "Do you know a lot of famous people?" he asked at last.

"Me?" Shuibai said. "Well, I've met the Fire Lord and the Fire Chief of Alla Far, but that's all. You'll get to meet the Chief, too, if you're a good boy."

The boy's eyes were wide. "I will?"

Shuibai laughed. "Let's go. It's too cold to stand around talking."

They entered Alla Far, capital city of the New Queendom of Hu Shen, and found the roads swept clean by servants. Oxcarts rumbled along the road. *Taran* warmly dressed in cloaks and hoods maneuvered their horses up the highway towards the Palace

District to report for the day's duty. A few tired *taran* and night servants were wending in the opposite direction, heads bowed with fatigue after a long night of service. It was the sort of scene to end up on a woodblock print if an artist had seen it.

At Chief Byan's home a young woman Shuibai didn't recognize opened the door; Zashi's sister-in-law he guessed. She was petite and pretty, with a long dark brown braid of hair tied in a loop with a large pink bow. She wore a long pink gown tied with a red sash. "Is Fire Chief Byan at home?" he asked her.

"No, he has gone to the Rag District to make inspections," she answered him politely. Her brown eyes were watchful. "Can I help you with something?"

"Is Fire Watchman Mizaka home?"

"Yes, but he just got home from work and he's sleeping."

He handed over the piece of paper he had written his poem on. "Will you give him this note? Tell him it is from Fire Warden Shuibai of Low Marsh."

She accepted it and nodded. "Yes, Fire Warden."

"I am going to the Fire Court now. I have to make a report." He wanted to say many things, so many that he didn't know what to say, so he said, "Just tell him I stopped by."

"I will."

Shuibai and Kanko went further up the Capital Road. It was mid-morning by the time they reached the Fire Court. Shuibai gave his name and errand to the guard, who passed them into the courtyard. The buildings of the compound were laid out in a horseshoe shape; to the left side was the barracks, to the right was the stable. The mansion house was at the top of the horseshoe, opposite the gatehouse. A wall ran all the way around the compound, and the space behind the buildings was broken into several smaller courtyards, including a private garden. The boy's eyes were very wide as they entered the palatial estate. He pressed close to Shuibai's side. Shuibai smiled down at him. He remembered his own awe at the first visit. It still made him anxious to come here, but he was getting used to it. The *taran* who circulated about the premises were only human after all, albeit violent and sensitive about their rank.

The front door of the mansion was opened by a majordomo with the short hair of a commoner. He wore plain dark purple clothes with an orange sash and trim. Shuibai repeated his name and business, and he was admitted to the house, but his boy was sent around the corner to wait in the kitchen. Shuibai removed his wooden sandals and stepped up onto the polished wooden step, then entered the house, bowing as he did so. He was taken down a hall, then the majordomo spoke into a closed room, and Shuibai was admitted. The majordomo withdrew. Shuibai dropped to his knees and kowtowed low. He kept his head down. All he could see was a thick cloth mat in the center of the floor, with an orange cushion peaking out from underneath the Fire Lord's green clothes. A writing desk was before the lord. It was basically a large tray with legs and handles so that it could be moved easily. It bore an ink stone and ink pan, several brushes, and paper.

"Fire Warden Shuibai of Low Marsh," the Fire Lord said, remembering him this time. "You're late."

"My apologies, Noble Lord. I wanted to complete some of the tasks you assigned me before making my report."

"I'll hear your report now, but keep it short. In the future I expect you to show up on the appointed day. I'm a busy man, and I schedule these things for my convenience, not yours."

Shuibai decided now was a good time to give a gift. Barely lifting his eyes he extracted the scroll case from inside his clothing and slid it across the floor. "I have brought a small gift in token of my appreciation for your magnanimity."

A bare hand pulled the case toward the Fire Lord and Shuibai found himself staring. He had never seen the Fire Lord's ungloved hands before, and he was fascinated by the perfect, pale, smooth, clean skin and neatly filed fingernails. Shuibai always got ink smudges on himself when he wrote, but judging by the deft motions of the Lord's hands, he never smudged anything. The Fire Lord lifted the case and turned it over, inspecting the workmanship with a discerning eye. He opened it and looked inside as well.

Shuibai dared to lift his eyes a little further, and saw that the Fire Lord was casually dressed, shockingly casual for a *taran*. It was plain that he had not been expecting visitors today. His green willow robe was elegant, and the sleeves were tied back with white silk strings so that his forearms showed. His divided skirt was a smooth heavy silk in a clear but subtle shade of green, not like the murky greens that were so common among the lower classes. He was kneeling with his feet tucked beneath him as he worked at the desk. His queue was wrapped around his neck and the end hung down in front; it was tied with a white ribbon. He wore a green half mask that covered the upper part of his face. He had a high forehead and a strong jaw, darkly shadowed by a beard even though he was neatly shaved. His nose was straight and his cheekbones were cliffs above lips that had a tendency to sneer, though this did not in anyway diminish the terrible beauty of his *taran* image. Shuibai had seen men of low birth wearing far less clothing and had never paid any attention to them, but the Fire Lord's appearance struck him with a strong emotion he could not identify. The man was handsome.

"A scroll case?"

"Yes, Noble Lord."

"You made it?"

"I did."

"Very practical. Looks like a good piece of campaign equipment."

Shuibai almost fainted with relief. He had been afraid the Fire Lord would treat his gift with contempt; he was profoundly grateful for the man's forbearance.

"I got the idea because I often carry a scroll when making inspections." Shuibai opened his own scroll case and withdrew the document he had been keeping. "It was impossible for me to memorize each place I had inspected, so I started writing them down. I made up a system of numbers so that I could keep track of them and go back if I needed to."

He unrolled the scroll across the floor. "I started inspecting near the Narrow Way, since that was where the fire was. As you can see, most establishments did not abide by the fire code. I made a note and went back to them, selling buckets. So now my apprentice and I work several days a week making buckets, then we go out and do a day of inspecting and by the end of the day all the buckets are sold. They pay me and send their apprentices in the evening to get their buckets."

He continued speaking. "I haven't finished the town. It's going to take me all winter to do that. I haven't gone back to check up on violators who refused to buy buckets or pay their fines. I thought it better to survey the town as well as I could, then go back and fill in the holes. It will be late spring before you can expect each establishment to abide by the bucket edict. I'm sorry, but it can't be done any sooner. I have been thinking about hiring some help, but I don't have enough money." Shuibai bowed to the floor, knocking his head against the wood. "I'm sorry I have not been able to do better, Noble Lord. Please forgive me."

The Fire Lord picked up the end of the scroll and laid it across his desk. Reading from right to left and top to bottom, he ran his fingers along Shuibai's crude printing and read his notes. "So you know the status of every property in your district?"

"Only the ones that I have inspected," Shuibai clarified.

"Yes, but by summer you'll know them all."

"I'll have them all written down."

"I am impressed by your record keeping." Nobody had ever claimed to be impressed by anything Shuibai had done before. He didn't know what to make of it. "If only my other wardens were as zealous in carrying out their duties." The Lord sighed heavily. "Have you established a fire company yet?"

"No, Noble Lord. That was not part of my instructions," he replied cautiously, his moment of optimism truncated by fear that the Fire Lord was going to punish him for this lack.

"Every district should have one."

"Your pardon, Noble Lord, but isn't it the duty of the town council to establish one if they think it necessary?" He fought to keep the panic from his voice.

The Fire Lord smiled grimly. "*I* think it necessary. I think you do, too. I am authorized to take steps to suppress fires and prevent looting and other disorders. I'm ordering you to start a fire company."

Shuibai's heart sank. "But sir, how do I do that?"

He waved a hand. "Don't bother me with trivia. That's your problem, not mine. I want effective fire companies in all the suburbs, and I'm tired of all the petty squabbling and minor rebellions. Deal with the council."

"With all due respect, sir, I think they'd pay more attention to you than to me."

"I am only one man, who does not have the time to meet and coddle every single councilwoman in the thirty-seven boroughs of the Capital District! Which is why I appoint Fire Wardens."

Shuibai was getting desperate. "A prominent woman has apprised me that the Councilwomen believe they appoint their own wardens."

"Do they? My appointments are written with the tip of a sword, and my authority comes from the Black Prince. Tell them they can appeal to the Golden Emperor if they feel the need."

"There's no way I can make them do what they don't want to do. You can." His voice was rising.

The Fire Lord cocked his head to one side. "You want a show of force?"

Shuibai suddenly remembered the bloody boots of the last *taran* that was sent down to Low Marsh. He hastily said, "Force isn't necessary, sir. But a financial stipend would help solve the manpower shortage."

The Fire Lord laughed silently through his teeth. "I like the way you work, little man." He pulled his desk back to him and wrote a quick letter. "Will three silver pieces a week be an adequate wage? You'll need to pay your own expenses out of that, of course."

Three pieces of silver was ninety pennies a week. A week! "Yes, sir, that will be fine," he agreed.

The Fire Lord finished writing the letter and handed it to him. "Present this to the paymaster, then come up once a month to collect your pay."

"Thank you, Noble Lord. You are most generous." Shuibai bowed all the way to the floor again.

"Did you find the other arsonist?"

"No, sir. I have learned that his name was Agan, but nobody seems to know him or where he is. I doubt we will be able to apprehend him."

The Fire Lord stroked his chin thoughtfully. "I do not like being balked on this or any matter. I have patience, and I am willing to play the game of fox and lion if need be, but this matter begins to irk me."

"Your pardon, sir, but if you would tell me what the other arsonist said, it would be helpful." Shuibai remained crouching on his hands and knees, giving the aristocrat a hopeful look.

The Fire Lord's mouth soured. "Unfortunately, I cannot. He was not alive when he arrived. I have corrected my retainers concerning the proper handling of prisoners."

Shuibai was relieved that the Fire Lord did not condone the viciousness of the men who had made the arrest. He was beginning to think that the Fire Lord was not such a bad fellow for a *taran*.

"Any more revolvers?" the Lord asked.

"Nothing, sir. I'm sorry."

"If you do learn anything about them, no matter how minor, you send a runner with the information immediately."

"Sir, I know they're contraband, but why do they matter?"

"Can you imagine what an army with such weapons might do? Especially if they are pitched against the Imperial Bodyguard, who is equipped only with swords and arrows?"

"But who would want to do that?"

"That is the question, isn't it?"

Shuibai gaped in horror. "But the Golden Emperor is the life of His people! How could anyone even think such a thing?"

"You're an honest man, so your mind is not prey to vanity and jealous ambition. Suffice to say, the Golden Emperor was too merciful; He let too many of His enemies live. Now there's no telling which of them is plotting against Him. But that's not your worry. Go on back to Low Marsh. Build a fire company."

Shuibai rolled up his scroll, put it away, and bowed himself from the room. He found his boy in the kitchen eating sticky rice and drinking tea,. He helped himself to a bit of refreshment as well, then presented himself to the paymaster and was added to the payroll. The payroll was a very long scroll with hundreds of names on it. Most of them were *taran*, and Shuibai doubted that so many *taran* were needed for the fire service. But as he had discovered, the principal occupation of the Fire Lord was not the fighting of fires, but the ferreting out of rebellion.

CHAPTER 13: THE ADMINISTRATION OF JUSTICE

Shuibai and Kanko returned home from the Fire Court to find the shop in a shambles. There was no need to unlock the front door; it had been kicked off its hinges. The interior of the shop was wrecked. The shutters had been axed open and his meager household possessions shredded. His poster of the Lantern Bridge was ripped to pieces, the few sticks of furniture reduced to kindling, his buckets axed, his clothing and bedclothes torn, the feather stuffing of his second-hand pillow strewn across the room like a snowstorm. His tools had been thrown in the mud of the alley and his money box had been overturned and the coins spewed across the floor.

Stonily Shuibai turned to the boy. "Go find me a carpenter. Tell him the Fire Warden wants him immediately."

Kanko ran from the shop. Shuibai wondered if he would come back. He sat down on the edge of the flooring and stared out through the broken shutters at the street. Who had done this he didn't know. It was obvious to him that they were trying to drive him away, though why they wanted to do so he couldn't imagine. He was cold and hungry after his journey uptown; he was angry and frustrated. He didn't know what to do to make the attacks stop. He didn't think there was anything he could do, unless he hired a full time guard. With his new salary he might be able to do so, but the guard would take most of the salary, leaving him poor again. But maybe it was necessary. Who to hire? He trusted no one.

A carpenter returned with the apprentice. He was a tall muscular man a few years older than Shuibai with a long brown mustache trailing down beside his mouth and hair pulled into a short pony tail at the back of his head—a common hairstyle for laboring men who wanted to keep their hair out of their faces as they worked. "What happened here?" he asked.

"You know as much as I do. Board it up so I don't freeze tonight."

The carpenter left and returned with boards while Shuibai swept his floor and picked up the broken pieces of crockery and furniture. He dumped the porcelain fragments in the marsh at the foot of the lane, then swept the others into the fire and lit it. His hearth blazed merrily and warmed the room, but he had no blankets to sleep in nor any change of clothing. Fortunately his expensive uniform had been saved because he had been wearing it. He reached into his pocket and inventoried his property: he had the inspection scroll, which would have been an incredible labor to replace had it been lost, his purse, and his silver fan. The carpenter boarded up the front and built a makeshift door, then promised to return in a few days to replace the shutters and build a real door. Shuibai paid him, then sat and wondered why the invaders had not bothered to steal his money as long as they were at it. While he was warming his hands over the fire someone rapped on the doorframe. He opened the front door and there was a strange boy with a note for him. He tipped the boy and told him to wait.

The poem said, "Although I am sure that he will not be coming, in the evening light when the locusts shrilly call I go to the door and wait." Shuibai could barely decipher the calligraphy, even though Mizaka had taken care to use a simple form in deference to his limited education. Below that a natural hand had written, "I'm sorry she didn't wake me. Will you come again?—Zashi."

Shuibai's heart crumpled at the poetic rebuke, but sprang to life again when he realized Zashi wanted to see him again.

He retrieved a torn scrap of paper. "By this scrap of paper you can see that my misfortunes have not ended. Someone ransacked my house while I was at the Fire Court." He couldn't think of any poetry, so he just wrote, "Please ask your father to call on me. If you were with him I would like it." He gave the note to the boy and told him to take it back to Zashi.

Shuibai got some old clothes and blankets from a rag dealer very cheap, and he and the apprentice slept together for warmth. The night was uncomfortable and cold, but even so, someone was knocking on the front shutters before they woke in the morning. Shuibai opened one panel cautiously, and looking out, saw a troop of *taran* filling the street outside his shop while a sergeant banged on his shutter with the hilt of his dirk. The *taran* were all armored, their winged and horned helmets and demonic war masks making them look as if the Underworld had opened up its gates and spewed forth devils.

The Fire Lord raised one mailed hand and pointed. "What happened here? Chief Byan said you were attacked again." So Shuibai opened the makeshift screen further and pointed to the boarded up rear wall, the lack of furnishings and his own shabby clothes, and told him what had happened.

The lord said grimly, "The town has not apprehended the arsonist, Agan, either. It is time for them to pay the price for defying the Fire Lord."

Shuibai looked at the armor with its broad panels like shields that covered arms and legs, the broad metal chests, the brightly colored ribbons that laced it all together, and most of all he looked at the halberds with their scarlet tassels and the swords with their hilts bound in gold and silk. The halberds curved like wicked smiles, and his heart fell. "What are you going to do?"

"Summon the Council," barked the Lord.

Shuibai put on sandals and his uniform and went out into the snow. The apprentice followed close at his heels. Shuibai didn't know who all the Councilwomen were, but he knew some, and when their servants looked out and saw the *taran* backing him up, they hurried their mistresses out of their warm beds. The first Councilwomen taken were forced to give up the names of the others, and after a hour of heavy knocking and barked commands, thirty hastily dressed old women were dragged from their homes and huddled together in the Broadway Market under the blades of the *taran*.

The Fire Lord began immediately. "You, Headwoman Oroni. Why have you not turned over the felon Agan who is wanted for arson? To protect him is to share his guilt!"

She was a beldame of at least fifty years, with her hair twisted up into a chignon above her magenta night robe. She wore black divided skirts and high wooden sandals, and was shivering in the cold. She spread her hands placatingly. "We have not been able to find him, Noble Lord."

"Bah. This is your town, you know every nook and cranny. If you don't, you should be replaced by someone who does." The Fire Lord's white horse pranced restlessly, disturbed by the anger in his master's voice.

The Broadway Market was a square surrounded by shops. A large stone well with a wooden handle was at one end of the square, while a few booths had been set up around the edges. In fair weather the whole market was packed, but in winter business was much slower. Word had gone through the town like fire; the tramp of horses' hooves and the jingle of bridles had alerted the citizens that something was afoot. Gossip carried the tale even farther and a slow sneaking crowd was appearing at the edges of the square and in the windows to watch, faces hidden behind sleeves or under hats. The air was cold and crisp, and the horses' hooves cracked icy puddles. The mud lay frozen in ruts. Steam issued from the mouths of men and beasts.

"I am going to hold the Council hostage until the felon Agan is delivered to me," the Fire Lord barked at the Headwoman.

"Of course we all want to apprehend the felon, and if you would allow us to—"

"Silence! I've been a patient, forgiving man, and you selfishly take advantage of my good will to thwart my Office." He stood in his stirrups. "Hear me! All of you! We have come for the arsonist Agan! If you do not yield him to the law, then you are all guilty of the crime, and all are liable for punishment!" He reseated himself and turned to Shuibai. "Pump the well."

Shuibai hastened to the pump. The handle was stiff with the cold, but after a half dozen strokes it loosened up. Water began to flow. It was a large well; the bamboo spigot emerged about shoulder high and fell into a large stone basin used to water four animals at a time. The Fire Lord issued a short order, and two *taran* dismounted, picked up the Headwoman and threw her into the trough and held her down.

"Drown her," the Fire Lord told Shuibai.

He stopped pumping. "I can't. I'm not *taran,*" he replied in horror. He stood back, expecting the blade to bite his own neck in payment for his insubordination.

"Feh. Peasants. You, take the pump handle." He gestured at one of his men.

The indicated *taran* moved over and began to pump. The old woman shivered violently as the cold water splashed across her body. Icy water rapidly soaked her clothes. Little by little the water rose in the horse trough. As the water crept up her body she craned her neck, lifting her face up above the surface. But the *taran* held her down so that her back was against the bottom of the trough. Eventually the freezing water lapped over her mouth, then her nose. She flailed helplessly, her claw-like hands grabbing the sides of the trough and pulling hard, but the *taran* warrior was twice her size. After a long struggle, her body went limp. Bubbles burbled to the surface. No one moved, no one made a sound. The only noise was the snorting of horses. Breath steamed out of the mouths of the watchers, who otherwise might have been mistaken for statues they stood so still.

The *taran* let her go then and stood looking down at her submerged body. They shivered from the water that had splashed them, for surely no human sentiment moved them. The demon masks showed neither pity nor mercy. The Fire Lord looked down impassively. Then he did a thing which terrorized them all: he bared his face to them. He tucked his helmet into his elbow and grinned at the remaining Councilwomen, who quailed in terror. "I am going to drown you one by one until the culprit Agan is brought to me. I show you my face so that you may see that I am sincere in my oath. We will wait a few minutes before we continue."

Rising in his stirrups he pointed and cried, "These are your Councilwomen! They are responsible for the proper conduct of all citizens! They are the ones who pay the price for your rebellion! Give me the arsonist Agan and I will release them!"

He sat down and replaced his helmet. Long minutes ticked by. The *taran* shifted restlessly. The Fire Lord's tension communicated itself to his horse, who tossed its head and nickered, prancing in agitation. The old women whispered together, but they did not know where to find the wanted man. A quarter hour ticked by. The Fire Lord pointed at an old woman in a navy blue nightgown. "Drown her."

An older man stepped from the crowd. He bowed and scraped his way forward. "I am the arsonist Agan," he whispered. He was a man of mature years with iron grey hair and a thick comfortable body. His face was lined and weathered.

The Fire Lord regarded him in consternation. "I thought you were younger." He motioned to Shuibai. Shuibai sidled up, trying to stay out of sword's reach. The Lord motioned him closer with a glare. When he was close enough, the Fire Lord bent down and asked, "Is that the man? Answer me quietly."

Shuibai whispered, "No."

The Fire Lord sat up. He looked at the women huddled before his weapons. He looked at the townspeople staring at him. He pondered. "Very well. Arrest him. Since he has admitted his guilt, we will execute him on the spot."

One of the Councilwomen raised her hands to her mouth and covered a cry. The old man did not look at her or any of them, instead he closed his eyes tightly and let the mounted *taran* lift him off his feet and carry him forward.

"Drown him," the Fire Lord said.

"Mercy!" shrieked a Councilwoman as she dropped to her knees and held up her hands. Powder blue sleeves fell back, exposing thin white arms.

"Silence!" the Lord barked. "Gag her," he ordered one of his men. The designated *taran* pulled a handkerchief from his sleeve and tied her mouth. With a second handkerchief he bound her hands behind her back. She knelt crying on the frozen mud, the tears tracking down her face while the old man was led to the well. The *taran* heaved out the body of the drowned Headwoman and threw the old man into the water. They pushed him down, but he didn't fight. They pumped a little more water into the trough, and he drowned slowly and silently. Shuibai wept.

When the body lay limp, the Fire Lord said, "Justice has been served. Hang the bodies for public examination. So perish the enemies of the law."

Ropes were procured and the two slaughtered old people were hung by their heels from a veranda roof. They were left that way with their arms dangling and their skirts falling around them, the indignity of the position part of the punishment. But the Fire Lord wasn't done yet. He intended to drive home his authority so that they would never balk again. He pointed to Shuibai.

"This is my Fire Warden for your town. Obey him as you obey me." All eyes were suddenly fixed on Shuibai. He wished he could turn to vapor and blow away. "Remember this: interfering with a fireman in the course of his duties is subject to summary execution. The laws are established for your protection. Without them the entire city would burn. It is concern for your pathetic lives that motivates me. I expect your full cooperation."

He used his fan to signal his troop and they rode away. The townsfolk remained immobile until the bright forms disappeared down the road and the sound of hoofbeats died away. As soon as they were gone, the Councilwomen released the weeping woman, who lunged for the corpse of the old man. She tore her hair and wailed, "My husband, my husband!"

The other Councilwomen gathered around her. "He saved us all from a terrible death. He will be remembered for this."

Shuibai turned and walked away. People gave him angry, sidewise looks, but no one spoke to him, not with two corpses hanging close at hand. It was all so clear to him. The Fire Lord would be able to close the case and claim success. The other *taran* would hail him as a glorious leader. The people of Low Marsh would cooperate with him—for a little while. The Golden Emperor, if He ever turned His mind to such worldly things, would see the illusion of an effective fire service. It was a satisfactory outcome all around—except for the dead, the widow, and Shuibai.

CHAPTER 14: THE LADY OF THE KNIFE

The execution of the elders left Shuibai depressed and appalled. He moped around the shop and snapped at the boy as he cut the leathers. Shuibai could not bring himself to work on the buckets with his own hands, but eventually he grew ashamed of his paralysis and began to make some purses. Then the Fire Lord's promise of wages stung him, so he laid them aside half completed and made a scroll case, but that reminded him of the Fire Lord as well. Everything he thought to make had some warlike and bloody application. He grew desperate and understood the motivation of monks who swore off all worldly activities and were content to sit and pray on the side of the road, waiting for someone to throw something in their begging bowls. He examined his role from every angle, and concluded that he had not directly done any harm, yet, if he had acted more effectively, he could have prevented harm. Maybe someone cleverer than himself could have ferreted out the arsonist's hiding place, or perhaps someone more ruthless than himself could have beaten the secret out of those who knew, but neither conniving nor violence were part of his character. He could not fault himself for things he was not, but the responsibility weighed heavily on him. He should have done something.

Finally, at midweek, he put on his uniform and sent his boy ahead to the Garden of Earthly Delights where the gangster Jozatha was supposed to keep his apartments. He took his mother's letter of introduction as well as his copy of his appointment by the Fire Lord. He doubted a gangster who was accustomed to intimidating people would be much impressed by the papers, but they were all he had. He thought about taking a gift, but stubbornly refused; the man's minions had wronged him. If anyone was owed a gift, the gangster owed one to Shuibai. So he set his jaw and resolved to be firm.

The Garden of Earthly Delights was a handsome edifice, rather old, and added onto over the years. It sat with its porch directly on the street with its wooden shutters slid back to reveal screens made of sheer silk, which rendered the lights and perfumes of the interior ghostly and enticing. The first room was a tobacco room where men and women sat and smoked, dreamflower as well as tobacco;

as such it was little different from other tobacco rooms, though the decor was richer and the servants prettier. Shuibai let himself in. He found it very warm inside, so took out his fancy silver fan and waved it in front of his face. He was used to the frugal chill of his own apartment.

A petite hostess dressed in pink approached, the long skirts of her robe trailing on the floor behind her. She had her hair done up in an elaborate style with several pink lacquered combs and pins holding it all together and little silver ornaments glinting in the light. Her faced was powdered white and her cheeks rouged pink, while her eyebrows had been shaved and smudged onto her forehead with makeup. On her the artifice looked entirely charming, as if she were a puppet or a painting, not a real person. Shuibai was taken aback; it had not occurred to him that the phrase 'painted woman' was a literal description. He had thought it referred to women worthy of being painted.

"I'm Fire Warden Shuibai, here to see Master Jozatha. I sent my boy ahead with word."

"Oh yes, Fire Warden," she bobbed. "We have been expecting you. Please do come in and enjoy yourself. Camellia Blossom will take care of you."

She showed him a spot at a little low table. He sat upon an indigo blue cushion and looked around him. Everyone was better dressed than he, but nobody paid any attention to him. Rice wine arrived, delivered by a young woman with small breasts pushing against her pink robe, and her hair piled on top of her head and ornamented. Her face was also richly painted. She smelled of flowers and moved with fluid grace. He mumbled his thanks, sipped his rice wine, and worried. He had expected the door to be slammed in his face and garbage flung at him. He was suspicious of the courtesy.

She offered him lobster tails sauteed in butter and served in their shells, octopus in purple sauce, various kinds of fish, including saltwater fish that had been brought to the capital alive in barrels, pickled vegetables carved into the shapes of flowers and arranged in a bouquet, and skewers of chicken dripping with golden brown sauce.

"Do I have to pay for this? Or is it a gift from Master Jozatha?" he asked suspiciously.

Camellia Blossom tittered like a little bird. "This is the hospitality our house always shows to notable persons when they are so kind as to honor us with their presence."

Shuibai didn't know what to make of that. "I'll take the chicken," he said at last. She set the plate before him. It was a rectangle of blue ceramic and was accompanied by an artfully mismatched small bowl of sauce. "Vegetables?" she asked. He nodded. Pretty soon she had transferred half the contents of her tray to his table top, delivered a warm wet washcloth and pair of inlaid chopsticks, and departed. She returned promptly, refilled his rice wine, and remained kneeling beside his table, serving him whatever he looked at before he even thought to reach for it.

"How long have you been a Fire Warden?" she asked conversationally.

"A few weeks," he replied.

"You have already distinguished yourself. We admire you."

"Do you? No one else has said so."

"There is to be a one act play about it, or so I have heard. The actor Bunofore is to play your role." She smiled sweetly at him. "But he is not handsome enough for the role."

He could not have been more astonished. "But I did nothing."

She lowered her head, and looked warily about her from under long lashes. "You spared the life of my brother, and for that I thank you, even if no one else does." She poured him another cup of rice wine.

"Brother?" He could not think of anyone he might have saved.

"At the Broadway Market. When Karopa offered himself as a sacrifice, and you told the Fire Lord it was the one he sought, you saved my brother and the Councilwomen, too. You are a hero!" She whispered softly.

"Agan is your brother?" he asked stupidly. His stomach was hollow. They had entirely misunderstood and attributed to him something he had not done.

"Hush. We have told the truth when we have said that we have not so much as spoken his name here. No trace of him remains."

"What happened to him?"

"He went away. His employer was displeased with him."

"Who was that? Jozatha? That's what people say."

"Would you care for dessert?" Her face was a charming mask.

"No thank you."

She bowed to him and rose in a smooth motion, padding away on her stocking feet. He pondered what she had said. It preyed on his mind because he was not the sort to claim honors he had not earned, but he didn't know what to do about her mistaken belief that he had protected her brother. While he was lost in cogitation the hostess arrived and bowing to him, said, "The Lady of the Knife will see you now."

Shuibai rose and followed her nervously. "I want to see Master Jozatha," he attempted to explain to her back.

She ignored him and led him down a hall and onto a porch at the rear of the building. The porch overlooked a small courtyard surrounded by the black wooden screens of private rooms. A single wisteria tree held arching limbs over the white sand where a woman was dancing. She was stripped to the waist, wearing only a divided skirt of black silk. Her shirt was tied around her waist, the details of which were lost in the darkness. White paper lanterns were strung from the eaves, but only a few of them were lit so that the lady was a shadow across the white gravel. Her leather boots crunched and scraped as she slid through the motions of her dance; the knives in her hands flickered in the faint light. He stood and stared. He had never seen anything like it.

After a while she lowered her knives and sheathed them, then walked up to the edge of the porch. The porch was a couple of steps up; she stood looking up at him with her chin lifted. Her hair was long and black and she wore it in a braid like a *taran* warrior but it was tied in a loop with a red ribbon so that it did not hang loose as was the *taran* privilege. Her features were very handsome, with broad cheekbones, almond eyes, and a high forehead. She wore her eyebrows naturally and used no cosmetics. Sweat sheened her sallow skin, and her nipples were erect in the evening coolness. Small brown aureoles circled the nipples and he glanced at them, noticed the firmness of her breasts and shoulders and found himself to be wiry and underfed by comparison. She smiled faintly, then lifted her shirt and slid into it.

"So you're the new Fire Warden," she drawled. She didn't sound impressed.

"I'm here to meet Master Jozatha," he replied firmly.

"Are you? Nobody gets to see him unless I think they need to. I'm his bodyguard." Although she spoke the *taran* dialect, her southern accent was slower and rougher than the singsong accents of the Capital; consequently everything she said sounded contemptuous.

Shuibai had been baffled by the luxury which surrounded him, but now he relaxed. The trappings were different, but the game was the same. "I have no trouble obtaining an audience with the Fire Lord when I need one. He takes his prerogatives as Fire Lord very seriously, as everyone in this town should know by now. I would hate for him to get the idea that Master Jozatha was disrespectful."

She threw him a contemptuous look. "It's a brave man that expects somebody else to defend his honor. Or don't you think you're capable of standing up for yourself?"

"If I was capable of standing up for myself they wouldn't have beaten me in the street and burned down my shop. I'm a man of low degree with no resources. Why the Fire Lord picked me to do this work I have no idea, unless the Spirits moved him. But the work is important, even if I am not. I am determined to do my best to carry out my duties, and I am not ashamed to admit that I need help doing it."

She slipped off her boots and climbed the rough hewn stone steps to the porch as she spoke. "That's refreshing. Most men don't admit they're worms."

He had thought he'd made a good speech, but she'd knocked his legs out from under him with a few words. He couldn't think how to answer, so he decided to push on. "There was another chimney fire this week. Fortunately the family detected it right away. They got a wet mop and swabbed it out. Fire is not a matter of luck or fate like people think it is. Their own actions create the fires, and their own actions can confine them to simple blaze that is easily extinguished, or they can panic and let it run rampant through the city. My job is to make certain people know what is expected of them, and to make certain they have the equipment to do it. I'm not asking much. Buckets at every house. Respectful attention to any notices I post about fire safety. It isn't hard, and much good can be gained by doing it."

"So you take it upon yourself to make the laws?"

"No, I am enforcing the fire code. I don't make it up."

"And where does the fire code come from? The Fire Lord?"

"Yes. As directed by the Black Prince, of course."

She laughed. "And you run to Chuja-don and tattle about everything that happens down here. You're his little lap dog."

"I didn't ask to be appointed warden."

"Then resign!" she snapped.

His jaw dropped. Of all the things he had thought of doing, resignation had never crossed his mind. "If I resign, who will replace me? Will that person work as hard as I do? Will the town be better off? I don't think so. I won't resign."

She drummed her fingers on the sheath of her knife. "I am in error. I have overlooked your diligence and your dedication. Of course you are a hard worker. Forgive me for not honoring your accomplishments. Allow me to suggest that a deputy might be of great use to you. Your deputy can be assigned to certain tasks that do not need your personal attention, and will thereby relieve you of the burden of your duties."

He stared in stupefaction. "It's just a matter of counting buckets," he hemmed. "It's not so hard. I can't afford one anyhow."

She smiled sweetly. "The Council is going to be in an accommodating mood. A salary for a deputy is not so much to ask. What of yourself? How much does the Fire Lord pay you? We'll double it."

Her sudden turn of mind astonished him. He didn't want to accept her offer; he was afraid it was a like a basket with a snake in it. Open it up and be bitten. "I can think of someone who would do very well as a deputy," he hedged.

Her brow darkened. "I'm sure the Council will have their own recommendations. Someone trustworthy."

"Oh," said Shuibai as the light dawned. "You mean, someone to spy on me."

Her hand caressed the tiger that adorned the sheath of her knife. "Think of it as someone who is knowledgeable about things you do not understand, and who can who can prevent you from falling into error."

"I know my duty."

"So do I," she hissed, losing patience with him. "You're a slow and stupid peasant who has caused me no end of trouble!"

Shuibai took one step backwards. "Then I think you'd better be blunt, because I don't know what you're talking about."

Steel whispered as she jerked her knife from the sheath. She glided up to him and he backpedaled rapidly. His back slammed against the wall and he was trapped. The point of the blade came to rest an inch from his left eye. His eyes were locked on hers, and her eyes were like two black pits of damnation. "Then allow me to make it clear: do it our way. There are no other choices. You live only as long as you are useful to us."

"I understand," he whispered. He understood nothing but the threat.

She took his fear as consent and stepped back. She slid her knife back into the sheath and smiled grimly at him. "Now you know why I lost my place among the *taran*. I prefer the reality of steel to the vapidity of politics. I have no patience for useless things. You will take our money and you will avoid certain neighborhoods as we instruct you. We will encourage cooperation with your fire code in other matters." Her hand caressed his chin. "You will be beholden to us. Sometimes, we will need something from you. And sometimes you will need something from us. Perhaps you would like us to inform the boys on the street to leave you alone? Would that be good?"

"That would be very good," he choked out. "What's it going to cost me?"

She waggled her fingers at him. "Oh, nothing at the moment. But later on, if I need a favor, you'll oblige me, won't you?"

He remained plastered to the wall. Several things were clicking through his mind, not the least of which was, *Why didn't she kill me?* Surely that would have been the simplest solution of all. Why bother with threats, orders and bribes, unless he had something they wanted? But he had nothing, nothing at all. He was bewildered.

"I will meditate on all your good advice," he croaked. He edged carefully along the wall and slipped to the door. A knife thunked into the wall by his ear and quivered. Another knife thunked into the wall on the other side. He turned slowly around to face her. If he thought she had disarmed herself, he was mistaken, for she reached under her shirt in back and withdrew a revolver. The metallic creak was loud in the night as she drew back the hammer. She held it beside her cheek with the barrel pointed at the moon.

"Meditate *now*. You have five seconds."

He gulped and nodded violently. "I will obey your orders," he gasped.

Her frown faded and she smiled in satisfaction. "I thought you would see it my way." Carefully she lowered the hammer. She returned the revolver to the back of her sash, hiding it under the voluminous shirt. Reaching into her sleeve she pulled out a purse and counted coins. "How much are your wages now?"

"Ninety bronze pennies a week," he replied.

She counted out six silver coins. She cupped his hand in hers and pressed the coins into it. "Gangsters are a brotherhood. Where others are bound together by blood, gangsters are bound together by money. As the *taran* love fame and glory, so does Jozatha love the coins piling up in his coffers. As a *taran* who disgraces himself is put to death, so we put to death any person that costs us money. I trust you understand."

"Perfectly."

"Go away now. And don't be so nosy."

He fled full down the hallway with the silver burning in his hand. He didn't wait for the hostess; he tore out the front door and ran down the street like a terrorized rabbit.

CHAPTER 15: THE STOREHOUSES OF MUNIFICENT HAPPINESS

The weather was mild and sunny with a crisp lavender-blue sky overhead. Shop girls were gossiping together, delighted at the sunshine and fair weather. People waved to him and greeted him as he strolled along the Low Road. So close to home he was instantly recognized. He liked it. But he was well aware that a week ago they had not been so friendly. The Lady of the Knife had been true to her word. He was surprised to discover how much influence she had. It was a relief to not have to worry about getting mugged, but her patronage worried him all the same. He was afraid of the cost the strange woman with the sharp knives and the sharp tongue would extract from him.

Eventually his path led down to the wharfs, a neighborhood he had not yet inspected. He was simply walking, strolling about, getting a feel for the area. He would come back later with his scroll and pencil. The warehouses and chandler's shops were mostly roofed in orange tile and plastered in white stucco; the buildings had yards that separated them from each other, and none of them was over two stories tall. Fishermen, sailors, and artisans of various sorts lived in little cottages lining the lanes that ran behind the warehouses, and they all had the sailor's dread of fire. It compared favorably with the newer parts of town where buildings were jammed together and getting taller all the time; there the construction was rapid and often shoddy, and the buildings were frequently subdivided into warrens of little rooms jammed with families and sweatshops.

He thought he might be able to find a sympathetic ear down here, might even acquire the backing of a powerful businesswoman who had influence with the Council, a woman who could exhort her colleagues about the importance of fire safety and persuade the council to fund a fire company.

The Crane River was running full and cold. The sampans rode high where they were tethered to the wooden docks. They were painted with bright colors and looked like a giant had dropped a handful of celestial blossoms into the river. More sampans and skiffs plied the river. A line of merchant junks were tied up at the quay, and water spilled from one of the square-sterned ships as sailors pumped the bilge.

Looking at them Shuibai remembered the idea he had had about the water pipes and corner pumps. Was a bilge pump any different than a water pump? They both served the same purpose: moving water from where it was to somewhere else. Suppose it could be hooked up to bamboo pipes to somehow move water to a fire. He approached the nearest boat, a small sampan. A woman was sweeping the deck. She was dressed in a padded cotton jacket of blue stuff, dark blue knee pants, socks and a conical straw coolie hat on her head.

"Excuse me," he said bowing. "But are you the owner of the boat?"

When she looked up he saw that she was a middle aged woman with a deeply lined face and greying hair. "Yup."

"Do you have a bilge pump on your boat?"

"Nope."

"Do you know anybody that does?"

She pondered. "Junks."

Shuibai turned and looked over toward where the larger ships were tied up to heavy timbered piers that jutted into the water. "One of those?"

"Yup."

"Thank you." He had more questions but decided to save them for someone more loquacious.

He hiked over to the first junk. It was as big as a house and its deck was above his head. It was rigged with accordion-pleated sails, but at the moment the sails were furled. The hull was painted a rusty red color and had two large ferocious eyes painted on its sharp bow. Its stern was blunt, square and tall. He looked nervously up the gangway. Junks were major property; any woman who owned one had to be rich. He didn't mind talking to poor people, but people richer than himself bothered him a lot. He didn't know what to say. "Hi, I'm Fire Warden Shuibai. Give me your pump." They'd throw him off the boat.

For that matter, he didn't even know what a pump looked like. All he knew was that when he went to the well and worked the handle water came out. His confidence crumpled. He turned and went into a nearby noodle shop. It was a small, tidy place where low tables with orange tablecloths were surrounded by round straw cushions. A waitress waited on him as he bought some lunch in the form of steamed noodles with a fried egg on top. Eating made him feel better, so he bought some tea and asked the her. "Say, do you know who owns that junk?"

The woman was plump and tired-looking with long brown hair pinned up with yellow combs. She wore a yellow robe, dark green sash, and worn leather slippers. She had a baby in a cradle while a little boy in blue was playing under the counter. Shuibai had come after the usual lunch room trade so they were alone as she changed the tablecloths.

"Which one?" she asked.

"The first one, with the fierce eyes."

"Oh, that's the *Frowning Junk*. It belongs to the Munificent Happiness Company. All their ships have different faces. The *Drunk Junk* is one of theirs too."

Shuibai laughed in spite of himself. "The Drunk Junk?"

She rolled her eyes and grinned. "I didn't see it myself, but I heard about it. It seems that when Master Jozatha was a young man he persuaded a certain woman that he was qualified to command a ship, so she bought one for him. He hired a crew made up of his friends. Well, they bungled their way into the river, bouncing off half a dozen moored ships along the way and making the other captains very angry. They called him an imbecile and shook their fists at him, but he just waved and said, 'It's not my fault, the ship is drunk!'" She grinned at him. "So around here whenever something doesn't go right, we say, 'It's not my fault, the ship is drunk!'"

Shuibai was delighted. He put three bronze pennies on the table and said, "That was a very fine story. Do you know any others?"

She grinned and looked away, but it was clear she was pleased. She refilled his tea without even being asked and settled herself on the other side of the low table. "One day I was sitting at that table over there. That one right there, in the corner. I was doing the books. This is my mother's shop. After so many years, the ledger book has gotten very thick. So I was sitting and trying to balance the accounts while my husband Agan was sitting on the other side of the table drinking cinnamon tea and trying to distract me. I felt something bump against my knee and I ignored it because I thought it was his hand. Then this skinny brown rat scrambled up the table cloth right onto the table and stood in the middle of my ledger book. I screamed and jumped up. Agan stared at the rat and the rat stared at Agan. Then quick as a wink, he grabbed the edges of the book and slammed it shut. Wham! Well, the rat was dead of course, just like that. We all laughed and started calling him the 'Rat-Slaying Hero.' He was very proud of himself so he hung it by the tail in that doorway over there. We thought it was terrible of him, but we let it hang until his back was turned. I threw it in the garbage. He was mad at me then." A shadow crossed her face.

Shuibai told himself that in a town the size of Low Marsh there had to be a dozen men named Agan. "So where is he now?" he tried not to sound too curious.

"His employer sent him away on business. He's been gone a long time. I don't know when he's coming back."

"Did he have a sister named Camellia Blossom?"

"Oh, that's Ryuza. They call her 'Camellia Blossom' in the restaurant where she works. Do you know her?"

"Yes. I think I've met your husband. Where does he work?"

"The Munificent Happiness Warehouses." She spread her hands. "Everybody around here works there, used to work there, or will work there."

"I could use a good job," Shuibai's heart was beating rapidly. He tried to sound casual as he asked, "What kind of things do they sell?"

"Oh, well. Master Jozatha buys all manner of herbs and things. He's the biggest dreamflower merchant in town. Medicinals, tobacco, all kinds of stuff that stinks and has to be carefully handled. It's not like regular warehouse work. You have to know a little alchemy, make sure the goods are treated right according to the Zodiac and the Way of the Sages. He brings in the raw materials, refines them and blends them and makes them into something useful. Ever smoke Good Luck Tobacco? That's one of his brands."

"I don't smoke," Shuibai replied.

"You should try it, I smoke it all the time. They mix a little bit of dreamflower in it so makes you feel cheerful and energetic." She went behind the counter, got her pipe and pouch, and lit up.

"Do they make guns?"

She shook her head. "That's illegal."

"Gunpowder?"

"I don't think so. No fireworks."

Shuibai rose and put his empty bowl on the counter. "Thank you very much for all your help."

"Say hello to Camellia Blossom for me," she replied.

"I will. What's your name?"

"Papi. What's yours?"

He hesitated. But she'd been kind to him he couldn't lie to her. "Shuibai," he replied. "Goodbye." He hurried away.

He passed a smattering of shops, taverns, and chandlers, then reached the warehouse district. The five Munificent Happiness Warehouses were lined up side by side along Quay Street, which ended at the river. The warehouses were large and commodious and surrounded by a high stucco wall. One gate was open, so he stepped towards it, only to be greeted by a fierce brindled dog chained in the opening. He hushed the dog, but it continued to growl low in its throat. He sidled closer and it barked and lunged. Shuibai leaped back and the dog was yanked off its feet as the chain caught it short. Shuibai retreated out of attack range.

"Hey you!" A large skinny man wearing a dark green jacket and black pants approached. "What are you doing there? Be on your way!"

"Please sir," he said bowing lowly. "I was wondering if you had any jobs available."

The man looked him over. He was tall and older, with a nose that had been broken at least once. He had brown deep set suspicious eyes and short cropped grey hair. He grabbed the dog's collar and held onto it. "Step forward," he snapped.

Shuibai stepped forward, stopping short out of deference to the dog. The man looked him over. "I haven't seen you before."

"No, sir," Shuibai said. "I live in the Iris Bottom and I used to be apprenticed to a tanner, but I want a better job."

"Are you a runaway?"

"No sir."

Shuibai wouldn't meet the man's eyes, which was proper behavior in a social inferior. Keeping his eyes in the vicinity of the man's powerful chest he noticed a couple of things, first, that the man was very muscular in spite of his thinness, and two, that he had a bulge in his broad sash. A gun-shaped bulge.

"Got a written introduction?"

"No sir."

"We only hire reliable men," the man said coldly. "Get lost."

Shuibai continued playing the role of the desperate job seeker. "Sir, if you would be so kind as to give me a chance—"

"Beat it! Before I loose the dog."

Shuibai turned and ran, his heart beating wildly. He tore down the block, then finally slowed and looked over his shoulder and decided he was safe. He mulled over what he had learned, but wasn't sure what use it would be to him. He walked down the first side street, and going the long way around made his way back to the waterfront.

It didn't take long to find a ship's chandler; there were several of them lined up along the quay. Touts—teenage girls in long robes —stood at the doors inviting passersby to enter the shop. Female captains tended to business while male sailors roistered in the taverns. He approached the first girl, who wore a long bright blue robe decorated with images of ships under full sail obscured by clouds of fog.

"I'm looking for a ship's bilge pump, do you sell them?" he asked her politely.

"Oh, you mean a water engine," she replied. She smiled condescendingly at him.

"A water engine? Well okay. Do you have any water engines in stock?"

"No, but we can order one. When would you like it?"

"How much does it cost?"

"Three hundred silver pieces."

Shuibai rocked back on his heels in shock. "That's too expensive! I can't afford that!"

"If you're interested, we have a small used water engine we took in trade when we refitted the *Ice Runner*."

"Is it in good condition?"

"Yes, we've cleaned and serviced it."

"How much?" he asked, bracing himself for sticker shock.

"Fifty silver pieces."

Fifty silver pieces was the equivalent of fifteen hundred bronze pennies. Shuibai's heart sank. 'There's no way I will ever have that much money,' he thought to himself. To the girl he said, "Thank you very much. I'll keep in mind."

He checked with the other chandlers, but the story was the same. New water engines were prohibitively expensive, but none of the others had any used engines. If only he could persuade the Councilwomen to pay for it! But he didn't have much hope of that.

Absorbed in worry, he strolled blindly. Following the quay past its end, he discovered the waterfront was being expanded along the river below the cemetery. Heavy wooden doors led into warehouses burrowed into the side of the hill. A phalanx of seven black ships was moored along the new extension of the quay, flying black flags edged with long thin white triangles like the blades of dirks. The flags bore a white glyph which Shuibai couldn't read. The ships were quiet. A watchman occupied a shed at the foot of the dock, so Shuibai walked down to him.

"Excuse me, I am Shuibai, the Fire Warden of Low Marsh. May I inquire the name of this business?"

The watchman was warming himself over a brazier while he reviewed a lurid picture book about a famous sword fighter. He was dressed in a warm black coat over knee pants and knee socks and sandals. The hem of the coat and the hem of the sleeves were edged with skinny white triangles. "The Black Ice Company."

"Who is the proprietor?"

"Nalazaki is the manager, but the Black Prince owns the company."

"Oh," Shuibai said in astonishment. He tried to grasp the thought of a Celestial engaged in commerce, but his mind boggled. *Taran* disdained business; persons of good birth did not haggle over price. Merchants were parasites who made their fortunes paying craftsmen less than their labor was worth while selling products for more than they cost. In spite of their fortunes they ranked just above untouchables on the social scale. "What manner of enterprise does the Black Ice Company conduct?" 'Business' was a dirty word, so he avoided it.

"We sell ice."

"Huh?"

"Once it gets a little colder we'll be harvesting ice off the Crescent Moon Lake. We store it in those warehouses over there, dug into the side of that hill. The ice keeps until summer when we sell it. This dock is a hive of activity then."

Shuibai's jaw dropped. "How to you prevent it from melting?"

"Oh, a lot of it does melt. But we pile a mountain of it into those cellars, pack it well with sawdust, and enough of it survives until summer to make a nice profit. Then these ships load up and carry it to the customers in Alla Far."

"Why here? Why not do it in the Capital?"

"Real estate is cheap down here. So is labor. Besides, there's more traffic further up the lake, so it takes longer for it to freeze and it doesn't freeze smoothly." He waved in the general direction of the Crane Marsh, "Over there the water is pretty calm and shallow and freezes up real nice."

"Oh. Well, that doesn't sound like a fire hazard. Thank you for your time." Shuibai wandered away, muttering, "Ice in summer, what will they think of next?" Then he stood stock still in realization that in Low Marsh money was thicker than blood. Who was the principal purveyor of those sensual little luxuries that made life bearable? Jozatha. He ran back to the noodle shop.

"Papi," he asked breathlessly. "Does Jozatha sell ice?"

She rolled her eyes and answered obliquely, "Ice is an Imperial monopoly."

"So there's only one ice company and that's the Black Ice?"

"Officially, yes."

He wasn't sure he knew what was going on, but he was beginning to get an inkling. He, Shuibai, as a Fire Warden, was a subordinate of the Fire Lord, who was a retainer of the Black Prince, who had a monopoly on a business Jozatha wanted a piece of. Financial rivalries could be every bit as bitter as the feuds among the *taran* clans, but were not governed by the bounds of *sanaka* and etiquette. Hence the automatic hostility he had received. They thought he was trying to muscle in on their turf and they resented it.

"Papi, listen to me. I'm Shuibai, the Fire Warden of Low Marsh. If your husband will talk to me, I'll do my best to protect him from his enemies."

She jumped up and grabbed the baby from its cradle. "Go away! Leave us alone!"

"Papi, I won't tell the Fire Lord about you. No one will bother you." He could readily imagine what the Fire Lord might do to the wanted man's family, seeing as how he had ruthlessly executed two old people who had not committed any crimes.

She was near to tears. "You tricked me!"

"Papi, I'm sorry. I won't tell anyone. I swear it."

She grabbed her little boy by the hand and dragged him into the back room. "Go away!" she shrieked from the other side of the curtain. He heard busy noises, like cabinets being opened and their contents rifled. He turned his back, knowing it would be better for her if he knew nothing about her taking flight. He quietly left the shop. When dragons fought, it was the poor whose lives were turned to shambles.

CHAPTER 16: CONSULTATIONS & VISITATIONS

Over the course of the next several days letters and gifts arrived. The finest gift was a porcelain liquor set with five cups and two small bottles decorated with cranes sent by Councilwoman Radaun. The bottles were full of fine plum brandy as he discovered when he uncorked one. He was in no mood for liquor so he put it in the cabinet. The letters were friendly congratulations and excuses as to why they had not written earlier. There was even an invitation to a party. Several of the letters contained orders for large numbers of buckets, and the monies were duly delivered by journeywomen who brought apprentices with them to carry away the buckets. Shuibai made quite a bit of money and didn't have to go looking for any of it. It was all due to the Lady of the Knife.

The money weighed heavily on him. He kept the silver paid to him by the Lady of the Knife in a red cotton cloth separate from the rest of his money. Every time he opened the cabinet it mocked him with his hypocrisy. He spent none of it. He awaited his visit from Chief Byan with considerable impatience.

On the afternoon that the Chief was to arrive Shuibai gave Kanko a bonus of ten pennies and told him to go buy himself a new shirt and quickly too, as he expected company that evening. He swept and tidied the meager apartment. He tipped over a wooden crate and covered it with a green shirt. He tucked the sleeves underneath so that the true identity of the tablecloth was disguised. He fetched down the porcelain liquor set and it looked well on the improvised credenza. That made him feel better, so he whistled as he walked down to a nearby restaurant and ordered a fine dinner of lake scallops, brown rice, vegetables, and sweet buns to be delivered. It was a feast the like of which he had not had since leaving his mother's house.

Kanko was not back yet; he imagined the boy was skylarking, which didn't bother him, until he had to fetch his own water from the well. It was several blocks away and sleet was starting to spit down from a leaden sky. He hoped the weather would not discourage his guests. If Zashi didn't come—he told himself not to think about it. He pumped his water, filling up two large buckets, and as he pumped he noticed an advertisement for a theater;

fittingly enough the play was called *The Great Fire of Low Marsh*. Not that the author had bothered to ask Shuibai anything about the fire. Entertainment was not restrained by small details like facts. So it was that Low Marsh got its first taste of high culture.

Back home he heated water in a kettle and washed himself with a sponge; the boy came back dressed in something red and tasteless. He was only a boy so it didn't matter what he wore. "Wash up," Shuibai said without heat. "We have guests coming and a fine dinner is on the way. Scallops and vegetables. I shall serve the plum brandy the Councilwoman sent me as well. Wash up and mind your manners."

He dressed himself in his fire uniform. As the orange dragon settled about his shoulders, it felt natural, as if it was supposed to be there. He was impatient. What if Chief Byan didn't come after all, or worse, didn't bring Zashi with him? He sat sulking by the brazier and would not let Kanko touch the dinner when it arrived. Instead he set it on the hearth to keep it warm and sunk his head in his collar while the tantalizing spicy aromas wafted through the room. Kanko, dressed in his new red shirt, squirmed endlessly, eyes moving from Shuibai to the food and back again.

Finally the boy could not stand it any longer, "When are they coming, Master?"

Shuibai lifted his head. The word rang like a bell in his skull, *master*. He was not Shuibai, useless extra son anymore. He was Master Shuibai, Fire Warden of Low Marsh. He sat up straighter. "Light the lamps," he said. He had only two and they were simple white paper balls with a candle stub inside. The boy took a taper from the hearth and lit them. "Set the table now."

The dinner table was a low square of rough wood, scarred with the marks of the knife when Shuibai cut his leathers. He cast another one of his old shirts over it: a clean tan and green one in a bamboo pattern. Kanko set one of the paper lamps on the table, then laid out a stack of plain bamboo chopsticks. He was transferring the food from cardboard boxes to cheap wooden dinner plates when someone rapped at the door. Shuibai leaped to his feet and padded across the wooden floor in his stocking feet. Opening the door, Zashi and Byan, along with a boy carrying a lantern, were in the vestibule.

"Hello, good to see you! Welcome! Please come in," he greeted them with a bow.

"Thank you for the invitation," Zashi replied formally, bowing back.

"Good to see you," the Chief remarked as he sat on the step and pried off soggy footwear. "Miserable weather. But it'll replenish the cisterns if it really rains. We could use it." He paid the urchin with the light, who bowed and went away.

They left their open umbrellas in the vestibule along with their wet wooden sandals and socks. They were both wearing trousers and were soaked to the knees. "Come in, come in, we'll get you dry," Shuibai said heartily.

He motioned to Kanko, who came over and collected the dirty wet footwear and took it to the kitchen to wash. The firemen removed their uniform coats, revealing heavy cotton shirts beneath. Zashi was wearing a tasteful purple shirt so dark it was the color of a ripe plum patterned with oversized peonies in pink and white. His father was wearing a more plebeian outfit of brown in a natural weave. Neither of them matched their uniform coats. It didn't matter, *taran* habitually wore their lord's or lady's uniform coat over their family colors, regardless of the clash. The coats were hung near the hearth and began to steam. "I can offer you dry clothes, although they are poor things," Shuibai offered.

"Let's take off our wet trousers at least," Zashi said. They did so, and the shirts they had tucked into them were standard robes that fell all the way to their calves. Narrow plain sashes tied around their waists held the shirts closed. The trousers were rather racy, seeing as how the material did not hang together in one indefinable mass like the divided skirts did. Trousers made it clear that a man had two legs. That in turn reminded Shuibai what else a man had between his legs. He flushed at such immodest thoughts and hastily took the damp pants to the kitchen. He pinned them to the clotheslines where they spent the evening slowly dripping and drying. Recovering his composure, he offered the firemen plum brandy. They accepted gratefully and settled around the table.

"It smells delicious," Zashi said.

"It does indeed," Chief Byan heartily agreed.

The three men and the boy gathered around the table. They sat cross-legged on the bare floor since Shuibai had no cushions, but they didn't mind. They were firefighters and used to hard conditions. They tucked into the heap of scallops and vegetables and rice with keen appetites. Nobody spoke; the sounds of chewing and slurping filled the air. Sometime later, after much scraping of plates, they came up for air. The brandy had done its work so everyone of them was relaxed, warm, and content.

"I'm glad you came. I know you're very busy so I'm deeply grateful. I hope I'm not wrong to say I feel like you are friends." Shuibai gave them a shy look.

Byan belched contentedly. "That's only because you have not met any other firemen. We are a brotherhood. Of course we came. Didn't I tell you he was one of us?" he asked his son.

"Yes, you said something to that effect," Zashi replied diplomatically. Chief Byan drained another cup of brandy and Shuibai smiled and refilled it for him.

"Unfortunately, I have been put in a difficult situation," Shuibai said, broaching the subject of his worry. "The gangster Jozatha has bribed me."

"The Dream Seller?" the Chief asked. "What did he do that for?"

"I don't know. I'm surprised he didn't have me killed. I think they want something from me, but I don't know what. Nothing was taken when my apartment was broken into. I thought at the time that they were just trying to intimidate me, but why didn't they confront me directly then?"

"Interesting." Zashi remarked.

"I also learned that the arsonist Agan has fled, but I don't know where." He omitted telling them how he knew.

"I thought he was executed by the Fire Lord," Zashi murmured.

"Yes, that's what they say. But the man the Fire Lord executed was not the arsonist, and he knows it. But the matter is settled to the satisfaction of the *taran*, I guess."

Byan rolled his empty cup across the table. "The *taran* do what the *taran* do. That's not something for us to worry about." He set the cup upright and held it for another refill. "Leave it be, Shuibai. The Fire Lord is happy. The town is obedient. It's settled." Byan was regarding him with intense black eyes. He had drunk enough that his pupils had dilated so that he had no irises left. "If the arsonist comes back, which I doubt, you can worry about it then."

"So what am I to do about the bribe? It's sitting there on the shelf."

"Spend it," Byan replied promptly.

"But, isn't that a violation of the trust the Fire Lord places in me?"

"Is it? Graft is the norm, Shuibai. You'll be a poor man forever if you try to stay honest. Weigh the two against each other, and whenever a decision needs to be made, favor the one with the weightier coin."

Shuibai stared at him in horror. "But sir. What if they want me to neglect my duties?"

Chief Byan shrugged. "The risk is on their own heads. If they want you to overlook certain pieces of property, they can only blame themselves if they burn down, no?"

Shuibai gaped in horror.

Zashi interjected dryly, "Father is being cynical and a little drunk. But the point is, these are matters each warden has to settle for himself. There is nothing wrong with making money off your position. You should if you can, otherwise you'll have no way to fund your office. But I will say, if you accept their money, you should give them exactly what they pay for and not one iota more."

"I can't do that. I'm not smart. My poor head would explode if I tried to keep track of every little bribe and preference they want. My duty as Fire Warden is plain. It's poor work, but it's honest and it's easy enough, in the sense that I understand what the Fire Lord expects of me. I can see the good that comes of it. I can't accept anything that would compromise it."

Chief Byan wrinkled his brow. "Shuibai-don, this isn't your battle. You've been caught in the middle. It isn't a matter of principle but a political struggle between the old and the new. Between that no account Black Prince and his newfangled ideas and the old-fashioned, reliable way of doing things."

"Don't discourage him," Zashi said. "A virtuous man is a rarity that ought to be cherished."

"I want him to live a long life," the Chief replied.

"All I want to do is to establish a fire service in Low Marsh. I was hoping you could help me with the fire watchtowers. I don't care about politics!"

The Chief must not have really believed what he said because he abandoned the argument. "We'll walk around tomorrow and have a look-see. I'd be happy to advise you about the watchtowers. I wish the other appointees were half as diligent as you."

"Other appointees?"

"The Golden Emperor has ordered the fire laws for the City to be extended to all of the Capital District, so the Fire Lord has been going around appointing Fire Wardens. Fourteen new ones! You're the only one that's even trying to accomplish something and has the wits to do it. The rest of them have done nothing, have quit, been fired, are embroiled in petty feuds with their neighbors, are incompetent, lazy, corrupt, whiny, or always running to the Fire Court to beg for money. I'd like to flog the lot of them." Chief Byan sounded a tad disgruntled.

The wind rattled the new shutters, but it was warm inside. Sleet pattered against the walls and they could hear the children in the upstairs apartments romping through the building. The fire glowed on the hearth and the brandy glowed in their veins. They were well into the second bottle, and most of the contents were inside the Chief.

Shuibai dropped his jaw. "Really?"

Zashi spoke. "Well, it's not quite as bad as the Chief makes out, but yes, you've distinguished yourself compared to the other new appointees. It surprises everyone that Low Marsh should be doing so well."

Shuibai flushed and ducked his head. "I'm trying the best I can."

"The weather reminds me of the Golden Swan Teahouse fire," Byan began. "It started when a maid knocked over a lantern and spilled the oil into the bedclothes. Whoosh! The whole room was burning, women were screaming, and by the time we got there the whole house was burning. We knocked down as much as we could, threw water on what was left, and prayed for it to rain, but it just spit on us. Not enough to quench the flames but more than enough to freeze our balls. We were all sick after that fire—even little Zashi."

"When was this?" Shuibai asked.

"Ten, fifteen years ago."

"I was twelve at the time, so fourteen years ago, Father," Zashi put in.

"You were fighting fires at twelve?" Shuibai asked in astonishment.

Zashi explained, "I was a cat. My job was to carry the lantern and serve the beer. An apprentice fireman, if you will."

Cats were young boys who worked for pennies lighting the way for travelers at night—like the one who had escorted the Chief and his son. Supposedly the linkboys could see in the dark, like a cat, but Shuibai had done that job often enough to suspect the boys were sent ahead so that they would fall into any holes and thereby warn the adults. He'd sprained his ankle a few times in that line of work. "Beer?" he asked, encouraging them to go on.

Chief Byan grinned. "Yes, beer. Beer is the soul of the firefighting trade. It's thirsty work, you know. You don't dare drink the water, but beer is healthy and it improves the fighting spirit of the men. Men will gladly work for beer when there isn't enough money in the world to motivate them. Speaking of which, pour me some more of that very fine brandy." He lifted his cup to Shuibai.

Shuibai poured. "I am not much of a drinker myself. I had always thought it led to disorderly conduct which is injurious to the public peace," he replied.

"A fire is injurious to the public peace." Byan knocked back his brandy and held it out for another. "Once it's broken out you need your firemen. In order to do the job, you have to keep them wet— inside and out. Water on the outside to protect them from the flames, and beer on the inside to protect them from the heat. Believe me, young man, firefighters are rarely burned by the flames, but many of them drop from the heat. Beer keeps them on their feet!"

Zashi intercepted the brandy bottle before Shuibai could refill the Chief's cup. "Have some tea, Father. Leave a little brandy for the rest of us!" His voice was a gentle tease.

Chief Byan was looking the worse for the alcohol. "Sorry about that, son, but it's very fine brandy." He belched to show his appreciation. Zashi put the teacup in his father's hand and Byan drank it, not noticing that Zashi did not take any more brandy for himself.

Shuibai looked at the drunk Chief with dismay, then gave Zashi an anxious look. "You're sure about the beer?"

Zashi nodded. "It's hot work, Shui-lan. It's lamentable that men become rowdy when intoxicated, but it's a wonderful motivator. There is nothing like free beer to attract volunteers."

"It soothes their aches and pains as well," the Chief added in a voice that was beginning to slur. His head nodded on his neck.

"But where does the beer come from?" Shuibai asked, anticipating yet another drain on his financial resources.

"Grateful shopkeepers and homeowners."

"I don't think gratitude is very common in this town."

Byan bellowed with laughter and slapped his thigh. "It's rare enough in all parts! Sometimes they need to be 'reminded.'"

"Oh. You mean, like the way they need to be 'reminded' about the buckets?"

Byan winked broadly at him. "Exactly. It's for their own good, after all." The Chief lay down on his side on the floor and pillowed his head on his bent arm. His eyelids were heavy and he yawned. "Ah, good food, good brandy, good company. This is how a man likes to spend his evenings." His eyes closed and began to snore softly.

Shuibai looked him over dubiously. "Zashi, I think your Honored Father has been overcome by the brandy."

Zashi was smiling softly. "It happens. He'll have a headache in the morning, but no matter. You mustn't mind him. Beer and cynicism are occupational hazards. He doesn't really mean half of what he says. But I'm glad you're serious about your work."

Their eyes met and they stared at each other for a long time. Suddenly Shuibai looked at the apprentice. "It's time you went to bed."

Kanko made a noise of protest, but he obediently went to the cupboard and unrolled his mattress. They laid it beside Byan and rolled him onto it. "You'll have to share your blankets with the Fire Chief," Shuibai told him. There simply weren't enough beds or blankets to go around. So Kanko draped his blankets over the snoring chief and snuggled next to his broad back. The larger man was a natural furnace and the boy soon decided a warm bed was worth the snoring.

Shuibai blew out one of the paper lamps before schooling his voice enough to say, "Zashi, you'll have to share mine with me," in what sounded like a normal tone of voice. There was no question of Zashi leaving while his father was passed out on Shuibai's floor. Besides his trousers were still wet and the night was rotten.

"I don't mind," Zashi replied.

They unrolled Shuibai's thin mattress and laid out the green and purple patchwork quilt. Shuibai removed his fire coat and hung it up, revealing a plain grey shirt, then removed his divided skirt, which he was starting to view as a rather old-fashioned garment even if he had paid good money for it. Zashi crawled under the covers and held the blanket open for Shuibai, who crawled in next to him. They lay on the narrow mattress, each of them so close to the opposite edges he was in danger of falling off. Even so there was scant space between their bodies. Zashi propped his head upon his hand and the pose reminded Shuibai of the Chief. But the son was taller and more refined, and his grey stare in the dim light ensnared the younger man. Shuibai stared back, then shut his eyes, not knowing what he should do next. He had often shared a bed with a couple of his siblings—homes in Low Marsh were small and fuel was expensive. Everything was shared and conserved. But sleeping with an older sister he could kick when annoyed was very different from sleeping with a handsome young man that snarled his emotions.

Zashi laid down on his back and put his hands under his head for a pillow. Pillows were a luxury Shuibai could not yet afford. "You're a strange man, Fire Warden Shuibai," he murmured.

Shuibai discovered he could move again and laid down gingerly beside him, staring at his profile. "How is that, Watchman Mizaka?" he asked, imitating Zashi in tone and inflection. He had no idea what to do or say, so tried to do and say nothing. Besides, what would he do even if he did something? He had no clue. It had been a long time since he had played the children's game of Catching Frogs. In that game the girls had run after the boys and it was considered embarrassing to be caught and kissed—especially if the girl shrieked, "Frog! Frog! You kiss like a frog!" Such experiences had not prepared him for the reality of a handsome fireman in his bed on a cold winter's night. Nor the intensity of his feelings.

"You never do what I think you'll do. You're not like other men. Which is just as well." Zashi closed his eyes.

Shuibai didn't dare ask what other men did that Zashi didn't like. Did they reach out and touch the lean chest as he longed to do? He squelched the thought. Zashi was a guest under his roof, the son of an important man, a man who wished Shuibai well and who was willing to help him—and who was passed out less than six feet away. He'd better not do anything that might alienate the only friends he had.

"I left the lamp burning," he mumbled. Rising from bed, he went to the table and blew out the light. The room was dark with only the orange glow of embers on the hearth to light him back to bed.

"Sleep well," Zashi murmured, then turned over on his side. Shuibai stared at the pale peonies over the purple shadow of his shoulders, then got into bed. Though his body burned with heat, he lay very still. He wrapped his arms tight around his chest. He wanted to rock himself like a baby, but he made no motion for fear of disturbing Zashi. He lay awake for hours, watching the embers die out and listening to the snoring of the Fire Chief. Finally the room grew so chill that he carefully snuggled closer to Zashi, his back touching the other's back, and the warmth of Zashi's body helped fend off the cold of the night. That innocent contact gave his heart surcease, and he finally fell asleep.

CHAPTER 17: SHADOW WARS

Early the next morning, Shuibai, still huddled under the blankets, ordered Kanko to build up the fire then go to the well. Rank has its privilege. Miserably Kanko dawdled about getting dressed, but at long last he left the shop with four buckets slung over a pole balanced over his shoulder. It was raining, so he wore a straw raincoat and conical straw hat that made him look like an ambulatory haystack. Chief Byan snored on. Shuibai and Zashi had a slice of morning to themselves.

"Did you sleep well?" Shuibai asked politely.

"Well enough." Zashi replied. He quoted an ancient poem, "'Night that ends so soon: in the shallows still remains one sliver of the moon.' It seemed to me that you were restless." He stretched, inadvertently revealing his scars; he pulled his sleeve over his crippled arm so that his maimed hand didn't show. He moved stiffly. The cold had settled in his scars and made them ache, but he wouldn't admit it.

"I was cold until I moved closer to you," Shuibai replied, trying to match Zashi's polite disinterest.

"Were you?" Zashi suddenly looked at him and there was a light in his eye. "I thought so." Then his expression closed down again. "Tea?" he asked.

So Shuibai dragged himself from bed and found a bucket that had a little water in the bottom of it. He broke the ice on it, then poured it into the copper teakettle. He set it on an iron spider nestled amid the coals. He warmed himself at the fire and didn't look while Zashi made use of the chamber pot. Then Zashi came to the fire and Shuibai said, "I appreciate the friendship of your father and yourself."

Zashi didn't answer for a long time, then at last he said, "I like you, too. You're a simple man, but not coarse. Just uneducated. It's refreshing sometimes."

"Do you have to leave right away?"

"Yes, I suppose I should. I promised my Reverend Mother that I would help around the house today since I did not have to work last night. There are any number of things that need fixing."

"Some breakfast first?"

"No, I'll stop in a noodle shop along the way. If I eat and walk at the same time it will keep me warm."

"What about your father?"

Zashi turned to look at him. "Let him sleep. When he wakes up, feed him and show him around town. He'll tell you what you need to know about the watchtowers. Ask him anything. He's a good man."

Zashi pulled his trousers from the clothesline and stepped into them, and this time Shuibai did watch him. He memorized the long length of hairless leg and the pattern of scars that marked it. He watched how the burned left hand grasped like a mitten with the thumb pinching the cloth against the side of the first finger. Zashi used his right hand and left thumb to put his socks on, then carried his sandals to the door. They were tall sandals, the bars under the soles at least a hand's breadth high, but that had not been high enough to keep his feet dry last night.

Shuibai helped him into his fire coat. "I'm sorry it was so wet last night. It was good of you to come out in such miserable weather."

"We took the short cut down the Wet Lane. I must say, it lived up to its name!" Zashi joked.

"Before you go—"

"Yes?"

"Nothing really. I found some calligraphy in a second hand shop. I thought it was pretty, but I don't know what it means. Will you read it to me?" He didn't want Zashi to leave.

Zashi smiled crookedly and set the sandals down. "All right. What is it?"

Shuibai reached into his sleeve and pulled out the silver fan.

Zashi took it into his hand and snapped it open with a flick of his wrist. "It's a good fan," he commented. "You can't do that with a cheap one." He turned it over and glanced at the crescent moon crest. His eyebrows shot up. "Where did you get this?"

"It was in a package of odd lots I bought. It was old clothes and things that had belonged to a soldier who threw them out."

"This is the Moon Crest of the Silver Lineage. This was made for use in the Silver Imperial Household."

"Yes, I thought as much. I guessed perhaps a lady had given it to a soldier."

Zashi shrugged. "That's possible." He turned it over and glanced at the calligraphy. "It's a very fine hand. And it's very long for a love poem!" Then his eye noted the red seal at the lower left. He bent to inspect it more closely. "This is the seal of the Silver Prince, the One who became the Golden Emperor! If this is a love poem, it isn't for a handmaiden!"

"Really?" Shuibai crowded close. The Imperial Families rarely made direct proclamations; They usually worked through the feudal hierarchy. Consequently Shuibai had never seen any of the Imperial seals.

Zashi pointed at a detail of the sign. "The Seal remains substantially the same generation to generation, but each succeeding princess or prince alters it to be uniquely their own. The Imperial Herald keeps track of all of them."

The silver paper seemed to shimmer with an ethereal light. Did some aura of the Divine linger about it? Or was that only Shuibai's imagination? He was afraid to touch it now, afraid his untouchable status would dim and pollute it; yet he had carried it on his person for several days and it had not lost its luster. "The Golden Emperor held this fan?" Shuibai asked in awe.

"Yes, but in the days before He was Emperor. He would have been young at the time. Younger than you, even. Still, that the likes of us have come into possession of something from the Celestial Court—" Zashi's voice caught in his throat.

"What does it say?"

Zashi laughed ruefully. "I am not as expert as you believe, Shui-lan. It's a beautiful hand, but I can hardly read it." He moved to sit down on the edge of the floor with his feet on the dirt floor of the kitchen. Shuibai settled next to him and leaned over his shoulder, not even trying to read the elegant, ethereal hand. Zashi frowned and concentrated, sounding out the words to himself as he struggled to elucidate meaning from the slim liquid lines. His face grew pale and he stopped mouthing the words. He scanned the several lines silently, then looked up with a wild expression. He slammed the fan closed.

"What is it?" Shuibai asked.

Zashi didn't answer. "Burn it. Burn it now. They'll kill you and me too if they know we've seen this. That dealer, did she know the fan went into your hands?"

"Yes."

"Then you've got a short life expectancy."

"But what is it?"

Zashi bit his lip and looked away. "It's better if you don't know."

Shuibai tugged on his bad arm. "Tell me!"

Zashi raised his maimed hand to fend him off. The sleeping Fire Chief snorted and rolled over.

"This is the ruin of Golden Emperor if it winds up in the hands of His enemies. The Hero of the West is a liar!" Zashi spread open the fan with shaking hands. "Our Hero lost. Do you hear that? He lost. There was no smashing victory over Pangu. He lost and He paid tribute: ten thousand ingots of sacred silver. He holds the Barren Lands as a vassal from the Kingdom of Pangu, and they provided Him with an army to defeat the General of the Eastern Gate. This fan is the record of His surrender."

"But, the Final Battle, the glorious conquest, the earthquake, the Mandate of Heaven descending upon His shoulders . . ."

"A pack of lies." Zashi threw the fan across the room. "He's nothing but a usurping upstart and a pawn of Pangu. Did you ever wonder why He confirmed a foreigner in the Black? Now we know. They own Him. He sold out His country for the sake of a throne. He's not an Avatar, there's nothing holy about what He did. He's a pretender, a usurper, a traitor . . ." Bitter lines contorted his face. "And to think I thought the reign of a male emperor might herald an era of peace and justice. I used to admire him. I was a fool."

Shuibai bent and spread the fan open. "It says all that?" he asked in astonishment.

"It defines the terms of the surrender and specifies the date for payment of tribute. The Silver Prince staked His life as bond that the terms would be kept. If He fails the terms, they kill Him. He signed it with His own seal and His personal name: Garathan. No one outside the Imperial Palace knows His name. Mere commoners like us would be killed if They knew we knew it. We have violated the sacred taboos and polluted the person of the Emperor." He laughed hollowly. "Not that it matters, since He's a fake."

"Maybe they forced him."

Zashi shot him a contemptuous look. "Only cowards are taken prisoner. It's the *taran* way. Doesn't the old poem say, 'Men here are as savage as giant vipers, and strut about in armor, snapping their bows'? Victory or death. *Sanaka ha tessa*. Death before dishonor."

"Yes, but—He did something good, didn't He? The Fire service? Doesn't that count? He's been a good ruler, hasn't He?" Shuibai could not grasp the immensity of the Golden Emperor's crime. If the Emperor was a fraud, then the Fire Lord was a fraud, then Shuibai the Fire Warden of Low Marsh was a fraud . . . His mind rebelled.

Zashi folded his arms and tucked his hands inside his sleeves. "No. His government is illegal. The real Avatar is out there somewhere and when It claims Its place the Pretender will be torn down. Do you want to be on the side of the Pretender when that happens?"

Several choice epithets regarding the Avatars and Their ancestry went through Shuibai's head, none of which he voiced. It would have been blasphemy and sedition to say such things. Sulkily he replied, "I like Him better now that I know He's just a man and not a god. A man I can deal with, but how do you argue with a god?"

Zashi smiled in spite of himself. "With difficulty?"

Shuibai straightened up. "Maybe there is no Avatar. Maybe it's just men and myths."

"The Avatar might be young. Maybe it is the Silver Princess. We may have to wait twenty years for It to grow up and assume Its rightful place. But believe me, I know. The Spirits are real."

Shuibai was getting stubborn. "I believe in what I can see, not fairy tales."

Zashi shoved his burned hand under Shuibai's face. "You've seen this!"

Shuibai cupped Zashi's hand and folded it in on itself. He kissed the scarred knuckles. "I've seen it. But that doesn't change how I think."

Zashi crumpled. "Promise me you'll burn the fan? I don't want you to end up dead."

"It belongs to the Golden Emperor. We should give it back. Especially if it's as important as you say."

Zashi made an exasperated noise. "Oh, sure, the Emperor always gives appointments to untouchable peasants from Low Marsh!"

Shuibai set his jaw. "The Fire Lord could get in."

"Don't you dare trust him with this. Don't you dare trust anyone. Not even Chief Byan."

"What?" a bleary voice asked.

Zashi stepped away. "I was just saying goodbye, Father."

"Where are you going?" Byan asked, groggy but awake.

"Home, Honored Father. I promised to help Mother today."

"Is it raining?"

"Yes."

"Take my umbrella. Yours is no good."

"Thank you, Father."

Shuibai ushered the elegant young man into the hallway where he stepped into his sandals. Speaking in a low voice, Zashi said, "I'd like to visit you again. We can talk about this later. I'd invite you to my mother's house, but it's always so busy there. There's never any privacy."

"You're welcome to visit me any time," Shuibai immediately replied. "I want to see you again, too."

Grey eyes met his full force and he was trapped in them. He hung in the doorway, ready to fall at the slightest sign from Zashi, but Zashi scooped up his father's umbrella and said, "Thank you for your hospitality. Father will help you draw up the plan for your fire company. Remember what we talked about. Good day, Fire Warden Shuibai."

"Good day, Fire Watchman Mizaka."

Zashi let himself out into the street and the canvas curtain fell shut behind him. Shuibai withdrew into his shop and shut the wooden door.

"He likes you," Byan said suddenly. "He was always a quiet boy, but a good worker. Since his accident, he's been even more quiet. But he likes you."

Shuibai grinned like an idiot. "I'm glad. I like him too."

"Now, breakfast." Byan was a practical man. If he had overheard the discussion about the fan, he gave no sign of it.

Kanko arrived with the buckets of water and they heated them, washed and shaved, then got dressed and departed. The Chief and the Warden hunched under dripping umbrellas as they walked up the Low Road. "Where can I get a good view of Low Marsh?" Chief Byan asked.

"The Lantern Bridge has an excellent view all along the river," Shuibai replied.

So they went up to the Lantern Bridge. Byan had a ring of passkeys that fit all manner of locks; one of them fit the door inside the Lantern Gate and they climbed up inside. The gatehouse was a fortification; hence the long room across the top of the gate was equipped with arrow slits. Holes in the floor enabled things to be dropped on anyone caught beneath the gate. A massive portcullis was raised, ready to fall if the gears were released, but they were thick with coagulated grease and the whole machine was covered in dust.

"The Lady of the Highways has been remiss," Byan remarked. "I shall mention it to the Fire Lord."

"Why?" Shuibai asked, not seeing why the Fire Lord would care about the bridge.

"Lady Nayabashi is the Lady of the Highways," Byan replied.

"Oh. So they tattle on each other like children?"

Byan grinned. "Constantly."

Looking down through the holes in the floor they saw farmers crossing the bridge on their way to market, although not as many as usual. The weather was keeping some of them at home. "The price of dreams is going up," Byan noted. Shuibai understood that remark well enough; the dreamflowers were gathered from the marsh, dried, weighed, ground, packed and shipped from Low Marsh. Prices always rose in winter when it was nearly impossible to find the brown and withered stalks amid the other frost-blackened vegetation.

A trapdoor in the ceiling of the gate gave access to the roof. A wooden ladder was hung on the wall and they set it up and climbed up. The trapdoor was heavy from the weight of clay tiles that shingled the roof, but Byan heaved once and the door opened. He was careful to lay it back against the roof without slamming. Had he broken any tiles then the Lady of the Highways would have cause to complain about him, and since the Lady was a *taran* and Byan was not, it behooved Byan to be careful. Although perhaps it was the Lord of Hangovers that was exacting such mindfulness from the Chief.

They peered out of the roof. Clouds lowered over the town and dark smudges of soot streaked upward from hearths and forges. From this distance the clamor of the smiths and the rumble of the sawmill was muted almost into melody. The cold and fetid marsh air washed away some of the human stink. Shuibai pointed out the stark white timbers of a new building.

"And that is the new entertainment house. It will be four stories tall, with a restaurant and tavern downstairs, and private rooms above. It will be the tallest building in Low Marsh when it is completed."

"Who owns it?"

"I don't know."

Byan gave him a level look. "As a Fire Warden you need to know your city intimately. If there is a fire you need to be able to notify the property owners. And more importantly, if you know who owns what, then it is easier to ferret out the perpetrators of arson."

"You mean, rivals burning each other down?"

"It happens. Nowadays it usually goes unpunished too, unless the victim survives and exacts his own vengeance."

"That's appalling."

"Isn't it? Which is why we used to have a Secret Police. To discover and punish those who offended the Celestials. Which fortunately for the common folk was usually other *taran*. But the Black Prince abolished it. The country is going to hell. A male Emperor, a foreign Black Prince, a gazette—the city is developing a mania for the odd and unusual. Things are just not right. It makes our job harder. Too many shadow wars." Byan completed his survey of the area and climbed back down into the gatehouse. Shuibai followed him. "One watchtower should do you." He explained his suggestions.

"How much do watchmen get paid?" Shuibai put the thought of politics out of his mind and concentrated on practicalities.

"Fifty pennies a week."

Zashi was a pauper. But he still lived with his parents, so the fifty pennies was all his to spend. Still, he had not bought such handsome clothes on that wage.

"Does Zashi work another trade?"

"No. But his mother is generous. Fire service does not pay well, Shuibai. If my wife and daughters did not have such good jobs, we would be poor. Most of the men that will come to you as firemen will be poor, too. Well off folks want nothing to do with such dirty, dangerous employment."

Shuibai shrugged. "I was already untouchable from working in the leather trade."

Byan slapped his shoulder. "Feh. If you don't get dirty doing it, it's not really work."

They climbed down from the Lantern Gate then sought refuge from the cold rain in a nearby tea shop. The Fire Chief laid out the organization of a fire company and promised to send Shuibai a copy of the fire code and regulations. He even volunteered to pay the copying fee himself. They sketched a map with eight wards to serve the town. Two trained firemen in each district would be the core from which the fire service would be built. These two men would respond to all fires in their wards and organize the bucket brigades and direct demolition and salvage efforts. They'd be responsible for finding and training additional men.

Byan dictated an advertisement before he left which Shuibai took to a printer. The printer had pre-carved glyphs for most of the words; Byan had kept the message short and simple for the semi-literate populace. Shuibai was not a good reader himself and was grateful. The printer charged extra to carve a couple of needed blocks, but Shuibai was able to pick up the posters the following morning. They were almost poetic in their simplicity:

Wanted: Strong, brave men
who are afraid of nothing and willing to prove it
by fighting fires.
With good comrades and plenty of beer
the disasters that have lately threatened
our town will be ended.
Report to the sign of the Swan and Bucket in Small Lane.

Shuibai stamped them all with his swan and bucket seal, then he bought some glue and he and Kanko went around gluing them to the well housings and other public kiosks. The weather had dried up, although it had not cleared off. The wind was fitful and raw. He stayed clean and dry, but not comfortable. He kept thinking about Zashi and the ache in his heart would not quit. Finally he made a decision. He wrote a note and dispatched the boy with it.

"I have recently posted notices seeking men for the formation of a fire company. I would appreciate the help of experienced men in establishing the company, so if you are available I would like to hire you."

That done, he thought he had better make an appointment with the Councilwomen. Somebody had to pay for the new fire company.

CHAPTER 18: SILK PURSES

Kanko cut leather for buckets while Shuibai interviewed prospective firemen. Most of them withdrew after learning there was no pay involved, but a few of them seemed serious minded and inclined to view firefighting as a worthy cause. Some seemed highly motivated by access to beer and wanted to know how much and how often. Shuibai wrote down every name and made notes to himself. He told them that in another week he would post the roster of accepted men and alternates in the usual places. Further instructions about when and where to meet would be posted then. In the end, he had less than a dozen men on his list, mostly from the wards along the river, and less than half of them seemed suitable. He selected eight as his first cadre of firemen and listed the others as alternates. It did not bode well. He bought a keg of beer and advertised it, and found that it increased the number but not the quality of applicants.

On the third day after he sent his letter of request to Zashi, he got a note back. "I would be delighted to accept employment with the Low Marsh fire company when funding is available for a watchman's job."

Shuibai kept the runner waiting and wrote back immediately, "Funding is available immediately for an Assistant Fire Warden. The position pays seventy pennies a week." He intended to use the stipend he received from the Fire Lord to cover the wage. That would make him destitute again, but for Zashi he was willing to be poor, if only it would bring him closer. He added a note, "I have an appointment tomorrow mid-morning with the Council to discuss the fire company budget. If you are willing to be my assistant, please be present for this meeting. I need your expertise."

Zashi showed up first thing in the morning, dressed in his uniform, complete with dark purple trousers and a conical straw hat with badge on it. Shuibai grinned from ear to ear, while Zashi bowed and said, "I have decided to accept your generous offer of employment as the Assistant Fire Warden of Low Marsh."

The day was crisp and fresh, the temperature well above freezing, and the wild geese whirled overhead, their honking audible even over the clamor of the workshops. The Fire Warden and his assistant set off together, each of them in their fire coats, orange dragons wrapped around their shoulders. They fell into step, Shuibai babbling happily.

"I'm so glad everything is finally coming together. I expect they'll approve the budget I ask, after all, they don't dare risk the wrath of the Fire Lord. Not again. Not only that, but the Lady of the Knife promised to support the fire code as long as I don't bother them, so there is no reason why they shouldn't agree."

Zashi just smiled, basking in the other man's enthusiasm.

The Council was meeting upstairs at the Lotus Blossom Inn, the usual host for such gatherings. The high wooden rafters were heavily carved and painted. Smoke made blue clouds around them. The Council was composed of approximately thirty matrons arranged in a circle around a bronze brazier that provided the room with heat and light. Its fumes added to the cloud gathering under the roof. Shuibai's heart sank when he saw his mother there. When had she been selected for the Council? He hadn't heard. He hadn't been home in a long time. The women were arranged in a circle, reclining or sitting on cushions, half of them smoking, with several teenage girls waiting on them. The girls would learn the art of politics by keeping their ears open and their mouths shut.

"Fire Warden Shuibai. I'm Headwoman Vaadayasin." The new Headwoman bowed respectfully. She was a short, soberly dressed woman in a dark green robe decorated with snow-laden pine trees and a brown sash. "Allow us to show you our hospitality. We missed you at the party last weekend."

"I regret that my duties did not permit me to attend. I have been consulting with Fire Chief Byan with regards to the establishment of our fire company. Allow me to introduce Assistant Fire Warden Mizaka. He is an experienced firefighter and the son of Fire Chief Byan."

Zashi bowed politely. "I'm delighted to make your acquaintance."

The women gave Zashi some sharp looks but didn't comment. Instead the Headwoman said blandly, "I see you boys have initiative. Allow me to present you to the Council."

And so, by emphasizing their youth and gender, she put them firmly in their place. They had to trail along with her, bowing to the reclining women who didn't get up, but who simply lifted their hands in acknowledgement. The women reacted to them as if they were about as interesting as the floorboards. That is to say, useful, but hardly noticeable.

Shuibai felt his ears burning, but Zashi remained courteous. "It is always a pleasure to meet such distinguished Old Women as yourselves," he said as the two young men took their seats. Several of the councilwomen were old enough to qualify for the honorific 'Old Woman,' and several of them were vain enough to think they deserved it, but the others looked at him sharply as if they suspected sarcasm. Zashi's face was schooled to bland politeness.

But the Headwoman knew she had been served tit for tat, so when a teenage girl in a long pink robe knelt and offered her the first tray of refreshments, she fluttered her hand. "Guests before elders, Amadun-lan."

The girl bowed and crossed to the young men, offering the tray of pickled vegetables and nut rolls. The nut rolls were rolls of rice wrapped up with seaweed and chewy green betel nuts; Shuibai helped himself to two of those. He was hungry enough to want more, but afraid to look greedy in front of the councilwomen. He glanced at Zashi to see what he did, but Zashi merely picked up some vegetables and a rice roll with his chopsticks. He smiled prettily at the girl. "You're doing very well," he told her. She ducked her head and giggled in embarrassment. She returned to the Headwoman to serve her, and from there served around the circle.

A second girl brought in a tray with cups and plum brandy. Shuibai wanted to dive right into the food, but he restrained himself to follow Zashi's example, not eating or drinking until Zashi did so. Zashi waited until all the women were served, and not until the Headwoman lifted a morsel to her lips did he eat. At that point the courtesies were satisfied and chopsticks began to rattle in the dishes as the food was consumed with pleasure. A second tray was brought around with raw fish and rice rolls and everybody got a couple of pieces, then a crispy sweet desert was served.

At that point the Headwoman lighted a large pipe, puffed to get it going, then proceeded to pass it around the circle. Shuibai and Zashi each were obliged to take a large puff and pass it on. Shuibai coughed self-consciously, while Zashi was careful to keep his injured hand hidden in the folds of his robe as he smoked the large pipe one-handed. The blue haze at the ceiling became thicker and lower. At last the requisite amount of food, alcohol, and tobacco had been consumed. Vaadayasin began to speak.

"We are delighted to meet your new assistant, Fire Warden Shuibai. I was under the impression you were planning to hire a local man."

"Most of the men will be local, but I thought it important to have someone experienced in the fire service to take the position, seeing as how I am not so experienced," Shuibai replied.

His mother snorted. "That's an understatement."

The Headwoman held up her hand, but did not look at Shuibai's mother. "We are surprised that a son of Chief Byan is willing to take service in Low Marsh," she remarked somewhat pointedly to Zashi.

Zashi replied diplomatically, "My father considers it a beneficial arrangement, as it will enable good cooperation between Low Marsh and the fire companies of Alla Far. I realize that these arrangements are new to you, and that therefore you have no reason to expect much good to come of them, but under Fire Lord Chuja and Fire Chief Byan such improvements have been made in the Capital that fires have been reduced from nine a day to seven a day. In other words, as inconvenient as the fire codes may seem, they are effective at protecting valuable property. There is no reason why Low Marsh should not experience the same beneficial arrangement."

"It's another new tax regardless of what rhetoric you wrap it in," Shuibai's mother snapped. "This is a Free Town, and it is not lawful for any lord or lady to levy taxes upon us."

"A moment, please," Vaadayasin said to her. "Allow me to ask some questions. Perhaps all will become clear when we have the complete details before us." They all waited in respectful silence while she framed her questions.

"I think I speak for all of us when I refer to the Town Charter and do not see fire service listed among the obligations we render to the Golden Empress, or in these latter days of the law, the Golden Emperor. Lord Chuja is not a man of our city. His mother holds no land here, and neither does she own any chattels in this town. We are at a loss then to understand why it should matter to the Fire Lord how we govern our own affairs."

Shuibai looked at Zashi, who answered easily. "All charters require you to obey the Golden Sovereign, and we know that you are dutiful subjects who adhere to Imperial Will as best you can. The administration of an empire is a complex thing, so the Golden

Emperor has given responsibility for the fire service and many other humanitarian projects to the Black Prince. The Black Prince, with the approval of the Golden Emperor, has appointed various lords to administer these duties. Specifically, Lord Chuja has been appointed Fire Lord of the Capital District and is responsible for enforcing fire codes within it. The Capital Fire District is defined as being the same as the Capital Highway District, namely that territory bounded by the Crescent Lake, the Northeastern Highway, the Southern Highway, and the Crane River, including the bridges. So you see, the Fire Lord is the humble servant of the Golden Emperor, and Low Marsh is within his jurisdiction."

A woman with greying hair and a navy blue robe glared at him. "It is an unreasonable interference and not in the charter."

Shuibai spoke up. "You maintain the Low Road, don't you? This is no different than that obligation."

"Maintenance of the road is specified in the charter," she replied. He wished he could remember her name, but there were too many of them.

"It's the same thing—" he tried to say, but the Headwoman Vaadayasin held up her hand.

"We will review the charter." She spoke to the first girl, who left the room. A few minutes later she returned with a large ceramic scroll case, glazed in red, and sealed with the Imperial Sun seal. It was very old, in a style no longer seen in common use. The gilded seal was a sort of puzzle lock which the Headwoman carefully manipulated until it opened. The two halves of the lock folded back and she unscrewed the lid, which was sealed with a black cloth placed between the lid and the jar. She laid aside the lid and the cloth, then reached into the case and carefully removed the scroll. For over two hundred years the ceramic case had kept the Charter safe from worms, rot, water, and fire.

Carefully she laid the scroll on the floor, and the people crowded close. Few of them had ever seen the Charter, although the case was paraded through the streets during the Winter Festival, the anniversary of the founding of Low Marsh. "Not so close!" she warned them. "Don't even breathe on it. The moisture from your breath will damage the paper."

The paper was thick, stiff, pure white rice paper that time had not dimmed. The ink was very black, the letters old-fashioned in form, the language archaic.

"Read it," Shuibai suggested.

"It's long," she replied.

"It would be good for all of us to hear it in all its details," Zashi commented.

So the Headwoman commenced to read, pausing from time to time to decipher strange glyphs.

"In the ancient days when the people first came out of the moon and settled in the land, the Spirits were moved to inhabit the dreams of women, and so obtained an understanding that surpasses human understanding with regards to the workings of the world. In those dreams the Spirits found things which seemed to Them good and desirable, and so granted that an Avatar should be born among the people, and She was made Empress of all the lands.

"Ever since that day when the august Empress made Her abode in Ton Far where the holy mountain rises, every Sovereign born to us has exercised sway over all beneath the skies, each One in Her turn ruling the old land of the Shen. But the Barren Empress sinned against the Mandate of Heaven, and the land turned to desert. Then the Spirits had mercy upon the people and a Prince was born to lead us to the sky-filling land at the foot of the green mountains where the earth is rich. He exercised sway over all beneath the skies from the Imperial Palace where the wavelets ripple upon the shores of the Crescent Moon Lake and the water breaks on rocks. Rural though it was, and distant from the Old Capital of Ton Far, it was here that a new Empress was born. Here Her palace was built wherein dwelt the New Sovereign, the divine Avatar of the Sun; here soared the mighty halls when haze veiled the sky above the luxuriant growth of springtime grasses, and the spring sun shone strong upon the site where stood the great stone-built palace—the place we glory to see."

They sat rapt in silence, listening to the ancient tale. In their maturity they had forgotten what it meant and dismissed it as a fable for children, but the voice of the law was speaking and it would not let them forget where they had come from, nor how they were bound to both their history and their future by the power of the Spirits, as personified by the One who wore the Gold.

"So it was that the Avatar of All Things gave life to each dream, and all the Avatars were born into the world, each to the person who best embodied the principles of the Spirits, and who was a fit instrument to commune with Them, for the minds of ordinary women could not well abide them, and were driven into madness. So it was that the Sun, who sees all and rules all, was made the administrator of the government and the happiness of the people was in the hands of Her Avatar. The Golden Lineage has descended without break through the entire history of the Old and New Queendoms, and is the authority by which this Charter is made and sealed by the Golden Empress, on the ninth day of the second week of the eleventh month in the thirteenth year of her reign, which is the astrological year of the Gilded Dragon in the Cycle of Wood in the Fifth Eon; and given in grace to the inhabitants of the place known in the world as the Town of Low Marsh.

"That firstly, the inhabitants protest their love of *sanaka,* and do vow to uphold it in a fit manner, and to be obedient to the Oracles, and most diligent in their service to the Golden Empress whenever She shall require it of them;

"That secondly, the Golden Empress shall set no Lady over them, but leave them to govern the affairs of their town as they see fit, in accordance with the principle of *sanaka,* and that the Empress shall deny the claim of any lady or brigand who attempts to gain title to the place through any means whatsoever;

"That thirdly, the town of Low Marsh shall tender to the Imperial Treasury a poll tax of one silver coin per inhabitant, excepting infants under the age of two years and infirm persons unable to engage in labor, beggars, monks, and other persons who contribute nothing to the welfare of the community, said payment to be made at the anniversary of the signing of the Charter . . . "

There was more; the maintenance of the Low Road which passed through Low Marsh was specified along with the maintenance of the post station; there was a prohibition against soldiers being lodged within the town; a pledge of free passage for anyone in the Imperial service; assurance of the town's right to levy taxes on goods passing through it; a pledge that the town would not harbor criminals, rebels, or runaway servants, and would turn them over to anyone who asked for them; the right of the Golden Empress to draft common soldiers in times of emergency with the rate of pay and number of days of service specified; the right to petition the Empress for redress; and last but not least, eight prayers a year to be offered for the welfare of the Golden

Empress, Her Consort (who in those days was the Black Prince), and Her Children. Fire service was not mentioned.

"Just as I thought. It says nothing about providing for a band of ruffians called firemen," Shuibai's mother pronounced.

"It orders you to obey the Empress," Shuibai responded.

"If it isn't in the Charter, we aren't obliged to do it," the Old Woman in navy blue opined.

Headwoman Vaadayasin carefully rolled up the scroll and placed it back in the case. "I suspect that if we petitioned the Golden Emperor, He would tell us that it is His Will that we obey His Fire Lord."

"But He can't do that! The Charter says we're allowed to run our own affairs as we see fit!"

"But He did do it. He appointed Lord Chuja as Fire Lord and Lord Chuja appointed Shuibai-don as Fire Warden, and you are sworn to obey the Gold," Zashi replied, nailing down the case.

Shuibai's mother switched her baleful glare to Shuibai and said, "This is your fault, meddling in affairs over your head."

"Who *is* she?" Zashi asked him.

"My mother," Shuibai replied sourly.

"No wonder you don't live at home."

"Mind your manners—" she snapped, but Vaadayasin interposed, "She is the Councilwoman from the newly established Iris Bottom ward."

"You've annexed the Iris Bottom?" Shuibai asked.

"Yes, we approved it earlier this week. The town has been growing, and some of our more prosperous citizens thought they could avoid their civic obligations by moving outside the town limit."

"But doesn't the Iris Bottom fall within the Cherry Hill fief?" Shuibai asked.

"We have arranged a satisfactory settlement with the Lady of Cherry Hill, and she has agreed to lease the land to us."

Zashi leaned and whispered in Shuibai's ear, "That's Nayabashi's mother. Now what?"

"I shall have to inform the Fire Lord of the change in the boundaries of my district." Shuibai was not confused; the motive seemed transparent to him. They'd arranged things specifically so that his mother could henpeck him to death. No son, not even the Golden Emperor, could gainsay his mother. Luckily for the

Emperor His mother was dead. Fleetingly he wondered if the rumors that He had killed His own mother were true; staring at his own mother Shuibai understood the appeal of matricide.

"In the meantime," Zashi said, smoothly picking up the pieces. "We will commence building the watchtower and training the firemen. Please tell us where the watchmen should report to collect their wages."

"Wages?" asked the Headwoman.

"Men, or women, if any can be found, willing to undertake such poor work, must watch every night from dusk until dawn. Chimney fires and roof fires are the most common kind of fires. When they happen at night they can burn through an entire house without any of the unfortunate victims ever waking. A man can't stand a watch all night and work all day too, so they must be paid."

"We will take your suggestions under advisement and let you know our decision by Winter Festival," Headwoman Vaadayasin replied.

"That's two months away!" Shuibai protested.

"These are weighty matters that must be given due consideration." The Councilwomen were smirking and nodding their agreement. It was plain that some of them would 'meditate' upon the subject from thence to eternity. Shuibai would never see the color of their money. He started to protest.

Zashi elbowed him. "Naturally we understand. However, you must understand that we be vigilant in our inspections. Since the Councilwomen set an example to their community, we will commence with you."

"I bought my buckets already," said a plump woman who wore a dark green robe and blue sash.

Zashi looked at Shuibai, who nodded confirmation. "I'm delighted by your cooperation. If all of you have passed the bucket inspections, we can move onto the ladder and chimney inspections," he said pleasantly.

"What?" demanded Shuibai's mother. "What are you talking about?"

"A box of sand must be kept by each hearth, forge, or other source of fire. A ladder long enough to reach the roof must be kept by each establishment that is more than one story high. Chimneys must be kept clean. Further, it is forbidden to use a thatch roof on any building with an open hearth. There are quite a few regulations. Fines vary anywhere from five pennies to a thousand pennies per offense. We will naturally carry out weekly inspections as proof of our devotion to duty and vigilance against the fire dragon."

"So you're going to harass us with your codes until we do things your way, eh?" Councilwoman Omian scowled.

"Thugs," Shuibai's mother started in. "Trying to intimidate us. It won't work."

"Please, enough," put in the Headwoman. She was ignored.

"I won't allow this—this—uptown popinjay to poke his nose into my business. As for you, little boy," she glared at Shuibai, "You're going to get your hide tanned!"

"No, he's not," Zashi objected.

"I will damn well discipline my son as I see fit, and if you get in the way I'll have your mother tan your hide, too!"

Zashi's smile grew more ferocious. "We are duly appointed firefighters carrying out our duties. If you interfere with us, you will pay the penalty provided by law."

"Intolerable!" Shuibai's mother seethed. "Insupportable! You can't do this!"

Councilwomen nodded.

"We're going to!" Shuibai replied, getting hot.

Zashi said coolly. "You're welcome to appeal to the Fire Lord if you think it necessary. Do you remember what happened the last time he intervened?"

Shuibai and his mother stared at one another across the space, and two bright pink spots appeared high on his mother's cheeks. She was livid, her jaw clenched in rage. "Never did a mother have such an ungrateful son! I should have beaten you more often. I was too tender-hearted, and this is how you repay me!"

He leaped to his feet and stood over her. She scooted back from him. He clenched his fist, but he did not strike her. Instead he pointed at her. "I'm not going to put up with your threats any more. You're a viper that bites its own tail if it can't bite someone else. Stay out of my way. Don't interfere with my business. You're such a spiteful old creature. I hate you!"

His anger rang from the rafters and left a stunned shock of silence. She jumped up and cracked her fan across his face, leaving a red stripe where it lashed him. "Meddler! Bungler! Fool! Ingrate!" she cried.

He slapped her face as hard as he could. He didn't think about it; it just happened. Her heel caught in the cushion and she staggered backwards. He pushed her hard and she sprawled across another councilwoman who scrambled to get out of the way. He followed up with a kick to her ribs and pursued her as she scuttled away in a tangle of blue-green robes.

Zashi was suddenly at his side, his hand gripping Shuibai's elbow. "Enough, Fire Warden Shuibai. Let's leave this place."

"Barbarian!" his mother howled.

He stopped and looked at her. "If I am, it's your fault. You raised me."

The council broke into little knots. A few town mothers comforted the Councilwoman from Iris Bottom, while others stood stone-faced beside Headwoman Vaadayasin, who glared at them. She spoke through tight lips. "Leave—now."

They descended the steps, and someone, they weren't sure who, yelled, "And don't come back!"

As they emerged on the street Zashi burst out, "Frost on a horse's bones! Everything they say about Low Marsh is true. It's a narrow-minded, hidebound, filthy, stinking hole. You should leave. You're too good for these filthy peasants. Come stay at my mother's house. We'll get you a job in the Capital. Not all people are like this."

Shuibai stepped away from him. "Is that how you think of me? A filthy peasant? I'm Untouchable, you know. I work in the leather trade. I live in a filthy low place. I'm the son of a family of butchers. I don't know any poetry, and I can barely read. More than that, I am a fool because I thought . . . never mind." He started walking.

Zashi trailed behind him but did not overtake him until they had reached the corner of the street where he lived. Shuibai stopped and let him catch up. He wouldn't look at him though.

Zashi touched him with his burned hand and said, "I am untouchable, too." Then he entered the narrow street. Shuibai followed him down the muddy lane to his own door, and let them in.

CHAPTER 19: THE HOODED WOMAN

When Zashi learned that Shuibai was turning over most of his meager salary to him, he was appalled. Shuibai wouldn't accept it back, saying that he would simply have to sell buckets to make his own living and hope for the best. The gangster's wage remained sitting untouched on the shelf. It was agreed that since Shuibai could make buckets and Zashi cut a more imposing figure, Zashi would do the inspections and bring the bucket orders home to Shuibai. Zashi was able to persuade some of the more recalcitrant business and homeowners to comply with the fire code. He felt no compunction about bullying them if necessary, and made his threats in such elegant and subtle language that most were intimidated, but not offended. Consequently, they liked him.

Every day he went out, and every day he came back limping with his face drawn in lines of pain, but he never complained. Kanko would bathe him and rub him down. Shuibai longed to perform that favor himself, but body service was commonly assigned to servants, and besides Shuibai didn't think he could prevent his hands from trembling. He resolutely attended to his work, choosing instead to rivet the day's crop of buckets, the hammer banging down repeatedly in a noise that drowned out thoughts and overwhelmed any physical sensations he might be experiencing.

Zashi was shy during his rubdown. He would keep a cotton robe wrapped about himself, exposing only the limb that was in the process of being washed and oiled. He drank tea sweetened with cinnamon brandy if they had it, and after an hour or so he would feel better. Then he dressed casually, the lines of pain eased from his face, and he talked to Shuibai about what he had seen and done, and went over his notations on the scroll.

There was no discussion, but another mattress and set of bedclothes appeared, and bit by bit some of Zashi's personal items came to inhabit the space. The bachelors settled in together without discussion, the boy keeping house and running their errands, while the two of them put in many hours of hard work, barely earning enough to eke out a living.

A woman came weeping down their street. The front screens were closed and they paid little attention to her, but gradually the weeping grew nearer and they could make out her words, "Fire Warden, Fire Warden! Somebody please show me the house of the Fire Warden!"

Somebody slid a window open and shouted, "The one with the bell, you stupid wench!"

Shuibai rose and slid back the paper screen and then the wooden shutter. Cold air rushed into the room and Zashi and Kanko scooted over to the hearth where they stood warming themselves. "Over here," he called to her from the window.

She was limping as she walked, her long skirt trailing on the dirty street, her coiffure torn to shreds, long tresses trailing over her shoulders and down her back. Her robe was made of elegant stuff in the color known as 'autumn mist over the moors,' and it was falling down one arm. Her persimmon colored sash was badly tied, wrapped around her waist and knotted in an ugly lump without a bow. Her makeup was smeared and ran down into the collar of her robe, and the white under robe was stained with red. In the lamplight spilling into the street he recognized the waitress.

"Camellia Blossom?" he asked. "What happened?"

She looked up, and he saw that she was not torn like a woman in mourning. She was battered, her nose broken and bloody, her front teeth knocked out, and the mess running down her neck was blood as well as makeup. "They made me say where my brother went, and they are going to kill him!"

"Who?"

"The Hooded Woman!"

He looked up and noticed that cracks of light were showing where a few people had slipped their screens open just enough to spy on the street. "Come in. You look awful."

He helped her step up onto the wooden floor. She stumbled and he caught her. She was light and frail in his hands like a broken bird. He slid the shutter and screen shut and ushered her across the floor to the hearth. She slumped on the planks.

"What happened?" Zashi asked.

"Kanko, bring us some water and a washcloth," Shuibai said.

"Please help my brother, they're going to kill him!"

"Who?" Zashi asked.

"Where is he?" Shuibai asked.

"At an inn by the Lantern Bridge," she cried. "The Hooded Woman was angry, and they made me tell where he was."

Zashi brought brandy and she gulped it and coughed. "Who's the Hooded Woman?" he asked her.

"The Lady of the Knife," Shuibai answered.

"No, not the Knife. The Knife is an ex-Iris soldier from down south. The Hooded Woman is from the Capital. I don't know who she is. An important *taran*. She told the Lady of the Knife that it was her fault for losing the fan in the first place, then she told the Dream Seller that he and his men were bungling idiots, and she demanded that he kill my brother for revealing the revolver to you. He said it was nothing, that you were a stuffed shirt that would never amount to anything, but she said Agan had to die to keep their secret safe."

"They beat you?"

"Yes. I wouldn't tell. She said she would ruin my face and she did!" Camellia Blossom was gasping for breath. "When I still wouldn't talk she told the Lady of the Knife to cut me." She wrenched open the neck of her robe and showed the bloody line drawn across her ivory breast. "So I talked."

Shuibai remembered the knife glittering an inch from his eye. "It's not your fault. She would have killed you." He was pulling on his hat and Zashi was putting on his coat. "Kanko, stay with her. Give her whatever she needs. Zashi, sound the alarm."

Shuibai grabbed his fire coat and dressed quickly while Zashi slid back the screen, picked up the beater that hung by the cylindrical iron bell, and hammered three swift taps. The sound echoed loudly in the narrow street. It being evening the town was mostly quiet and the metallic clangor carried a long distance. The sound was strange and people stuck their heads out their windows. "What's all the racket?" they called down.

Zashi repeated three rings three times, then went back inside to get his own coat. As he passed Shuibai who was striding forward with a stout fireman's pike in his hands, he asked, "Just out of curiosity, who are we trying to rescue?"

"The arsonist Agan."

Zashi spun around. "Why?"

"Because he knows other people's secrets."

"I see your point."

151

The first firefighter came running pell mell down the street a moment later, his conical straw hat concealing his face. He wore a sensible heavy cotton coat of dark green, with leggings and wooden sandals. "Where's the fire?"

"No fire, we're going to arrest an arsonist." Shuibai's blood was up and he paced impatiently along the edge of the wooden floor, waiting while five more firefighters showed up over the next several minutes. That gave him eight, counting himself and Zashi, which he judged to be enough. Two of the men had brought their axes with them. Suddenly the crack of distant gunfire shattered the night. They all stood still as four shots echoed over the marsh.

The little party froze in tableau. "What was that?" a short burly firefighter with an axe over his shoulder asked.

"Murder, if I'm not mistaken," Shuibai replied grimly. "Let's get moving. Maybe we can catch a rat."

They ran up the street at a jog trot. They turned onto Low Road and their wooden sandals clattered loudly. People looked into the street and called, "What's up?"

Shuibai grinned like crazy and called, "The Low Marsh Fire Company is answering a call!"

The mothers called their children to the window and pointed, "Look! There goes Chief Shuibai and the Low Marsh Fire Company!"

Glancing around himself Shuibai saw his grin echoed on excited faces. The men were panting as they ran along, caught in the excitement of the moment. It didn't matter what they were doing, all that mattered was that they were doing it. No matter what happened, they'd have bragging rights. A street sweeper, a brewer, a leather worker, a cripple and a motley collection of day laborers were making history, and they knew it: Low Marsh's fire company was answering their first call.

A few minutes later they arrived at the intersection of the Great Southern Highway and the Low Road. A miscellaneous cluster of inns, a post station, livery, teahouses and souvenir sellers were built at the edge of the town of Low Marsh. The huge red lantern that gave the Lantern Gate its name was glowing brightly, but the thing that interested Shuibai most was the hooded figure mounted on a great black horse. She whirled to watch him approach, but her face was masked and there was no insignia on her sleeves. Her jacket was of rich black brocade, and her divided skirts were thick and heavy. Her curved sword hung blade up in her sash, and her hand went to the hilt. In that position she could draw it in an instant and take his head off, shake the blood off, and return it to its scabbard before his head hit the pavement. The *taran* practiced things like that.

"Who goes there?" an aristocratic voice rang out in challenge. A party of female *taran* whom Shuibai had never seen before accompanied the Hooded Woman. One of them kicked her horse forward to bar his way. Behind and above them a flickering glow leaped behind the translucent paper screens in the windows of the upper story of an inn.

"Fire Warden Shuibai and the Low Marsh Fire Company," Shuibai called back in answer. He pointed to the inn. "We've come to fight the fire." He didn't doubt for a moment that the gunshots, the fire, and the sinister women were related, and that somewhere in the middle was the very dead body of the arsonist Agan.

"An accident. A guest was smoking in bed," the Hooded Woman said. Her language was so formal, so strange, so very high society that Shuibai could barely understand her. Why a Celestial should take part in the murder of an arsonist he didn't know and wished he did. Silver fans and women warriors and all manner of trouble were descending from the Capital to his little town and he didn't like it.

"With your permission, we'll take care of it," Shuibai replied.

The Hooded Woman's horse curvetted; the smell of smoke and burning meat was making him skittish. She watched the flames eat up the paper window, then flick up under the eaves. "Very well. We will leave you to your work. An accident of the most ordinary sort." She placed a whistle between her lips and piped an ear piercing call. Her squadron formed up, she put spurs to horse, and the troop galloped north along the highway. Several figures were left standing on foot, and Shuibai found himself face to face with the Lady of the Knife.

"You served with the Iris Battalion during the war, didn't you?" he asked her.

"Don't ask questions, Fire Warden Shuibai. Now is when you earn your silver and our forbearance."

"I hear you," he replied. Then he turned his back on her and shouted, "Form a bucket brigade!" He detailed a man to find a path down to the river while a couple of his men ran up along the highway crying, "Throw out your buckets!"

Buckets were lobbed with alacrity, and once the Lady of the Knife and her sullen, tattooed companions withdrew to watch, the local inhabitants sprang to action. Shuibai was glad of the firemen; it made a big difference to have the help of people who had a clear idea of what they were supposed to be doing and who weren't panicking over their own property. The local citizens were drafted to form a bucket brigade, then Shuibai and Zashi entered the burning building. Flames crackled over head.

Shuibai called, "Is anybody inside?" No one answered him. Pipes and teacups were left in the main room, so he suspected that the Hooded Woman had emptied the inn before making her attack on the arsonist.

He climbed the steps into a haze of grey smoke. His bucket brigade followed him up the steps, and Zashi was right at his heels, giving him advice. "Check the door for heat. Be careful when you open it, the sudden rush of air will cause the fire to flare up. Let us soak you first." Zashi poured a bucket of water over the front of his coat and sleeves, getting him halfway wet, and two more buckets of water were dumped on him, drenching him thoroughly. More buckets were passed. The bucket brigade was working.

Shuibai looked around, saw that everyone was as ready as they could be, then took a deep breath and slid the door slowly open, and looked into the room. The straw mats on the floor were burning, the bed and bedclothes were burning, and the inert figures on the bed were blackened by flames licking over them. A pipe was in the nearer figure's right hand, the clay cracking into pieces from the heat. The pictures on the walls were burning, and so was the wall around the window.

A rank, pungent stench, like overcooked pork, rolled over him. He gagged and staggered, and put his sleeve over his face. Zashi shrugged, unimpressed by the charnel smell. "You'll get used to it," he said.

Shuibai shouted, "Water!" in a hoarse voice, and the first bucket was passed to him. He tossed it, and Zashi said, "Drive the fire outward towards the window and away from the center of the house. You can herd it like an animal by the way you place the water. This isn't so bad. Just a mattress fire."

'Not so bad' was a relative term. As far as Shuibai was concerned the room was a fiery hell. But there was no time for fear. The buckets came at quick intervals, and he tossed the water. Each time the flame would retreat a bit, then reclaim part of what he had quenched before the next bucket arrived.

"It's going into the roof," Zashi said. "That will be a problem. I'll tackle it from the outside, you keep going here. Don't let it trap you."

Zashi went downstairs, shouting for a ladder. The roof was tile, but the fire was beneath it, in the wooden eaves. Nobody had a ladder. Zashi shouted at the gangsters, "You there, don't just stand there, make yourselves useful!"

The Lady of the Knife pointed at herself, then laughed derisively, as if she had never heard such a foolish thing. Zashi and another townsman started hunting through the yards and sheds in search of a ladder.

Meanwhile, inside the inn, the fire was eating into the walls. Shuibai told the closest fireman, "Get your axe. Drag the debris into the middle of the room where we can throw water on it. Don't let it get through the walls."

So the man, who was known as 'Axe' ever after, pulled his axe from his belt and used it as a hook to yank burning things down from the walls and fling them into a heap on the burning bed. Shuibai tossed bucket after bucket of water. Smoke stung his eyes and throat, and his arms turned to lead. The buckets kept coming, occasionally adorned with river weeds or rocks, and he kept chasing the fire toward the front wall and away from the interior walls. He understood Zashi's advice: the building was full of flimsy walls and textiles and all manner of things that would burn merrily, gutting the building. The exterior walls were sturdier, and even if the fire did breach them, it would be licking at air with nothing else to burn. Some time later, he had no idea how long, he met Zashi at the window.

Zashi had secured himself with one leg threaded through the rungs and his foot tucked under, while men on the ladder below him were passing buckets up over their heads to him. He had to toss the water up into the eaves. His head was practically in the fire because his scarred arm wouldn't lift any higher. But in spite of the awkwardness they extinguished the fire and no major structural damage had been done. Zashi's face was blackened with smoke and his eyes were red-rimmed and running. His uniform was wet and filthy.

"You look like a troll," Shuibai said. He didn't bother to ask where the ladder had come from; he trusted Zashi's resourcefulness.

"You should see yourself. You look worse," Zashi retorted. His voice was tired, in spite of his good spirits. He crawled through the burnt window and stared down at the corpses. "Do you know them?" he asked.

Shuibai didn't want to look at the bodies of the victims, but he knew he had to. He walked over and carefully studied the blackened skulls, but there was nothing to recognize. Just oval lumps. Several firefighters and members of the bucket brigade gathered in the room and watched him as he used an axe to peel back the ashes of the bedclothes. The quilt was heavy and had not burnt completely; he found a few fragments of clothing scorched but intact. He carefully peeled them away from the charred flesh. A swatch of fabric was bright yellow, and he said, "This is Agan's shirt."

"Smoking in bed," said one of the firemen.

"Everybody out," Zashi said. "The Warden and I will take it from here. Go clean up the mess."

They shuffled out.

Shuibai didn't want to do it. His stomach was riling him, but it had to be done. Distastefully he peeled off a layer of scorched fabric. He tried not to breathe the stinking air as he blew ashes off the body. Using the cloth he tried to clean off the face, but the charred meat was unrecognizable. The forehead was pierced by a single round hole. He moved to the second adult corpse, and found that it too had been shot through the forehead. Between the two adults was the tiny form of an infant, also shot, and on the far side of the bed, the small frame of a child.

"Shot to death, and the fire set to cover up the murder. They didn't want us to be able to identify him, and they wanted us to think it was an accident. That's what the public announcement should be," Zashi said.

"I knew these people," Shuibai whispered. "Papi and her children. I frightened them and they ran to him. I didn't mean to, but now they're all dead."

Zashi pursed his lips. "Let's see if we can find his gun."

They searched the burned room, but they didn't find any guns. They guessed the killers had taken it. However, they did turn up a box of unexploded ammunition. It was warm to the touch and they counted themselves lucky it had not gone off in the fire. The box was stamped with the red seal of the Maiko Fireworks Company.

"Maiko, that's in Cherry Hill," Zashi said.

"Why are they meddling down here? Why can't they keep their troubles to themselves?" Shuibai complained. "What did we ever do to deserve this?"

Zashi limped across the charred floor. "The Lady of Cherry Hill ceded the Iris Bottom to Low Marsh, and people in Low Marsh hate the Fire Lord. Perhaps their antipathy has a reason above and beyond their resentment about the intrusion on their traditional liberties."

"But who is the Hooded Woman? Do you suppose that was the Lady herself?"

"No, the Lady of Cherry Hill is old. Furthermore, if she wanted somebody dead she wouldn't need to do it herself. She can hire it done."

"Hire a *taran* as an assassin? That doesn't make any sense."

"It does if the assassin is a member of the Secret Police. The Secret Police wear no insignia."

"But the Black Prince disbanded them, so how could they— Oh. That would be a motive for them to dislike everything connected with the Black Prince, wouldn't it?" Shuibai admitted. "But why here, why us, why Low Marsh, why guns? It still doesn't make any sense!"

Zashi put the still warm box into Shuibai's hands. "You have a problem, Shui-lan. The Lady of the Knife made it very clear that they want you to overlook whatever happened here. The Fire Lord, however, I'm sure would be very interested to know these details. It's time to choose sides, and either way, you could wind up dead."

Shuibai went and looked out the window. The Lady of the Knife was standing with her arms wrapped tight around her as if she was cold. She was flanked by several ruffians in gaudy shirts. They were waiting for Shuibai to exit the building.

Shuibai said, "I have a plan. They don't know Camellia Blossom came to me, and with a little luck, they never will." He hefted the box of ammunition in his palm. "Suppose she takes this to the Fire Lord and tells him everything she knows? We can't protect her, but he can."

Zashi's eyes were red-rimmed and his face was covered with soot, making his slow glad smile all the brighter. Shuibai thought he would gladly die for a smile like that. "Ah, Fire Warden Shuibai, you are brilliant. By all means, let us send the girl to the Fire Lord."

Shuibai put his hand inside his sleeve and fondled the silver fan. It mocked him, and he wondered if he should send it with the girl. But he said nothing, and in the end, the fan remained where it was, troubling him with things that were beyond his control.

Chapter 20: The Silver Fan

By virtue of their uniform coats Shuibai and Zashi were able to gain admittance to the Shrine of the Moon on the day of the celebration of the birthday of the Silver Princess. The Princess was turning two and so acquired legal status as a human being. Infant mortality being so high, children who perished before the age of two were legally classed with miscarriages. As such they inherited no property or claims, and therefore could transmit none—a crucial distinction among the upper classes where children were often fostered with relatives or patrons who gained control of their properties. It had a virtue for the lower classes as well—only the most obvious cases of infanticide were investigated. For people without a reliable form of contraception, birth control tended to be practiced after the fact. Therefore the second birthday of the little princess, Heiress of the Old and New Queendoms of Ton and Hu Shen, was an event of considerable importance.

Shuibai and Mizaka hiked up the Low Road through the town of Crane Marsh and hence to the Southern Gate of Alla Far; the Moon Shrine was located a short distance inside the Southern Gate. They spent a cold morning shuffling their feet as they stood in line. The line of well wishers wended out the Gate of the Moon and down the street for several blocks. The pilgrims were composed about half of *taran* of insufficient rank to warrant VIP status and half retainers and servants in livery. The general public would not be admitted until after the ceremonies were performed.

It took an hour for Shuibai and Zashi to reach the gate, which stood open, and was flanked by a cadre of armed and armored guards, brilliant in the mirror polish of silvered armor. Their helmets were topped with crescent moons extending up into wicked spikes, and their faceplates featured slanted, narrow eye slits, hooked noses, and thin mouths. Their armored skirts rattled as they shifted position while their curved halberds rested against their gleaming shoulders. They wore the uniform jacket of the Moon Guards over their armor, but the jackets hung open to dazzle the eye with the brilliance of their panoply. Their swords were turned blade up ready for an instant draw; they were the honor guard, but among the *taran* that was a serious obligation. Should anyone attempt a palace coup they would be expected to die fighting. Shuibai hunched down inside his collar and wished he could melt into invisibility. They stood still as the Moon Guards frisked them. The Guards' metal gauntlets were articulated and moved deftly over the boxy shape of their fire coats, patting them down and feeling their sleeves; the two young men were unarmed and unarmored and so allowed to pass. The *taran* who passed through the gates were inspected also, but were allowed to keep their blades.

"What is the point of inspecting us if they're going to let weapons in anyhow?" Shuibai asked out of the side of his mouth.

Zashi leaned close to Shuibai's ear. "Guns."

Shuibai shivered. "I guess that means word has been passed up the chain of command about our discovery."

The Celestials in their palaces had been unreal to him until he passed under the watchful gaze of the Moon Guard; he had not thought any further than the Fire Lord. But naturally, if Lord Chuja were a loyal retainer, he would have passed word to his superiors. It bothered Shuibai to think that his actions reverberated all the way to the Imperial Palace; he had liked it better when the Celestials were far away, irrelevant, unmoved, and uninterested in mortal affairs—most especially the doings of one insignificant leatherworker who was just trying to stay alive and earn a living. He twitched as if he had a bug crawling up his spine.

The grounds of the Moon Shrine were cramped; the Silver Mint, the Moon Shrine, the Moon Palace, and numerous offices crammed the space, with the result that the forecourt was too small to admit any sort of crowd. The grey gravel was raked smooth and contained two moonflower trees not in bloom at this season. Their leathery leaves had turned greenish brown and were rolled up tight against the morning chill, but as the morning warmed they partly unfurled.

The only open space was a plot to the side of the shrine exactly big enough to rebuild the shrine when the time came, which would be very soon. The shrine itself was built in the old style with a sharply peaked thatched roof and owl-headed roof beams supporting the eaves. A wide veranda ran across the front and a broad set of steps carried the line of pilgrims up to the porch. The fountain was reached by a paved path that led from the gate across the gravel to the veranda steps. It was offset to the side, and the line bent to take each pilgrim to the fountain to perform their ablutions.

A place became available at the fountain and Zashi moved forward, washing his hands in the cold water, then rinsing out his mouth. He waited respectfully as Shuibai stepped forward and removed his sandals and woolen socks. Shuibai sat on the low ledge that ran around the fountain and rubbed his feet with cold water, the excess dribbling into the gutter that ran around the foot of the fountain. Then he washed his hands and face and rinsed out his mouth. Most of the pilgrims that day performed the minimal ablution on account of the cold, then hurried up the path to the shrine. Shuibai and a few other hardy souls went barefoot.

Zashi shook his head. "I didn't know you were the pious sort. You don't really have to do that, you know."

Shuibai held his socks and sandals tightly in his left hand. "I've never been here before. And, you know." Zashi looked puzzled. He continued in a strained voice. "There are other people from Low Marsh here, people who know me. Who know that I'm untouchable. I don't want them to have any excuse to throw me out."

The orange embroidered dragon moved uneasily as Zashi hunched his scarred shoulder inside his uniform coat. "No one is paying any attention to us."

Shuibai put his right hand into his sleeve and clenched the silver fan; his heart raced as he reviewed his plan. Enter the shrine, pray, make an offering. The fan was wrapped in a piece of bright paper; no one would recognize it. He would simply drop it with the other offerings and leave. Later, whoever sorted through the gifts to the little princess would find it. What would happen to it then he didn't know, but it would no longer be his responsibility. With so many offerings made on this day no one could trace it to him. He stood in line, waiting his turn, staring blankly at the shrine without seeing it, but even though the enormity of what he planned to do weighed on him, he could not bring himself to pray. He left that to Zashi who counted his catechism on his fingers.

Finally they reached the steps and Shuibai added his footwear to the shelves that ran along the foundation of the porch; at this point everyone had to remove their shoes. Zashi and several other men and women toed off their boots and sandals. Shuibai hardly noticed them. He was in a daze, jaw clamped tight to endure the endless wait until they had their turn inside. *Taran* in full formal clothes moved around him, green and purple and yellow and gold and orange and black and all the myriad colors of day and night. Several incenses wafted over him, rich dark patchouli, lighter sandalwood, orange blossom and other aromas he had never encountered before.

He dared to glance about himself and saw hundreds of *taran* and servants in livery, the line extending across the courtyard, out the gate, and up the street further than he could see. He had never seen so many *taran* together at once; *taran* of every noble household, a veritable who's who of the Shen aristocracy. These were just the low ranking retainers and servants; the Great Names and their entourages would arrive separately at a more convenient hour of the day. No need for Ladies of great Rank to spend hours waiting in line in the morning chill with dew clinging to their skirts. In such a splendid and varied crowd the presence of a soldier of the Iris Battalion close in line behind him did not impinge upon Shuibai's consciousness.

The two firefighters took their places at the foot of the steps. In a few minutes the line moved forward and they climbed up onto the porch of the holy shrine. At this point the *taran* disarmed themselves of their longswords, placing them into the racks that nearly covered the front wall of the shrine. There was a small votive table before the racks where the *taran* knelt and made their first prayers, lighting incense. Incense was forbidden in the interior of the shrine by ancient custom. Nothing would stand between the pilgrims and the Spirits once they entered the Shrine, not even the thin haze of incense.

The entrance was closed with silk screens of dove grey, ornamented solely by the crescent moon with the full moon in its arms—the insignia of the Moon Priestess and Silver Princess. Lamps glowed inside, and the shadow play made people seem ethereal and insubstantial. They were silhouettes devoid of color, the distinctive hairstyle of a *taran* there, the voluminous skirts of a lady here, all in silence. The shadows kowtowed, the highest heads bowing all the way to the floor, then shuffled sideways to make their offerings and further prayers. After a few minutes the exit doors opened at the far end and the pilgrims streamed out in awestruck silence. A moment later the silk screens in front of Shuibai and Zashi slid open.

The priestesses were women in formal light grey robes with white and black accessories; their brocades were full and stiff but graceful, like dolls. The silks whispered as they moved, gliding across the polished wooden floor. They wore their hair long and loose, covered by gauzy veils that covered their heads and fell down their backs. Their faces were covered in white make up, sloe eyes lined with black, exaggerating the shape, while their eyelashes had been shaved off. Their eyebrows had likewise been shaved and repainted in thin arching lines, while their eyelids had been painted with palest pink all the way up to the eyebrows and across the bridge of the nose in a way that gave the illusion of a mask, while a small rosebud of color in the center of their mouths gave the illusion of small, perfect lips. They were adorned with pearls, ropes and ropes of them, that hung one below another from their collarbone to their waists, although in their voluminous garb no anatomical features were discernible.

They did not speak, but one on either side counted pilgrims, and when a group of about a hundred had entered, they slid the screens shut behind them. The pilgrims kowtowed with their faces to the floor. The susurration of cloth announced the arrival of more priestesses, then the High Priestess spoke the prayer in the archaic Chan language. The choir sang in clear piping voices and Shuibai didn't understand a word of it. The dialect used for religious ceremonies was ancient and used only by the Celestials for formal occasions. Shuibai peeked between the bowed bodies before him and saw that several of the singers that made up the choir were in fact boys. Male and female they were dressed all alike, though the boys did not have the rosebud lips of the women. Instead they had bars of pink that ran along their jaws on either side, but other than the fine points of their makeup, their voices were so pure and their faces so pretty that they would have been mistaken for girls.

Shuibai did as the others did, mumbling his responses a second behind them, and finally rising up when the others rose. The choir parted, lining up on either side of the sanctuary. A low wooden railing divided the pilgrims from the sanctuary. There was nothing in the sanctuary, nothing at all. No statues, no artwork, no clutter, nothing like the rude pagan shrines Shuibai had occasionally seen. Instead there was a large wooden cabinet in the center of the rear, flanked by a pair of dove grey banners bearing the crescent moon insignia of the Silver Princess. The cabinet doors stood open, but the opening was covered over with a luxurious cloth of grey brocade that shimmered in the lamplight.

The High Priestess spoke again, this time in comprehensible speech. "Behold the abode of the ineffable Spirit, Who is unnameable by human names, Who is unseeable by human eyes, and Who is unheard by human ears, but Whose works are apparent to all. Long life and honor to the Avatar who alone can withstand the perfect presence of the Spirit of the Moon. Long life to the Silver Princess!"

"Long life and honor," the pilgrims intoned. Shuibai glanced sideways to check Zashi's reaction; the other firefighter was staring with parted lips, his gaze locked on the shrouded shrine. A flush of color pinked his cheeks and a line of perspiration gathered on his upper lip. Then his eyes rolled up inside his head, alarming Shuibai. The pilgrims shuffled sideways to approach the offering table and Shuibai tugged on Zashi's arm, but he was immobile. His hand was clenched on the prayer ribbon he had meant to offer.

Patting his friend's shoulder Shuibai said, "Are you all right?"

Zashi made no reply. Shuibai looked around the room, but nobody seemed to notice or care. He didn't know what to do, so he decided to do what they had come to do. Carefully he pried the white prayer ribbon from Zashi's hand and made his way to the offering table.

Shuibai was at the rear of the crowd making their offerings; he kept glancing back at Zashi. At last the crowd thinned and moved to the next station. As he took his place, another straggler, the Iris soldier, her head wrapped in a white silk shawl, bowed her head low and counted her prayers on her fingers. He opened and smoothed out the paper on which Zashi had written his prayer, and feeling guilty, scanned the characters. Zashi's hand was neat and elegant, and though Shuibai could not make out every character, he got the gist of it. It was a poem by an Ancient Poet:

> Mine is not a love
> as plain to see as rice ears
> in the autumn fields,
> but never is there a time
> when he is not in my heart.

Shuibai's heart thumped hard, then he folded up the piece of paper again. It was wrong of him to have read his friend's prayer; but all the same, he was not sorry he had. Zashi was an enigma that he desperately wanted to understand. Yet having read the prayer, he was not certain he understood any better than he had before. He carefully placed the folded prayer amid the many other offerings; the big table was nearly buried with all manner of prayer ribbons, trinkets, flowers, small parcels, coins, rice cakes, candies, fans, and the other odds and ends.

He bowed low and made a prayer. His emotions were whirling; his own inarticulate prayer was something like, 'Don't let anything bad happen to him.'

It took him a moment to collect himself, then he reached into his pocket and withdrew the green wrapped fan. Zashi had neatly lettered, "For the Golden Emperor," upon the wrapping paper, in the hopes that would help the article find its way to the proper person. Shuibai placed it on the offering table and as he did, a great weight lifted from him. It was no longer his problem. What would happen to it now he didn't know, but it would no longer trouble their lives. A measure of peace descended upon him, and he turned to the entranced Zashi. He tugged gently on Zashi's sleeve as the exit door opened and people bowed again and made their exit. "C'mon, it's time to go," he whispered to his friend.

Movement caught his eye, and glancing up, he saw the green glove of the Iris soldier move from the offering table to her sash, and the parcel he had left was gone. He froze. The woman glanced casually his direction, checking to see if she was observed. Their gazes locked, then the Lady of the Knife smiled coldly and bowed mockingly to him, and glided to the exit.

Panic stitched through Shuibai; he yanked viciously on Zashi's maimed arm and hissed in his ear, "The Lady of the Knife took the fan! We have to get it back!"

Zashi's eyes snapped open. "What?" he asked blankly.

Shuibai dragged him to the exit. As they stumbled out of the shrine and down the steps, the green and purple figure of the Lady of the Knife was already striding away. Since she carried knives, not swords, she had not needed to stop with the other *taran* to retrieve their blades. Shuibai grabbed up his footwear and ran down the pavement after her. Zashi called, "Wait!" as he tried to step into his sandals.

Shuibai was in a panic. His plan which had been so carefully made and so patiently executed had been finessed by a rogue. He tore into the street, and looking left and right, saw the Lady of the Knife striding down the street towards the Southern Gate. A troop of horsewomen waited at the gate; they were all clad in black and wore hoods without any insignia.

The Lady of the Knife approached the black figures with swift steps and there was nothing Shuibai could do to overtake her. As he watched in anguish, she held up the little green parcel and the Hooded Woman accepted it and tore it open with impatient fingers. The green scraps fell away, and dark aristocrat turned the fan over in her hands several times; then snapped it open. The Moon insignia was plain upon it and she smiled with cruel delight as she read what was written there.

There was nothing he could do against a troop of *taran*. He turned his head as he heard the limping clatter of wooden sandals on the road behind him; Zashi caught up to him and asked, "What happened?"

Laughter rang out as the Hooded Woman stood in her stirrups and displayed the open fan to her cohorts, then she bent and kissed the Lady of the Knife full on the mouth. Then she snapped the fan shut and pointed at the two firemen. "You're too late! Now the Neutral Ladies will rally to us! Death to the Pretender and His foreign whore!" She put spurs to horse and the black garbed troop charged up the road toward the capital, scattering pilgrims before their hooves.

"Now what?" Shuibai asked, his face ashen.

Zashi shrugged, "It's out of our hands. It was a mistake for the fan to even come to you. Now everything is back the way it used to be."

"Not quite." Still holding his footwear in his hand, he walked over the cold stones to approach the Lady of the Knife.

She looked at him in surprise. "What do you want?"

Taking one sandal firmly in his right hand he hit her across the face as hard as he could. "You don't deserve that uniform and you know it. You're a disgrace."

Her hand went to the hilt of her knife that protruded from her sash.

His voice dripped contempt. "You don't have the right. You aren't *taran*. You're one of us. A commoner. What did you think you would accomplish by betraying the Emperor? Do you want a civil war? Are you so selfish that all you care about is your own preferment?"

Her brown eyes were blazing and her teeth were clenched. "You don't know a damn thing about me! You don't know what hell I've gone through because of you! I should kill you right now!"

"Go ahead. But there's about three hundred witnesses, and some of them are Iris soldiers. What is the penalty for pretending to be a *taran*?"

"I hate you. I hate you as much as the Emperor, you stupid peasant!" She tore the shawl from her head in fury and cast it upon the ground. He realized with shock he had made her lose face.

"I never did you any wrong. It was your own fault if you erred and paid the penalty."

"The Emperor cost me everything I ever cared about. Honor, rank, love—and you're helping Him!"

She shoved him hard, her foot hooking around his ankle so he toppled to the pavement. He tried to roll away, but she pounced on him and her fist connected to his jaw. He saw stars and her fists pounded into his face, then Zashi was there, trying to grab her arms and pull her off him. Several green and purple Iris uniforms ran forward; they had not been close enough to hear what the altercation was about, but they had watched, and now that somebody wearing the same uniform was in action, they came to join the fray. The Lady of the Knife looked up, saw her old comrades bearing down, leaped to her feet, and ran.

The *taran* came to a confused halt. "Was that who I think it was?"

"No, it couldn't be," they said to each other.

Zashi helped Shuibai to his feet. One of the soldiers accosted them. "You there, what was this all about?"

Shuibai, knowing full well he was sealing her doom, replied, "That was the Lady of the Knife. The one who used to be an Iris soldier but was disgraced. I told her she had no right to wear the uniform."

There were three of them and they stiffened. "Dammit, it *was* her!"

"I told you so," another replied.

"What are we going to do about it?"

"A little street justice, I think."

"But the Princess' birthday?"

"Damn the Princess, She'll have another birthday. This must dealt with. Our honor depends upon it."

The three took off in pursuit of the disgraced warrior.

Shuibai sat on the pavement to wearily don his stockings and shoes. Zashi knelt beside him. "What were you thinking? She could have killed you!"

"I hope *they* kill *her*," he replied.

Zashi touched his bruised jaw. "Don't pick fights you can't win, Shui-lan."

"I won that one," Shuibai replied grimly. He picked himself up. "Maybe she'll think twice about picking a fight with me now. Let's go home."

Zashi stood still. "I'd rather stay a bit."

Shuibai glanced at him, then did a double take. "Why? I'm freezing. My face hurts too."

Zashi gestured apologetically with his good hand. "There's going to be a ceremony. I can't be inside for it, but I can hang around in the courtyard. Maybe I'll see something."

"Like what?"

Zashi cradled his injured arm in his right hand. "Didn't you feel the Spirit present in that place?"

"No."

Zashi flashed him a weak smile. "Silly me. I should have known better than to ask. I suppose it's my imagination playing tricks on me. But still, don't you think the others felt something?"

"I don't think the Lady of the Knife felt anything holy," Shuibai replied. "If the Spirits were real I can't imagine they'd let her steal something right off the offering table, and right in front of the priestesses, too."

Zashi crumpled. "Let's go home. My poor brain is tired."

CHAPTER 21: VAIN IDEAS

Shuibai was working in the shop when a note arrived. It was addressed to 'Fire Warden Mizaka,' and the hand writing was strong and feminine. A pang of jealousy struck through him, so he opened it. The poem was cribbed from classical sources.

"Although my feet never cease running to you on the path of my dreams, such nights of love are never worth one glimpse of you in your reality." It was accompanied by a note, "Meet me at the Lantern Bridge at sunset this weekend." It was stamped with the seal of a local brewer of rice wine.

Shuibai very carefully refolded the note along its original lines. He resolved to say nothing about it and to pretend he hadn't read it. Zashi had certainly never given him any cause to think they were anything other than amiable coworkers; it was inevitable that such a dashing young man would attract the attention of women. He was vaguely aware of the brewer, a woman in her thirties, successful in her trade, prosperous, with several children and several ex-husbands. Marriageable. Zashi's prospects were modest, but that was immaterial to a woman who lived in comfort. Zashi had something that was hard to come by in Low Marsh: he had class.

Zashi arrived home a little early from his round of inspections. He was tired and footsore, and he listed to one side because his shoulder and leg hurt. He did not complain, but lines of strain showed in his face. He walked across the wooden floor to the step down to the kitchen, then sat down on the edge of the floor and stretched his feet toward the hearth. He pulled a leather purse of Shuibai's making from his sash and put it on the floor beside him. He laid down the scroll. "The fines and day's report."

Shuibai gestured to Kanko, "Go to the well and bring some water."

The boy, who was wearing his gaudy red shirt and a pair of cast off breeches tied up with cord, found his worn out straw sandals, put on his tattered coat, donned an old straw hat, and hurried off without saying anything.

Once the boy was gone, Shuibai reached into his pocket and brought out the letter. "This came while you were gone."

He slid it across the polished wooden floor with his fingertip as if it were a dead beetle he was flicking into the trash. He was dressed in his old green willow shirt with a black and brown striped sash, sitting cross-legged at the low table where he was piecing brightly colored scraps together to make another quilt.

Zashi opened it up and scanned it quickly. "It's nothing." He tossed it into the kitchen fire. He got up and stepped gingerly across the cold dirt floor of the kitchen, took down the teapot and cups, and set the teakettle on the iron spider. Kanko arrived shortly with the bucket of water and set a pot to heat for Zashi's usual rubdown. Zashi unrolled a sleeping mat and laid down. He seemed more tired than usual.

"You should go," Shuibai said, surprising himself. He had not intended to admit reading the note; his jealousy did not want to give any support to another's affection. He took a perverse pleasure in hurting himself.

"You read it?"

"You should think of marriage," Shuibai went on, hurting himself again.

Zashi laughed bitterly. "She hasn't seen my hand."

Shuibai heaved a sigh of relief. "Perhaps you're right."

The resulting silence was far more intimate than any words they had shared since Zashi had moved in. Shuibai wanted badly to say something that would bring Zashi out of his self-imposed exile, but he didn't know how. At first he had thought it was some flaw in himself that made it to impossible to reach the other man, but now he saw that the flaw was in Zashi, and it centered on his scars. Zashi did not want anyone to see his injury; cripples were unclean. He kept his hand hidden with such practiced ease Shuibai no longer noticed that he was hiding it. At the moment he was lying on the mat, his left hand tucked into the flap of his robe where it overlapped his sash. It was common for men to rest their hand there, especially in cold weather. Not a bit of the hand or forearm showed. Shuibai suddenly realized that no one in Low Marsh knew that Mizaka, Assistant Fire Warden, was crippled.

He glided across the worn wooden floor and sat down cross-legged beside the other man. He didn't know what to say, but he saw that although he was a poor man he had nonetheless given Zashi something that could not be bought at any price. He had given him normality.

"Were people cruel to you about your arm?"

"They were kind, and they pitied me. They avoided looking at me. I often heard their voices drenched in pity, 'There goes Mizaka, the one who used to be so handsome.'"

"I think you're still handsome."

Zashi sat up and cradled his arm against his chest. He patted his brocade sleeve. "As long as you don't see this."

"Even then."

Zashi was silent a long time. "Well, perhaps that's because of where you live. You're not used to pretty things down here."

Tears welled up in Shuibai's eyes. "I've seen you at your mother's house, and I thought you were handsome then, too."

Zashi spoke softly. "You're kind to me. You give me real work to do. I appreciate that. Yet I know that if this were a better place, it would have no room for one like me."

"Alla Far is a much nicer place to live."

"In Alla Far I only saw the servants going home late and heard the complaints of tired parents. Here I can hear the marsh lapping at the foot of the path and the sweeps creaking as the boatmen go singing along the river." He spoke lightly, which was his usual way of avoiding something he didn't wish to speak of.

"I suppose that's another poem."

Zashi laughed in genuine amusement, although his expression was still strained. "No, that's just me being picturesque."

"You had a job and a family in Alla Far."

Zashi's almond eyes darkened. "So they say. I'll tell you this, those watchtowers are foolishness. Most of the time the watch is asleep, or worse yet, huddling in some tavern over a hot fire and a bottle of warm wine. You shouldn't waste your money on them."

Shuibai was surprised to hear the system criticized. "But it must work, or why would they do it?"

"Because they are afraid of fire and superstitious about it. We're supposed to watch for flying dragons, you know. But that's not how you find a dragon. They are born in the flames and fly away. By then it's too late. Fire doesn't come from the sky. It comes from men. From pipes and forges and arson and lamps and foolishness. So many fires are started when sparks jump from a hearth, or when embers catch in a wooden chimney. More are started when someone falls asleep or is drunk with a pipe. When the fire devours enough it takes on a life of its own and gives birth to a dragon. Where they go after that I do not know."

Shuibai pulled his knees up to his chin and wrapped his arms around them like a child. "Do you really think the dragon is real? Or is it just a story?"

When Zashi finally spoke it was in a low, intense voice. "I've seen it, Shuibai. Some firemen think it's superstition, or poetic license, or delusion. But the dragon devoured me and I lived. It comes to me in my dreams sometimes, and the beauty terrifies me. Sometimes I think it would be so easy to reach out and tip over the lamp . . ."

"Start a fire on purpose?" Shuibai was horrified.

Zashi's face closed tight. "I didn't say that. I merely noted that accidents happen easily."

He turned his back deliberately on Shuibai, picked up his mattress, and moved it all the way to the front of the little apartment. The draft from the shutters made it cold up there. Kanko brought a bucket of hot water and a cloth to him, but Zashi shooed him away with a flick of his hand. He washed himself, furtive and alone, his shoulders hunched beneath his robe, the washcloth scrubbing violently across his scarred skin, irritating it so that it turned red and puffy. He didn't undress, just peeled back the robe enough to reach his skin, keeping himself turned so that the scars were not visible to either of his roommates. He wouldn't look at them.

Shuibai watched him from a distance, then rose and walked over to him. "Have you ever set a fire? On purpose?"

Zashi glanced at him. "No. When I was a child I played with the lamps, but I never had an accident. I outgrew such childish experiments."

Shuibai heaved a great sigh. "I'm glad. I could not bear to think you had."

"Lots of children play with fire. It's pretty and interesting and easy to get hold of. But eventually a child learns the ways of the world and he grows up. At least, some do. Some people grow up to be fools."

Shuibai sighed. "This is true. But you aren't one of them."

Zashi flashed him a tortured look. "I am the biggest fool of all." Once again he turned his back on the younger man.

"But Zashi," Shuibai said plaintively.

Zashi sat with his arms wrapped around his knees, shrunk into a tight little ball of arms and hunched shoulders.

Shuibai put his hand upon his shoulder. "I wish you would talk to me."

Zashi barked a short laugh. "I can't talk to anyone. Nobody understands what is happening to me."

"Well, couldn't you try?"

"I have tried, Shui-lan. But you don't believe in the dragon. Therefore there is nothing I can say to you."

"Do I have to believe? Couldn't you tell me about it, and I'll listen and not say anything?"

Zashi picked at the frayed edge of his pallet. "I don't think so. It bothers me too much. It's better not to think about it if I can avoid it. I would get upset, and you would say something. You know you would say something. You're not very tactful."

"I didn't mean to hurt your feelings."

"I know, Shui-lan. I know. It's not your problem. Really. It's nothing for you to worry about. It's my problem. You've been very kind to me, and I am grateful to you. I love you like a brother."

"You're much nicer than a brother," Shuibai said.

Zashi unfolded a little bit. "You only say that because you have a terrible family!"

"I know!" Shuibai replied. Zashi gave him half a smile. Shuibai smiled shyly back. "I would like to consider you as a brother."

Zashi turned to face him. "Comrades against the dragon, metaphorical or otherwise."

"Yes, however you want to put it."

Zashi reached out with his good arm, and leaning forward, hugged Shuibai. Shuibai's arms went slowly around his body and they held each other for a long moment. Shuibai felt his heart hammering in his chest, felt Zashi's warm embrace, felt emotions boiling up inside him that he had no words to express; worse, that he was afraid to express. The enigmatic Zashi had finally made himself clear. If brotherhood was what he wanted, then that was what Shuibai would give him. He asked nothing for himself. His heart stung, but he buried his own feelings.

"I'm sorry I'm such an odd person," Zashi apologized.

"You don't seem odd to me."

"Thank you." Zashi settled back on his mattress. "I think I'd like to have the boy rub me down after all. I'm very tired."

"Certainly." Shuibai rose and motioned to Kanko. "Assistant Fire Warden Mizaka is ready for his rubdown now." So Kanko fetched the massage oil and approached, and Zashi slid his shirt down his back but did not disrobe.

A strange thing happened then, and it had nothing to do with any of them. The earth trembled. They sat very still, waiting for it to repeat and it did. The earth shook with short sharp motions and the prints on the wall jumped on their strings and the dishes in the cupboards rattled. Water slopped from the teakettle and hissed in the coals. Tools bounced on the table and fabric slid over the edge like a slow motion waterfall of bright colors. The vibration was silent. It came as a series of short, sharp jerks that made the shutters rattle. It was not like any trembler Shuibai had been through before. It lasted for as long as they held their breaths, then it was over.

Zashi smiled and the two of them righted the things that had toppled over. "They say there's a dragon in the earth and every once in a while it stirs in its sleep. Pray it never wakes." His voice was light and his mood had lifted; there was nothing like an earthquake to make a man's self-pity seem trivial.

"I hope not," Shuibai agreed. Zashi settled down for his rubdown again and Shuibai started dinner preparations, but about the time Shuibai was frying vegetables in oil the earth shook again. The shakes were sharper and stronger this time, and more things bounced in place or toppled from the shelves. Pictures fell. Kanko stopped rubbing and Zashi sat up. The boy huddled with his chin sunk inside his collar. His face was frightened and he chewed his sleeve ferociously.

"If it gets any worse, perhaps we should go outside." Zashi spoke calmly, but his face was white. He dressed quickly. The shaking stopped, only to be followed by several more small jolts. Embers shook loose and fell from the hearth, landing on the dirt floor of the kitchen where they glowed harmlessly. Shuibai extinguished the cook fire and the stray coals with the bucket of water they kept by the hearth for the purpose.

Zashi shoveled half-cooked food into a bowl quickly. "Hurry up and eat," he advised. "Those jolts will have started some house

fires for sure. Grab yourself some supper then don your uniform .
We'll be going out."

"Perhaps the burning will be a lesson to them," Shuibai said
sourly, stuffing his mouth with incompletely cooked rice.

"It's never been a lesson to them. Not in a thousand years,"
Zashi replied, chopsticks clicking as he shoveled up crunchy
chunks of vegetables.

"Should I sound the alarm?"

"Yes, do. We'll have the crew ready that much sooner."

Shuibai shrugged into his coat as he stepped outside. He struck
the bell thrice, which he repeated three times: the general call for
the company. While he did that the ever practical Zashi scraped the
sticky rice from the bottom of the pan and molded it into rice balls,
which he wrapped in a napkin and put in his pocket.

CHAPTER 22 : THE MAIKO FIRE

The Low Marsh Fire Company assembled over the course of the next quarter hour. The original men who had fought the fire on the Southern Highway were supplemented by another five men, one of whom was a tall, gangly man of middle years with ginger hair. They all laughed when they saw him. Although he had the slanted eyes and small nose typical of the Shen, his complexion was pale and freckled.

"Hey, hillbilly, is it true what they say?" Axe asked. "That you all fornicate with your sisters and eat like pigs and that's why you look like that?"

"Not at all," the ginger-haired man replied. "We fornicate with the pigs and eat like our sisters, which is why we're not nearly as fat as you lowlanders." He punctuated his remark by poking his harasser right in the paunch.

They all laughed, and Axe rolled his eyes and looked like he was going to take offense, so Shuibai jumped in. "I don't care who you sleep with as long as you fight fire like men."

Nods of assent went around the group. Shuibai breathed a sigh of relief. Insult contests were a frequent form of entertainment among the laboring class and generally resulted in fistfights and the harboring of grudges.

"All right, let's form up," Zashi said. "You, Red," he pointed at the ginger-haired newcomer, "You're a ladder man." He pointed to another tall man about the same height, "You're another ladder man. It's in the crawl space. Get it. You, you're another axe man. You and you and you and you, you're in charge of the bucket brigades. You and you, you're hook men."

The implements were passed out. The hooks were heavy iron crooks with ropes attached, but the axes were ordinary axes. The ladder was a wooden ladder about twenty feet long with dowel rungs, painted creamy white.

"Where did that come from?" Shuibai asked in surprise.

"An anonymous donor after the last fire," Zashi smoothly replied. He neglected to mention that the donor was unaware of her generosity—there was no point bothering the Fire Warden with trivia. The company needed a ladder and they had acquired one.

"That was nice," Shuibai commented, suspecting nothing. "I wish I had known. I would have liked to have thanked her."

"You were busy with more important matters."

It was true. He had been distracted by the girl Camellia Blossom, the box of ammunition, and the message he had sent to the Fire Lord. He was glad Zashi was taking care of business. "Oh. Carry on then."

The motley crew all froze at the sound of hooves rattling in the main street. Bells jingled on the bridle, announcing an Imperial Post rider. A moment later the horse and rider turned the corner, hooves skidding in the dirt as the rider reined up hard to keep the horse from stumbling. The figure wore a flared helmet with a brass ornament above the faceplate and the yellow and white vest of the post service over her family uniform of blue. "You there," she shouted, reining up. The bay horse checked violently, foam flecking from its mouth. "I'm looking for the Low Marsh Fire Company!"

Shuibai stepped forward. "I'm Fire Warden Shuibai. What can I do for you?"

"I've got a message from the Fire Warden of Cherry Hill. The Maiko Fireworks factory has exploded. Cherry Hill is burning. Your help is urgently needed. I'm going to Crane Marsh and from there to Alla Far. Riders are going to every fire company in the Capital District. Bring every man you can." The horse blew violently and shook itself.

"We're on our way," Shuibai replied.

She nodded curtly. "Good luck. You'll need it." She started to turn away, then paused, "The wind is from the northeast, in case you hadn't noticed." With that she touched spurs to the horse's flanks and bolted down the Low Road.

They all looked at each other with white faces. Cherry Hill lay northeast of Low Marsh; if the fire crossed the Southern Highway, there was only the woody hollow of Iris Bottom between Low Marsh and the conflagration.

"We'd better get going," Shuibai said.

"Send the boy Kanko to the town mothers and tell them the news," Zashi said. "Tell them to pump the wells now and fill as many cisterns and buckets as they can. Tell them cut a fire break in the Iris Bottom."

The boy ran with the message and the Low Marsh Fire Company trotted up the road with their implements over their shoulders. Reaching the Lantern Gate they looked north and saw the long sweep of highway pointed almost directly at the red glow in the sky, a glow as scarlet as dawn but in the wrong place. The distant hill was crowned with an orange radiance and a pillar of black smoke blotted out the stars while the habitations of human beings were impossible to distinguish. The heart of the fiery glow was almost white at its center, surrounded by a nimbus of orange-red auroras. It didn't even look like fire; it was so immense that it looked more like veils suspended from the sky to shimmer over the hills.

The company halted and stared. "We're going there?" somebody asked in disbelief.

Shuibai's heart quailed. What could human beings possibly do against such a titan?

Zashi was assessing the situation with a practiced eye. "I don't think it's crossed the highway," he opined. "If that's the case, we can demolish the neighborhood and create a fire break."

"We?" Shuibai asked.

"Every fireman in the Capital District is being called out. We aren't doing it alone. We never do it alone. We always do it as a team, working with each other and the other fire companies." He shrugged. "No one told you it was going to be easy."

Shuibai exhaled a large breath. "We have our work cut out for us."

The breeze was mild but steady. It carried the smell of burning wood and flakes of ash. The closer they got to Cherry Hill, the more refugees they met streaming away, and the more ash fell from the sky like a black snow. It created a fine dust underfoot that puffed up with each step; it clung to their eyelashes and mixed with their sweat to turn their faces black and bleary before they even arrived. The wind became gusty and burning brands dropped out of the sky. Then they were in Cherry Hill where the buildings along the Southern Highway were built four and five stories high and crammed with merchandise from the four crossroads of the empire. They could look up at a red and smoky sky, and they could hear a roaring in the distance like a mighty cataract, but they were not yet close. Porters and merchants labored like frantic ants to try and save the valuable goods from the warehouses; merchants gladly paid tenfold wages for the hiring of carts and laborers. The highway was choked with people. The company pushed through the mob, shouting their throats raw, crying, "Make way for the Low Marsh Fire Company! Make way for Fire Chief Shuibai!"

Nobody paid them any attention, except for one man who stumbled and fell under the ladder. "You fools! The dragon will get you too!" he yelled. The ladder men trampled right over him and kept going.

Adrenalin had them in its grip. Nobody dared to stop or think because if they did they would turn tail and run. The mindless rhythm of one step after another carried them forward. Zashi led them down side streets to find the fire front.

They came out on a wide avenue that ran east toward the red heart of night. Buildings were built side by side, their eaves touching over tiny alleys, or else with shared walls. There were no yards or any green spaces. The firemen ran out into the street only to be caught by an immense gale that ripped the hats from their heads and lashed their coats about them. Debris composed of shingles and unidentified objects flew through the air overhead and was sucked into the maw of the fire. Looking up the street they saw flames three blocks away. The roar was deafening. Hurricane force winds ripped shutters from their frames and sent them sailing down the street to disappear into the inferno. Buckets were ripped from their hands and several of them lost their balance and fell. They broke and scattered, but Zashi leaped and snagged the coat of Red, who was knocked head over heels as the wind tore him off his feet. The two of them struggled back to the safety of the side street.

The company huddled together in the lee of an apothecary shop. Their hearts thudded in their chests while the awful inferno roared. They couldn't hear each other as the howling wind rushed in to fill the scarlet void. Looking up they saw chunks of roof sailing very high in the air, lifted aloft by the mighty updraft created by the conflagration. Worse than that, convection currents carried flaming brands into the upper air and flung them across the city. Some of them extinguished themselves before landing on the roofs below, but others carried the glowing spark of destruction to new neighborhoods. As they huddled together in the side street embers scattered across the intervening three blocks to light a dozen smaller fires. Buildings with tile roofs resisted the initial onslaught of flame, but their wooden shutters and window sills had nooks and crannies into which bits of burning debris settled. They too would succumb to the all-devouring beast.

"Now what?" Shuibai mouthed, his words impossible to hear.

Zashi stuck his head out and studied the scene. Shuibai reluctantly put his head out too and got clipped by a sailing wooden slat. His leather hat, firmly tied under his chin, was badly warped, but it gave his head a little protection. He stared and saw to his horror that the street itself was burning. It was a prosperous neighborhood and the street had been paved with large wooden blocks fit tightly between wooden curbs and mortared with tar. Wooden boardwalks and porches would have sheltered shoppers and businesswomen during inclement weather but were nothing more than fuel for the fire. Everything was burning. Worse still, in the moments of their confusion, another block had fallen prey to the red beast. The facades and timbers melted away as if they had been made of wax. All that remained were the shimmering waves of heat and the roar that filled their skulls. Color ceased to have any meaning; everything was the color of flame. Those buildings which had not yet caught fire were bathed in a fiery light, forerunner of their doom.

In the middle of the shimmering cataract of wind and fire, a single figure lurched to a fifth floor window and leaned out. A young woman, her long hair tattered by the wind, looked desperately left and right.

Shuibai leaped as if stung. "The ladder!" he cried, the wind tearing away his words. He grabbed their shoulders, then pointed out into the street. They looked at him like he was a madman. He leaned close to them and shouted directly in their ears, "A woman!"

They nodded and grabbed one another's coats. With four men to wrestle the ladder they stepped out into the maelstrom. Zashi stood rooted to the spot, his experienced eye having already told him that the ladder was too short. But the Low Marsh Fire Company struggled across the street and set the ladder up against the house, so he followed with his sleeves wrapped protectively around his head. The heat was a wall that blistered exposed skin and the straw hat of one man burst into flame. He tore it loose from his head and the wind sucked it up. It was consumed to ash before it even reached the fire.

The young woman, a servant girl not more than fifteen or sixteen, climbed onto the window sill and perched with her short blue night robe hiked up around her thighs and thick white smoke billowing out around her. She clung to the window frame and looked desperately back into the room, her wind-torn black hair a curtain across her face. The roof above her was burning, the drop to the street was five stories, and the ladder didn't cross half the distance. She looked down at them with fear in her eyes, and they looked up at her, knowing there was nothing they could do.

She jumped.

They heard the impact—a dull, sick, wet thud that churned their stomachs. With the wind roaring and the fire thundering maybe they heard it in their bones rather than in their ears, but they heard it all the same. Nobody could look. At last Shuibai looked down at his feet and saw the broken pieces of what had been a young woman cracked upon the ground. He leaned into the wind and hiked away, waving for his company to follow him. Tonight fire was king and it was beyond the power of mere mortals to stop it.

CHAPTER 23 : FIRE BREAK

The fire ate through the blocks almost as fast as they could run. They loped along, their brief brush with fire having turned their clothes black with soot. The streets were too narrow to stop the fire; the Southern Highway was the only thoroughfare wide enough to give the firefighters a chance to create a fire break. Cutting back and forth through the neighborhoods they came out on the Southern Highway quite a bit north of where they had come in. Once on the highway they pushed through the sightseers and refugees in search of an authority figure. They had no right to demolish buildings in Cherry Hill; the city that had grown up at the Imperial crossroads lay just outside the Capital District. Given the political situation, Shuibai thought it unlikely that the Lady of Cherry Hill would be willing to forgive and forget if one of the Fire Lord's minions demolished her prime commercial district, fire or no fire.

They met *taran* on horseback in the lavender uniforms of the Eastern Guard. The General of the Eastern Gate was personally charged with safeguarding the Golden Emperor; by extension he was the ultimate law enforcement officer in the Capital District. During times of unrest his duties included putting down rebellion anywhere it occurred in the nation. That the Eastern Guard had been called out told them that the Emperor Himself was afraid. If the wind held, the southern suburbs of Low Marsh and Crane Marsh would perish, missing Alla Far, but if the wind shifted a little, the Golden Emperor would be scrambling for a boat to take Him safely across the Crescent Moon Lake. The capital would vanish in a sea of flame. No wonder the Eastern Guard was called out.

The highway was packed with traffic. The *taran* used their closed metal fans as truncheons and beat their way through the throng, but the street was too jammed with carts and citizens to easily part. They could all hear the roaring in the distance; the wind was streaming overhead like an ash-laden flood. Thick black smoke blotted out the sky. The streets were full of smoky haze and bits of charred paper floated through the air. Cloth flapped and dust rose, making them cough and choke.

"It's getting close!" Zashi shouted.

The crowds abandoned their merchandise when the sparks started dropping among them. Panic set them to flight and they ran headlong in one great mass, streaming northward along the highway, trying to get away from the glowing sky.

"Stick together!" Shuibai shouted.

They hung onto each other's sleeves. They made no progress against the crowd but stood like a rock, the screaming human wave breaking around them. Suddenly the press of bodies ended and they were left alone except for the dervishes who twisted and wailed. The firefighters gathered themselves and trotted forward, running southward on a path that paralleled the front of the fire.

It was dark under the smoky pall and their lanterns were little help. They could see were the storefronts but not well enough to know what goods they sold even though they were no more than two fathoms away. A line of grimy forms appeared out of the lurid orange gloom of a side street. They were exhausted firefighters, carrying axes and pikes over their shoulders. They were led by a foreman whose head hung low.

"Hey, Cherry Hill! Low Marsh has come to your aid!" Shuibai called out in a voice made rough by all the smoke he'd eaten.

The foreman looked up, and his crew took heart at the sight of a reasonably fresh company come to help them out. "Tear it down!" he shouted. "Tear it all down!"

That was enough authorization for them. The hook men ran up four flights of stairs and leaned out the windows to set their hooks in the front facade, then threw the ropes down into the street. They retreated to street level, then a team of firemen, heaving hard, pulled the facade loose from the face of the building. They went in again, crooked their hooks around the supporting pillars and yanked them out, bringing the house down. The flimsy shops and houses were built with timber frames and paper, fiber, or wooden shells; the pillars were footed on large stones with no foundation. The design was cheap and easy to build and flexible enough to withstand the shock of frequent earthquakes, but succumbed easily to a demolition crew—or fire.

Shuibai peeled off his bucket brigade men and sent them up the highway to look for civilian volunteers. The rest of his crew ran up and down stairs, coughing in the thick atmosphere, clutching their chests when the air got particularly bad. Legs ached from climbing so many steps, shoulders ached from throwing their weight onto the ropes. One by one the buildings came down, with bales of cotton goods, bundles of household items, and baskets full of trinkets showering into the street as the warehouses and stores toppled. Someone had left a lamp burning in one of the buildings, which flared up in the debris and was quickly quenched; after that they made a point to quickly inspect each building to make sure the hearths and lamps were extinguished.

Fire companies congregated along the Southern Highway, all of them knowing that the highway was the only road big enough to make a fire break. It was paved in stone, not wood, and some of the establishments along the highway had tile roofs, not wood or thatch, and some of them had even been stuccoed with fire resistant plaster. Some of the establishments had their own wells, and some of them even had pumps.

In a small miracle, Shuibai's bucket men returned with a straggle of citizens, mostly young men, but a few women, with buckets, who began to pump water and carry it to the debris. Before all the buildings along the east side of the highway could be demolished, the fire caught up with them.

Without the wall of buildings to shield them, they looked directly into the maw of the fire. It spread for blocks north and south along the Southern Highway. There was no escape; it filled the eastern horizon. The smoke and heat was so intense it was like drowning in lava: thick, scorching, and unbreathable. The men's lungs hurt, they were coughing incessantly, their bleary eyes streamed tears. When they sneezed their snot was black. If any of them could gather enough saliva to spit, that was black, too.

The heat was so intense water turned to vapor and evaporated before it hit the ground. One civilian screamed and beat at his clothes as the cheap cotton fabric caught fire. His voice was a tiny cry in the deafening roar of the flames. One bucket brigade broke and scattered, dropping the buckets and running for their lives.

"Come back, come back!" Shuibai cried, but no one could hear him.

Zashi caught his arm and motioned him away. They gave up trying to soak the debris; the fire was too vast, too insatiable. Instead they retreated to the opposite side of the street where they threw water on the store fronts. Men climbed to the roofs. Using brooms they swept embers from the roofs. The ashes and embers fell into the street like a fiery waterfall. Many of the buildings had tile roofs, which thwarted the insinuating caress of fire, but men were needed to wield long-handled mops to wet the windowsills where burning debris gathered and ignited the translucent oiled paper window panes.

"Go up there!" Zashi shouted in his ear.

Shuibai climbed up a ladder to a porch roof, then climbed another ladder to a rope, which dangled from the ornamental head of a ridge pole, and joined the men on the roof who were sweeping like berserk housewives. Awnings and veranda roofs burned, fire lodged under the eaves. Shuibai was pointed to a stretch of steeply slanted wooden roof. He scrambled from spot to spot, stamping out the sparks or using a broom to sweep them over the edge. He discovered that if he kept the embers moving they didn't catch in the wooden roof, but if they lodged someplace a moment later a flame would leap up. He chased sparks across the sloping roof, falling occasionally into the gutter that ran between his roof and the next one. He lost his sandals, his feet hurt, his hands were scorched, each breath ripped from his lungs. He lost all sense of time and didn't dare look at the conflagration. Occasionally he collided with another firefighter as they dived for the same fall of embers, but he had no conscious awareness of anything beyond the aching fatigue of a body that protested yet another fall on the harsh shingles, and the exhaustion of arms that never stopped moving.

A long—very long—time later he stopped to catch his breath. He lifted his head and saw the debris on the other side was a smoking ruin decorated with orange flames—but the fire had not leaped the highway. He could hear men talking in hoarse scratchy voices now that the fire was no longer roaring and the gusty wind no longer threatened to rip him off the roof. Dawn was breaking, lurid and orange, but laced with lavender. The fire sulked through the morning, hemmed in by the line of the Southern Highway.

Eventually he discovered he had fallen asleep standing up, but no new sparks had landed during his period of oblivion. The civilians returned, bringing beer and rice cakes, so he crawled down the rope to the ladder to the street. He drank the beer gratefully, sucking down an entire ladle full without drawing a breath. He was dehydrated, his skin was parched like paper, his uniform was full of charred holes, and he was exhausted. The firefighters mobbed the boy with the beer, and as the alcohol hit their systems, their spirits revived and they became jolly. They started making rude gestures at the smoldering ruins, then turned and showed their bare butts to the flames, then laughed and slapped each other on the back. A scorched fire officer in a fragment of uniform detailed men to return to the roofs to keep watch and sweep, but Shuibai and Zashi were given a break.

Zashi was blackened from head to toe and only his white grin and bloodshot eyes could be distinguished. Shuibai knew he must look just as awful. They clasped each other in a crushing bear hug, and Shuibai, in an excess of emotion and beer, kissed him on the mouth. Zashi kissed him back. Nobody paid any attention to them.

The beer ran out, so firemen started breaking open the shops in search of more alcohol. They felt they had earned it. Out of the corner of his eye Shuibai recognized the burly form of Axe as he broke open the front shutters of a shop. Shuibai broke loose from Zashi and ran after the man shouting, "Stop that! No looting!"

Axe and his fellow heroes looked at him in open rebellion. "We want more beer!" they demanded.

He relented. "Beer, okay. But don't touch anything else."

The shops were quickly plundered of alcohol and food. A tavern was broken open and kegs of beer were rolled out and the barrels axed open, while dozens of civilians and firemen started dunking cups, ladles, even their hands into the kegs and scooping out the drink. The Low Marsh company was right in with them. They had put in eighteen hours of non-stop work in terrifying conditions, they had checked the fire, and now they were celebrating. Not even a chilly, soot-stained autumn day could squelch their jubilation.

Zashi slapped his arm. "It's time to go home—before they get drunk and pass out. Nobody's eaten anything all night."

"I couldn't eat. I didn't even think of food," Shuibai said.

"Get them together, now, before you've lost them in a drunken orgy." He reached into his pocket and pulled out one of his sticky rice balls. "I still have one left. Want it?"

Shuibai, who wanted nothing better than to lay down and take a nap, nonetheless stood up and shouted, "Low Marsh, Low Marsh, form up!" then shoved the rice ball into his mouth and swallowed it after chewing only twice.

The Low Marsh company grumbled, grabbed more beer, and staggered down the road behind their officers. They retrieved their tools, but since they couldn't identify their own hooks and axes in the mess, they simply appropriated the ones that happened to be closest at hand. In this way they ended up with a red ladder instead of a white one. However, they had arrived with a ladder and they left with a ladder, so it was all right. The people cheered them as they passed, and women blew kisses to them and boys waved. They discovered something they liked every bit as much as beer: glory.

They limped and strutted, waved to the crowds, and shouted their brags in hoarse voices ripped raw by the fire, "Here comes Low Marsh, best fire company that ever was!"

The trek home was much longer than the run to the fire. It was all downhill, which helped, but once they left the fire behind the adrenalin gave out and the day was cold. All of them were burned in places and the wounds festered with a fiery heat that gave them fevers. Their clothes were reduced to rags and the wind blew through them. Most of them had lost their hats and mittens, their sandals, and even their socks. Some of them were soaking wet from working the bucket brigade. They were all exhausted, coughing and hacking from the smoke.

Zashi was canted over, hugging his crippled arm to his chest, limping along at the back, falling further behind with each step. "Go on without me." His voice was tight with pain.

"I won't leave you," Shuibai answered. "I won't leave anybody. We stick together, no matter what."

Zashi leaned heavily on him and spoke in a low voice. "All during the fire it hurt so bad I thought I couldn't go on. But I had to. You were counting on me. But I can't walk anymore. I've got to sit down. Please, just let me rest."

Shuibai whistled sharply. The company, which had been straggling forward obliviously, muddled to a halt and looked back. Shuibai gestured for them to gather around. They tapped each other and pointed. Not knowing about Zashi's old injuries, they thought he had gotten hurt during the Cherry Hill fire. They clustered around him in a concerned knot.

"Hell, I can't get any colder than I already am," Axe said and took off his coat. He and three other fellows held it as a sling and offered Zashi a ride. He demurred, but they prevailed upon him and he sat down gratefully. The company took turns carrying him in the makeshift sling. Finally they reached their home town.

"Baths on me," Shuibai said, as they came abreast of a bath house. He knocked violently on the door. The bath keeper stuck her head out of an upper window and yelled, "Go away, we're not open!"

"I'm Fire Warden Shuibai. I order you to open up for the Low Marsh Fire Company. We've just fought the Great Fire in Cherry Hill."

"Firemen?" she asked.

"Our comrade is injured!" one of the men called.

"Open up, we want a bath!" somebody else shouted.

"In a minute, in a minute!" She withdrew her head and slammed the shutter shut. They waited. A moment later she was at the front door letting them in.

"Do you have any beer?" Axe asked her.

She did, and they got gloriously clean and drunk at Shuibai's expense. Nobody objected when the Chief and his Assistant retired to a private bath as befitted their rank, so Zashi was able to soak without revealing his scars.

CHAPTER 24 : AFTERMATH

All the fire chiefs and fire wardens in the Capital District were meeting at the Fire Court. Interior walls had been removed to open one wing of the Fire Lord's house to create a room large enough to hold them all. A number of *taran* lords were there, seated in two factions facing each other across the aisle down the middle to the dais. Shuibai and Zashi were surprised to see the Fire Lord seated at the head of the faction to the right hand of the dais. A lady he didn't recognize was seated across from him at the head of the faction seated to the left of the dais. The firemen were set in rows behind two ranks of *taran* who were dressed in their handsome, voluminous winter garb, their formal black hats perched on their heads giving their shadows on the wall a raptorial silhouette, while the scent of many perfumes wafted through the room. The atmosphere was close and tense. The long swords had been politely racked in the hallway—a necessity considering the subject to be discussed was going to be a touchy one. But the *taran* did not disarm completely; they maintained their long dirks, steel folding fans, and other small weapons that were an essential part of every gentleman's apparel.

Translucent paper screens decorated with the scene of the Great Fire of Alla Far that had burned so many centuries ago aptly suited the subject of the audience. The dais was covered with luxurious black cloths, prepared especially for the occasion.

Whispers passed along the line and Shuibai and Zashi were quietly slipped into position next to Chief Byan, who, as head of the Alla Far Fire Company, was seated behind the Fire Lord. Shuibai was nervous at being placed so near to the head, but nobody objected. The stiff *taran* backs in front of him were a wall of silk. The warriors paid no attention to the shuffling going on behind them—that was the duty of the guards who stood along the walls.

From his vantage point Shuibai could see that the Fire Lord and the lady seated across from him were engaged in a staring contest. Each of them was splendidly decked out, the Fire Lord in his uniform coat with the orange dragon embroidered upon his shoulders, and the opposing lady in a white set of clothes embroidered with branches laden with cherry blossoms, bound with a red silk sash, also patterned with cherry blossoms. From this Shuibai guessed she was Lady Nayabashi, daughter of the Lady of Cherry Hill. She wore an old-fashioned mask of Balanced Judgment, which had narrowed eyes and a long nose, revealing only her chin and down turned mouth.

The *taran* on each side exchanged muted whispers that could not be heard by those opposite. Tension grew, but at last the majordomo announced, "His Highness, Lord Brice, the Black Prince, Avatar of Death, and Priest of Night."

The cloud-dwelling prince entered the room on stockinged feet. For the second most powerful man in Hu Shen, a member of the Imperial inner circle, and a purported Oracle, He was rather plebeian in appearance. He was average height, with a medium build and pale skin, clad in thick black brocade comprising the obligatory formal divided skirts and a heavy black coat lined with black silk over a long sleeved robe, with a bit of black sash visible in the front where the coat was open. Even His socks were black. He was Night personified and His presence cast a pall over the gaudy *taran* peacocks. He stood at the foot of the aisle and lowered His hood, which revealed light brown hair cropped short like a commoner. He didn't look Shen at all—more like one of the western barbarians. He wore a black Raven mask that covered everything but His mouth and chin, and the mask had metal feathers that swept back past His ears and over His head. Two clawed feet thrust down past His chin, and a beak thrust out from the middle of the face. His eyes were hidden by eye slits that were almost invisible in the feather pattern of the mask. He wore no insignia and carried no sword. He had a black folding fan thrust into His sash but was otherwise apparently unarmed.

Shuibai swallowed hard. The unknown Hooded Woman had dressed the same, was she a retainer of the Black Prince's household? The intricacies of conspiracy made his head swim. Who was allied with whom, and to what purpose? What secret ambitions were disguised as service to another? Did the Black Prince even now carry the silver fan that would be the Golden Emperor's undoing? Although the Black Prince was his master's master, he felt no loyalty towards the man, only fear and suspicion.

'The Black Prince is trying to get You killed,' he wanted to say to the Golden Emperor, but he had no way to reach that august personage. Why would the Emperor believe him? The Emperor trusted His chief advisor—had even made the man Regent for His child in the event He should die untimely.

Everyone kowtowed, the *taran* faces hovering a hair's breadth above the polished wooden floor while the commoners made sure their noses were pressed to the wood. They heard the rustle of the Prince's skirts as He passed down the aisle. A spicy, pungent cinnamon incense floated through the room. There were several quick footfalls as His retainers took up their places.

"Please rise," He said. His voice was inelegant and strangely accented. The rumors were true: He was a foreigner.

They all straightened up. He had two bodyguards who wore black and white zigzag face paint, short hair, and carried short spears, showing that they were men of common birth—masks, swords, and horses all being the prerogative of the *taran*. In spite of their lofty place in Shen politics, the foreign-born Black Prince and His personal retainers were not entitled to the ancient regalia of the warrior class.

Later Shuibai learned the bodyguards were called 'Sergeant Left' and 'Sergeant Right' because of their habitual positions near the Avatar of Death; positions they held due to their fanatical loyalty. They stood on either side of the dais and were dressed in practical trousers and jackets and unusual rubber-soled socks. Shuibai wondered if the ancient custom of removing shoes when entering a building had started as a method of rendering combat more difficult should the mercurial *taran* lose their tempers. It seemed like it would be impractical to sword fight while slipping across the polished floor in stocking feet. The Guardians of Night had found a way around that particular difficulty.

The Black Prince lifted a black-gloved hand in greeting. "The blessings of the Night upon you all," He said formally. Then He turned to the Fire Lord. "Fire Lord Chuja Harada, please proceed."

The Fire Lord bowed in acknowledgment. "Let me begin by saying that we are surprised and gratified that You have taken Your attention from loftier matters in order to give us the benefit of Your wisdom. It is unexpected and Your generosity is appreciated." He used the divine 'You' to address the Prince; the man was an Avatar.

The Black Prince waved his hand. "Don't stand on ceremony on my account. We'll be here all day if we have to go through the Fifteen Niceties and the Forty-Seven Obligatory Literary Allusions.

Let's just hear about the fire." He eschewed the use of the formal dialect; in fact, His speech could even be called coarse. He was not an impressive specimen.

Somebody, very softly, said under their breath, *"Barbarian."* Nobody moved, and Shuibai hoped he was the only one who had heard the insult.

The Fire Lord spoke into the silence, "Your . . ." he groped for a polite word and couldn't find one, so he switched tacks, "concentration upon the task at hand sets a good example for us all, My Prince." Having smoothed over the Black Prince's breach of etiquette as gracefully as he could, he moved on. "It was my original intention to investigate the Great Fire in Cherry Hill—"

"I object," Lady Nayabashi interjected.

"Why?" the Black Prince asked.

"Cherry Hill does not lie within the Capital District and as such Lord Chuja has no authority over the matter."

The Fire Lord spoke up smoothly. "With all due respect, I had intended to hold this meeting purely for my own informational purposes. By understanding the disaster that has befallen Cherry Hill I can take steps to be certain it does not befall Alla Far. Since the Golden Emperor has made it clear that He desires the establishment of a fire commission, such an investigation seems a very proper first step in carrying out His Will."

Lady Nayabashi shot Lord Chuja such a look of hatred that Shuibai thought they would come to blows in an instant, but Lord Chuja remained bland, his lip slightly curled.

"When the Golden Emperor actually establishes His fire commission, we will cooperate. But in the meantime, you overstep your authority," the woman countered.

The Black Prince raised His hand. "We understand. This meeting is purely educational and will not attempt to fix blame. The information acquired will be presented in full to the fire commission, once the formalities establishing that body are completed."

Lady Nayabashi glared at him. "Cherry Hill is not part of the Capital District. This Court has no authority over this matter! You have ridden roughshod over our ancient fealty, and we will not tolerate it!"

The Black Prince crossed his arms. "In that case, you can leave, and we will go on without you."

Her eyes glittered behind her mask and she ground her teeth. "This is not a lawful court."

"I'm the Black Prince of Hu Shen. I wish to know about the Great Fire in Cherry Hill. Indulge Me." He switched to the formal dialect to make his authority clear.

She gave him such a baleful look that Shuibai almost felt sorry for the man. She ground her teeth and bit back words. "If it is purely for Your Own amusement," she said, adopting the formal dialect, her voice reeking of sarcasm, "then of course I am happy to entertain You." She looked like she'd rather eat His living heart, but He didn't seem to notice.

"Good! Let's proceed. Chuja-don, carry on."

"I would be most appreciative if Fire Chief Pokodin of Cherry Hill would share his report with us," Lord Chuja replied.

Chief Pokodin was sitting behind Lady Nayabashi, so the Black Prince gestured with one gloved hand and said, "It would facilitate communication if you would step into the aisle."

Nayabashi didn't object even though she looked like a storm about to break. Pokodin stepped around the packed room and kowtowed his way up the aisle. His voice was high pitched and nervous.

"I am the Chief Fire Warden of Cherry Hill, and have been so for five years. We have never had such a disaster as this one. Interviews with survivors suggest that the night watchman at the Maiko Fireworks Factory dropped a lantern, but I have not been able to find the watchman. The factory was well supplied with gunpowder and was stockpiling fireworks to be used in the winter celebration. This set off a chain reaction with several powder magazines and a great number of pyrotechnic devices exploding. When they did, they shook the earth like an earthquake and flung fire into nearby buildings. It was breezy that night, so the sparks carried quickly into other buildings. That part of the city is quite old, with many buildings jammed close together, wooden roofs and wooden streets. Streets were narrow and the fire rapidly raced out of control. Many lives were lost as flames leapfrogged from house to house, trapping people and cutting off escape. It happened at night, so many people were asleep and didn't wake until fire was roaring through their houses. I notified the Lady of Cherry Hill immediately, and asked permission to call for support. She gave her permission and dispatched Imperial Post riders to all the neighboring towns. The nearest fire companies arrived within a half hour. All told, about six hundred firefighters responded." He paused to catch his breath, then rushed on.

"However, the fire was running out of control. It was impossible to check it in the close confines of the neighborhood, so it was decided to sacrifice several blocks in order to get ahead of the fire and pull down buildings along the Great Southern Highway to make a fire break. This was done. Buildings, many of them as tall as five stories, were pulled down along an eleven block front. The fire was checked at that point, and burned for eighteen hours before it ceased threatening other property. The wind carried sparks and started several dozen other fires, which were extinguished by civilians.

"About one sixth of the buildings in Cherry Hill burned." He bowed. He did not elucidate the dead and homeless, such trivia were irrelevant to the ladies and lords of the land.

"Thank you," said Lord Chuja. "Next I would like to hear from Chief Byan."

"A moment," said Lady Nayabashi. "How did the fire start? Was it accident? Or arson?" Her voice was harsh.

"I think it would be more helpful to hear all the reports before we start asking questions," the Black Prince said mildly. "Once we hear the complete story I'm sure some questions will be answered while others will be raised." He gestured, and Chief Pokodin fled back to his seat. Lady Nayabashi bestowed a look of undisguised loathing upon the Black Prince.

The hearing went on a long time, with each participating fire chief giving an account of what he saw and what his company did. Everybody refrained from speculation and stuck close to the facts, but Shuibai could not resist the opportunity of concluding, "So it is my opinion that if the towns were obliged to install a water pump on every corner, fires such as this would not get out of control." That got him a few quick looks, but the next speaker was called, and he returned to his seat. The reports went on for most of the morning, and the Fire Lord's scribe filled up an entire scroll with shorthand notes.

When the floor was finally opened for question, Lady Nayabashi demanded, "I want answers. I find it strange that a night watchman would *accidentally* drop his lantern in precisely the right place to blow up an entire factory. Gunpowder is carefully stored to prevent such accidents, so how could this happen?"

"If you wish me to investigate this matter in more detail, I will be happy to do it as a favor to your Lady Mother," the Fire Lord replied with unbecoming relish.

"I am not asking you to investigate, I am asking you for answers!" Nayabashi roared, losing all patience. Her retainers winced.

Lord Chuja remained impassive. "I cannot answer your questions unless I investigate."

The Black Prince held up his hand. "Enough. No one is attempting to trespass on the Lady of Cherry Hill's right to administer justice within her own domain. I'm sure that Fire Lord Chuja will be happy to provide a copy of today's testimony for her to use in her own investigation."

The Fire Lord nodded curtly. "As You say, My Lord," his use of the possessive adjective reminding the rest of them that they were not vassals of the Black Prince, and hence, entirely dependent upon His good will. He owed them nothing, and out Ranked them in every way—even if He was an ill-mannered person of foreign birth.

"The guilty must be punished!" Nayabashi persisted, glaring straight at Lord Chuja.

The Black Prince raised His gloved hand in a placating gesture. "The purpose of this meeting is to evaluate the fire code and to prepare a defense against future calamities. I will not tolerate rivalries," he added, giving the two aristocrats a stern glare.

"You play favorites," Nayabashi seethed, glaring at the Black Prince. "You come to our country with Your corrupt practices, You overturn everything that is sacred, and order Your puppets to destroy everything that matters to the great houses!"

"That's ridiculous," a *taran* on the Fire Lord's side of the aisle retorted.

"We know who's trying to ruin our Lady! This fire is the latest mischief!" one of the Cherry Hill faction retorted.

Voices clamored with accusation and insult.

"Silence!" roared the Black Prince. The tumult died down. "I know you don't like me, Nayabashi-don, but I don't give a damn. I've built a hospital for the sick and crippled. I'm spurring the enforcement of the fire code and the development of fire companies. I demand that women and men give their loyalty to the common good instead of the gratification of their own vanity. I hire women and men based on merit, not their political connections. And I do not tolerate any underhanded thing at all!" He paused to gather his composure. "If you have an accusation to make, make it in the Court of Justice. You had damn well better have evidence to back it up, real evidence. Facts, not feuds."

In the ensuing silence the Fire Lord stripped off his glove and flung it down in front of Lady Nayabashi. "They insult me by insinuating I am somehow responsible for an act of arson. I will not tolerate such a blot on my honor."

"I will receive your glove at a more convenient place and time," Lady Nayabashi snarled. She rose abruptly, didn't bow, and rudely turned her back on the Black Prince and stalked down the aisle. Her retainers quickly scurried after her, casting haughty or guilty looks about them. The Cherry Hill Fire Chief looked apologetically at Chuja's faction, and bowing and scraping, followed them out.

When the screen slid shut and they all drew a breath, the Black Prince stepped forward to pick up Lord Chuja's glove and threw it back at him. "Idiot! What did I just say? Are you deaf? Is your vanity more important than the security of the realm?"

Lord Chuja calmly picked up his glove and donned it, saying, "Is there any difference between the two?"

That stumped the Prince. "What do you mean?"

"I uphold Your Office. You uphold the Office of the Golden Emperor. If I am affronted, then that impairs my ability to render You the service You are due. If Your retainers cannot do what is expected of them, then You canot fulfill Your obligations to the Emperor."

"If you kill Nayabashi in a duel, that deprives the Golden Emperor of the Lady of the Highways. That is not the proper way to serve Him!"

"That is none of my business. I am only concerned with my conduct and that of my retainers. If Nayabashi had kept her face, I wouldn't be obliged to kill her, so it's her own fault."

"Dammit, you could have ordered her out of the house and that would have been good enough! Now you are committed to a stupid duel. This resolves nothing and only worsens the rift between the two houses!"

The Fire Lord folded his arms across his chest and looked stubborn. "I will of course obey You in all things. But I cannot undo what has been done. I won't tolerate her baseless accusations."

The Black Prince caught the panel of his sleeve in his two fists and twisted it forcefully. He schooled himself to speak levelly and explain the obvious. "All of you must learn to hold your tongues and open your ears. If you're so busy quarreling with your rivals, how will you hear what has not been said? Why didn't Chief Pokodin answer the question about arson?"

The Fire Lord repressed a smile, but he did not answer the question.

Shuibai burst out, "Because he's been bought." He was absolutely certain it was no coincidence that he had sent a box of ammunition marked with the Maiko Fireworks Factory seal to the Fire Lord, and not long after, the factory had blown up.

The Black Prince looked past the silk shoulder of Lord Chuja. "Who's that?"

Fire Lord Chuja glanced behind him. "Fire Warden Shuibai of Low Marsh. A very effective fireman."

The Black Prince motioned to Shuibai. "Come here and talk to me."

Shuibai started to move toward the aisle where everyone had given their testimony, but the Black Prince tapped the dais next to him. Sergeant Right moved slightly to allow Shuibai to sit on the dais with the Prince. They all stared at Shuibai, more astonished by the sight of a man of low birth sharing a dais with a great prince than they had been by the issuing of a deadly challenge. Shuibai perched on the very edge, careful not to touch the Prince's brocades that were spread around him.

"So you're the Fire Chief of Low Marsh?"

"Your pardon, Noble Prince, I am only a Fire Warden. Nobody has appointed me Chief."

"Why not?"

Shuibai shrugged. "The Councilwomen of Low Marsh do not see the need for a fire company."

"Feh. I do. I'll tell them so. Now, why did you say that about Pokodin?"

Shuibai thought over his situation very carefully. "A woman in a black hood told me my silence was appreciated. Perhaps she made a similar remark to Chief Pokodin."

The Black Prince drummed His fingers on his thigh. "I see. What insignia did she wear?"

"None that I could see, Noble Prince." Retainers of the Black Prince were the only *taran* who traveled without insignia. Nobody missed the implication.

"She didn't do so at my direction. Interesting. What did she say to you?"

Shuibai looked beseechingly at him. "If it please the Noble Prince, these matters are over my head."

"But not over My head. Continue."

The Fire Lord rescued him. "If it please My Lord, there is something You ought to know that cannot be discussed in open court."

The Black Prince drummed His fingers some more. "Very well. Fire Warden Shuibai, I release you. Chuja-don, you and I are going to have a long talk."

Everyone except Lord Chuja and the Prince's bodyguards shuffled out, and nobody knew any better than they had before what was actually going on, but that didn't prevent them from speculating wildly. As for himself, Shuibai was glad to be out of there. He and Zashi slipped away before anyone could tell them to stay.

Chapter 25 : The Jade Demon

Because of his maimed hand Zashi was no longer able to handle the carving tools of his former trade, but a writing brush required only one hand. He bought paints and a long, narrow blank scroll made of thin wooden slats. It was very light, but sturdier than paper would have been. Gold cord stitched the slats together. It could be rolled up, which was another reason Zashi chose it. He laid the scroll on Shuibai's work table and began to paint in strong, curving strokes. The form of a fire dragon appeared in outline, its sinuous lines twisting back upon itself. Flames wreathed it, smoke billowed about it in a great cloud, and a small burning city made a smudged line across the bottom. The constellation known as the Crown capped it. While he worked Shuibai bought some good cypress wood and built a cabinet along the side wall between the kitchen and the front door. A low shelf and a high shelf and two vertical wooden boards defined the space. When Zashi's painting was completed they hung it in the cabinet. Zashi lit a stick of incense and stuck it in a small brass burner. The fragrant aroma of cypress smoke drifted through the room. Zashi remained on his knees before the image in deep meditation. Shuibai knelt beside him, and in a minute the apprentice Kanko came and knelt also.

"The dragon is named Kwaji," Zashi remarked, his burned hand resting upon his thigh. They did not contest him; if anyone knew the Dragon's name, he did.

A superstitious chill went down Shuibai's neck. He compared it to the fear he had felt when the Lady of the Knife had held her glittering point an inch from his eye. She had terrorized him, but he saw nothing awesome about her; she was merely arrogant. A dozen images from the fire flickered through his mind: the despairing look of the girl before she jumped, the hurricane wind that sucked everything into the maw of the inferno, the streets burning, the flaming embers scattering through the sky like a flock of demons, and Zashi's form crumpled with exhaustion and pain. He began to shake and gasp. He gave way to grief, hugging his arms tight about his chest, swaying back and forth as his overwhelmed brain finally released the shock. He had thought he was made of sterner stuff but staring at the terrible beast hanging in the night gave him an intense awareness of the paltriness of human life. Nothing he did mattered in the grand scheme of things. There was no justice, merely an arbitrary assemblage of days, each laden with good or ill according to the whim of an uncontrollable destiny. He leaped up and rocked like a dervish. The boy Kanko counted his prayers on his fingers, and Zashi stared at the thing he had made as if oblivious to all else.

Finally Shuibai sucked in a great breath and sat down on the wooden floor with his legs folded in front of him. No one mentioned his loss of composure and he didn't apologize. Grief was the one emotion exempted from the strict rules governing proper conduct.

"How do you know?" Shuibai asked, continuing the conversation as if there had not been an interruption.

Zashi gave him a strained look. "I just do. How do you know that this place is called Low Marsh, or that the sun rises in the east? It's just the way things are. You don't know when Low Marsh came to exist, and you don't know when the sun started rising in the sky. As far as we can tell they have always been this way."

"But how can you be sure, and if you are sure, what does it mean?"

Zashi adopted the light tone he always used when he did not want Shuibai to consider something too carefully. "I suppose it means I shall have to say some public prayers, maybe erect a prayer stone."

That was a reasonable answer and put Shuibai off the real question. It was so reasonable he was a little ashamed that he hadn't thought of doing so himself. Zashi went over to the table and came back with his brush, and in black strokes added an arcane sign to the upper left hand corner of the painting. Shuibai could not read the archaic characters, but he memorized them. "What does it say?"

"The sign is an old one, and it means 'great fire'. The dragon will be reborn again and again in endless disastrous incarnations until it has a proper Avatar to channel it. Meeting the Black Prince helped me to understand what is being asked of me."

"It seems a matter for the priestesses to settle," Shuibai said dubiously.

"The Spirits choose whomever they will."

Shuibai looked him over carefully. "You're not going to become an Oracle, are you? That would be inconvenient."

Zashi laughed suddenly. "But it would pay better than Assistant Fire Warden, eh?" Then he quoted an old poem, "Determined to fall a weather-exposed skeleton I cannot help the sore wind blowing through my heart." He washed out his brush carefully. "Me? An Oracle? I don't think so."

Shuibai wasn't convinced. He wasn't happy about the Dragon hanging in his house either, but wouldn't contradict Zashi by removing It or rolling It up. Instead he went out and bought some more cypress boards and built a set of doors to cover the image. The smell of fresh-cut cypress wood and incense lingered in mute testimony of the thing he hid but could not deny. The Dragon hung in darkness, waiting patiently in the knowledge that It would be released another time.

Shuibai immersed himself in work, designing a leather hat that would withstand the appalling conditions of the fire zone better than the straw hats of the men. The result was a conical leather hat with a suspension web inside it to prevent his sweaty skull from warping the shape of the leather. It was fastened with metal rings and a leather strap that was easier to operate than the strings that had tied the old hat.

"What is it?" Zashi asked.

"A leather fire hat. Those straw hats are no good. What do you think?" He put it on.

"Looks all right," Zashi said. "Can I try it?"

Shuibai passed it over. Zashi put it on. He looked up. "You can't see up very well, and you have to be able to look up when you're at a fire. Stuff falls down all the time." Shuibai took the hat back and cut away a semi circle from the front. "Now it looks like a *taran* helmet," Zashi commented.

"You don't think I'll get in trouble with the *taran*, do you?" Shuibai asked in sudden worry.

"I don't know. I think a leather fire hat is a good idea, but maybe you better get permission from the Fire Captain before you wear it."

Shuibai tried the hat on again, then trimmed the front edges so that they didn't stick out like tusks—*taran* helmets were often ornamented that way. The result was more of an oblong hat, which looked rather strange, but it provided good visibility in front and protected the nape of the neck. Falling coals wouldn't be able to drop down inside their collars. "Let me paint a fire dragon on the back, then it won't look like military helmet," Zashi suggested.

"No dragons, I've seen enough of them. Make it a swan and bucket like my insignia. We ought to have uniforms made up like that too. In fact, we should paint it on all our equipment so we can tell what belongs to us. Things get awfully mixed up at a fire."

Zashi brought out his brushes and paints and spent some time laboring over a design to be used on the Low Marsh uniforms. When it was ready he showed it to Shuibai for his approval. It featured a swan with its plumage spread out in a fan shape, its beak pointed down to grip a bucket. It was the same design Shuibai had executed, but much more artistic.

Shuibai smiled. "You're very good, much better than I am."

"You like it?"

Shuibai stared past the art and looked straight at Zashi. "I like it a lot," he replied.

Zashi got to his feet and rummaged in the closet. He pulled out his best set of clothes, the dark purple set with the peonies on the shoulders. "I am going to go get us some new uniforms, Fire Warden Shuibai."

"We can't afford it," Shuibai replied automatically. He'd paid old debts, bought some more equipment, and laid in a store of groceries. The money they'd earned at the Cherry Hill Fire was gone.

"We both need new fire coats. You deserve it. You should look your best when you go up to those fire commission meetings."

"Oh, they don't care what I wear. It doesn't matter."

"You deserve a good coat anyhow. I shall do my best to find a donor who is willing to support the heroic Low Marsh Fire Company. It won't cost you a thing."

"How do you expect to do that?"

Zashi flashed his brilliant smile and Shuibai almost dropped his awl. "I'll use my charm and wit. Don't wait up. Flattery takes time."

Shuibai eyed him suspiciously. "Exactly what are you planning to do?"

Zashi didn't answer as he checked himself in their small mirror. He cut a dashing figure, and Shuibai's eyes ate up every inch of him. Then he donned his stitched and mended fire coat, and hid his maimed hand in his sleeve. "Wish me luck."

"Good luck," Shuibai replied unwillingly.

Zashi was gone all evening and into the night. When he returned Kanko and Shuibai were asleep, their mats laid on the wooden floor and the fire carefully banked. He laid his mattress on the floor in front of the dragon's shrine. Shuibai heard him moving and woke up. "Zashi? Did you have any luck?"

"A little. Remember the brewer who sent me the note?"

"Yes."

"I spoke to her."

"All night long?"

"Long enough."

In spite of himself Shuibai asked, "Is she pretty?"

"She's pleasant. Why do you ask?"

"I wondered . . ." But he couldn't say what he wondered. His heart wrenched. "I shouldn't have asked."

"Do you disapprove?"

"No, I understand. I was never any good at charming women myself, but, well. It's useful, I suppose."

Zashi sighed. "You do disapprove. You think it's wrong for a man to use his looks to try and get things from women, don't you? But then, women want things too. It's a trade."

Shuibai turned over and buried himself deeper in the coverlet. "If you had waited a bit, we might have found the money ourselves."

"I don't want you going up to the Fire Court looking like a beggar. You're a good fireman. You deserve better."

"Patience is a virtue," Shuibai mumbled. "I'm not vain. Material things don't matter. You shouldn't have done it, not for me."

Zashi heaved a long sigh. "Truth be told, I didn't mind. It's been a long time since I've been with a woman. I was nervous, but I didn't have to take my clothes off, so it was all right. She's really rather nice."

Shuibai rotated violently from one shoulder to the other. His face burned and his eyes glared in the darkness. "Was it so easy?"

"Don't be jealous. It won't last long."

"I'm not jealous!"

Zashi laughed softly. "All right then. I'll pretend you're not."

"I'm just concerned about your welfare," Shuibai mumbled, his face burning. Hurtful things leapt to the tip of his tongue, but he bit them back. "Do you have to do it in the evening? Or can you do it while I'm gone? I'd rather you were home when I come back from the Fire Court. It isn't easy quarreling with all those people. Everyone of them wants exceptions and reductions that will make the new fire code useless. They say it will cost too much, they say it won't work. They argue constantly. They haggle like pawnbrokers. Even the *taran*. It's disgraceful."

Shuibai hated the petulant tone of his voice, hated the fact that Zashi had a lover, and hated the fact that it was a woman with money even more. He wanted to hammer nails through both of them.

"All right. I'll try to see her tomorrow while you're gone." Zashi yawned, wrapped up in his blanket, and drifted off to sleep.

Shuibai didn't like himself or the way he was reacting, and came to understand why jealousy was called the Jade Demon. It was cold and hard and easily carved into pretty shapes as he told himself lies about why he should have his way in this matter. He didn't sleep at all. Dawn found him exhausted and bleary-eyed, so he got up before the others, stoked the hearth and boiled water for morning rice and tea. When Zashi rose and started shaving he wanted to say something gracious by way of apology, but he didn't have the words. So he just said, "I'm sorry I was rude to you last night."

Zashi paused with the razor in his hand. "You weren't rude. Just plainspoken. I appreciate that about you. As a matter of fact, I'm a little worried about how it's going to go. Eventually she's going to want to see me without my clothes. Then she will be very disappointed." He brooded. "You're right. This is a bad idea."

Shuibai sat down on the edge of the wooden floor next to him. Zashi was kneeling on the dirt floor of the kitchen and using the edge of the wooden floor as a low table for his basin and mirror. "One day we'll have enough money to afford a proper washstand, eh?" Zashi joked, changing the subject.

"Maybe. Some day. How much are the uniforms going to cost? Maybe I can borrow from one of my sisters," Shuibai replied.

"We didn't talk about money. We talked about everything except money. We both had to save face, you know. I had to pretend to be taken by her charms, and she had to pretend she wasn't desperate. She's not so bad looking, you know, but she's not so young either. Women like to be flattered. It seemed okay at the time, but now I feel bad."

"It would be rude to hurt her feelings now. It might be better if you did whatever she expects you to do."

"You think so?"

"I have no idea. I've never been with a woman."

Zashi grinned. "Never?"

Shuibai shook his head. Zashi laughed silently. "Not even the girls in the shop where you were apprenticed?"

"Ugh, my sister and nieces? No way."

"You're missing out on something good, you know." Then he quoted an old poem, "'Whipped by a fierce wind and dashed like the ocean waves against the rocks—I alone am broken to bits and now am lost in longing.' Isn't that a wonderful poem? That's how love should be."

Shuibai rose in agitation. "I don't feel like I've missed anything. Women are nothing but trouble."

"Ah, but they're such a delicious form of trouble."

Shuibai clamped his jaw hard. No word came out. He saw half a dozen ways he could hurt Zashi, but he turned his face away and busied himself by stirring the rice mercilessly. Water slopped out of the kettle and hissed in the fire. At last he said politely, "Your mother is a very nice woman."

"Yes, she is. You ought to ask her to find you a wife. She's good at that. She'll find you a sweet woman, not like these harridans down here." Zashi resumed shaving.

Marriage? The prospect of being tied to a woman's apron strings terrified him. "I'd rather throw myself off the Lantern Bridge than marry a woman."

"Going to be a confirmed bachelor, eh?" Zashi teased him.

"I have to get ready to go to the Fire Court," Shuibai said, jumping up. The future of his love life was not something he wanted to think about. He washed rapidly, the cold water shocking his skin, then pulled on his old green willow clothes and the mended fire coat over them. He donned two pairs of socks in an effort to keep his feet warm on the trek up to the Fire Court.

"You work too hard, Shui-lan. You should think about yourself from time to time. A romance would be good for you. There's plenty of women that would like your attention. You're quite the hero these days."

"I have no interest in women."

"Surely there is someone you admire, if only from a distance."

"Yes," Shuibai choked out.

"So tell me! I'll write you a poem to send to her. Then she'll think you're charming."

"It isn't a woman, Zashi."

A little silence reigned. "I see. Some pretty boy, then? An actor or a wrestler maybe? Not Kanko, you never pay any attention to him!"

"No, don't be silly. He's just an apprentice! It's someone I can't mention. I wouldn't even know what to say to him. So I don't say anything."

"You should declare yourself. He might reciprocate."

"No, I don't think so. He's not like that. He likes girls. So what point is there?" He finished dressing and crossed to the door. He paused on the threshold. "I don't mind, you know. I never did expect to find somebody to be with. I didn't think I would ever meet somebody I liked that much. So it's already more than I expected. It would be foolish not to appreciate what I've got, wouldn't it?"

"You sound like you have it all worked out."

"I guess I do. I'll see you later."

"Goodbye."

"Goodbye, Zashi-lan."

He stepped through the door and closed it carefully behind him. He stepped into his sandals and pushed out into the street, his head spinning. Did Zashi guess? He didn't think so. He didn't think he was playing dumb on purpose because that would have been cruel. But Shuibai didn't want him to know. Because if he said it in plain words then Zashi would have to say, "Sorry, I'm not interested in you that way." He knew it was true, but it would hurt to hear the words all the same. Better to avoid the issue and be content with what he had.

CHAPTER 26 : THE LOW MARSH FIRE COMPANY

The town mothers were pleased to see Shuibai and Zashi in their new uniforms at the Council meeting; they were no longer parading the Fire Lord's authority through a Free Town. Shuibai had no idea whether the Black Prince had intervened on his behalf or not, but he hoped not. He wanted to think the town mothers were coming around on their own. His mother was not present at the meeting for which Shuibai was grateful. Headwoman Vaadayasin welcomed him and offered him a cushion in the place of honor opposite her; he and Zashi settled down. A girl in a sky blue robe and orange sash knelt with a tray. They helped themselves to dried squid and seaweed sauce. Several of the Councilwomen were smoking their pipes and the tendrils of aromatic haze wound around the exposed beams of the ceiling. Pale sunlight glinted on the oiled paper screens of the windows while a brazier in the center of the room provided warmth.

Headwoman Vaadayasin was dressed in a deep violet robe with some sort of tree print in black and a black sash. The deep color suited the white in her hair. "Master Shuibai. We have been most impressed with your work on the Great Fire of Cherry Hill. I speak for all of us," there were nods all around the room, "when I say that we are keenly aware that if it was not for the dedication of the Low Marsh Fire Company, the fire would have jumped the Southern Highway and ravaged our town. Low Marsh could not withstand such losses; the town would be utterly wiped out. Therefore, we want to ask, Master Shuibai, if you will accept the title of Fire Chief of Low Marsh, and establish a good and proper fire company for our town."

Shuibai was momentarily stunned. Then he said, "Yes, of course."

The Headwoman nodded to the girl, who turned behind her and lifted a wooden box. She crossed to Shuibai, skirting the brazier, then knelt before him and laid the box on the floor in front of him. She unlatched it and lifted the lid, revealing scarlet silks. She folded back the padding to reveal a silver speaking trumpet.

"Please accept this as a token of our appreciation and as a symbol of your rank," the girl said in a singsong voice, clearly reciting a formula she had been required to memorize.

Shuibai stretched out his hand and lifted the silver trumpet. It was as long as his arm from fingertip to elbow and had a black leather strap to carry it by. Zashi whispered in his ear, "I told them the proper symbol for a chief's authority."

Shuibai looked at him. "You knew?"

"They sounded me out first. They made no promises, but I guessed they would go through with it."

Shuibai tilted the trumpet and looked at the marks engraved upon it. He was not well versed in letters, but he had a pretty good grasp of vocabulary related to the fire service. The inscription read, "Presented to Master Shuibai, first Fire Chief of Low Marsh, in the year one thousand and thirty four since the founding of the Old Capital of Ton Far."

"Now I won't have to shout myself hoarse at fires," he said, lifting the speaking trumpet. "Thank you. I am honored." He bowed low.

They bowed back to him. "The honor is ours."

From there they got down to business. Low Marsh Fire Company got its budget—but only half of what Shuibai had asked for. He got his salary and Zashi's salary, and finally breathed easy on his personal finances. For watchmen he hired four of the men who had been with him at the Cherry Hill fire. The other men he appointed as unpaid Fire Wardens within their wards. His experienced men were disproportionately taken from the area along the Low Road, but he decided that was all right because that was where the bulk of the buildings were concentrated. Since he had no money for watchtowers, he ordered them to walk around the neighborhoods to keep an eye on things. Each was provided with a staff painted red and tipped with a brass hook as a sign of their authority; in addition they carried a wooden noise-maker with them to sound the alarm should it be necessary.

Shuibai also received the keys to the city along with the speaking trumpet and title of Chief. The keys were wrapped in a bright red piece of silk printed over all with green birds and white blossoms. Dozens of keys: iron keys, brass keys, bronze keys, all strung together on a large brass ring. Some keys were small, some were large, and each of them opened a door somewhere in the city.

Paper ribbons were tied to the keys, naming the door they belonged to. Noticeable by its brazen weight was the key to the Lantern Gate. The whole collection weighed several pounds and hung heavy on his belt. When he got home he would make a leather baldric so that it would hang on his hip like some men hung their swords.

Once the formal niceties were accomplished, the town mothers stalled. They vetoed his plan for installing pumps on every corner as foolish, expensive, and impractical. They refused to pay for the construction of a watchtower. They insisted that the fire code not be enforced any more strictly than it already was, meaning they were willing to let him inspect chimneys and buckets, but they weren't willing to let him enforce any building codes, not even on new property.

Even so, there was a different attitude in town. This time when women saw him on the street in his new coat, they waved and pointed him out to their children. "There goes Fire Chief Shuibai!" Children ran after him holding up their hands and crying, "Stamp me, stamp me." So he opened up his seal box and stamped them with his official seal. They ran away giggling with red ink on their hands. A group of tattooed roustabouts working to load a wagon cheered him as he went past. Some women waved buckets with his swan and bucket symbol on them and yelled, "I've got mine!" He smiled and nodded at everyone and felt as if he had grown six inches taller. He walked with an unconscious swagger.

Zashi grinned broadly as he limped along beside him. "You're a hero. I think you're more famous than Chief Byan right now."

"Oh, I couldn't be that famous," Shuibai instantly replied. "This is just Low Marsh, after all. Still, never in my life did I think anything like this would happen to me. I think this must be the happiest day of my life."

A handsome matron woman stepped off the boardwalk and approached them. She was accompanied by two girls, one a mere child, the other poised to cross the border into womanhood. The little girl was wearing a very pale pink winter dress with a pink and blue plaid sash, her older sister was wearing a bright pink dress with a purple sash. The mother was dressed in a pearl grey robe with a bright pink sash. The girls had their hair bobbed short while the mother had her hair done up in an elaborate coiffure ornamented with lacquered combs. They had wrapped white silk shawls around their heads on account of the cold. They each carried an oiled paper umbrella over their heads because of the rain that was threatening. The matron bowed and the little girls bowed like puppets on the same string. The effect was indescribably charming, and Shuibai smiled, predisposed to like the family. He was in an expansive mood.

"Good afternoon, Fire Chief Shuibai," the mother said. "Good afternoon," the girls echoed in their piping voices.

"Good afternoon to you too," Shuibai replied cheerfully.

Zashi spoke. "Allow me to present Mother Rikasa, the brewer who donated the money for our new uniforms."

Shuibai's face froze as he realized he was face to face with Zashi's lover. "You are very generous, and we are in your debt," he uttered, feeling like his throat had turned to stone.

Zashi smiled and nodded. "We appreciate your help. The uniforms are very smart. Even the Councilwomen liked them."

Mother Rikasa simpered and batted her eyelids at Zashi. "You know it was my pleasure."

Shuibai felt all his good will evaporate, replaced by an urge to strangle her.

She smiled sweetly at Shuibai and said, "I have brought a gift in honor of your promotion, Fire Chief." She held up a small wooden box. "Marmalade," she said. Again the sweet smile. "I was hoping that you would let Zashi-lan have some time off to celebrate with his friends."

Marmalade was imported from the far south lands and was one of the more costly—and highly appreciated—treats enjoyed by the Shen. Not only that, marmalade was prescribed as medicine for stomach maladies as it was quite effective at quelling nausea. The marmalade trade was brisk and pricey, with demand always exceeding supply. It was a handsome gift. Shuibai received the box with numb hands. "I am stunned by your generosity."

The matron smiled prettily and said, "My daughter works for a merchant. We get marmalade quite often." She hooked her arm into Zashi's and drew him away, "Tell us he doesn't have to show up for work tomorrow, please?"

Shuibai swallowed hard. "He deserves a day off. He is a very hard worker." He was staring hard at Zashi, and Zashi shrugged abashedly.

She bowed, the silk scarf fluttering about her face. Her hair ornaments jingled. The smell of orange blossoms wafted about her. "I knew you were kind. I could see it in your face."

"Thank you, Chief," Zashi said as she drew him away.

"I've got a fine lunch all prepared," she was telling him, Shuibai instantly forgotten.

The new Fire Chief stood in the street a long time watching them walk away. He had to admit they made a handsome couple. The woman had been attractive, her daughters were pretty, and her clothes tasteful. She was a good match if Zashi wanted to get married. Shuibai had a knot in his stomach, so he went home and ate some marmalade on a rice cake, but it didn't make him feel any better. He gave the apprentice the day and night off and sent him away with a little money to spend. Then he sat in a corner and brooded.

He wasn't left alone for long. He'd only been home a short time when someone knocked on the shutter. He opened it to discover the Lady of the Knife. She was dressed in bright blue trousers with a navy blue coat over them. A blue scarf was wrapped around her head. "What do you want?" he demanded.

"I understand you had an interesting conversation at the Fire Court."

"I told them nothing I was forbidden to say."

"And yet, interesting motions have resulted from that conversation. Accordingly, Master Jozatha requires your presence. Now would be a good time."

She appeared to be alone, but it didn't matter. She was quite capable of taking him by force if need be. He looked up and down his little street, but the shop fronts were closed against the cold. There were no witnesses. No one could help him.

"I can't leave. I'm the only one here. If the alarm is rung I have to answer it. My assistant has the day off."

She frowned at him. Her eyes were brown and her brows were very fine. She was a strikingly beautiful woman as well as dangerous. He wondered if she was still in disgrace, or if her recovery of the silver fan had redeemed her. But if she had been redeemed, why was she still in Low Marsh? "I can force you to come," she threatened.

Shuibai sat down cross-legged in the opening. "I shall not resist. I know I don't have a chance against you in a fight, so there is no point in struggling with you. But there is nothing you can say that will make me leave, either. I have a duty to attend and I won't abandon it."

"Bah. You are an idiot. There is no need to be difficult."

"I am not being difficult. I have a very clear understanding of my duty."

"I'll carry you if I have to," she threatened.

"Go ahead. But it might attract attention if you were to be seen carrying the Fire Chief bodily through the streets. I doubt the Hooded Woman would approve."

Her eyes snapped. "You know nothing!"

"That's very true," he agreed.

She fumed. "I could club you over the head and throw you in a cart."

"Go ahead."

"Bah. Men," she grumbled. "It would be more convenient if you would just visit the Master."

"It would be more convenient if the Master would come to me."

He slid the screen closed and latched it. His heart beat wildly. He half-expected her to burst through the shutters, knives glittering in her hands. But she didn't. He waited a long time, then peeked into the street. She'd gone. He rose and paced around the small apartment, then decided to write a note and leave it in the alcove with the dragon picture—just in case Zashi came home and he wasn't there. There was no telling what she might do.

For that matter, he did have one resource. So he stepped outside and rang the assembly code. His firemen answered his call within minutes, and it gratified him to see them come when he called. He smiled at them and said, "Master Jozatha has invited the Low Marsh Fire Company to call on him. We're going to the Garden of Earthly Delights. You, Red, stay here in case anyone sounds the alarm. You know where to find us if we're needed. Remember, interfering with a fireman in the course of his duty is a felony punishable by death, so if you need me, don't allow anyone to stand between you and me."

Red's slanted eyes were wide. "What's going on?"

Shuibai looked them over, then said, "I wish I knew. We're going to try and find out. Take up your tools."

The axes and hooks were passed out and the men looked very sober. "Is there going to be a fight, Chief?" Axe asked him.

"Probably," Shuibai replied. "Watch out for a woman in blue, she's a dangerous knife fighter. Kill her if you can."

Tabuza, a skinny guy who was going bald stepped forward. "Point her out to me and I'll keep her busy."

Shuibai looked him over. "How?"

He shrugged. "I served in the army when we fought Pangu in the Barren Lands. I don't say I'm any good at combat, but I ought to be able to keep her busy long enough for somebody else to stab her in the back."

"You served out West? What unit?"

"Second Infantry. I was drafted. If it weren't for the Black Prince, I'd be dead."

"Why?"

"He got medicine from the foreigners that cured my infection. I had the Red Fever. So you see, I'm more than happy to serve in the fire service. I figure I owe him."

"You know him?" Shuibai asked.

"Not personally. There was a whole bunch of us in the field hospital when he came around and made arrangements for our doctor to get the medicine."

"I'd like to hear more about it, but not right now. Can you find yourself a partner to deal with the Lady of the Knife?"

A brief consultation resulted in a short, burly man named Faua agreeing to partner Tabuza. He carried a hook over his shoulder. "She tries anything, we'll get her."

"Oh, one other thing. She's pretty. Don't let that stop you."

Nods all around. Some of the men looked grim, some looked worried. "We won't fight if we don't have to, eh, Chief?"

"No, but I want some answers. However, I don't want to get killed either. We'll see how it goes."

They walked briskly up the Street of Good Fortune to the fancy quarter with the bordellos and restaurants and liquor stores and gambling parlors and opium dens. The Garden of Earthly Delights had closed its shutters on account of the cold, but Shuibai and his men walked in. "Keep your shoes on," he ordered, remembering the lesson he had noticed while visiting the Fire Court. He wanted good traction in the event of a fight.

The hostess greeted them and he spoke politely to her. "Fire Chief Shuibai and the Low Marsh Fire Company are calling upon Master Jozatha as requested. Please inform him that we are here."

"He's busy right now—"

Shuibai took an axe from the nearest man. "We are here on official business. You can cooperate, or we can take action."

She regarded the axe in his hands warily and backed up. "I'm sorry, but—"

Shuibai swung the axe and rent a great gash in the paper wall that separated the vestibule from the main room. He hooked the axe on the frame and yanked it, snapping the wood and dropping the whole torn mess to the floor. Patrons looked up from their tables in shock. "Everyone out!" he bellowed. "We are doing a complete inspection!"

He walked through the torn debris and kicked over the nearest table. His firemen followed him, pulling the pictures from the wall and kicking over the tables. The patrons fled. Shuibai selected a fine wooden cabinet and sank his axe into it. Porcelain dishes were stacked inside and cascaded in a grand crash as he toppled the cabinet.

"I'll tell him you're here!" The hostess shrieked and fled upstairs.

Shuibai formed his men in a circle with him closest to the steps. They bounced on the balls of their feet, waiting for fighters to stream out of the back hall or down the stairs. The Lady of the Knife flew halfway down the steps, saw Shuibai and halted, her stocking feet slipping on the polished wood. She grabbed the railing for balance. Shuibai smiled to see it.

"I have made arrangements to see that my post is covered while I chat with your Master," he told her. His blood was up. With a dozen armed men backing him up he was not afraid of her. Not yet. She glared at him, then gnashed her teeth. Then she shouted up the stairs, "Hey, boss! It's the Fire Chief! He's armed and he's not alone!"

"What in the hell does he think he's doing?" a male voice drifted down.

Shuibai grinned viciously and swung the axe, severing the banister near her hand. She drew one of her knives and backed up one step. "You better ask him yourself before he wrecks the joint!" she shouted back, not taking her eyes off of Shuibai.

Jozatha descended the steps. He was a big man, large with muscle and fat. He had heavy jowls and wore his very black hair all the way to his shoulders, just long enough to irritate the *taran*. He wore a green willow robe and dark green trousers in the uptown style. He surveyed the scene, noting the armed firemen and the damage to his restaurant. Several men slid down the steps with him and Shuibai lifted his axe menacingly. "Send them back upstairs. I don't want to see them. Just you."

Jozatha gestured them away and his henchmen retreated far enough up the steps to be out of Shuibai's sight. "What do you want?"

"Who is the Hooded Woman?"

Jozatha laughed through his teeth. "You don't need to know."

"I'm tired of people with weapons threatening me. She's behind you, I know that. I want to know who she is. I don't like sneaks. If she's a *taran,* she's a coward."

The Lady of the Knife snarled at him like an angry cat. Jozatha folded his arms over his great chest. "On the contrary, I think it is you who owe me some answers. We had a deal."

Shuibai turned to his firemen. "Wreck the place. Wreck it all." They ripped apart the walls, broke into the kitchen and the private dining rooms, shredded the fine artwork, knocked out the windows, and reduced the first floor to flinders. Jozatha followed them with eyes of hatred, but he didn't speak.

"Who owns you? Who's the woman that bought you a ship and makes you do her dirty errands? Is it the Hooded Woman?" Shuibai asked, hefting the axe. The Lady of the Knife glided down the steps and onto level footing. She adopted a guard position, her gleaming blades held backwards in her hands so that the metal lay along her forearms.

"You told me you were a brotherhood of money," Shuibai told her. "You told me you didn't like it when you lost money. I can wreck this entire house and send you to ruin. I can wreck every piece of property you own in this city. How expensive do I have to make it before you decide to talk?"

"Lady Omo," Jozatha said at last. "It's not a secret. You could have found out yourself if you'd been clever." He sneered contemptuously at Shuibai.

"If it's not a secret, then why did you keep it from me?" Shuibai replied in exasperation.

"You can't walk in here and order me around. This is my place."

Shuibai hung his axe over his shoulder. "I just did. Next time I ask you a question, I expect an answer." He gestured to his men and they climbed out through the broken front wall. Shuibai stopped on the threshold and asked, "What clan is Lady Omo?"

"Sakoro, you idiot," the Lady of the Knife spit at him.

"I see," said Shuibai. He walked away, not commenting to anyone. His men followed along behind him, watching over their shoulders in case anyone followed them.

"Who's Sakoro?" Axe finally asked him.

"The ruling clan of Cherry Hill," Shuibai replied.

"Oh. So, what's that got to do with anything?"

"They despise the Fire Lord. And hence, because we are his minions, they despise us."

"Inconvenient. Why do they hate the Fire Lord?"

"Because he's the Black Prince's retainer."

"Why do they hate the Black Prince?"

"Because He's a foreigner."

"Ah."

CHAPTER 27 : BAMBOO PIPES

Zashi surprised Shuibai by returning that evening. He had expected him to spend the night with his lover. Zashi came in quietly and hung his coat on the wooden peg near the door. He slipped off his fine clothes and folded them up neatly and put them away in the closet. Dressed in just his white under robe he went to the kitchen and put the tea kettle on. He didn't speak. Shuibai followed him and seated himself on the edge of the floor. Shuibai was dressed in his old green work clothes with sturdy cotton socks on his feet.

"What happened?"

"She proposed marriage."

"And?"

"I showed her my hand."

"Yes?"

"She said she didn't mind."

"She didn't?"

"No, she didn't."

"What did you say?"

"I told her I had to ask my mother."

"Did you? Ask her?"

"Not yet. I'm trying to make up my own mind. Then I'll ask my mother to smooth things over, one way or the other."

"You're not going to do it!"

"Well, I think I should."

"Why? You have a good job here. Things are going well. You should have seen it! I found out who the Hooded Woman is!"

Zashi lifted his head at last. "You did?"

"Lady Omo of the Sakoro clan."

"Nayabashi's sister. Well, that makes sense. So this is just part of the feud between the Fire Lord and Lady Nayabashi. It doesn't concern us. That's nice to know."

"I wrecked Jozatha's restaurant, so there might be repercussions."

"What?" Zashi spun to face him.

Shuibai told him the whole story. Zashi shook his head miserably. "Now you've made them angry, Shui-lan. They won't forget or forgive. You've given them a reason to dislike you above and beyond your tangential involvement in the Fire Lord's affairs. My friend, you were foolish."

Shuibai was nettled. "But now I know who the enemy is."

"Bah. We knew the Sakoro clan was the enemy. Dammit, Shui-lan! I can't get married. I have to look out for you. You're so naive!" He sat by the hearth and regarded Shuibai with an expression that was composed of equal parts affection and exasperation.

"I'm not naive," Shuibai mumbled. "I was very commanding. You should have seen me."

Zashi snorted. "Bah. Shui-lan, it is better to charm people than to anger them. People will do things because they like you that they won't do just because they should. Angry people will do things because they're mad and won't care whether they're right or wrong."

"I thought I accomplished something," Shuibai grumbled. "Isn't it useful to know that the Hooded Woman is Lady Omo? She was just dressing that way as a disguise, not because she was a member of the Black Prince's household."

"Lady Omo dresses that way because she was the Captain of the Secret Police under the Deceased Black Princess. You've just pissed off the most dangerous woman in the Two Queendoms."

Shuibai's jaw dropped. "You didn't tell me!"

Zashi lost his temper. "You're such a peasant! Didn't tell you? *Everybody* knows Lord Brice fired her when He ascended to the Black. Don't you pay attention to something other than your own belly? Damn peasants. You are such narrow-minded, provincial, short-sighted, ignorant, uneducated, selfish—"

"I'm not."

"Shui-lan—"

"Don't yell at me! Just explain it to me. I tried to figure out by myself and I blew it! Why don't you stop putting on airs and tell me something useful?"

"Shuibai, if you think—"

Shuibai leaped to his feet. "I gave you a job, *cripple,* that's what I think! I hired you expressly so you could teach me what I don't know! If you won't, then dammit, I'll fire you and find someone who will! I'm fed up with politics. I'm fed up with your high and mighty attitudes. I'm sick of your girlfriend. I hate you!"

Zashi went white.

Just as suddenly as he had burst out, Shuibai collapsed. "I depended on you. Don't abandon me. Don't get married. I need your help. I'm sorry I screwed up. I always screw up when you're not around. You should be Chief, not me. You were raised for it. I'm just a stupid peasant. I never asked for this job. You should have it. You're good at it."

Zashi clasped his burned hand in his good hand and rested them both in his lap. He bit his lip and wouldn't look at Shuibai. "We shouldn't quarrel," he said at last. "We have been good friends until now. We shouldn't quarrel. I am very aware that your generosity brought me my current good fortune. You're a good chief, Shuibai-don."

"If I have accomplished anything, it's because you always told me what to do."

They glanced at one another. "We worked well together," said Zashi.

"I have enjoyed your company," Shuibai said shyly. "Even the poetry."

Zashi looked abashed. "I was putting on airs. It's not like I've been educated in a proper school, you know."

"You improved my mind."

"I like to think I've been a positive influence."

"Yes, you've been most helpful. I'm sorry I lost my temper."

"I apologize for thinking of myself before my work. You are right to be dissatisfied."

Shuibai took a deep breath and let his shoulders relax. "Well then. I want to buy some bamboo. Will you help me test an idea?"

"Yes, but we'd better take a bodyguard. Can I suggest that in the future you ask my advice before antagonizing powerful people?"

"Well, you were with That Woman, and the Lady of the Knife showed up and threatened to carry me off, so I had to do something quick."

"What did she want?"

"I have no idea."

"It would have been useful to know," Zashi remarked dryly.

"Next time I'll ask them wait until you come home before they threaten me with bodily harm."

"Now you're being sarcastic."

The next morning was a bitter cold day with snowflakes drifting down. Shuibai and Zashi bundled up in their uniforms and donned wooden sandals with four inch soles to keep their feet out of the mud and slush. They hiked the short distance to the lumberyard. They were the only customers that morning so they had the undivided attention of the sawyer. He was happy to answer their questions and show them bamboo in various sizes. Bamboo had the virtue of being hollow, except for the knuckles every few feet. The largest bamboos were as thick around as a man's biceps and more than five fathoms in length. Shuibai and Zashi hefted one and found it unwieldy, but easily moved by two men. They consulted. Shuibai favored the larger diameter bamboos in the belief that the pipes would have to be nearly as big around as the buckets in order to carry the same amount of water.

"No, I don't think that's right," Zashi answered. "Because you have only one bucket to cross a fathom or so of space."

Doing the math in his head he figured out how many gallons of water the bucket brigade could move, then calculated the capacity of the large bamboos. He pointed at the medium sized bamboos. "There, those ought to carry as much water as a bucket brigade." The indicated bamboos were about three and a half fathoms in length, and tapered from a diameter of about three inches to about two inches. They hefted a length and found it light enough for one man to carry, but because it was flexible it drooped at the ends. Two men could carry it conveniently. In fact, if they were lashed together, two men could carry an entire bundle of the rods. The bamboos were five pennies each and for an extra tuppence the sawyer agreed to drill them out and deliver them.

Back at the leather shop Shuibai laid out leather and stitched up a four foot length of hose. Each end was flared to fit over the spigot and the end of the pipe regardless of its size or shape. A dozen pipes were delivered late that afternoon as the sun was going down. Red, who was out of work at the time, dropped by to shoot the breeze. They sent him to round up a couple more firemen. Word got around and all the firefighters stopped by on their way home from work. They were hungry and thirsty so Shuibai sent Kanko to a noodle shop for a great pot of noodles and vegetables and a gallon of tea to feed them. It wasn't much, but it was a free meal and poor men like them were always in favor of free meals. While they ate Shuibai explained his gadget to them. They were eager to try it right then and there.

Fire service might have been a demanding unpaid job for most of them, but it was an interesting interruption to the grind of their daily lives and gave them a sense of pride. The occasional free meals, bonus money, and beer were their only pay, but they discovered that telling tales about the fires they'd fought gained them the attention of their coworkers, not to mention, female admirers. For a man who worked as a human beast of burden, the opportunity to stand up like a man and be a hero had tremendous allure.

Dinner done, the ladder men carried the bundle of bamboo pipes several blocks uphill to the nearest public well at the intersection of the Street of Good Fortune and Cross Way. To save themselves some effort they untied the bundle and dropped pipes in the street in a trail alongside the gutter. Being practical laborers they were always quick to discover the method that involved the least amount of effort for themselves.

"Hey, Red, put 'em together!" Shuibai directed.

So Red and another fireman worked jamming the ends together. The smaller end fit inside of the larger end and with a good push stuck together.

Shuibai left Zashi behind to supervise the laying of the pipe while he carried some rope and the leather hose pipe to the well. The street was busy with day shift laborers going home for their supper while prettily dressed waitresses and entertainers were reporting for the evening shift. A few windows opened in the upper stories and some partially dressed male courtesans leaned out their windows to see what was happening. "Hey, what's that crazy Fire Chief up to now?" they asked each other. A knot of spectators gathered; the entertainment district was peopled by curious folks who had seen everything from dancing bears to duels over women and were eager for another novelty.

Shuibai had come to that well because it was closest; now he was having second thoughts. Succeed or fail, the word would be all over town; gossip was the favorite local sport. It was too late to pack up and leave—there was nothing to do but proceed and hope his invention worked. At the well he fitted the end of the hose over the spigot and tied it tightly with the hemp rope he'd brought. Then he tied the other end around the end of the first length of bamboo.

The men fiddled with the pipes, finagling them to get them all laid out in a straight line and it occurred to Shuibai that inserting flexible leather hose sporadically along the line would enable the pipe to bend around obstacles.

When all the pieces were fitted together he called up Tabuza and Axe and told them to pump. The leather section became turgid as it filled with water and the bamboo creaked. Water leaked from each joint, but that didn't bother Shuibai. Water was flowing. He ran to the foot of pipe a hundred feet away and crowed with delight as water streamed out the end.

Shuibai grinned and cavorted. "I told you it would work! We can make enough of this stuff to reach anywhere in the city!"

Zashi smiled.

The water flowed from the pipe into the gutter that ran down the middle of the street and Shuibai reached down and lifted up the end. The bamboo flexed awkwardly. "See? We can take the water to wherever we need it and fill the buckets right close to the fire."

"As long as it's downhill," Zashi agreed.

"There are three wells in Low Marsh. Most neighborhoods are downhill from at least one of them. Still, we're going to need a lot of pipe." Absorbed in thought, he placed his hand over the end of the pipe and let it spray through his naked fingers. They chilled instantly. He jerked his finger out of the stream, then slowly covered the mouth of the pipe again. Water, constricted by his fingers, shot forward in a long arc.

Shuibai grinned. "The stream becomes more forceful when it is restricted."

He lifted higher, pulling the flexible bamboo pipe up to thigh level, but the weight of the water combined with the resilience of the bamboo made it unwieldy. Nonetheless, he was able to spray the water in a long low arc.

"Mizaka-don, help me," he asked. Zashi lifted the lower part of the bamboo and they were able to spray water onto the roof of a one story building. A woman threw back her screen, shouted, "Hey, there, what do you think you're doing?" Then she gaped at the spray from the bamboo hose that was raining down on her house. Suddenly two pipes came apart at the joint, splashing the two young men.

Zashi leaped as if he had been stung. "Cold!" he yelped.

Shuibai was laughing. "It's all right, it's all right. I'll make another leather sleeve for this end and then it will flex and not come apart."

"Do it again," Zashi demanded. "Let's see how high we can get it."

They jammed the ends back together and tried again. The stream faltered; pumping was strenuous work and the men at the well were getting tired. In spite of the cold they were sweating. They swapped in two fresh men who pumped with a will. When water flowed again Zashi and Shuibai picked up the length of bamboo pipe and tilted it upwards. Zashi put his hand over the mouth of the pipe, and the spray shot high in the air. The water was so cold it hurt, but he turned the hose against the second story of the shops. He tried compressing the stream with both hands, but he could not get a strong enough stream to make it to the eaves. Nonetheless, he was sure that with a wooden nozzle or similar object they'd be able to get it onto the roof of a second story building. Bystanders applauded, the advantage of being able to shoot a stream of water higher and stronger than a bucket was obvious to everyone.

Suddenly pressure was lost and the water disappeared. The firemen yelled in dismay. Shuibai and Zashi turned around and saw the leather hose had burst at the pump. Water was pouring down the street from the ruptured hose. The stitches had snapped from the pressure. "Damn. I'm going to have to rivet it," Shuibai said. Riveting would be more expensive and more time consuming, but much sturdier. The two firemen at the pump staggered away, blowing hard. "I'm gonna throw up," Red complained mournfully.

"Get away from me," Axe retorted, shoving him away.

Tabuza, who had already had a turn, agreed. "It made my stomach hurt. You're going to have to have about six guys taking turns or they'll be puking all over."

"But it worked!" Zashi exclaimed. "It really worked! We have to fix it and make it sturdier, but it worked!" he exclaimed, slapping Shuibai on the back.

"We can draft the neighbors to pump the wells instead of carrying buckets," Shuibai added.

The firemen pounded him on the back and laughed loudly, "We can really knock down some fires now!"

"Yeah, let's burn something and try it out!"

"Hey! Not yet," Shuibai interjected. "We have to fix it first. But okay. This weekend gather at my place, and we'll haul the equipment down to the Iris Bottom for a real test."

Shuibai bought a map of Low Marsh, a commodity that cost him a pretty bit of money, but which quickly proved inadequate for his purposes. He updated the map, noting additions and prominent buildings. He also noted all the locations of the wells, public or private, that he knew about. If there was a well close to a fire scene he was going to use it, private property or no. He corrected errors of location and nomenclature, and then he took his corrections to the mapmaker and commissioned a new map. He also stopped by the sawyer and ordered one hundred lengths of bamboo pipe, then he went home and made ten copper riveted leather sleeves for bending the pipes around corners and over obstacles. He hired a turner to make him a pair of wooden nozzles that would screw onto the end of his pipes. To make sure they'd fit he had to select two pipes as the designated hose ends and mark them.

The one hundred pipes made a tremendous pile, which occasioned the purchase of a wagon with big wheels and two tillers, one at each end so that it could be negotiated through tight turns in the narrow streets. The ladder was hung on the side, buckets were hung from hooks added to the underside of the wagon bed, and axes, hooks, and ropes were lashed to the other side. It required six men to pull it, and a man to operate the rear tiller.

Shuibai pulled his hair because now they had lost the advantage of speed and maneuverability. He thought about stashing pipes at various locations in the town so they would be handy wherever they wanted, but he was afraid of vandalism and theft. He thought about establishing another fire station, but he didn't have the money. Instead he depended upon his watchmen. Each watchman patrolled the streets of his ward from nine in the evening until five thirty in the morning. Each watchman carried a staff to symbolize their authority—which was also useful for self-defense should they be set upon by ruffians, which happened more frequently than they would have liked. The watchmen had discovered that there were any number of people abroad at night, many of whom did not care to have an authority figure questioning them about their nocturnal activities.

Shuibai exhorted his watchmen to greater diligence and trained them to make inspections and set quotas for them to meet, but told them to leave the people traveling the streets alone. The watchmen did not assess the fines themselves; instead each morning they came to the fire station and had breakfast while Zashi received their reports and followed up personally. Many householders and shopkeepers found that the first visitor of the day was Deputy Chief Mizaka, accosting them over some infraction of the fire code with his usual mixture of charm and coercion. This increased the fire company's revenues in the form of fines and sales which persuaded Shuibai that watchmen on patrol were a superior system over watchmen stuck in a tower. His system cost little and brought in revenue, as compared to the Capital's system, in which the watchmen cost money but produced nothing.

Unfortunately, he had no good place to store the wagon. He had to park it in the filthy alley behind his home and cover it with a tarpaulin. He worried ceaselessly about thieves, and his neighbors, after assuring him that they greatly admired his ingenuity and dedication, politely informed him that they didn't appreciate tripping over the wagon on their way to the privy. It did not fit entirely within his own little yard and slopped over into theirs. He pulled his hair and promised to make other arrangements as soon as possible.

Zashi smiled ruefully and remarked, "Chief Byan says he doesn't mind fire at all, it's the little stuff that drives him to despair."

CHAPTER 28 : DEMONSTRATION

How the Fire Lord found out about the test Shuibai didn't know, but bright and early the clatter of hooves made him slide back the shutter and there he was. The aristocrat's dragon was an extraordinarily fine piece of embroidery work and so life-like it seemed ready to leap from the fabric. His coat was open to show his breastplate, his gauntlets were studded leather mittens, and his sword was carried in the ready position. His retainers were dressed equally well with as much armor as could be concealed under their clothes. It was rude, and in some cases, illegal, to go about the Capital in full armor, but the Fire Lord was not making the mistake of underestimating the anger of the Sakoro clan. Chief Byan and several firemen from the Alla Far Fire Company trailed him on foot, trotting to keep up with the leisurely pace of the horses.

"I understand you have invented a clever device for dousing fires," the Fire Lord began at once.

"I have been experimenting," Shuibai admitted. "But I have a great deal of work to do before I could recommend it to your attention, Noble Lord."

"I understand. But I'm interested. What I've heard is very promising and I want to see it. I always knew you were a resourceful man." The white horse tossed its head in apparent agreement.

"I shall have to call out the company, Noble Lord. The equipment is rather bulky. If you would be so kind as to clear this street, it would be helpful."

The *taran* retreated to the Low Road and waited while Shuibai rang the bell, clanging out the code for assembly. It was earlier than he had intended, but there was no help for it; the Fire Lord hadn't consulted him about the schedule. Shuibai went into the house and donned his own fire coat and hat and leather mittens, then he and Zashi returned to the street.

"These are new," the Fire Lord commented.

"With all due respect, sir, we thought it would improve the attitudes of the town mothers if Low Marsh used its own uniform instead of the Capital uniform. It's a Free Town," he said apologetically. The white swan was embroidered upon a dark grey mass of smoke clouds, its head pointed down with a bucket in its beak. It tail and wings were fanned out above it. The composition was dramatic and distinctive and Shuibai felt proud and conspicuous each time he donned the coat.

"I have no objection. The uniforms look very smart. You've made a number of innovations, I see. The hats are unique."

"Straw hats burn too easily, sir."

He nodded. "I see. Yes. You take your work seriously." He pointed at the toggle buttons angling across the breasts of the coats. "And these?"

"I got the idea off of some old clothes from Pangu. The old style fire coats can gape open. We make sure they stay closed this way." He showed him the narrower sleeves and longer skirts, all of which improved the mobility and defensive capacity of the coat. "I think it would be even better if the coats could be made of leather, but I haven't had time to try it yet."

Chief Byan looked over their turnout coats and hats, and said, "I can see the utility, but it's rather awkward to require unpaid volunteers to go to such expense."

"All it takes is money," Shuibai sighed.

"Where does the money come from?" Chief Byan asked.

So Shuibai told him about the fire watchmen and the fines that Zashi collected, and also about the funds from the Council, and the various donations that had been arranged. The wagon, for example, was provided by one of the firemen who was a cartwright by profession. Shuibai had paid the cost of the materials while the cartwright donated his labor.

"Right now we're trying to persuade the Council to provide us with a shed large enough to house the wagon and hold meetings of the company because my house is too small."

Chief Byan nodded, but he was busy making his own calculations about how to adapt the system of patrolling watchmen to his own district. Especially if it made money for the company.

The firefighters, having expected Shuibai's call, arrived in a matter of minutes. The company was resplendent in their new uniforms. Each fireman wore a leather fire hat with the swan design on the back, as well as dark grey trousers and leather mittens. They had adopted trousers instead of the divided skirt not only because it was cheaper and more practical but also because it was more stylish. Shuibai thought perhaps he was being vain, but at the same time, each man seemed proud to wear the uniform. They had worked hard for the privilege. The Alla Far firemen, by contrast, were rather ragtag. They all wore uniform coats, some of which were worse for the wear, with short pants and knees socks of mismatched colors showing beneath the coats.

Shuibai counted heads, came up with the right number, and said, "Noble Lord, we are assembled, if you would like to begin the demonstration."

"Yes, please. Carry on."

Shuibai gestured with his silver speaking trumpet and gave a command, and a team of men ran around the end of the block and into the alley where the fire wagon was stored. They rolled it out of the muddy alley and onto the Low Road. They drew up abreast of Fire Chief Shuibai and waited for orders.

"Shall we proceed? We're going to the Iris Bottom," Shuibai told the Fire Lord.

The Captain pulled out his fan and made gestures; his company of *taran* formed into columns of two with the herald at the forefront. Traffic on the Low Road parted for them and Shuibai and his company followed them down the road. People opened their windows and waved. "There goes our Chief!" somebody called. The firemen waved back.

Shuibai led the company. He was nervous, which meant he had a tendency to walk too fast, so he had to keep looking over his shoulder to make sure he hadn't left them behind. Chief Byan and his associates followed behind the Low Marsh company, then the citizens of the town followed them.

Shuibai ran up to the Fire Lord and told him, "Turn left on the Upper Road!" There were no street signs, so at Shuibai's signal, the Fire Lord kicked his horse forward and made the turn, using his fan to signal his men. The whole cavalcade turned up Upper Road until they came to Broadway and thence to the Wet Lane. Once in the Wet Lane the going got heavy. The mud and narrow spaces and ruts caused the men pulling the wagon to curse mightily. Four more firemen helped shoulder it through the rough spots.

As they passed the well Shuibai yelled into his trumpet, "Lay a line!"

Two pipe men started throwing pipes into the street, which startled the *taran* horses and made them shy. Two more firemen stooped and darted to screw together the pipe ends and insert the leather elbows where needed. A *taran* leaped his horse over a fence to avoid the firemen. Chickens and small children ran squawking as the horse trammeled across the yard and leaped the brush fence into the next garden. The fire company made it to the meadow below the flower farms without any mishap. Shuibai had been drilling them.

Word ran through the town very quickly and the Councilwomen arrived in ones and twos. The well dressed matrons with their girl servants huddled under varnished paper umbrellas to watch the preparations with consternation and curiosity. It was drizzling steadily and the ground underfoot was wet. The little stream that ran between the meadow and the flower farms was brown and turgid. All was dark and damp, except for the chrysanthemum fields, which were blooming in spite of a recent frost. Farmers were at work cutting the blooms to sell to the perfumers; later they would cut the leaves and sell them to apothecaries. They paused in their labors as they saw something that they had never been seen before: the Low Marsh Fire Company at work.

Shuibai bowed to the Fire Lord. "With your permission, sir, we will begin."

The Fire Lord nodded. "Carry on."

An old cart loaded with kindling had been placed in the meadow the day before. It stood next to the stream and was covered with a tarpaulin to keep it dry; Shuibai pulled the cover off. He called, "Bucket men!"

They sorted themselves out with four men carrying buckets taking up a place beside the stream. Red was their leader. They filled their buckets and stood ready to spring into action if the pipes failed.

"How pipe?" Shuibai asked. Practice had reduced commands and questions to a minimum of verbiage.

"Tight," came Zashi's response.

"Charge the line," Shuibai commanded. The word was passed up the line and the pump men started pumping. It took a minute for the water to reach the nozzle.

"Water," reported the hose man. He kept the nozzle closed, waiting for the Chief's order.

Shuibai cleared his throat. "Set the fire, Mizaka-don."

Zashi was carrying a small terra cotta pot with embers in it. Using small iron tongs, he took out some embers and got a fire going. It spread through the old clothes and broken things, growing up large and vigorous in spite of the dampness of the air. The horses snorted uneasily and the *taran* tightened their reins to keep them steady. Shuibai let the bright orange flames lick through the trash until they were burning strong and tall.

"Water!" Shuibai called. "Lay a stream!" The nozzle man turned the nozzle and water arched out. He passed it over the cart from front to back soaking it thoroughly. The fire hissed and crackled and a cloud of steam rose up. The fire was quenched within econds. The hosemen continued to soak the wagon with water and Shuibai called, "Any sparks?"

Zashi replied, "None, Chief."

"Water off and stand by." Shuibai told the nozzle man, who twisted the nozzle. The water stopped. The wooden nozzle leaked, but Shuibai didn't care about that. His system worked!

Fire Lord Chuja rode forward and Shuibai warned, "Please stand back, we're not through, Noble Lord." The Captain reined up short but did not retreat.

Shuibai called out, "Hooks!"

"What are you doing?" the Fire Lord asked him.

"Overhauling the wreckage, sir. Sometimes fire smolders deep inside, only to flare up again. We're making certain it's out."

Two men with hooks ran forward and tore the charred debris out of the cart bed and spread it around on the ground under the watchful eye of the hosemen. Tendrils of smoke rose up from the charred goods, so the hosemen played a stream of water over them for good measure. Shuibai, Zashi, and the Fire Lord on his horse inspected the cart. The bed was singed but not burnt. The collection of old clothes and broken furniture and trash that had been loaded in it were only partially consumed by the fire.

The Fire Lord asked, "Is it true that you can throw water onto a roof?"

Shuibai called, "Charge the line!" and the message was passed. The pump men started pumping again. To the hosemen he said, "Straight up." The fire officers and *taran* moved back.

The pump was not far away; they got good pressure. The nozzle turned and a narrow jet of water shot at least seven fathoms into the air.

Shuibai spoke. "You'll notice that because of the powerful stream the men don't have to get as close to the fire as a bucket brigade does. This preserves the men from harm as they fight the fire. Because of this even great conflagrations that are too hot to be approached by a bucket brigade can be fought by means of a stream of water."

"How far?" the Fire Lord demanded.

"Level it," Shuibai told the hosemen. The stream shot more than a ten fathoms before breaking up and falling to the ground in a plume of rain.

"Amazing!" exclaimed the *taran*. "This is a truly useful invention, Fire Chief Shuibai! Instruct Chief Byan in all the particulars. I shall recommend the establishment of such pipes in each town."

"Cease water," Shuibai ordered. The command was passed to the pumpers, who gratefully stopped pumping. "Break pipe," he ordered. The pieces were taken apart, drained, and loaded in the wagon.

"The men are obedient to your orders," the Fire Lord commented.

"I've been training them. A fire is dangerous. They have to know what to do and do it right. A little bit of water in the right place will quench a fire that would otherwise race out of control. We aren't very good yet. We need more practice."

"Keep me posted. Next time you invent something wonderful, do let me know instead of leaving me find out through the grapevine."

"Sir, it wasn't finished. We had some problems the first time. I wanted to make sure everything worked before informing you. It's expensive, too. We had to make it."

"How much?" The Fire Lord reached into his sleeve and pulled out his purse.

"Oh, I think we should have at least a thousand pipes. With the ends threaded so they screw together they're twenty bronze pennies each. That would be, um . . . "

Zashi spoke, "Eight hundred pieces of silver."

"Yes. And I'm still trying to convince the town mothers to add more pumps to the water service or buy a portable pump like they use on ships."

"Here, let me make a donation." The Fire Lord dropped his purse into Shuibai's hand.

"You are very generous," Zashi replied for Shuibai. The young chief stood stunned by the weight in his hand.

Shuibai recovered himself and put the purse in his sash. "We have beer and rice cakes at my house if you would like to refresh yourself, Noble Lord."

The Fire Lord said, "I'll return from here. I regret that I will miss your hospitality. However, I would appreciate the escort of Deputy Chief Mizaka."

Zashi looked surprised but presented himself as ordered. With a worried look over his shoulder at Shuibai, he fell into step beside the great white horse of the Fire Lord. Shuibai watched him go with trepidation.

"Why is he doing that?" Shuibai asked Byan.

"Politics," Byan replied. "The Fire Lord understands that there are things he can't ask you, so he's going to ask Zashi-lan instead. That way if you are ever questioned you can truthfully say you have not discussed it with the Fire Lord."

"Will Zashi be all right?"

"Yes, I think so. He's wise enough about keeping his mouth shut, and courteous enough not to appear stubborn and intransigent, even though he is." Byan smiled lopsidedly at Shuibai. "I love my son, but he is not the easiest man to get along with. Moody, and given to flights of fancy. Always was, but it got worse after . . . Well, you know."

"He is fortunate to have a father like you," replied Shuibai, who had very few recollections of his own father. His mother had never formally married; her succession of 'husbands' had been at her convenience.

Byan put a ham-like hand on his shoulder. "You care for my son, don't you?"

Shuibai was tongue-tied. He had no idea what to say, so he opted for a simple truth. "I like him very much."

Byan slapped his shoulder. "He likes you, too, but he won't admit it."

Shuibai was shocked. He had made a habit of not wondering what Zashi was thinking because once he started it kept him awake all night and he never did figure it out. "Do you think so?" he managed to say at last.

"Mark my word, he does. You've given him his manhood back. He used to mope around the house being useless and unhappy, so I got him the watchman's job. He was faithful to his work, but he didn't like it even though the work needed doing. You've given him real work. Physical, mental, maybe even spiritual. He needed that. You're good for him."

"Oh, I see. Yes, I think he's a very fine man. I have always thought so."

"Feh. Don't be so shy. I've seen the way you look at him. You should say something."

Shuibai blushed scarlet. "I don't."

"You do." He produced a ceramic flask from his sleeve. "Brandy?" he offered, grinning at Shuibai.

Shuibai accepted the flask and took a long hit off of it. His eyes watered and he coughed. Chief Byan swigged down some brandy, then winked and said, "Take my advice: he's a sentimental boy. Get him drunk and quote poetry at him. Then you can do what you want."

"I really have to go now." Shuibai was blushing to the ears as he fled.

CHAPTER 29 : SKULL MOUNTAIN

The ashes of the Cherry Hill fire had smoldered for a week, and the Low Marsh Fire Company had an unexpected infusion of cash when the Fire Chief of Cherry Hill was obliged to pay wages in order to get the volunteer companies to return to overhaul the smoking debris and extinguish the flames that persisted in the rubble. The fire had burnt out a swatch of seventy-two blocks from the Maiko Fireworks Factory to the Southern Highway, more than a thousand structures had been destroyed, and four thousand people were left homeless. The area that burned was a heavily built industrial and commercial neighborhood, which left fifteen thousand people jobless. Property losses ran two million silver pennies.

Over five hundred people were presumed dead, including seventeen firefighters, twelve of whom had died when fire had overleaped their position and cut off their escape. The others died later of injuries to the lungs that had made them vulnerable to pneumonia. Zashi had a lingering cough, but Shuibai bounced back after a few days of coughing up black phlegm. It had not occurred to him to fear the smoke; it had seemed an insubstantial nuisance rather than a threat in its own right.

Cherry Hill, a city of sixty thousand inhabitants, was not able to absorb its losses. The homeless, the orphaned, the jobless, and the bankrupt crowded into the nearby towns. A shanty town sprouted in the woods between the Iris Bottom and the Southern Highway as women who had once been mighty merchants were reduced to scrounging blackened boards to prop up their now filthy silk robes as tents. Their serving men deserted them and they sent their little daughters to beg in the streets. Beggars were everywhere; monks, thieves, and prostitutes proliferated. Within two weeks the pity that had first opened doors to the unfortunate had been replaced by anger and resentment. Property owners stood guard to drive away the destitute with sticks, but even so, chickens, dogs, pigeons, pigs, rice, bread, vegetables, fruit, beer and wine were stolen and consumed.

The Fire Lord sent Shuibai word to meet him on the Capital Highway at Iris Bottom one morning. His message had no more information than that. Shuibai and Zashi took the long way up the Southern Highway to the Capital Road rather than taking the short cut up the Wet Lane. They wanted to see the condition of Cherry Hill for themselves. Acres of blackness blotted a gaping hole in the city; the space consumed was nearly as large as the town of Low Marsh. A layer of charred debris lay waist high. Merchant houses that had once reared lofty heads towards the sky were reduced to a blanket of ash in which no thing survived. Crockery had cracked to shards from the heat, the timber had been reduced to charcoal, the flammable goods were no more than black dust. The silence was absolute. No bird sang. No person spoke. No figures moved through the acres of desolation. Death reigned in a grim glory unmatched in human memory.

Then, as the day warmed, a line of laborers appeared. Drafted from among the homeless and jobless, they were rousted out by Eastern Guardsmen. The *taran* drove them to places along the grid that had been dug through the rubble. Like a swarm of ants they began to toil by hand, shoveling up debris and loading it into baskets, which were carried to carts, which were pulled by teams of men. The debris was taken to a field north of the Iris Bottom and piled up. The refuse heap was quickly named Skull Mountain. The neighbors said that at night you could see mystic fires upon it, surrounded by cavorting demons.

"It started at the Maiko Fireworks Factory," Shuibai said at last. "Do you think—"

"I think it was the earthquake that started the fire," Zashi replied quickly. "I don't dare think otherwise. Not when the Fire Lord is our lord."

"But the bullets were made there. And a few days later—"

"Shui-lan, please don't say such things, or we'll end up dead too."

"It isn't fair!"

Zashi rounded on him. "Fair! Since when did 'fair' have anything to do with it? How could it be fair? The Spirits rule over humanity, the *taran* rule over commoners, the women rule over men, the powerful rule over the weak. Where is there any trace of fairness?"

Shuibai sunk his head deeper in his collar. "It still isn't right."

"War, fire, famine, pestilence, the world is a place of suffering. Get used to it."

"I can't."

Zashi stopped in his tracks. "I can't either." They looked at each other. There wasn't anything either of them could think to say, so they trudged on. "At least I am a fireman," Zashi said at long last. "I am asked to save, not destroy. Whatever my flaws, I think in the long run the good I do will outweigh the bad."

They turned down the Capital Highway and stopped at the top of the Wet Lane, which at this point was only a track through the woods, steep and rugged and harboring frost in the shady spots. The trees were threadbare with tattered leaves rattling desolately in the fitful breeze. A watery white sun glared weakly through a grey winter haze. They stood together, stomping their feet in a vain effort to restore warmth and blowing on their hands. Their charcoal grey uniforms were as dreary and desolate as the surroundings.

As the herald approached they got down on their knees beside the ditch and kowtowed, putting their faces in the cold dirt. The swan insignia on the grey uniforms made them immediately recognizable. Horse's hooves clattered on the stone road before them, and Shuibai and Zashi looked carefully up without raising themselves, scooting back a little, prepared to crawl into the ditch if necessary. It was the Fire Lord.

"Fire Chief Shuibai, Deputy Chief Mizaka. Please rise." They lifted their heads but did not get to their feet. "His Grace the Golden Emperor requests your attendance as He tours the Burned District."

The Emperor himself? They stared up in frank astonishment. Zashi recovered his wits first. "It is our pleasure to serve Him however He requires," he said. Shuibai was tongue-tied. He had no facility with *taran* courtesies. They had no time to think. More heralds were arriving, followed by riders and banners and a drum keeping time. The Fire Lord's company was merely His vanguard.

The Fire Lord and his soldiers waited on foot on the side of the road, and when the Emperor approached, they knelt in the three point kowtow: one foot, one knee, and one fist upon the ground. It was a soldier's pose. The Imperial cavalcade surrounded a figure dressed in gold and red and white, obscured by the Imperial Bodyguard that surrounded Him. When the Imperial party drew abreast of the kneeling Fire Lord, it stopped. The Imperial hand clad in red silk raised and beckoned languidly.

The Fire Lord stepped inside the ring of golden horses that carried the Imperial Bodyguard and knelt again. He remained bowed until told to rise. No one else could hear the Emperor's voice; He spoke in tones so soft even the Fire Lord had trouble hearing him. The Fire Lord's tenor voice was firm and clear and they could hear his responses to the questions the Emperor put to him. "Yes, Your Majesty. These are the men I told you about."

The Golden Emperor spoke again, so the Fire Lord turned around and beckoned to the two commoners. "Please approach."

Shuibai and Zashi glanced at each other in stunned disbelief. They rose, and bowing every other step, approached the line of mounted Bodyguards and knelt down again.

The unthinkable happened. The Golden Emperor turned His horse to approach the commoners. Not that Shuibai or Zashi saw Him since they had their faces in the dirt. The consternation of the *taran* was heard as a low murmur of surprise, the rustle of silks, and the creak of armor. A soft thud of horses' hooves approached the two commoners and an indescribably rich and pure incense wafted around them. The scent was sandalwood and aloeswood and things for which they had no names; it reminded them of the incenses they had smelled at the Silver Princess' birthday, only finer. Shuibai was too frightened to move, but Zashi turned his face ever so slightly so that he could see the gilded hooves of the Emperor's horse.

The Golden Emperor's mellifluous voice came to their ears. His tenor voice was the lilting cadence of the Imperial Court; the dialect formal and archaic and incomprehensible to those unschooled in the ways of the Celestials. When they did not respond, He graced them by switching to the ordinary speech of the *taran*. "Please rise. It is all right if you look at Me."

He was not alone. As soon as He had moved, the Fire Lord had jumped up and followed Him and hovered near at hand, uncertain whether he should stand or kneel as the Emperor violated protocol by speaking directly to the commoners. He opted to serve the role of a groomsman and put his hand on the golden horse's bridle to steady it. The Bodyguards remained as a screen between the Emperor and the firefighters.

Shuibai and Zashi lifted their heads but remained on their knees. They weren't supposed to look at the Emperor: He was sacred, awesome, and untouchable, a being that dwelled beyond the clouds and communed with gods. But He had told them they could. They stared at Him in stunned disbelief. The Golden Emperor was tall and lithe and handsome with a regal bearing. He was dressed in golden armor with a red brocade coat glittering with thread of gold embroidery over crimson divided skirts so heavy and voluminous that no trace of His person could be discerned through the fabric. The voluminous skirts tucked into the top of His red leather boot which was itself completely covered in gold filigree. The boot heel was gold. It was tucked into a stirrup just as elegant as the boot. The sleeves of His coat were like box kites and completely obscured His arms. The crimson coat was worn open over His golden breastplate, which was itself decorated with an embossed whirling sun disk that looked like a giant flower. The Emperor's face was masked in gold and a tall black cap topped His head.

He spoke again. "Come a little closer. Don't be shy; We are informal today."

"Your Pardon, Noble Emperor," Shuibai said in a cracked voice. "But I am untouchable. I cannot approach You." He remained kneeling where he was and put his face down to the icy road surface.

The several *taran* Bodyguards looked down on him from their horses. He could feel their disdainful eyes and he trembled. There was a strained silence.

"You didn't tell Me he was *ita,* Chuja-don," the Emperor said reproachfully.

The Fire Lord's orange dragon mask met the Imperial gaze calmly. "With all due respect, My Emperor, a great many men in the fire service come from the lowest castes of society. You are very gracious to lend Your Presence to such a humble endeavor."

The golden Sun mask betrayed no emotion; the Emperor was highly adept at the art of keeping face. After a slight pause He said, "Master Kung says, 'I will not grieve that men do not know Me; I will grieve that I do not know men.' Even the humblest of My people is still one of My people. You may approach, Chief Shuibai."

So the Imperial Bodyguards were obliged to stand aside for an untouchable. Shuibai crawled to the indicated spot at the feet of the Emperor's horse. He kowtowed in the mud.

"Please rise."

Shuibai rose a little but remained crouching with his shoulders bowed and his head down, not daring to look any higher than the Emperor's foot. He had an excellent view of the pointy-toed red boot and gold spur, settled into a wooden stirrup that had been gilded. The horse was covered with a crimson saddle blanket, and the saddle itself was crimson leather tooled and ornamented with golden ornaments. Golden fringe lined the edge of the saddle blanket. He guessed that the fringe alone had cost more than his uniform.

Again the mellow tones of the Imperial voice. "I have heard a great deal about you, Fire Chief Shuibai. Both Lord Chuja and Lord Brice speak well of you."

Shuibai lifted his eyes to the hem of the crimson brocade coat lavishly embroidered with golden chrysanthemums. It hung open, the gilded sword hilt in His sash holding it open in front. The Emperor's crimson leather glove rested on His thigh beside the sword. The glove was perfectly fitted to the Imperial hand. As a leatherworker Shuibai appreciated the supreme skill displayed in its workmanship. He lifted his eyes a little higher and saw the Emperor's long black braid lying over His shoulder and tied at the bottom with a golden bow. He wore the formal black hat that made a peak over His head, exaggerating His height, which from Shuibai's vantage point seemed immense. The broad black lace ribbons at the back of the hat offered the nape of His neck delicate protection. Lastly Shuibai looked at the Sleeping Sun mask which covered most of His face, but which showed the lower third of His face, a fine, closely shaved jaw; firm, sensuous lips; and the lines of determination that were beginning to make themselves felt at the corners of His mouth. Shuibai was shocked to realize the Golden Emperor was a man no older than himself.

Shuibai forced some words out. "I am greatly assisted by my Deputy Chief Mizaka. He is the son of Chief Byan of Alla Far and a very experienced man."

"Is that him?" The Emperor nodded to Zashi, who was still kneeling outside the Bodyguards, staring in rapt awe at the Golden Emperor.

"Yes, Noble Emperor."

"Invite him to join Us."

So Shuibai beckoned to Zashi. Zashi approached with his eyes bugging out of his head. He knelt in the road and bowed deeply.

"May You live a thousand years. You are too gracious, Noble Emperor."

"Walk with Me," the Emperor invited, taking their assent for granted. He kneed His horse to walk slowly along the road. The two firefighters walked with Him, and His retainers kept a polite distance as they moved along with him.

"Chuja-don tells me that you have invented a clever device for fighting fires. I am interested and would like a demonstration for My Own benefit. I am vexed by the multitude of opinions being expressed about the nature and efficacy of the firefighting service, so I have decided to see things for Myself. I understand you were at the Cherry Hill Fire."

"Yes, Noble Emperor. The entire Low Marsh Fire Company participated with valor. They are good men."

"You are fortunate. My experience is that reliable men are in the minority." The Imperial voice was dry.

Zashi spoke up. "Chief Shuibai brings out the best in men."

Shuibai flushed at the praise. The Golden Emperor glanced down with a smile. "That is a rare ability. You must tell Me your secret. I wish I could bring out the best in men. The Spirits know I try."

Shuibai's jaw dropped. He whispered hoarsely, "I am no one important. I cannot command their obedience. I can only try to show them how it benefits them."

The Emperor mused, "That's difficult, isn't it? People are stubborn. They don't like change."

Shuibai glanced up at the gilded aristocrat. "But, You're an Emperor. You can make them."

The golden horse walked a few steps slowly before the Emperor finally answered. "If I try to make people do things they don't want to do, they revolt. Maybe not with weapons, but they revolt in their hearts. Like you, I must persuade them that it is in their best interest to do as I say."

"Oh no, Your Grace. You are the Emperor. You speak, and it must be done."

The Golden Emperor smiled down at him. "You have a noble heart, Chief Shuibai. I wish I had more men like you."

"Me? I'm not noble. I'm untouchable."

Zashi walked silently beside Shuibai, listening to him talking with the Emperor.

The Golden Emperor stopped his horse and turned in the saddle to stare directly at Shuibai. "Look at Me," He commanded. Shuibai gave the golden Sun mask the briefest of looks. The Emperor leaned down and grabbed his chin. "I said, 'Look at Me.'" The red gloved hand held his chin in a powerful grip. Shuibai stared in shock.

"Noble Emperor, please, You defile Yourself. I am untouchable!" He quailed but he couldn't escape the Imperial hand.

The Emperor did not release him. "Not any more. I have touched you."

Shuibai whispered, "No," in protest.

"Chief Shuibai. Are you more powerful than Your Emperor?"

"No, of course not."

"Then it is My touch that transforms you, not your touch that transforms Me. It is not in your power to change Me because I am the Avatar of the Sun. Therefore, if I touch you, it is because you are touchable. You are not *ita* any longer."

Shuibai stared helplessly back at the golden mask. "I don't understand."

The Emperor released him and stripped off His leather glove. He reached for Shuibai again, and Shuibai dodged. Lunging, the Emperor got him by the collar and dragged him against the side of His horse. Holding him there, the Emperor very deliberately placed His bare hand on Shuibai's cheek. Shuibai flinched and looked up. Perhaps it was the sun behind the Emperor's head, but He shone with a radiant light that blinded Shuibai. The Emperor spoke. "I am the Light of My people, Chief Shuibai, and you are one of My people."

Shuibai blinked. He could not comprehend the Emperor's words. "But You're a mighty king. You live far away. You aren't like us."

With a sigh The Emperor released the fireman. Shuibai pressed his hand to his cheek where the Emperor had touched him. He had no idea what it felt like; he was too stunned. The Emperor looked sad. "If I am any sort of king, then I hope I am a merciful one. It is My duty to keep My people safe and alleviate their suffering."

That the Golden Emperor might actually care about the people of His realm had never entered Shuibai's mind. "Is it true?" he whispered through lips parched with fear. He stared up at the man.

The Golden Emperor smiled at him. "It is true."

Shuibai swallowed hard. "We tried to send You something we found, but it was stolen."

"What thing?"

Shuibai spoke lowly so no one else could hear. "Noble Emperor, it was a silver fan with the seal of the Silver Prince upon it. With calligraphy on the back. I found it in a box of junk from the Western War."

"Who took it?"

"A disgraced *taran,* formerly of the Iris Battalion."

The Golden Emperor looked sharply at him. "Don't say anything more, Chief Shuibai." The Emperor pulled His glove back on and the corners of His mouth turned down in displeasure.

Shuibai bit his lip and lowered his eyes. "I'm sorry, Your Grace. We didn't know how to send it to You. We didn't dare entrust it to any person, so we handed it over to the gods to take care of it. We put it on the offering table at Your daughter's birthday, and the renegade stole it right off the altar."

The Emperor moved in agitation. The gold spur jingled and He tapped the horse's flank. Shuibai fell into step beside the horse as they walked along the road. The Imperial party continued escorting Him. "You could have given it to Chuja-don."

"I'm sorry, Your Grace. But I don't know who to trust. I should have burned it like Zashi said."

The Emperor heaved a heavy sigh. "I wondered where it was. I would have destroyed it, but it was stolen from Me."

Shuibai trudged along beside the imperial horse with his head down.

"Can you read, Chief Shuibai?"

"No. Zashi-lan read it to me. Part of it anyhow."

The Emperor smiled ruefully. "Well then. You know what it says. Were you shocked?"

"Yes," Shuibai replied honestly. A long silence ensued. The clip clop of the horses' hooves was the only sound. Shuibai said, "I don't pretend to understand these things, Your Grace. There isn't anything I can do about them. All I can do is my own job."

"That's all any of us can do. Even an Emperor. By whatever means come to hand. I will not explain Myself to you or anyone." He paused and looked down at Shuibai. "But I think you know how hard it is to do the right thing when so many are opposed to it. In such cases, one can only do what can be done and hope for the best."

They had came abreast of the first of the corpses. The cavalcade halted and the Golden Emperor dismounted and stood looking down at the bodies. Three little girls, neatly dressed and washed, were lined along the side of the road. They had rag dolls tucked in the crook of their arms.

"What happened here?" the Emperor asked.

"The destitute, the hungry, the sick, the cold, the homeless," Shuibai replied. "They are dying because they lost everything in the fire and have no way to live."

"But why are they left upon the side of the road?"

"Their families have no way to pay for a burial."

"Brice-don, come here," the Emperor commanded. The Black Prince dismounted and approached. Shuibai and Zashi had been so engrossed by the Golden Emperor that they had not even realized the Black Prince was in His party. The two Low Marsh firemen faded back as the dark prince approached. The Emperor turned to face Him. "You're the Avatar of Death. What shall we do about this?"

The Black Prince knelt on one knee in the dirt of the road and bowed His head. He made a mystic sign over the girls, then asked, "Are there very many?"

"Several dozen this morning," Shuibai replied.

"I'll take care of it," He told the Emperor as He rose.

Next they found the gnawed corpse of the old man. A dog growled at them as they approached. It stood over the body, brown hair bristling on its back. The Emperor stopped in His tracks. The beast bared its fangs at Him and snarled.

"The dog recognizes *taran,*" Shuibai said.

"How is that?" the Emperor asked.

"The Eastern Guards beat them with sticks and kick them to drive them off. But when the Guards have passed, the dogs come back again."

A line of laborers appeared, led by an Eastern Guard on a white horse. His lavender uniform was dusty already and he carried a whip in his hand. The laborers shuffled along, heads bowed, men and women and children, baskets on their backs. The Guard recognized the Imperial party and snarled, "Halt!" to his pathetic charges. "Kowtow in the presence of your Emperor!" he shouted at them. Stunned, they dropped their loads and fell to their knees and put their faces in the dirt. Their skinny butts stuck up and the ridges of their spines were sharp against the thin fabric of their clothes. The Eastern Guard sat rigidly at attention.

"What is this?" the Golden Emperor asked.

Shuibai pointed to the rising heap of blackness just off the side of the road. "They're going to Skull Mountain."

"And what is that?"

"The ruins of Cherry Hill. They're carting debris out of the city and dumping it over there. But I guess they've run out of carts."

"That is from Cherry Hill?" The Emperor gave the hill a second look. "It's immense!"

"They've barely begun. They've dug the major streets but they haven't uncovered the side streets or the private property yet."

The Golden Emperor gestured to the Guardsman. "Carry on."

The Guard saluted the Golden Emperor with his whip then turned to the laborers. "Up! Get moving, you worthless scum! Don't you dare look at the Emperor!"

The groaning refugees lifted up their bushels of ash and debris and heaved them onto their backs again. They bent under their loads and trudged on, keeping their eyes down, but a few dared to glance out of the corners of their eyes as they passed. The stench of their bodies caused the Emperor to press His sleeve to His nostrils.

"It reminds Me of the war," the Emperor said. "I had not thought to see such misery anywhere but a battlefield."

The Black Prince nodded. "I'm afraid such scenes are all too common in Your country, My Emperor."

"I'll ride now," the Emperor said, turning back to His horse. A luxuriously clad retainer held His stirrup, and He mounted easily and settled into the saddle, taking the reins into His hands. The golden bells on His bridle tinkled merrily. He only glanced as they came abreast of the next corpses, and seemed unaware as beggars began to slip out of the woods to fall on the side of the road, right hands outstretched, pleading silently for His mercy. When He passed without stopping, the weeping began, and the moaning crowd followed forlornly in His wake, crying as they walked. The sound was a low keening noise that gave the devastation voice. The *taran* ignored them.

The Golden Emperor drew up short as the party turned the corner onto the Southern Highway and saw the vast sweep of darkness before them. Prince Porose, the General of the Eastern Gate, charged with safeguarding the internal peace, had declared martial law for the city of Cherry Hill. Cadres of lavender uniforms had moved through the shantytowns, sweeping up the homeless and the destitute and driving them in a mass toward the burned district. Two thousand refugees were enslaved to clear the debris. Like swarms of ants they toiled from dawn until dusk, fed two scant meals a day, and whipped when they staggered. Endless lines of scarecrow figures, blackened from head to toe by soot, emptied their baskets into wagons, or when the wagons were in short supply, carried them in long lines on their own backs. The Eastern Guards oversaw them, and their resentment at the dreary, filthy task made their hands heavy. At first they had been compassionate when charred bones were pulled out of the rubble, but time had quickly callused their hearts. Now the bones were just more rubble to be shoveled into baskets and carried away to the bitterly named Skull Mountain. The charnel stink was everywhere and it clung to the clothes and the flesh of those who labored there, even the Guards. No amount of bathing would get them clean again.

The Imperial party sat and watched for a long time. Then a figure in a lavender uniform approached. He had a dirty white silk cloth tied over his face to try and protect himself from breathing the filthy air.

"Uncle!" the Emperor exclaimed as the regal form of the older, grey-haired lord approached. "What are you doing here?"

The older man bowed. "My Emperor, You are kind to visit."

"This work does not require your attention," the Emperor chided him. "You should have left it to the Fire Lord."

"With all due respect, My Emperor, Lord Chuja's authority ends about two fathoms over there. As you can see, the fire did not leap the Southern Highway. The Fire Lord has no authority here."

"You could have appointed him to handle it anyhow."

The Black Prince spoke up. "That might not be wise. Lady Sakoro and her daughters are not on the best of terms with Lord Chuja."

The Fire Lord pushed his way forward, "I would be delighted to finish the work His Highness the Prince has begun."

The Golden Emperor looked at each of them carefully. "Speaking of Lady Sakoro, where is she? I sent word to expect Me."

"The Lady Sakoro sends word that she is in mourning and cannot approach You," the Prince replied.

The Golden Emperor's jaw set. "It does not seem to have occurred to her that I have made Myself ritually unclean by traveling through the Burned District. I shall have to be purified when I return home anyhow. She need not stand on niceties."

"These details should not be discussed standing in the middle of the street, My Emperor," the Prince chided the Golden Emperor. "You did not need to come here. It is unbecoming to the Imperial dignity."

The Golden Emperor was a sensitive man, bordering on the delicate, but the set of His jaw was stubborn. He said coolly, "Send her a message. Tell her that I appreciate her courtesy, but I am quite willing to overlook the inconvenience of her ritual pollution. Inform her that I shall be happy to send Lord Chuja to provide her with a personal escort, if necessary."

The Black Prince put his hand on the Imperial sleeve. "My Emperor," he said in a placating voice. "Do not be hasty. There is no point in provoking an open breach with her."

The Emperor switched into the formal Celestial dialect. "If We send Our Own herald, and she snubs him, then *We* have been snubbed. If We send Lord Chuja, and she snubs him, then that is just another piece of their feud, is it not? But We will have her know that her absence has been noted."

Lord Chuja smirked and practically purred, "I will be happy to convey Your message, My Emperor."

"Say it exactly as We have said it. You do not have permission to speak on Our behalf. You are a messenger only."

"I understand, My Emperor." He saluted. "By Your leave." It was granted and he leaped into the saddle and called his personal escorts. They put spurs to horse and tore off down the Southern Highway, scattering the laboring forms, and leaving a thin trail of sooty dust in the air.

CHAPTER 30 : IMPERIAL GRACE

The Golden Emperor watched the Fire Lord ride off then turned His attention back to the matter at hand. "Fire Chief Shuibai, I would have words with you. Walk with me." The Emperor swung down from His saddle and His Bodyguards formed a loose square about Him far enough away that they could not hear what passed between the two.

"Tell me about the Great Fire of Cherry Hill."

Shuibai nodded and licked his lips nervously. "The Lady of Cherry Hill sent out a post rider to summon all the neighboring companies. We had felt the earthquake, so we had turned out already, thinking there were bound to be fires as a result. We were the first of the outside companies to arrive in Cherry Hill, but the fire was already well involved when we got there. It created a firestorm, which is when the fire is so hot it sucks air into itself like a great blast furnace, and the onrush of wind is like a hurricane. It knocked us off our feet. In the moments it took us to recover, it gained a block. We were too close and embers were raining down on us and the wooden buildings were melting away like lard on a hot stove. So we ran back to the Great Southern Highway and joined the other companies in tearing down a fire break. That was where the fire was held until it burned itself out."

"How fast did you say it devoured a block?" the Emperor asked in astonishment.

"Not more than two minutes, Noble Emperor."

The Golden Emperor stopped and looked westward as He did the math in His head. At two minutes per block He had been ninety minutes from losing the Capital. "We had no idea how close to disaster We were."

"The wind held, Noble Emperor. It would have devastated Low Marsh and Crane Marsh and maybe the southern precincts of the Capital, but the main portion of the city would have been spared."

The Emperor glanced at him as he spoke matter-of-factly about the risk to his own home and people. "How long did the fire burn?"

"Eighteen hours until it was brought under control, but the ruins flared and smoldered for another week."

He shook His head. "This is intolerable. Why are they quarreling over the fire commission! What are they thinking? I shall instruct the Black Prince to pressure them."

"With all due respect, Your Grace, but I hardly think it is His interest to be diligent in Your service." Shuibai gulped at his own temerity.

The Golden Emperor smiled faintly. "You are not the only one who criticizes Him. But We know Lord Brice very well. We have the utmost confidence in His fealty and His ability. He is one of the stones upon which Our throne rests."

Shuibai looked desperately at Him. "My Emperor, if I cannot tell the truth to You, then to whom can I say it? Always I am told to keep silent, but I know what I know and I saw what I saw."

The Golden Emperor stared at him for a long time. Then He mused, "Master Kung said, 'He who heard the truth in the morning might die content in the evening.' I'll hear you, Chief Shuibai."

"The fan, the silver fan, with Your old seal upon it, was stolen by a woman in an Iris uniform and she gave it to a hooded woman in a black uniform without any insignia. The Hooded Woman cried out, 'Death to the Pretender.' It happened outside the Moon Shrine on Your daughter's birthday. They have guns, Your Grace. Revolvers that can shoot six times without being reloaded. They have killed and burned and lied and bribed and threatened. The ammunition came from the Maiko Fireworks Factory. Which is where the fire started." He turned and a broad gesture swept over the Burned District. "One of Your retainers burned them out. He did it for You. And You don't even know it. Who would dare to order such a thing but the Prince of Death?"

The Golden Emperor surveyed the ruins. What was passing through His mind Shuibai could not tell. He said shortly, "You lay a severe charge, and We tell you that you are wrong to blame Brice-lan. We will not hear such things again."

Shuibai's heart sank. "Yes, Noble Emperor."

But the Emperor had heard what he had to say, even if He did not share Shuibai's theory as to the responsible party. "It was an Iris warrior, you're very certain?"

"Oh yes, she was in uniform. Though she's been disgraced. Some other Iris warriors chased her, but I don't think they caught her."

"It went from her to the Hooded Woman?"

"Yes, Noble Emperor. The Hooded Woman is Lady Omo Sakoro. I made the gangster tell me."

"Our enemies are intriguing against each other, in which case there is nothing for Us to fear. But all the same." He turned and barked, "Captain Omel, recall your brother to the Capital at once. We want him posthaste." The Emperor clapped His hands. "Now, Johen-don."

The Captain of the Imperial Bodyguard bowed. "I'll send the word." He spoke to a retainer who produced a portable writing tablet. The Captain wrote a quick note, dried it, and sealed it. Then he dispatched the retainer to the nearest post station. "The message is on its way."

The Golden Emperor turned and looked toward the crowd that was filling the intersection of the Capital Road and the Southern Highway. When the people saw His head turn in their direction they cried out and raised their hands in supplication. A line of mounted Guards in lavender uniforms held them back.

"Uncle," He addressed the General of the Eastern Gate. "Open the Imperial granaries. Feed these people, all of them, whether they're working or not. See that they are adequately clothed. Open up the Imperial Wardrobe if you have to. How much are the laborers being paid?"

"They aren't, My Emperor. They're drafted."

"Pay them a laborer's wage. These are Our subjects, not slaves."

"That will be expensive, My Emperor."

"Would you sell the Imperial honor cheaply?"

"Of course not, Your Grace."

"Then do as We command."

He bowed deeply. "Your will is my will, My Emperor."

The Golden Emperor remounted His horse. As He drew near, the mob cried out in a great wail, "Mercy, Noble Emperor!" Naked hands reached out to Him who was a God on earth, beseeching Him for succor.

He stood in the stirrups and shouted in the language of the common people, "Listen to Me!" His voice rang like a golden bell, reverberating with Power. "I am Your Emperor, and I will care for you! You will have food to eat and wood for your fires. You will have wages as laborers for rebuilding Cherry Hill. When the city is rebuilt, you will have homes and jobs again!"

A ragged cheer went up. He pushed His horse forward, riding out alone, unprotected and unguarded. The *taran* wheeled their horses and pursued him in haste, calling Him back, but He ignored them and outpaced His Bodyguards.

"I am the Emperor of all the people, the humble as well as the mighty, the weak as well as the strong. I am the shield for those who have no shield, I am the lord of those who have no lord!"

The people cheered and clapped and whistled; they cried out, "Blessed Emperor, King of Peace, August Lord!" In a paroxysm of delight, they surged forward, surrounding Him, and trapping Him in their crush.

Dirty hands gripped His skirts and pulled while hungry faces thrust forward to kiss His boots. He put out His hands to balance Himself as they tugged and pushed, surging in waves of adulation, their hysteria cresting higher and higher, snatching at His fine coat, reaching for His hair, His face, His sword . . .

Captain Omel, Commander of His bodyguards, was already plunging into the melee, but it was too late. The Emperor's agitated horse reared and dirty hands pulled at Him; He toppled from the saddle. His brilliant form disappeared into the seething mass of humanity.

"Get Him out of there!" the General of the Eastern Gate shouted, standing in his stirrups. The Eastern Guards and the Imperial Bodyguards pushed forward, swinging closed steel fans like truncheons, beating the hysterical mob. The wounded staggered and fell, blood streaming from broken noses and cracked heads. The Emperor's horse bellowed in fury at the smell of blood and the sound of frenzy. Those at the rear of the crowd kept pushing forward, shoving more bodies in the maelstrom, while the lavender uniforms lost their line and found themselves the center of individual knots of violence, battering away as if they could clear the mob by brute force. Bodies fell under their hooves, children cried and women screamed, and hoarse voices of men sounded their agony. The form of the Golden Emperor was nowhere to be seen. The Emperor's golden horse bucked and kicked, lashing out at the press of bodies.

Shuibai clawed his way into the melee, stumbling and jerking, desperately trying to snatch for a piece of crimson cloth that might be His coat, fighting through the writhing forms, stepping by accident on fallen bodies, weighed down by the screaming dervishes that whirled amid the fray.

"Draw swords!" the Eastern Gate bellowed. There was a hiss of metal and bright flashes of light as the deadly *taran* swords were unsheathed. The screaming rose to a shriek of terror.

"No swords! You might hit Him!" the Captain of the Bodyguards bellowed back.

Some obeyed one man and some the other. Blood spattered in great arcs as the preternaturally sharp blades sliced through flesh and bone. The screaming swelled to a pitch that human ears could not tolerate and Shuibai threw himself down, arms over his head. He could not see Zashi and prayed he was all right; he prayed their fire uniform coats would save them from the swords of the *taran,* but he had no hope that it would be so. They cared about nothing but finding the Emperor.

He suddenly saw a red gloved hand sprawled on the pavement before him. Bodies leaped and struggled above it; the mob swirled in panic as those under the blades tried desperately to escape or fight back, while those at the back, not seeing what was happening, pushed forward, churning the ground into a chaos of blood and body parts. The General of the Eastern Gate shouted at the top of his lungs, "Disperse or die, you rebels!"

Shuibai grabbed for the red glove and missed; but the hand was not still. It shoved at the body on top of it, and a young woman reared up, crying, then her decapitated head went flying, raining blood on Shuibai and the Emperor. There was a momentary space and the Emperor rolled onto His side to try and get His knees under him, but Shuibai snagged His sleeve and shouted, "Stay down!" He did not want to see the Emperor accidentally killed by His own guards.

The Emperor yanked His coat sleeve free of Shuibai's hand. Horses hooves trammeled over Shuibai and he covered his head and tucked into a ball. The mob was coming apart as the confusion turned to panic and the refugees fled in all directions. Shuibai and the Emperor stayed down and covered their heads.

"Hold your places!" the Captain of the Bodyguards shouted. The Eastern Guards, splattered in blood, held the field. The wounded crawled blindly away, and the dead and maimed lay where they had fallen. The weeping continued.

"Sheathe weapons!" the Captain's command rang out. The *taran* flicked the blood from their blades then sheathed them.

"Dismount!" They swung down.

"Imperial Bodyguards, advance on foot!"

The lavender uniforms held their places while the gold and crimson uniforms began to pick their way among the several dozen bodies lying in the road. Red blood was everywhere, making it difficult to pick out the crimson and gold garments of the Emperor.

"Here He is!" Shuibai called. He did not put his head up.

"Who said that?" the Captain demanded.

Shuibai cautiously got to his hands and knees. There was no one within sword's length, so he sat up and called, "He's over here. He's hurt, I think."

The Emperor lay on His side, splattered with blood. He had lost His hat and His golden mask lay dented upon the ground several feet away. He sat up with grimace, leaning heavily on one arm and holding His other arm against His body as if it pained Him. His crimson coat was torn to shreds by the hysterical mob. Only a sleeve remained attached to His left side. His golden body armor was smeared with black soot and red blood. His hair was torn and His braid partially unraveled.

"Help me up," He said to Shuibai. Shuibai stood and offered his hand, and the Emperor's hand gripped his tight, and He lurched to His feet. A small cry of gladness went up when His retainers saw Him on His feet again. Then their cries turned to dismay when they saw that He was unmasked and His face was cut and bruised. The Emperor tasted blood and pressed the back of His glove to His cut lip.

"You're hurt!" Shuibai exclaimed.

"I've been wounded before. This is nothing." The Golden Emperor limped a few steps towards His bodyguards.

The Captain of the Bodyguards made a three point kowtow on the ground before Him. "Are You all right, My Emperor?"

"I'm still in one piece."

The General of the Eastern Gate arrived. "My Emperor, You should not have gone among these people!"

The Golden Emperor lost His temper. "You should not have starved these people! They aren't animals! They wouldn't have rioted if they weren't delirious at the thought of food and wages!"

"If the Emperor is unhappy with my service, He has only to say so and I will relieve Him of my presence." His hand went to the hilt of his dagger.

The Golden Emperor noticed the motion and snapped, "Your retirement is accepted!"

The General—the ex-General—hesitated, "I had intended—"

"I know what you intended, Uncle, and I forbid you to commit suicide. I will have order in My Own house if nowhere else."

Prince Porose snarled, "I will obey You in all particulars, as I have always done."

The Golden Emperor glared at him, then without taking His eyes off the older lord, said, "Captain Omel. Make certain that Our Uncle is kept comfortable in Our palace, and that he lacks for nothing until I have time to arrange a suitable place for his retirement."

The ex-General locked eyes with the young Emperor. "I rue the day that the Sun claimed You for Its Own. I will not defy the Will of Heaven, but I warn You against Your folly."

"Because you were the first husband of Our Reverend Mother We have spared you twice, Uncle. No matter what is said of Us, We have never spilled the Blood of Our kin, and We never will. Neither will We permit you to embarrass Us by committing suicide."

Lord Omel stepped forward and held out his hand to the older man. "If you will be kind enough to surrender your weapons, Noble Prince."

Prince Porose withdrew the sword and dagger from his sash and handed them to the officer in the golden uniform, saying, "You are the last of His old vassals, Johen-don. Soon you will be discarded, too, and *sanaka* will be dead."

"I have already yielded my inheritance to my younger brother, recognizing that his qualities are superior to my own. I have no regrets for allowing that which is better to replace that which is inferior. Now, if you are ready, Noble Lord, I shall escort you home."

"There has been no home for me since the Golden Empress died. Take me where you will."

The Captain turned to the Emperor. "You will be short handed if I leave, My Emperor."

"You cannot guard Us both at once. Take him away. I will fend for Myself." The Emperor looked at the disheveled Eastern Guards, who were watching intently as their lord was placed under arrest. "I grant permission for any *taran* who desires to follow his lord into retirement."

One by one the lavender uniforms dismounted and crossed to stand behind their lord. Not a single one of them remained in service to the Golden Emperor. The Golden Emperor rubbed a gloved hand across His bare face. "Go in peace."

Captain Omel was outnumbered about thirty to one, but he bowed deeply to the Emperor and addressed himself to his duty. "Gentlemen, if you will accompany me." The procession mounted up and turned down the Capital Road, following the Captain of the Imperial Bodyguards.

The Emperor watched them out of sight. "If it had been any other man, My Captain would be dead before they reached the city gates," He observed. "There go the two most scrupulous men in the country."

He sighed heavily and looked around Him. The Black Prince, Shuibai, Zashi, and a dozen Imperial bodyguards remained standing, while the street was littered with the dead and wounded. He knelt and with His Own hand closed the eyes of a girl of no more than six. The Black Prince, who was also the Death Priest, moved among the bodies. He bent and closed the eyes of some, making a sign over them, and to others who still lived, he spoke softly and said, "Help will come. You will be tended in My hospital." His voice was very gentle.

Shuibai had never heard the Black Prince use the Divine voice before, but now as He moved among the fallen, he saw that as the Emperor was the Avatar of all who lived, so too was the Prince the Avatar of all who died. As they watched, a young man struggled to hold his torn guts in place as the Death Priest approached.

The Black Prince knelt by his side and surveyed the wound. "There is no hope for you," he said gently.

The young man let out a despairing cry.

"Do you have family?"

"All dead," he gasped. "The fire . . ."

"I can ease your pain."

"Please!"

"Sleep now," the Black Prince said, passing his hand over the young man's face. The young man gasped and choked, then lay still. His features relaxed and he exhaled one soft sigh. Just like that, he was dead. Shuibai turned his back.

"You said the common people loved Me," the Golden Emperor said sadly, apparently addressing the Black Prince.

"They do love you," Shuibai said. "But they don't know you're only human."

They all looked at Shuibai in surprise. He was surrounded by Celestials who had never heard anybody address the Emperor as if He were anything other than a living god.

"I'm not human, I'm an Avatar," the Golden Emperor replied.

"Do the immortal gods bleed?" Shuibai asked reasonably.

The Emperor pressed His hand against His bloody lip again and looked at the stain on His glove. "You are unschooled in these matters. Avatars are the flesh that house the Spirit. You are right, that I, Garathan, am only human. But That which dwells within Me is Divine."

"Then it seems to me all men must be divine, for we are all possessed of immortal souls. I don't see why one should be privileged more than another. It seems that other than the accident of birth, you could have been me, and I could have been you."

"Not quite, Shuibai-don. The Blood is changed by the Presence of the Spirit. That change is inherited by Our children, and passed down through the generations. We keep the Imperial Bloodlines as pure as possible because an ordinary man would be driven mad if a Spirit came to dwell in him. We are bred to it. You are not."

Shuibai's lip got stubborn. He glanced at where the Black Prince was still moving among the dead and wounded. "He wasn't born into the Blood."

The Golden Emperor sighed heavily. "He's quite mad, too."

"You're only a man!" Shuibai cried out. "If You're a God, why did You let them tear You down? Why did You let Prince Porose rebel? If You are a God, how do You answer for all the evil that is done in Your Name?"

"If I am only a man, and not a god, is your question any different?"

Shuibai blinked. "What?"

The Golden Emperor limped over to stand directly in front of him. "Ask again. Ask Garathan, the man. How do I answer for what people have done in my name?"

"I don't know."

The Emperor laid His hand on Shuibai's shoulder. "That is why I am Emperor, and you are not. Because I am Emperor, everything that happens in the Two Queendoms is My responsibility. Everything! So My greatest duty is to seek wisdom in the hopes that I can do more good today than I did yesterday."

"That's every man's duty."

"But not every man accepts the obligation, do they? Most men look to someone else, then complain about what he does."

"Ye-es." Shuibai found his anger blunted and his questions baffled.

"Do you believe in Me, Shuibai-don?"

Shuibai shrugged. "I believe you're better than civil war." He did not use the Divine pronoun to refer to the man who happened to be Emperor.

The Golden Emperor smiled faintly and stepped back. "Then let Me show you something."

He removed His glove and held out His bare hand with the palm facing Shuibai. He stared hard at the fireman, who dropped his eyes dejectedly. "Look at Me, Chief Shuibai."

A soft golden light began to glow in the palm of the Emperor's hand. Shuibai raised his eyes and watched it as it grew and grew to become a globe larger than a woman's head, bright white in the center, yellow in its middle parts, and orange around its edges. "This is the Power of the Sun. With it I could immolate the world. But I don't. That is the purpose of an Avatar: to restrain the raw Power of a capricious Spirit, channeling it into positive actions whenever possible, and ameliorating the harm they do as much as possible."

Zashi drifted closer, staring in fascination at the glowing ball of light. Shuibai did not want to believe what he was seeing.

"Touch it," the Emperor commanded. Zashi stepped forward, maimed arm extended, and plunged his hand all the way to the elbow into the light.

A thunderclap resounded and the light vanished. The Emperor stared at Zashi in surprise. Shuibai was blinking and rubbing his eyes, trying to eliminate the afterglow burned into his eyeballs.

Zashi stood a moment with arm outstretched, then lowered his arm and gave a shudder that rippled all the way up his spine from his feet to his skull. Then his eyes rolled up inside his head and he collapsed. Shuibai leaped to his side and cradled Zashi's head in his arm.

The Emperor knelt beside him. "I'm sorry, I didn't mean to hurt your friend. He was rash! The Imperial Bloodlines must be kept separate for your protection as well as Ours. I would not have hurt you, but he surprised Me."

"Will he be all right?" Shuibai asked in a worried voice.

The Emperor peeled back Zashi's eyelids and looked at the whites, the only thing visible. He put His bare hand on the coat over Zashi's chest and felt his heartbeat. "He fainted. He'll recover. But make him rest for a couple days."

Then the Emperor laid His gloved hand against Zashi's face in a gentle caress. "These are My people, Shuibai-don. Everything I do affects them. *Everything*. No matter how small or thoughtless, it is magnified and reverberated through the Two Queendoms by the Power that resides in Me. But I am not omnipotent. I can't read the future. I can't read minds. The Power has limits. The biggest limit is the fear and affection of My people."

Shuibai held Zashi's cold hand in his. He said, "I'm not an educated man. I'm sorry to be so ignorant. I should keep in my place." He kept his head down.

"No, Shuibai-lan. Keep doing what you've been doing. We may be an Avatar, but We are not a firefighter. We can store rice in Our granaries to protect against famine, and We can lead armies to keep the enemy from Our gates, but until now We have been powerless in the face of fire. We look to you for succor. Please accept Our trust and continue."

Shuibai sat stunned. "I am only a man, not a god."

Garathan smiled. His swollen lip curved up and he winced as the bruised cheek moved. "I know exactly how you feel."

CHAPTER 31: DRAGON DREAMS

A couple of weeks later Shuibai was hammering copper rivets at his anvil in the kitchen. He didn't hear the knocking on his front shutter. Zashi, who was lying on his stomach on his pallet reading from a picture book, looked up, then crossed to the front screen. He slid back the paper screen, then the wooden shutter, and was surprised to see a courier in the Imperial livery of crimson and gold.

"I have a letter for Fire Chief Shuibai," the courier said.

"One moment." Zashi turned into the house. "Shuibai, you have an important message!"

Shuibai laid down his hammer and came forward, wiping his hands on his thighs. He was plainly dressed in his old green clothes while Zashi was comfortably dressed in his preferred purple peony jacket and trousers.

"I'm Fire Chief Shuibai," he told the courier. "What do you have?"

The courier did not dismount, just leaned forward. Shuibai stretched out his hand to receive it. "I'm instructed to wait for a reply," the courier replied.

"Can we get you some refreshments?" Zashi asked.

"Hot tea if you have it."

"Certainly," Zashi replied. "Please do come in. I'll meet you at the door."

So the courier dismounted and Zashi let him in, while Shuibai opened up the letter and tried to read it. He scanned the elegant lines of calligraphy and couldn't make heads nor tails of it. He waited until Zashi had settled the young man, who sat on the straw cushion Zashi offered him and looked around their little apartment with his nose in the air. Zashi signaled Kanko to bring a tea service with three cups and a teapot. Zashi poured with a graceful hand.

"Zashi-lan," Shuibai said. "Would you be kind enough to give me your opinion?" He didn't want to admit to being only semi-literate in front of the snobby young courtier. The courier was only a couple years older than Kanko and it rankled him to see one so young act so important. Even if he was a *taran*.

Zashi leaned his head close to Shuibai's and read the message softly. Sandalwood and other exotic aromas that they had learned to recognize as the Emperor's personal scent permeated the letter.

"Unto Fire Chief Shuibai of Low Marsh, Greetings. I have made inquiries but the Fire Lord tells me that your dispatches do not mention whether Deputy Chief Mizaka has recovered his health. Therefore, I am inquiring directly. Please tell Me that he is well and I will be content, but if he is not well, you must tell Me and I will send My physician to him," Zashi read.

They stopped to look at each other. "Well, this is certainly a case of the country raincoat and the city umbrellas telling tales!" Zashi exclaimed.

Shuibai had no idea what he was talking about. "Go on. What else does it say?"

"There is a poem, also."

"Read it."

"'One stroke of the hoe—they huddle uprooted, the violets.' It is by an ancient poet." Zashi passed him the Emperor's note. "Aptly chosen, and kinder than some of other ways He might have chosen to express Himself. He is a gentle man, our Emperor."

Shuibai sat back and rubbed his hands across his leather apron. "He's asking after your welfare; I understand that part well enough, but what does the poem mean?"

Zashi smiled. "Violets are a humble flower. Pretty, but a weed all the same. So when the farmer hoes his field, they get uprooted and destroyed. As our Emperor goes about His business, humble people sometimes suffer. It is the way of the world, but He is sensitive enough to notice."

Shuibai took the letter back and ran the fine paper through his callused hands. "He expects an answer. Will you write it for me, Zashi-lan?"

"Yes, of course." Zashi fetched the writing desk and ground the ink, mixing it carefully. He trimmed his brush before he began; he wanted no stray marks to mar Shuibai's response. "Do you know what you want to say? Or would you like me to help you frame your answer?"

"I can say it plainly enough. Tell him that we are not worthy of His attention, but since He asks, yes, you've recovered." Zashi posed his brush for a long moment, then exhaling gently, dipped his brush into the ink and began to write. His strokes flowed smoothly across the paper, and to his horror, the words that appeared on the paper were not the words that Shuibai had instructed him to write.

"As one Avatar to Another, know that Your touch has eased the burden of this vessel a little. You have no cause for concern upon that account.—Kwaji."

Zashi laid down the brush and stared at the words. The handwriting was not even his own. "I can't do this," he said in a strained voice.

"What's the matter?"

"Perhaps you'd better give him a verbal reply."

Shuibai was peering at the paper. "It looks nice. Did you misspell something?"

Zashi was getting agitated. He picked up the brush again. "Go ahead. I'll just write down a draft, then rewrite it better."

"I don't know what else to say. I already told Him everything that mattered."

"Well, maybe I can suggest something."

"Yes, please."

"A poem, perhaps. 'My eyes, which have seen all, come back, back to the white chrysanthemums.' Another classic."

Shuibai thought it over. "White chrysanthemums makes me think of the Emperor's coat."

"Yes, the white chrysanthemum is as much His symbol as is the whirling disk of the Sun."

"I like it."

So Zashi wrote it carefully. To his relief, the words were in his own handwriting.

Shuibai looked at what he had written. "It looks fine. Let me seal it."

Zashi hesitated, so Shuibai took the paper from him. Shuibai inked his seal with red ink, then firmly and carefully pressed it to the paper. He fanned the air above it with his hand, speeding the drying of the ink. Zashi watched him in disquiet. When the ink was dry, Shuibai fold up the letter and sealed it with wax. "Can you address it for me, please?"

Zashi carefully addressed it with a neat hand, then gave it to the courier. The courier put the letter in his sleeve, then retrieved his sandals and mounted up, his horse clattering away.

When he was well and gone, Zashi opened the doors to the Fire Dragon's shrine. Shuibai put away his tools, then paused in the middle of unrolling his sleeping mat, wondering what had gotten into Zashi. Zashi stood a long time staring into the interior, face to face with the thing he had made. Then he knelt and set a piece of incense in the censer. He seemed unaware of his surroundings, and walking like a somnambulist, crossed to the kitchen, stepped down onto the dirt floor, and lifted a twig from the wood box and lit it. Cupping his hand around the tiny flame to shield it he retraced his steps to the shrine. He knelt gracefully with only one small hesitation as his bad leg protested. Leaning forward, he touched the flame to the incense. It caught, and the smell of cypress wood drifted through the room.

Shuibai motioned to the boy Kanko. "Go to bed," he said quietly. "I'll sit up with the Deputy Chief."

Kanko dragged his mattress all the way to the front of the little house and burrowed under his bedclothes. The draft from the shutters made the front of the house much colder than the kitchen where he usually slept, but he wanted to be as far away as possible from the open shrine.

Zashi let the twig burn almost to his fingertips, then gave it one sharp shake to extinguish it. Shuibai decided to pretend that everything was normal, even though the hush that suffused the room was giving him goose bumps. It was not the usual evening quiet of a household going to its rest, but a watchful hush, as if unseen eyes were watching . . . and waiting.

He laid out Zashi's mattress a few feet from his own, neatly covered the two beds with green patchwork bed quilts, plumped the small square pillows, and waited for Zashi to finish his prayers. Zashi continued kneeling, staring into the shrine, a haze of incense surrounding him. Shuibai rubbed his eyes because the stuff was making them water and his vision was blurring. It made it seem as if Zashi was surrounded by a nimbus of amber light, and he knew that could not possibly be the case. Then Zashi rubbed his bad hand back over his hair, rubbed his eyes as if he were tired, and untied his sash. The outer robe of purple stuff slipped from his shoulders and pooled about him. The undershirt was a pale peach color of ordinary cotton, a little wrinkled and soiled about the neck from a day of wear. Zashi waved his hand in front of his face as if he was warm.

Shuibai on the other hand, found the house too cold for his taste. He would have liked to keep it warmer, but they had to be frugal with the fuel. Zashi rubbed his face again and made a noise. He stripped the outer robe entirely away, leaving himself clad in the thin cotton under robe. He folded the peony jacket under his knees as a pad and began to sway gently as he prayed. Pious people often swayed as they prayed, but it was not the sort of behavior he had expected from a man he considered to be more worldly than himself. Shuibai habitually neglected the spiritual rituals of life, but while Zashi gave them some attention, piety was not one of his distinguishing characteristics.

The room warmed a little. The light about Zashi grew brighter, and Kanko buried himself deeper under the bedclothes and turned his back to the room. Whatever was happening, it was something he wanted no part of. The room continued to warm. Shuibai rose and crossed to within a few feet of Zashi; he could feel the heat radiating from his form. Zashi made another uncomfortable noise, then stripped off the cotton under robe and tossed it aside. He was naked but for his loincloth, his discarded clothes disarrayed on the floor around him, his face flushed, his eyes closed, long black lashes lying along the translucent skin of his cheek.

Shuibai stared at the scars that marked his form from jaw to left knee. Zashi's left side was an alien map of bubbled and striated flesh, his arm scarcely human in appearance. The scars were darker than the rest of him and purple brown in color like old bruises. Shuibai did not remember them being so dark, but perhaps it was the light that made them seem that way. Zashi rocked harder, locks of hair swishing across his forehead as he shook, his shoulders flexing uncomfortably as if he carried a heavy burden. His respiration increased in tempo until his breath was coming in shallow gasps, and still the heat built.

As the heat increased, Zashi changed. The scars took on an iridescent light and formed themselves into rows upon rows of small scales, shining purple-orange in the strange amber light. Zashi's eyes were still closed; he seemed like a man caught in a fever, unaware of his situation, enraptured by his internal hallucinations. The maimed hand that was fused together like a mitten elongated and darkened. Black talons sprouted from claws connected by purple-black webbing. Tendons flexed and ran taut under the reptilian skin. Zashi's entire left side became alien, and where the purple reptile skin met the sallow skin of his knee, the image of a fanged head formed, lifted from his thigh, and snarled at Shuibai.

Shuibai stood shaking but did not retreat, even though the heat was like a furnace. He covered his face with his sleeve and reached out the other hand. "Zashi, please," he begged.

Zashi jumped as Shuibai's hand connected with his shoulder. The reptile skin was smooth and warm, like the finest grade of leather. Zashi's eyes snapped open, like a door being flung open to slam against the wall. Shuibai scooted around to where he could see Zashi's face. The left eye had become a yellow orb with a vertical slit for an iris. "Please don't do this," Shuibai begged, stretching out his hand again.

Zashi batted away his hand. "I have been 'not doing this' all my life!" he hissed. "Isn't that what the Emperor said, that every man has a duty but few heed the obligation?"

"I love you, please don't scare me this way."

Zashi blinked violently. "How could you love me? You don't even know what I am!" He lifted his talon helplessly. "Monster! Freak!"

"It doesn't matter what you look like, it's who you are inside that matters to me!"

"What I am inside is inhuman!"

"Don't say that!"

Zashi uncoiled to his feet with a sinuous grace that eluded him under normal circumstances. He flexed his arms and knees, twisted from side to side. "It doesn't hurt when I am like this. So many days and weeks and months I drag around my crippled body, all the time knowing that all I have to do is surrender to the Fire Dragon and my body won't hurt anymore. Can you imagine how that eats me, knowing that all I have to do is destroy someone else in order to escape my own misery? Isn't that monstrous?"

"Who told you life was fair? It is what it is. You are what you are. I'm sorry I can't make it better for you. I would if I could. I love you, Zashi."

Zashi clenched his talons into his hair and pulled hard, ripping out a lock. He let it fall. "I don't want to be this way, Shui-lan, but I don't know how to make It stop. It's chosen me and I can't escape. I could kill myself, but then It would go after someone else, someone less conscientious than me. It's driving me crazy. I have the urge to do terrible things. Sometimes it's so hard to leave the lamps alone, sometimes it's so tempting to destroy what I love!"

Shuibai stepped into the heart of the fire, closed his eyes against the glare and heat, and reached out even though he was afraid that touching Zashi would burn him. His hands connected with skin, reptile on one side, human on the other, and he pulled Zashi against him. He wrapped his arms around the glowing body and held him tight, skin scalding skin, blinded and afraid. But he didn't let go. Zashi clamped his arms tight around Shuibai, and whispered in fear, "I don't want to hurt you. What if I can't help myself?"

"It's all right if you do. I know you don't mean it. Just tell me that you love me." He found Zashi's lips. He pressed harder then, and their lips locked together.

He thought the fireball that bloomed in him was going to kill him, but he didn't let go. There was no more time for patience; whatever happened, happened, and it was better to declare himself and risk the danger than to walk away and live silent and afraid. Zashi responded frantically, clinging to him in fear and sudden unadmitted hope. The kiss lasted a very long time.

Shuibai was not burned. Instead he was filled with a kind of glow that made him sigh. He opened his eyes and found Zashi staring at him with wide eyes, both of which were humanly normal. The Dragon had become a great tattoo running the length of his body from shoulder to knee, the tail draped over onto his back and a clawed foot extending up his neck to his cheek. Zashi flexed his arm experimentally, then turned his wrist and inspected his hand. He unfolded the fingers one by one. A web of skin remained between each digit, but they operated independently of one another. The fingernails were very long, black, sharp and hooked.

"I'm all right," he whispered.

Shuibai smiled. "You always have been. You just wouldn't believe it."

Zashi exclaimed, "I did not imagine this!" running his hand along his left side.

"I know. I saw it happen."

Zashi stood up straight, then stretched his arms as far as they would go above and behind his head. He balanced on his left foot, the leg that had formerly been lame. "Look at me!"

Shuibai tackled him and deliberately knocked him over. They crashed to the floor and Shuibai suddenly tickled his armpit. Zashi laughed and thrashed, but Shuibai wormed his fingers in again and tickled him harder. Zashi kicked and rolled over, but Shuibai pursued him. He tickled his ribs, his neck, the backs of his knees, his armpits, his wrists, his stomach, anywhere he could get hold of while Zashi shrieked with laughter and rolled and thrashed on the wooden floor. He laughed and laughed, gasping for breath but still laughing even when Shuibai released him. They lay tangled together on the floor, relaxed and relieved.

"Oh Shui-lan, I do love you. But I didn't dare encourage you. I wanted to, but every time I thought about it, I'd have dragon dreams."

"It's all right. Now come to bed. The floor is cold."

Zashi shivered. "It *is* cold." He gathered up his clothes and put them on while Shuibai laid the two sleeping mats side by side and spread the quilts over both of them. Then they slid under the covers together. Shuibai desperately wanted to embrace Zashi again, but he was still uncertain. The embers on the hearth still glowed, and the cypress incense still drifted through the room. "I forgot to shut the shrine."

"It's all right," Shuibai replied. "We can get it in the morning."

"Do you know what this means?"

"Hm?" Shuibai was drowsy, but Zashi was still thinking too hard.

"I'm the Avatar of the Fire Dragon. But what am I supposed to do about it?"

"Um, channel the powers of the Spirit into constructive activities instead of destructive activities?" Shuibai was not entirely clear himself.

Zashi pondered. "I was raised a fireman. I believe in firefighting, and I believe in the Dragon. Perhaps that's why it chose me. But then again, why not Chief Byan, or you, or somebody else?"

"Me? I wouldn't know what to do with a Spirit. I didn't even believe in It. You're the poet."

"Maybe. All this time it's been there, and I've been afraid of it. I thought maybe I was crazy or evil or something terrible. Then you stood up to the Emperor and told Him He was just a man, and

He didn't get mad at you, He just showed you how It was. I had the most intense reaction."

"Yes, I saw. You fainted."

"No, before that. When I put my hand into His light; it was pure lust. I thought I was out of my mind. He had the Power and I wanted It so bad. I wanted Him, I wanted It, I wanted to devour Him—It—Them—to meld with It as One, to join with It body and soul . . ."

Shuibai tentatively put an arm across Zashi's stomach. "What about me? Or was it just, well, I know, I mean, I don't know, but, that is—"

Zashi rolled into his arms and kissed him hard. "I've never done it with a man, but for you, yes, I want you. I wouldn't trust anybody else."

"I've never done it with anybody, so you're going to have to help me."

"You start with kissing."

"Oh yes, I like kissing."

"And you go on from there." A long silence punctuated with sighs and rustlings ensued.

Kanko dared to peek out from under his quilt, and breathing a sigh of relief, picked up his mattress and dragged it back to his preferred spot near the smoldering hearth. He opened up the folding screen and set it across the middle of the apartment to give them a little privacy. He was glad that the two of them had worked out whatever it was that had been bothering them. He just wished they could have done it without the accompanying pyrotechnics. The floor was scorched and he knew who was going to have to scrub it in the morning.

CHAPTER 32 : RAID ON HAPPINESS

"Look at this!" Zashi said, hurrying in shortly before noon. He held a copy of the Imperial Gazette in his hand. He hastily put it on the table in front of Shuibai where the other man was working on yet another length of leather hose. The shoulders of Zashi's uniform coat were speckled with melting snowflakes and the leather of his helmet gleamed wetly. He spread the Gazette open before Shuibai. "It's a special edition. This news couldn't wait until the weekend and look what it says!"

There were various headlines. With Zashi's help he deciphered the formal script:

Imperial Gazette goes to twice weekly publication
Golden Emperor opens Imperial granaries to feed the hungry of Cherry Hill
Lady Nayabashi Sakoro released to familial service
Lord Jozeein Omel appointed new Lord of the Highways
Boundary adjustments in the Capital District
Golden Emperor revives Poetry Bureau
Lady Calimara appointed Poet Laureate
Lord Danno confirmed with Imperial Rank

"Eight pages of news! The Emperor has been busy since the fire!" Shuibai exclaimed.

"I think we know why," Zashi said dryly.

"Does it say anything about the General of the Eastern Gate?"

"No, nothing."

"But he's under arrest!"

"I don't think the Neutral lords would be too happy if they knew that, do you? The Emperor is keeping it quiet."

"That won't last. Word will get around."

"Yes, but the Emperor has a newspaper and His opponents don't. His version will predominate. At least for a while."

"What else?"

"Ah, I see the complete text of His dismissal of Lady Nayabashi." He read silently for a moment. "Tactful, and utterly gracious. Listen to this, 'We are glad to permit the Lady Nayabashi to withdraw into her own domain to assist her Lady Mother in succoring their people in this time of disaster, when by reason of the Great Fire so many of their people are in want, and there are so many details to be attended for the reconstruction of Cherry Hill' . . . blah blah blah . . . 'and to relieve her the burden of the Office of Lady of the Highways which she has faithfully performed' . . . and so on. It's several paragraphs long, entirely gracious, and makes it clear that Lady Nayabashi is no longer a person of any authority in the Capital. Ah, here's the appointment of Lord Jozeein Omel. Hm."

"Yes?"

"I thought the name sounded familiar, listen 'in those dark days when We were besieged by Our enemies in the Barren Lands, We were supported by four Noble Lords, namely, Lord Kizo Assaain, who serves Us loyally as the General of the Western Gate; Lord Gesshuu Homan, who gave his life in Our service; Lord Johen Omel, who serves as Captain of the Imperial Bodyguards; and Lord Jozeein Omel, Captain of the Mallard Battalion, a man of considerable strategy and acumen, who has served loyally for three years, seeking no preferment, but content to act as Our agent as We saw fit. But as much as We admire his gracious modesty, the disaster which of late has befallen Our country requires Us to call him out of retirement to take up active duty once again, this time as Our Lord of the Highways, charged with the administration of all the miles of Imperial roads, gates, post stations, and all other appurtenances which are necessary for the good communication and administration of Our Queendoms of Hu Shen and Ton Shen.' And so on."

"The Emperor is not a fool. He's nailing down His rule before it slips from His hands," Shuibai observed.

Zashi folded the pages together. "Blood will flow before it's secure."

"Then we had better do our part," Shuibai said grimly.

"What are you suggesting?"

"I think it's time to inspect the Munificent Happiness Warehouses, don't you?"

Shuibai descended the broad avenue toward Jozatha's warehouses with Zashi beside him and his fire company backing him up. They were dressed in their uniforms and armed with hooks and axes and crowbars. The foot of Wharf Street was congested as porters labored in a long line from ship to warehouse, carrying kegs in slings suspended from a long pole that was carried over the shoulders of two porters. The porters wore heavy cotton coats and knee pants with knee socks and straw sandals, and their jackets had heavily padded shoulders to protect them from the pressure of the poles.

Shuibai intercepted a porter. "Where's your boss?"

The porter didn't recognize the uniform, but he got down on his knees and set his load down and bowed. The porters behind him came to stop, and seeing the uniformed men fanning out around Shuibai, also set down their loads and knelt.

"Hey!" somebody yelled, and a foreman ran out of the gate of the warehouse compound. "What's going on here?" The foreman was a rat-faced man with a scraggly beard and mustache. He wore a conical straw hat tied under his chin, a dark blue jacket and trousers of better stuff than the porters could afford, white shirt and socks, and straw sandals. The sun was warm, but the fitful breeze was cool, and Shuibai was alternately too warm and too cold, depending on how the wind blew, and whether the sun hid behind a cloud.

"I'm Fire Chief Shuibai. This is the Low Marsh Fire Company. We're here to inspect your property."

"For what?" he snapped.

"The Golden Emperor has decreed a fire code applicable to the entire Capital District in the wake of the disastrous fire in Cherry Hill. We're in charge of enforcing it for Low Marsh."

The foreman glared at him. "Wait here."

The tableau remained. Porters continued kneeling and peeking out from under their coolie hats; the Fire Company milled impatiently.

Shuibai took a crowbar, and pulling a keg away from a clerk, pried off the lid. He tipped it over and the dark granules spilled into the street.

Zashi looked down at it. "Gunpowder. Your timing is impeccable, Chief."

The gate was manned by a female clerk who had been taking notes as the kegs paraded past her. The dog was elsewhere. Shuibai took a deep breath, and raising his hand, beckoned the company forward. The clerk looked alarmed. "You can't come in here!"

Shuibai pushed past her. "I just did."

She ran alongside him as he strode forward with long strides. "This is private property; you can't barge in here!"

"I found contraband being carried into the premises; now get out of my way!" Shuibai marched up to the first warehouse. He grabbed the great brass lever that operated the door and pulled on it, but it did not give. "Open it," he ordered.

"I won't. You can't come in here."

"Young woman, to interfere with a firefighter carrying out his duties is a capital offense. That means a flogging for you and death for any man who helps you."

She blanched. "You can't. You're just a peasant!"

He grinned viciously. "Try me."

She turned and ran, her green skirts kicking around her heels. "Boss! Boss!" she called.

Several men and women were coming out of the far warehouse. She ran towards them. Shuibai moved back to his firefighters and gave Zashi a hand signal. Zashi moved to the gate in response.

Jozatha came striding towards them like a thunderbolt. "What in the hell do you think you're doing?" he roared.

Shuibai grinned at him. "Making my tour of inspection. You should have expected me."

Jozatha was a fleshy handsome man with collar length jet black hair. He was dressed in the height of uptown fashion in royal blue trousers and jacket, yellow embroidered shirt, and yellow gloves. He crossed his arms. "We had an agreement."

"Not anymore," Shuibai snapped.

"You took my money."

Shuibai reached into his pocket and removed a purse. He shoved it at Jozatha. "I'm returning it. It stinks and so do you."

Jozatha raised his hand as if to hit Shuibai, but paused at the sight of a dozen firefighters backing up Shuibai. Then he glanced at the Lady of the Knife. She stepped forward, smiling archly.

"I can take them. Just say the word." Her hands went to her waist where the hilts of two long knives protruded from her orange sash. She was wearing blue clothes as brilliant as a peacock. Shuibai fell back two steps, out of reach of her bright blades. He lifted his hand. Zashi, standing by the gate, repeated his gesture, and beckoned.

The clatter of horses' hooves rang on the cobblestones of Wharf Street and all heads swiveled to see the Fire Lord come through the gate mounted on his white horse, flanked by two retainers with glaives in their hands. He reined up a few feet short of the tableau. More Fire Guards poured into the courtyard behind him. He gestured with his fan and the Fire Guards fanned out left and right to take control of the compound.

Shuibai said, "My Lord, allow me to present Jozatha, owner of this property. This lovely ex-*taran* is the Lady of the Knife." Turning to Jozatha he said, "I presume you are already acquainted with Lord Chuja Harada, the Fire Lord."

"I haven't had the pleasure," Jozatha replied sourly, "though naturally I have heard a great deal about him."

"Call out your employees," Shuibai said. "I want them all lined up over there." He pointed to the corner of the compound.

Jozatha gave Shuibai a look of pure hatred, then dispatched his underlings to call out the employees. Shuibai gestured for the Lady of the Knife and Jozatha to move over to the indicated corner, and they did, watching the Fire Guards warily out of the corners of their eyes. Lord Chuja detailed a guard to cover them, then as the employees started leaving the warehouse, they were herded into the corner along with their boss.

The fire company entered the first warehouse. It was dedicated to the storage of tobacco leaf. Huge bundles of the stuff were stacked in racks from floor to ceiling. They crossed via the rear door to the next building and found the tobacco cutting and grinding facility. Here the leaf was turned into cut leaf for smoking or chewing.

They crossed into the third building and found a facility devoted to the processing of dreamflower, which was not illegal. Dreamflower roots were dried and stored in the rear, then processed into smokable mixtures.

The fourth building was only partially filled with small kegs which were identical to the ones being transported by the porters. They were racked on shelves reaching toward the ceiling.

"The proof is in the pudding," Shuibai said, hauling down a keg. He broached the lid, and black powder poured out.

"Gunpowder," Zashi said in disgust. "And look over here." He scooped his hand into a bin of brass shells. "Cartridges. They're making bullets."

"They're making lots of bullets."

"Enough for an army, I'd wager."

Shuibai put the lid back on and heaved the keg up in his arms. He staggered out into the courtyard and set the keg down in front of Lord Chuja. He opened the lid. "This is what the porters are delivering today."

The Fire Lord leaned low from his horse. "Gunpowder, a controlled substance. Let's see your permits!" he snapped at Jozatha.

Jozatha glowered. The Fire Lord grinned. "I didn't think so. Unlicensed distribution of gunpowder is a capital offense."

"There's more," Shuibai said. Zashi opened his hand and showed several shell casings. "There's baskets and baskets of stuff in there."

The brass shells jingled as the Fire Lord took them into his hand and rolled them around together. "Making ammunition. That constitutes treason. I can execute you on the spot for that."

Shuibai lifted his hand. "Wait, Noble Lord. It seems to me that the gangster might be willing to save his life, for a price."

The Fire Lord, dressed in his purple and orange uniform, grinned. The orange demon mask he wore seemed frightfully appropriate. "You have an excellent point, Fire Chief Shuibai." He dismounted his horse, and dropping the reins, approached the prisoners. "I am not a patient man. Tell me where this came from and where it's going. If so, I'll release you, and you can run to wherever it is your kind goes when you're not wanted." He drew his sword. "Or I can kill you right here. You've been caught red-handed in possession of treasonous goods."

"We can make a deal," Jozatha said immediately, eying the bright length of the Fire Lord's sword. A second later a gun barked, and bright blood blossomed in his chest. His blood sprayed the Fire Lord as he dropped dead. The Lady of the Knife held her gun in two hands and said, "I'm leaving, and if you try to stop me, you're dead."

She sidled toward the nearest gate. A flick of the Fire Lord's head was all the order needed; his retainers swung into action. She fired immediately, downing the first man with a bloody hole in his armor just below the ribs. She fired three more times, and a horse screamed and went down, blood gouting from its chest while a *taran* wounded by the third shot lost his seat. There was a momentary snarl as the Guards tangled with the fallen animal; she seized the reins of a riderless animal and leaped into the saddle. She tore through the gate like hell itself was after her.

"After her!" the Fire Lord shouted. "You, you, you, you; bring her back alive!"

The indicated men charged after her.

Shuibai was not worried about the flight of the Lady of the Knife, she was just another pawn in the game being played. The Fire Lord was not interested in the lower class employees, but Shuibai figured they could be just as helpful as their boss. "You." He pointed at the foreman. "Tell me where the gunpowder came from."

"Don't know."

"What are you going to do with it?"

"Turn it into matches."

"That's an awful lot of gunpowder!"

"We're going to make an awful lot of matches," he replied insolently.

"You heard what the Fire Lord said. Unlawful possession of gunpowder is a capital offense."

He shrugged. "It's not mine. I just work here."

That nonplused Shuibai. He checked with Zashi. "Can we arrest him?"

Zashi spoke in a low voice. "We can arrest him, but he probably won't be convicted. Owning gunpowder without a permit is illegal, but then, he doesn't own it, does he? Jozatha owns it." They looked down at the dead man at their feet.

"Chief Shuibai!" the Fire Lord barked. "Have you finished your inspection?"

"No, Noble Lord. By your leave, sir. Zashi, check the last warehouse. I'll stay here." Zashi snagged a pair of firefighters, and they went into the last warehouse. Shuibai addressed the Fire Lord. "Noble Lord, what do you want us to do with the gunpowder?"

The Fire Lord almost smiled. "I'll confiscate it. Have your men transport it to the Black Ice Warehouses. They can keep it until the Black Prince decides what to do with it."

Shuibai bowed. "With all due respect, Noble Lord. I think it would be better if you took charge of the gunpowder. My men are not experienced with such materials and I would hate to have an accident."

Lord Chuja snapped his fingers at one of his retainers. "Round up as many of those porters you can find. They have work to do."

The retainers collected a motley crew of warehouse employees and porters to carry the confiscated kegs of black powder along the quay to the Black Ice warehouses. After some time, Zashi emerged from the fifth warehouse.

"What did you find?"

"Offices and lots of financial records." He held up a sheaf of papers. "I think the Fire Lord will want these papers."

So the two crossed over to where the Fire Lord waited with two Guards as the end of the line of laborers staggered away. "Noble Lord, we have found the gangster's financial records."

"Records?"

Zashi hefted a sheaf of papers. The Fire Lord took them and leafed through them. "Yes, I'm sure this will be useful," he said in a bored voice. "Box them up and send them to the Black Prince."

"Yes, Noble Lord. What should we do with the stuff that isn't contraband?" Zashi asked politely.

"Take it. Sell it. Use it. Dispose of it anyway you like. I'm declaring the property forfeit." He gave some orders to his retainers, who nodded.

Shuibai looked at Zashi and grinned. "You know what I saw in the gunpowder room? A pump. Let's go get it."

Zashi snagged Shuibai's sleeve. "Chief, there's something I need to show you."

Shuibai shook off his hand. "Later. Red, Axe, come with me." He turned and strode off to the #4 warehouse, not waiting for his deputy. Zashi made a noise of frustration, then followed him into the warehouse where he found the Shuibai studying the set up. It was a fixed pump, but the bamboo pipe ran down through the floor. The pipe was surrounded by a pair of wooden semi-circles with hand holds carved in them. Shuibai reached down, grabbed them, and heaved them up and out of the way. They were hinged with leather hinges and clattered onto the wooden floor. Water sparkled darkly in the dimness under the floor boards. "There's a big cistern down there!"

Zashi looked down. "Very wise of them, considering the flammability of gunpowder. But it's a fixed pump. Just what do you think you're going to do with it?"

Shuibai looked up from where he knelt. "Zashi-lan, imagine this is the floor of a wagon, and that's a well. Now imagine that we hook a line of pipes from the pump mouth and run them to the fire."

Zashi looked thunderstruck. "By the gods, it might work!"

"You see, if the pump is mounted on a wagon we can simply drive the wagon over top of a well, or alongside a stream, drop a hose into it, and pump like crazy. Presto, we have water wherever we want it!"

"If it's mounted on the wagon, the weight won't be a problem."

Shuibai gave him the thumbs up. "Help me get it out of here."

"Not now. Tell the guys to do it. There's something I really need to show you."

Shuibai looked puzzled. "Okay. What?"

Zashi crooked his finger at him. "Not one word. Get the men busy working. I don't want anybody to interrupt us."

So Shuibai gave the order and left the firefighters to the task of pulling up the pump. The Chief and his Deputy entered the fifth warehouse. It was divided up into several smaller rooms. Zashi led Shuibai into a room set off with wooden partitions. It was an office, with a desk and a wooden strongbox. The lock had been hacked open. Zashi threw back the lid. The box was full of gold and silver coins.

"And it's all ours," Zashi said fervently. "The Fire Lord said so. Anything that isn't contraband is ours to dispose of as we please."

Shuibai gawked. Then in an awed voice he asked, "Do you know what this means? We can build the water system I want!"

Zashi gave him a frustrated look. "That wasn't the first thing that came to my mind," he admitted.

Overcome with emotion, Shuibai said, "Just think of what we can do! We can hire more men! We can build more wells and cisterns! We can get more pipe and hoses! We'll have the best fire company in the Capital District!"

Zashi smiled lopsidedly. "Is that really what will make you happy, Shuibai?"

Shuibai threw his arms around Zashi and danced him around. "Yes! Oh, yes! We've finally got the money we need to do it right!"

Zashi withstood the dancing bear hug for a minute, then gently pried off Shuibai's hands. "Okay, Chief. Whatever you say."

The box was too big and heavy to be lifted, so they had to find empty kegs and fill them up with gold and silver. Once the kegs were sealed they assigned the firefighters to carry them back to the firehouse. They didn't tell the men what was in the kegs. When asked, Zashi just said, "You don't need to know. Not yet."

CHAPTER 33 : MURDER IN THE CANES

The Winter Festival arrived cold and clear with a sky so crisply blue it could have been pleated and starched. It was an auspicious beginning to the holiday but not a cheerful day. The Black Prince was traveling to Skull Mountain in order to hallow the ground. A new cemetery would be built to inter the remains of those killed in the fire of Cherry Hill. The visit had not been announced, but Shuibai had received a note from the Black Prince informing the young chief that he would be in the neighborhood, and that when his duties were completed, he wanted a demonstration of Shuibai's invention, the bamboo pipes for fighting fires.

Shuibai and his men waited at the top of the Wet Lane until the Celestial party approached along the Capital Road. A herald dressed in a black uniform and a man carrying a standard strutted along in front, crying, "Make way for the Black Prince! Make way for the Avatar of Death!"

The cavalcade traveled slowly, steam coming from the mouths of men and horses, the bullocks trundling along at the speed of a brisk walk. First came a rank of Ghostriders, the traditional honor guard of the Lord of Night. They wore black hooded uniforms without insignia and carried glaives in their right hands while their long curved swords hung from their sashes. The identities of the Ghostriders were concealed under plain black masks. There were only a dozen or so of them, supplemented by Sergeant Left and Sergeant Right, who trotted along on either side of the oxcart.

Fire Lord Chuja rode beside the ceremonial oxcart which was drawn by two hump-shouldered bullocks with gilded horns and purple traces. The Fire Lord, resplendent in his fire uniform, and four of his retainers, accompanied the Black Prince. All together there were some twenty armed warriors and half a dozen non-combatants. The few common folk knelt on the shoulder of the road to kowtow as the cavalcade passed.

Shuibai had turned out to greet the Black Prince with Red, Axe, and a new guy named Manata, leaving Zashi and the rest of the company on call at the house. As the herald approached, the firemen kowtowed. A Ghostrider reined up sharply in front of the firemen. "You there, who are you?" he demanded in the accents of the *taran* class.

Shuibai carefully lifted his head. "We are members of the Low Marsh Fire Company who have turned out as instructed to meet the Black Prince."

"Wait here."

The retainer wheeled his horse away in a flurry of black silk, pulling up beside the oxcart. The shutter opened to reveal a purple curtain and nothing of the interior. He spoke into the cart, but whatever conversation might have resulted was lost as gunfire erupted from both sides of the road. Horses bolted, shocked by the sudden strange noise. Several men fell dead or wounded in the first volley—but the fire did not slacken. One of the bullocks staggered to its knees, and the rear door exploded as the Black Prince leaped out of the cart and hit the ground rolling.

More gunfire splattered against the side of the cart while the Fire Lord wheeled his horse and shouted, "My Prince!"

The Black Prince wasn't waiting for rescue; He flung himself into the trees and disappeared. The trees which served to hide His assailants also served to hide Him, and He was lost in a moment. Blooded erupted from the belly of the Fire Lord's white horse and the animal screamed and reared. The Fire Lord reined hard trying to control it, but bullets slammed into the stallion's chest and belly, and the horse toppled. Lord Chuja hit the ground hard, the horse on top of him. If he cried out the sound was lost in the trumpeting of the dying beast. The horse struggled onto its side before collapsing, but the Fire Lord did not rise.

Shuibai and his firemen flattened themselves in place. As peasants they were not targets—as long as they didn't get in the way. Or so they hoped. Shuibai hissed, "Split up. Make yourselves scarce."

Shuibai kept his belly to the dirt and crawled into the woods where he suddenly encountered a set of black leather boots. He looked up, straight into the muzzle of a revolver, and flung himself aside. The gun barked, the bullet burying itself in the icy mud beside him. He leaped up and shoved against the shooter, knocking the figure aside and running into the trees. His men scattered and ran too. The new guy Manata, who did not know what to do, followed Shuibai.

"Pursue them!" a woman's autocratic voice rang out. "No witnesses!"

Shuibai ran for his life, but much too quickly the woods became the meadow in the Iris Bottom. He halted, and Manata nearly slammed into him. They both looked around wildly, but glancing up the hill behind them they saw figures dressed in black. Simultaneously they saw the orange spit of fire and the bark of the guns and hit the dirt.

"Into the briars, it's our only chance!" Shuibai exclaimed.

The briar patch was composed of billowing masses of thorns. In the dead of winter they were brown and brittle and leafless, but in the spring they would bloom in arching masses of white and pink flowers. Shuibai darted into a tunnel made by the arching briars. Thorns cut his hands and knees, lashed his face and snagged his uniform coat, but he forced himself on. Manata plunged into the canes a few feet from him, and he could hear him bulling through the undergrowth.

Somebody grabbed Shuibai's foot and he struggled, kicking back at the person who had caught him. "Bring him out of there," a male voice ordered.

Shuibai's sandal came off and his foot got free; he shot forward into the underbrush. Thorns buried in his knees and elbows and the pain was vicious, but he kept going, winding deep into the underbrush. In few moments he came to a clear spot in the middle of the thicket. The weeds beneath him were laced with dead thorns and vines. Manata crawled into the clearing from another tunnel. Shuibai listened carefully, but he did not hear the sound of pursuit.

"What do we do?" Manata asked in a whisper. Shuibai sat up and carefully extracted the thorns from his knees, shins, and elbows. Manata had fared only slightly better.

"I don't know. Hope they don't come in after us, I guess," he whispered back. Secreted in the center of the thicket they were invisible to their hunters. It was a dubious safety, but it was all they had. They could hear their pursuers discussing them. "That Shuibai person got away," one of the assassins said.

"No, he's in the briars somewhere," another one answered.

"I'm not going in there!"

"Me neither."

"Shuibai!" rang out a woman's voice. "Come out, or we kill this man!"

Red shouted, "Don't do it, Chief!"

Shuibai groaned and closed his eyes.

"Shuibai! Listen to this!" A pistol barked, and they heard Red's anguished cry, followed by a thump as he fell to the ground. They could hear his harsh breathing as he moaned in pain.

"Come out! Or I shoot him again!" the woman demanded.

Manata stared at Shuibai; Shuibai whispered, "If we come out, they'll kill us too."

"We can't just sit here!" Manata whispered back.

"I'm counting to three! One! Two! Three!" The pistol fired again, echoing through the hollow. Red was silent. Shuibai and Manata sat tight, clenching their jaws and grinding their teeth.

The next command was, "Fire the briar patch."

Shuibai and Manata jumped to their feet. "What do we do now, Chief?" Manata whispered in panic. Even standing up they were invisible to their pursuers; the canes with their wicked thorns arched above their heads.

"Move downstream," Shuibai replied. "Maybe we can get around them to the woods again."

Casting about the clearing they discovered that the briar patch was not the solid mass it appeared from the outside. Instead it was made up of clumps of shrubbery of various sizes whose arching canes interlaced together creating twisting tunnels littered with dead canes and snarled with bindweed. Thus they were able to slip slowly and quietly through the interstices. The thorns tore their clothes and flesh, but they kept going, navigating as best they could toward the bend where the stream met the woods and the briars ended.

Meanwhile, back on the trail, the marauders were discovering that setting fire to an entire briar patch was more work than they had imagined. They kindled a small blaze in the dead wood and it obliging ate at the nearby dead leaves and thorns, but it was not the racing inferno they had imagined. Winter's dampness had settled in the earth. The cane burned fitfully. They had to take flaming brands to different parts of the briar patch and light it again. Once they had the canes burning in half a dozen places they gathered to watch their handiwork. They ignored the limp form lying on the path, the white swan on his uniform torn and bloodied. The flames, almost invisible in the bright morning light, leaped up, crackling and hissing close by.

Shuibai and Manata reached the clear space that lay between the briar patch and the tree line, and checking left and right, darted across to the relative safety of the trees. "Split up," Shuibai said, "That way at least one of us should get away."

Manata melted into the trees while Shuibai paused to extract thorns from his knees. Slowly, he pushed quietly through the trees and came up behind some houses along the Capital Highway west of where the ambush had taken place.

A stray dog charged him. Shuibai leaped over a fence and tumbled into someone's vegetable patch. He accidentally trampled dark green leafy things left rotting in the winter garden. The dog jumped up against the withy fence, barking its head off while a woman ran out of the house and yelled, "Hey! Get out of my yard, you hoodlum!"

"Sound the alarm!" Shuibai called to her, "The Iris Bottom is burning!"

Panic stitched through the residents who started banging wooden spoons on pots to raise the alarm. This was not part of Shuibai's district; the woods they had crossed marked the western border of the Iris Bottom and the limit of the Low Marsh Fire Company territory. He watched in dismay as people ran hither and yon, collecting into clumps to debate their course of action, while a few others ran down the road away from the fire to sound the alarm.

"Where's the nearest well?" Shuibai asked.

It turned out the woman who yelled at him had her own well: a hole in the ground lined with stone. They had to lower a bucket on a rope to get their water. Shuibai ordered a bucket brigade formed up, but there weren't very many people and none of them seemed inclined to pay any attention to him. Putting his silver speaking trumpet to his lips, he roared, "MOVE! I, Shuibai, Fire Chief of Low Marsh, order it!"

Some of them had heard the name Shuibai before and obeyed. Slowly he got them formed up. He was cursing under his breath because he didn't have nearly enough people to reach down into the Iris Bottom, but the smoke could be clearly seen wavering up toward the sky in great grey tendrils. There was water in the Iris Bottom in the form of a public well with a pump, streams and bogholes, even cisterns on the flower farms, but the fire and assassins lay between him and the water.

Leading his bucket brigade through a trail in the woods, they came out into the meadow. Fire was leaping up three fathoms high from the briar patch. It was hot enough now to dry out everything around it and keep itself fed. The citizens hung back and would not approach. Worse, Red's body had been thrown into the briars and hung there, his uniform burning patchily. Black forms vanished amid the trees and Shuibai whirled, fearing that not even the presence of the bucket brigade would save him from a bullet between the shoulder blades.

"Move, you cowards!" he shouted at the bucket men, but their buckets of water fell uselessly short of the flames.

A dirt path ran alongside the flaming briars. The flames on the far side were low, just starting to nibble at the edges of the briars that jumbled the other half of the meadow. Heat shimmered in the air before him, beating on his face like the blows of a hammer on an anvil. He made up his mind and darted forward. He ran down the dirt trail between the two fires, holding his breath and covering his face with his sleeve. He burst suddenly into cooler air and lowered his sleeve; he had made it past the fire. On the other side he met women and men running down the road toward the fire with their buckets. "Sound the alarm! Form a bucket brigade!" The adults lined up at the pump, while the children ran along the twisting lanes shouting, "Fire fire fire!"

The Iris Bottom bucket brigade was much larger and better organized than the pig farmers on the other side. Men carried the full buckets to the fire and threw the water on, women and children passed the empty buckets to the well. Two brawny men pumped for all they were worth, then were replaced by two other men. One of the pumpers fell away from the pump and spewed his breakfast on the ground. More men went to the pump and Shuibai pointed at one of them and said, "You, you're in charge of the pump. Keep it manned." Pointing at someone else, he said, "You, run to Low Marsh and call out the fire company." Then he ran downhill to direct the firefighting.

The wind was blowing from the south in a gentle breeze, driving the fire slowly toward the trees and the Capital Road. That meant the Iris Bottom brigade was on the wrong side to curtail the advance of the fire while the paltry bucket brigade on the other side was throwing their water with little effect. If the fire got into the trees it would be beyond his ability to fight. The thin line of weeds betwixt the briar patch and the woods was narrow, but the wind was not great, so perhaps it could be made to serve as a fire break. If he could get a hose in there. He had a sudden thought, but it had to await the arrival of Zashi and the fire company to bring him the equipment he needed.

Shuibai had gotten used to having obedient, trained firemen and proper equipment; fighting a fire by the old methods drove him to distraction. It was not a bad fire; with the proper equipment he could have knocked it down in a matter of minutes, but the bucket brigade was barely able to keep the path open while fire consumed increasingly large quantities of briar patch. It was then that Shuibai saw the dragon. It rose in smoke and shimmering heat waves, its form so insubstantial that at first he was not even certain he saw it. The sun shone through it as though shining through a grey curtain. It was not orange as it was usually portrayed, but grey and drear and sinuous. It eyes were two burning embers and they looked at him. It had no limbs, only a great snake-like body that rose and rose, coil after coil winding up from the flaming vegetation, writhing into the sky. When at last it cleared the fiery oasis, it streaked into the sky.

Shuibai stood wordlessly. Around him the work of fire fighting continued. Nobody paid any attention to the sky. He wanted to ask, "Did you see that?" but the beehive of activity around him showed no sign of any miraculous happening. Just then he heard Zashi's voice crying, "Make way for the Low Marsh Fire Company! Make way!" The fire wagon had arrived.

One pipeline was quickly laid from the well to the fire. The men were well versed in this particular evolution; it was the exact same work they had performed when burning the derelict wagon during the demonstration. Shuibai had no time to worry about dragons. He seized Zashi's sleeve and cried, "Lay a second line from the Capital Highway to the fire!"

"Is there a well over there?"

"Yes, but no pump. Take the fire wagon, you'll need it."

"Where are the others?"

"Split up. I don't know where. You'll see Red on your way up. Don't stop, he's dead," Shuibai replied grimly.

"What happened?"

"Murder and arson. Don't turn your back on anyone dressed in black. We've got to stop the fire from getting into the trees. If they catch we won't be able to stop it before the Capital Road. The shantytown will burn." The shantytown was located a little further along the highway, between Iris Bottom and Cherry Hill. At least a thousand refugees still lived in the woods in huts made of trash.

Zashi's face was pale. "Yes, Chief."

Shuibai slapped him on his fire-marked shoulder. "Get moving."

Zashi signaled the wagon, and six of the firemen pulled it between the walls of fire, the trail kept open by the bucket brigade. When he came abreast of the burning flesh the stench assaulted his nostrils, but the form was too blackened to be recognizable.

"Keep going!" he shouted, dropping pipes and screwing them together with short violent motions.

One of the firemen noticed, "Leather hat!" Only firemen wore leather hats.

"Keep going!" Zashi shouted, dropping a leather elbow, its lashing trailing.

"It's a fireman!" The firefighters stopped and turned, milling in dismay. "It's one of ours!"

"Keep going!" Zashi roared. "Worry about it later! We've got to stop the fire before it reaches the trees!"

They reluctantly returned to the traces. "What happened? Who is it?"

"I don't know," Zashi replied. "Shuibai will tell us later."

The wagon was heavy and they labored hard to get the load up the trail to the highway. Members of the bucket brigade threw down their buckets and seized the sides of the wagon and helped push, and a couple of women grasped what was wanted and started screwing the pipes together. Zashi ran ahead of the fire crew, limping on his left leg, the pain reminding him that what the Spirits gave they could also take. He prayed to keep his strength long enough to do what needed to be done, then quit worrying about it. What would happen would happen.

He found Manata, and the two of them ran back to meet the wagon. The wagon was laying pipe down the road towards them, so he ordered Manata to lift the water from the well in buckets and pour it into the end of the pipes. Gravity carried the water downhill. Zashi ran back down the hill to the fire front. The heat was intense. Sparks jumped and flakes of ash rained down. He was glad of the leather hat that protected his head and neck. He met

Shuibai as he led the hosemen in a careful advance along the dirt path. They had quenched the advance into the eastern briars and confined the fire to the west side of the trail. Water gurgled in Zashi's hose. He twisted the nozzle for maximum force, but the gravity fed stream was a trickle. He groaned. Shuibai evaluated the situation in an instant.

"Zashi! Keep our trail wetted down! Protect our line! I've got good pressure so we'll attack with this line! Where's the wagon? We need more pipe!"

"Up there." He tagged a woman and sent her running up to order the wagon down again. They needed any pipe left in it.

The stream of water that trickled out Zashi's line wasn't good for much of anything, but it was wet and it kept coming. Unfortunately, he had also run out of pipe. He was forced to supplement with a short bucket brigade to cover the final distance while he waited for the pipe wagon.

"You, you, you. Get buckets." He drafted a few intrepid women, who hiked their skirts above their knees and tucked the ends into their belts. They went to work. They filled buckets from the mouth of the weak line and manually carried water to soak the path along which the pressurized line ran. Shuibai's line lay in the mud, leaking at its joints, its own leaking helping to protect it from the fire. Heat beat at Zashi as he labored to keep the trail wetted down and to prevent the fire from jumping into the eastern briars again.

The Low Marsh firefighters laid more line, cussing the inflexible bamboo. They quickly ran out of leather elbows, and were forced to attack the fire from an awkward angle. They tried to beat it back enough to allow them to advance along its face and get between it and the trees. But without enough leather elbows to bend around properly, they couldn't get a good shot at the fire. The eaves of the far woods caught fire.

Shuibai tagged Zashi and said, "You have command of the fire. I'm going to order the people along the Capital Road to evacuate. Don't let anyone get trapped down here. We'll rendezvous at the Iris Bottom well if we get separated. The dragon is loose."

"You saw it?"

"I did. I was never much for praying, but there isn't much else we can do."

CHAPTER 34 : MUTUAL AID

Shuibai hiked east along the Capital Road and accosted everyone he met. "We can't control the fire. You must evacuate."

The refugees streamed out of the woods with their pitiful belongings on their backs. They didn't know where to go. Shuibai checked the wind, and said, "Go south, across the Lantern Bridge. You'll be safe on the other side."

In a grim mood, he reflected that if the fire got out of control and burned northeast, it could only burn as far as Cherry Hill before it met the burned district where there was nothing left to burn.

Satisfied the refugees were warned, he turned and trudged back the way he had come. He limped heavily, blood was matted into the front of his coat, his face was scratched up, and his speaking trumpet was bent. One of his firemen was dead and one was missing, and all because of the murderous vanity of the *taran*. He cursed the entire *taran* class thoroughly and quietly under his breath. Yet when he found Lord Chuja's body lying in the road, the bloody carcass of the white stallion beside him, it stopped him in his tracks. All around him lay the shambles of the ambush; dead men, wounded horses, dark red splatters and mud on the fine silk uniforms. The ornate armor of the *taran* had not protected them from the fury of the guns.

A girl of about twelve was going through the sleeves of the dead men and pocketing the things she found while adults kept their distance. He almost shouted at her to stop, but then he recognized the pinched face of hunger clad in layers of fine robes that had become torn and dirty through weeks of winter living— she was a refugee from the Cherry Hill Fire. Shuibai shut his mouth without speaking. Maybe there was a little justice in the world after all.

"Chief! Chief!" Axe shouted, running down the road towards him, short legs pumping like pistons under his barrel body.

"Axe! You're not dead!"

Axe jumped over the fallen bodies without looking at them. The dead were of no concern to the living, not when fire was on loose. "I ran up to Alla Far and they're turning out!"

Shuibai slapped him hard on the back, nearly knocking him down. "Good work! That's exactly what we need! Now find me a well with a pump; we need to lay a line. When Alla Far comes up, I want a line run down through the woods right there, between that big tree and that shack. Send me a runner when they show up—I'm going down that trail over there. Zashi's at the bottom with the Low Marsh company."

"I passed an inn a couple of furlongs west of here. They have a pump."

"Good. Meet Alla Far, tell them what I want."

"Yes, Chief." Axe ran back the way he had come.

Shuibai picked his way through the dead men and animals. Wagons halted and surveyed the carnage. Nobody wanted to get near the dead bodies. Traffic backed up, and Shuibai, who had taken it for granted that highways somehow kept themselves clear, was appalled to discover a crowd of porters, merchants, and pilgrims milling at the bottleneck. Belatedly he realized what the Fire Guard was good for: traffic control. Unfortunately, the only visible members of the Fire Guard were lying dead in the road with their Lord.

"The road is closed!" he shouted at them. "Go back where you came from!"

Nobody obeyed. They had their own business and didn't want to change their plans. Shuibai twisted his hands in frustration. White smoke swirled up toward the brilliant blue sky. The smell of burning pine and flesh was fragrant upon the air. "You're in danger! The fire's coming this way!"

Frightened murmurs ran through the crowd, then a merchant ordered her porters forward. The men picked their way amid the bodies, twisting a path through the bloodstains and sprawled forms, their bodies bent double under the burden on their backs. Slowly foot traffic followed, squeezing past the stalled oxcart and the dead bullock. The other bullock still lived and tossed his head, snorting and shaking the traces.

A few minutes later the Alla Far Fire Company No. 5 arrived with their buckets, hooks, ladders and a wagon with two hundred feet of the newfangled pipes with leather fittings. Following Axe's directions, they laid a line from the inn, but they ran out of line before reaching the place where Shuibai had wanted them to turn into the woods. When the Low Marsh wagon was found, it still had pipe, so Shuibai told the Alla Far Company to use what they needed. The woods were too rough to admit the wagon, so the firemen ported bundles of pipe into the woods by hand. By the time the new line was set up, the fire had gotten a good hold on the woods and was burning merrily, traveling through the canopy and dropping burning brands into the underbrush to start more fires. But the forceful stream provided by the new line reached up and extinguished the flames in the tops of the trees, and a new front was established. The fire, not to be thwarted, broadened its attack and began to creep westward toward a clearing where a hamlet devoted to the making of charcoal was located.

"We need another line!" Shuibai called.

The Fifth's foreman replied, "We've got a spare spigot sleeve, have you got anymore pipe?"

Shuibai had already laid better than nine hundred feet of pipe, but yes, he had more pipe. Another crew was rounded up, civilians drafted to supplement the efforts of firemen, and another pump was found many yards further west along the Capital Highway. Shuibai ran out of pipe before the line was completed, so he sent a runner to Zashi ordering him to dismantle the line from the Iris Bottom well and transfer the pipe. More citizens were drafted to move it. During the moving several bamboo pipes had their threads broken and Zashi cursed and wished he had enough leather hose to simply replace the cheap but unwieldy bamboo.

Three lines were the limit; they had used up all their piping and one line had little pressure. Now it was down to the grueling test of time. Could they keep the exposures wet enough to prevent them from catching while the fire burned itself out? The middle line had the best pressure and was assigned the job of wetting down the canopy of the woods while the other lines washed the ground and brush. Gradually the flames ebbed, and Shuibai ordered the high pressure line to attack the fire directly. Steam rose in hissing, billowing clouds and the fire front began to retract. "Sounds like a dragon, doesn't it?" one of the hosemen commented.

"Ha, he doesn't dare stick his head out of his lair as long as Low Marsh is here!"

"Hell, you would have been shit out of luck if we hadn't shown up to save your asses!" retorted a member of the Alla Far company.

"Would not!"

"Would too!" He swung the pipe and sprayed the Low Marsh company.

Low Marsh sprayed them back, and immediately a tussle was on. Shuibai, who was on the fire ground at the time, yelled, "Stop it! Put that water on the fire!"

The two companies gave each other dirty looks, but returned to their business.

"Everybody helped fight this fire. Nobody can do it alone!" Shuibai admonished them. Chastened, they stuck to their work.

Fire Chief Shuibai was aching, wet, dirty, bloody, and cold. The fire didn't need his direct attention anymore, so he tagged the lead hoseman and said, "I'm taking a break. You're in charge until either Zashi or I come back. Keep your mind on your work."

Shuibai hiked up to the Capital Highway and found that a crew of untouchables had been drafted from the shanty town east of the fire. They had delivered the mercy stroke to the wounded animals and were moving the dead to the side of the road. A team of skinny men was tying ropes around the carcass of the Fire Lord's white horse to drag it out of the road. *Taran* in the uniform of the Fire Guard arrived. They inspected the bodies of the slain and plunged into the woods to look for the assassins. Surprisingly, the Black Prince reappeared, the elbows and knees of His fine clothes torn and muddy. Shuibai almost bolted when he saw the black garbed figure, mistaking Him for one of the killers, but the Black Prince turned toward him and called, "Shuibai-don!"

Shuibai presented himself, dropping to his knees in the cold mud and bowing deeply.

"Get up, I can't see you down there," the Prince said peevishly. Given the circumstances it was not surprising that He was not in the best of humors. Shuibai rose. "What's the situation?" the Prince demanded.

"The fire is under control. We'll have it knocked down soon. I'm looking for water for the men."

"We've got beer," the Black Prince said. He gestured. Shuibai spotted Zashi gulping from a ladle while a boy with a bucket of beer waited.

"Excuse me," Shuibai said, his manners deserting him. He ran to the beer bucket.

Zashi looked up in surprise, then grinned. "Hey! I was worried about you!" He scooped up a ladle full of beer and handed it to

Shuibai, who drank it thirstily. He was parched and gulped the
entire ladle in single draught. Suddenly the world spun and his legs
gave out. He dropped to the ground and Zashi knelt beside him.
"Chief? Chief? Are you all right?"

"I'm busted. You're in charge. I gotta sit down." Shuibai tore
off his helmet, plunked his butt onto the ground, stretched out his
legs, and leaned against a tree.

Zashi rested his webbed hand on Shuibai's shoulder for a
moment. "Okay, Chief," he said. He bent swiftly and kissed
Shuibai's sweaty, matted hair, then rose and walked quickly away.
Shuibai's eyes popped open, but he was too late. Zashi was already
walking off. Shuibai sat on the side of the road grinning goofily.

People wouldn't leave him alone. The Black Prince was the
first to ask questions in His coarse foreign accent, "Are there any
survivors?"

Shuibai looked tiredly up at him. "You, me, Manata, Axe. Red
is dead. The Fire Lord's dead. That's all I know."

The Black Prince squatted down. He was wearing a simple
black half mask; if He'd been wearing anything fancier He'd have
lost it during the ambush. "Left and Right are dead. They were
good men. They didn't deserve to die this way." He wasn't looking
at Shuibai. His gaze was turned inward.

"None of us deserve to die this way, not for the sake of the silly
taran," Shuibai snapped.

The Black Prince looked sharply at him. Shuibai didn't flinch.
The Black Prince deigned to explain. "Chuja-don was *taran* to the
bone. I tried to tell him he shouldn't be feuding with Lady
Nayabashi, but he was too damn proud—"

"It's your fault." Shuibai said shortly. He rose from his seat.

"Me? What did I do?"

Shuibai scowled at him. "You're so damned certain Your way
is right, aren't You? You're as stiff-necked as Lord Chuja. You
think You can do things the way You want and everybody has to go
along because You're the mighty Black Prince. Well, maybe You're
right. Maybe these newfangled ideas of Yours are for the best. But
You can't force people to be wise, and You can't force them to like
You. You have to earn it. None of You Celestials understand that."
Shuibai picked up his helmet and wiped the mud off with his
sleeve. Then he used his fist to punch it back into shape. His

punches were more violent than necessary but he found it hard to control his feelings.

The Black Prince was shocked. "Chief Shuibai, these people hate me because I'm a foreigner. I can't do anything about that."

Shuibai shot him a look of contempt. "I was an untouchable, which is worse than being a foreigner. They made me Chief anyhow, and I'm doing my best to deserve it." He replaced the helmet on his head, the swan and bucket logo gleaming whitely against the dark leather. "Maybe they care more about what You do than Who You are."

Shuibai wasn't done with headaches. A white haired matron accosted him and snapped, "You told us to evacuate for no reason! Now half my furniture is gone and it's your fault!"

"What?" he said stupidly.

She slapped him. "Looters! Where were the guards?"

"The Fire Lord was assassinated—"

"That's no excuse!"

"Well, I thought the fire was out of control. I didn't know Alla Far would be coming—"

"Well, you should have!"

Her words rang in his head like a gong. He should have known. How perfectly logical. He should know what kind of equipment the neighboring companies had and where it was located so that if he faced a conflagration bigger than he could handle, he could call for help. He'd been lucky because Axe had done the right thing on his own initiative. The neighboring companies could aid one another in times of crisis—but only if they knew what they were doing. They had to plan ahead.

That Axe had done the right thing was as much a product of Shuibai's training as luck; but Shuibai gave himself no credit for that. "You're absolutely right," he told the woman.

"My beer!" she suddenly wailed, spotting the boy with the bucket and the firemen lining up.

"Thank you. It was good beer." Shuibai walked away.

A strange man in an Alla Far uniform accosted him. "Chief Shuibai!"

"Who are you?"

"I'm Lanai, foreman for the Fifth Alla Far Company."

"Oh, sorry, I didn't recognize you. What can I do for you?"

"We laid a lot of pipe today."

"We certainly did."

"I was wondering if you could be persuaded to part with some of that piping."

Shuibai's brain began to click. "I suppose I might. I was admiring those nice brass nozzles you've got."

The officer grinned. "They are good, aren't they? How many pipes can I get for one?"

"Hm. Twenty-five."

"Highway robbery. Fifty."

"Thirty."

"Forty."

"Thirty-five."

"With two leather elbows."

"Done."

The swap was made and Shuibai admired the nozzle. It was half as long as his forearm and quite heavy. It could be twisted open and closed. The water would fan out wide or tighten to a narrow stream depending on how far it was twisted. Shuibai liked it a lot.

CHAPTER 35 : JUSTICE IS GOLDEN

The Black Prince accosted Shuibai again. "Fire Chief Shuibai."

Shuibai steeled himself and turned. "Yes, My Prince?" he asked politely.

"I need a courier. The Ghostriders are dead or wounded. The Emperor must be warned immediately about what happened here. I'm afraid that these assassins did not act alone."

"I can go," Zashi said.

"Good. I can give you a pass." The Black Prince rummaged in his pocket.

"I don't need one," Zashi said quietly.

"Huh?"

"I'm an Avatar too." With that he closed his eyes and his skin crawled, then he suddenly swelled up large and dark, reptilian amber eyes glaring at them. Where once there had stood a young man, a dragon hovered instead. The Black Prince stared in shock, then the dragon said in a voice like the roaring of flames, "I will carry your message." The dragon leaped into the sky and arrowed into the west, and Zashi dropped unconscious on the pavement.

Shuibai dropped to his knees beside him, looking back and forth, but the dragon had vanished into the west. The Black Prince knelt and lifted his eyelids; Zashi's eyeballs were rolled into the back of his sockets and only the whites were visible. "Did you know about this?" the Black Prince demanded.

"Uh, sort of."

"Sort of?" the Black Prince queried. "I think you'd better tell me about it."

"Well, he believed in the dragon even when I didn't. And then his scar turned into a dragon tattoo, and then he knew things that nobody else knew. And now this. I know that sounds peculiar, but I don't know how to explain it."

The Black Prince closed Zashi's eyes. "Being an Avatar is not an easy thing. He needs to be trained properly or it will destroy him. I will take him into my household and teach him what he needs to know."

Shuibai bit his lip. "Will he be all right?"

The Black Prince shrugged. "I don't know. It isn't easy for any of Us Who are ridden by the Spirits. With help, yes, I think so."

Shuibai cradled Zashi's head in his lap. He bowed his head deeply. "I don't want anything bad to ever happen to him. If you can help him, then he should go with you."

The Black Prince laid a gentle hand on his shoulder. "You love him, don't you?" Shuibai didn't meet his eyes, but he nodded. "Good. That's the best thing for him."

Shuibai looked up in surprise. "Really?"

"Yes. I don't promise you that it will be easy, because it won't. But if you really care about him, then in the long run it will be all right."

The General of the Western Gate was marching along the Capital Road; his troops came up in rank after scarlet rank. They were dressed in full battle armor with pennants jutting up from the backs of their armor, flying the gate and sunset insignia of the Western Gate. They halted at the carnage in the road, and the General and his aides rode out in front to survey the situation. Most of the bodies had been moved already, leaving only a few bloody spots and horse carcasses in the roadway. The Black Prince called out, "Lord Kizo! There has been an assassination attempt."

The General dismounted and inspected the shambles. "So the Emperor feared, though who told him, I don't know."

The untouchables had fled to the side of the road and hidden in the trees; the General of the Western Gate detached one of his aides with orders to complete the clearing of the road. While they worked the General of the Western Gate introduced a man who rode with him. "You remember Lord Jozeein Omel, Captain Omel's younger brother. He's now Lord of the Highways."

The man so designated wore brown trousers in the country style with the lower legs wrapped tight with cloths around his calves and thrust into pointy-toed brown boots. His jacket had a mallard insignia, and he wore brown armor laced with rust colored laces. He was positively dowdy next to the brightly colored urban *taran*.

"Yes, I remember very clearly. It's good to see you again, though I'm surprised that you made it here so quickly."

"The Emperor called me posthaste, so I rode express all the way from Ii province to Alla Far. He has briefed me on the situation, and Kizo-don is kind enough to lend me the troops necessary to carry out my duties until my own troops arrive. I'm afraid a regiment cannot be shipped by express mail."

"I won't keep you then. But this—" the Black Prince indicated the ambush site, "You need to know about. We suspect the Sakoro Clan—"

"I recognized her voice. It was Lady Omo, the Hooded Woman," Shuibai put in. They all looked at him.

"You're certain?" the Black Prince asked.

"Absolutely. I've met her before."

"Arrest her," the Black Prince said.

"Gentlemen, we have our work cut out for us. Let us be on our way." The General called his officers into a huddle and within a few minutes they had their orders.

Shuibai lifted Zashi's inert body and carried him to the side of the road. He sat on the ground and cradled him in his arms as he watched the scarlet ranks go marching past. The tramp of the soldiers' feet was loud and rhythmic, like the beating of a drum. It took a long time for them all to pass. When they were finally gone, he found a bucket with a little water in the bottom. He dipped the hem of his sleeve in the water and used it to pat Zashi's face.

Zashi's eyes fluttered open and he stared, then coughed and sat up. A dark shape hurtled through the air, then suddenly drew up short, and landed on its feet in front of them. It was a small lizard, purple-black and wingless, about a fathom long including the tail. It ran up to Zashi and raced around his coat, finally perching on his shoulder, its claws gripping the canvas coat, tail running down Zashi's back, head hanging down the front. The reptile looked at Shuibai with amber eyes and hissed at him.

"I don't think that's a normal lizard," Shuibai said in a strangled voice.

Zashi smiled and stroked its head. The lizard closed its eyes and puffed out its throat in pleasure. The creature became very relaxed as Zashi petted it. "No, it's not," he agreed. "I think I've got a pet now."

The crimson and gold banners of the Imperial party came into sight at that moment and Zashi rose to his feet. He did not kowtow, not even when the Golden Emperor reined up abreast of them. Shuibai's heart was thudding, but he remained standing beside Zashi, even though he was more than a little worried.

The Emperor wore golden armor that was laced with crimson laces. His armor shone in the brilliant sunlight, so dazzling bright it hurt the eyes to look upon Him. He regarded Zashi and the lizard, and the lizard lazed on Zashi's shoulder, unperturbed by the other Presence. "So You are the One who sent Us a message," the Golden Emperor said at last.

Zashi bowed as if to an equal. "I am Kwaji, the Fire Dragon." His voice was deeper and his accent archaic; it was not Zashi who was speaking.

The Black Prince stepped up beside the Golden Emperor and looking up, he said, "I've offered Him a place in My house so He can learn the duties of an Avatar."

"That's very wise. We appreciate all the services You have rendered Us, but We are most interested in an orderly queendom." His hand dropped familiarly onto the Black Prince's shoulder, and the Black Prince kissed the back of His hand. "If You will serve Our people as We serve them, then You are welcome for as long as You choose to abide among Us."

Zashi dropped to his knees and bowed, the lizard clinging tightly to his shoulder, "Thank you, My Emperor. I've tried not to cause any trouble. I've tried to help the people who were doing good." Zashi was speaking in his own voice now. "But it's been hard, because I don't really understand, and I've had the strangest impulses." He looked imploringly at Shuibai.

Shuibai knelt beside him and put his arm around Zashi's shoulders. "He's my Deputy Chief and a good one. I can vouch for him."

The two couples regarded each other for a long moment, then the Golden Emperor nodded. "Good enough. Brice-don, I think We've done as much as We can do. Let's go home." He offered His arm and the Black Prince took it, and the Emperor hauled the dark lord up onto the horse with Him, the Black Prince's arms going around His waist. The Emperor lifted His hand in farewell. "Peace upon you all," He said. Then He turned His horse's head and rode toward the setting sun, His bodyguards surrounding Him in a heavily armored phalanx.

CHAPTER 36 : FLOWERS OF WAR

Shuibai woke in the cold. He turned over, but Zashi wasn't there. With a sigh he rose and went to the hearth to stir up the embers and build a fire. Stepping into trousers and high-soled wooden sandals, he donned his fire coat and ambled out the back door and down the alley to the privy. Woodsmoke was heavy in the air. When he came to the bottom of the alley, he stopped and stared. Tendrils from a thousand cook fires rose in lazy dark columns above the opposite riverbank. A tent city had sprouted during the night, and here and there he could see the brilliant green and purple banners of the Iris Lord, one of the most powerful of the provincial lords, and leader of the Neutrals.

Shuibai stepped into the outhouse and relieved himself. Doing up his trousers, he stepped out and looked again. The scene was no mirage; an army was still encamped across the river. The war against Pangu had been far away, and aside from the increase in taxes to pay for it, had not meant much to him, even if his father had gone west as a laborer with the army. Now, however, war was camped right on his doorstep. As Fire Chief he wondered what would happen to his town and how he was going to deal with it, but as a man, he was terrified.

Staring at the army didn't tell him anything, so he went back up to his shop and let himself in. Kanko was awake and making breakfast, but when Shuibai returned, he went to the privy himself. He came tearing back, shouting, "An army, master!"

"I know," said Shuibai.

Pretty soon everyone knew. The residents who lived along the river could not fail to discover the ominous presence, and word swiftly flew through the town. More ominous still, a sudden clatter banged on the wooden shutter at the front of his shop. He and Kanko looked at each other, then Shuibai rose and went to the front of the shop. He slid back the paper screen, then the wooden shutter. A young man in the yellow, white, and black garb of the Imperial Post was outside on his horse.

"I have a message for Fire Chief Shuibai of Low Marsh. Is he here?"

"That's me."

"The Lord of the Highways commands you to attend him immediately at the Lantern Gate post station. He said to bring your maps and anything else that might be useful to him."

Shuibai's jaw dropped.

"Immediately!" the courier snapped.

"Yes, sir. I'll get my things."

The courier wheeled away and Shuibai went to gather up the maps he and Zashi used to enforce the fire code. "When Zashi shows up, tell him I've gone to the Lord of the Highways at the Lantern Gate. If he doesn't show up within the hour, sound the assembly code and tell the firemen to look for him. Tell them to fill all the cisterns in town as they do it. There might be a fight."

"Yes, master," the boy replied with saucer-sized eyes.

"Don't go outside. I don't want anything to happen to you."

Shuibai hiked swiftly to the post station. He had to push his way through the crowd of people gathered on the Low Road. Arriving at the front, he found *taran* guards in the yellow uniforms of the Imperial Post had fortified the gate and street. A sharp pointed spear blocked his way.

"You there! Get back. The bridge is closed."

"I've been summoned by the Lord of the Highways. I'm the Fire Chief of Low Marsh."

The guard passed him. Arriving at the post station, he was stopped once again and not admitted until word was passed inside and permission granted. A soldier escorted him across the courtyard and onto the veranda of the house that served as offices and sleeping quarters for the officers. A barracks to the left and stable to the right housed the post riders and their horses. The place was jammed with *taran* called up to supplement the usual post riders and guards.

Shuibai was admitted to an office in the left wing of the house. A bevy of *taran* in silk and brocade uniforms attended a man in much plainer dress. He wore brown hemp divided skirts tucked into calf high well-used brown leather boots. He wore a yellow surcote with black and white trim over it, but the surcote only partially covered the brown armor with its rust colored laces. A blue-green mallard mask of rustic workmanship covered his face. Like most *taran*, he wore his hair in a long braid, but his hair was thin and his braid was not as thick and long as some. He was a man in his prime, taller than average, stocky but not fat, and when he spoke, he did so in the nasal accent of the northern provinces.

"Rise, Chief Shuibai. We won't stand on ceremony. I'm told you have a recent map of the Low Marsh area, and that you yourself know the area very well."

Shuibai rose. "I have maps I've made for my own use, Noble Lord. I'm sure they're not as good as your maps."

The Highway Lord gestured to the map on the wall. "It's twenty years old. I don't know this area, but I've already found a dozen places where it's out of date."

Shuibai opened his scroll case and extracted his maps. "It's only Low Marsh, sir," he said apologetically. "That's my jurisdiction."

An aide took the maps in a black gloved hand and delivered them to his commander. Lord Omel perused them intently. "Every street and building in Low Marsh and the Iris Bottom. Very detailed. Yes, I see. Nothing outside it. Still, it's useful. I'd like to borrow them. I'll have my cartographer copy them and return them to you."

"Of course, Noble Lord." Shuibai bowed deeply.

"Come upstairs with me. I wish to ask you questions about the land around us."

So Shuibai followed the lord and his staff upstairs. The aides opened the sliding door to a sleeping chamber and they walked into the spacious room. It belonged to the commander of the post station and was elegantly appointed. All the sleeping gear was put away in the closet, so the floor was mostly clear. Another *taran* opened the window and they had a view of the Lantern Gate, the bridge, and the terrain on the opposite side. Iris Battalion soldiers were camped on both sides of the Southern Highway.

"How deep is the water above the bridge?"

"I don't know," Shuibai replied.

"What about below the bridge?"

"I don't know that. I'm sorry, sir." He backed away, afraid of the wrath of a thwarted *taran*.

"Don't skulk. Stay here by the window."

Mortified and frightened, Shuibai crept closer to the window, but tried to keep out of arm's reach of the Lord of the Highways. Not that it would do any good. He was trapped in a room with half a dozen *taran*. Whatever happened, he wouldn't escape.

"The river widens as it flows through the marshes. It would be bad footing, but it might be passable, especially if the marsh has frozen. What do you think?"

"I have no idea, sir. I've never been in the marshes."

The man turned to look at him. "They're right next door."

"I was never out of Low Marsh before I was appointed Fire Warden. Now I've been to Cherry Hill and Alla Far. Please forgive me for being a useless peasant, Noble Lord," Shuibai dropped to his knees and bowed to the floor.

Lord Omel dropped to one knee beside him. His blue-green leather glove lifted Shuibai's chin. "You only know what you know, Chief. Now stand up and don't be afraid." His baritone voice was kind.

Before Shuibai could answer, the sound of pistols cracked through the air and a clamor arose. The Lord of the Highways strode swiftly out of the room, across the hall, and into the opposite apartment. He flung open the paper window before his aides could reach it. Beyond the wall the banners of Cherry Hill were flying, all red and pink and white in the gloom of a winter morning. Drums reverberated and the clash of weapons sounded loud in the street outside. The lord said nothing. He whirled and strode out and down the stairs. His staff followed. Shuibai brought up the rear.

More shots echoed in the narrow confines of the street. The whine of bullets thunked into the masonry of the walls. Shuibai looked to the gate, but it was securely barred. He had never been inside the post station before, but he saw now that it was deliberately designed as a fort. *Taran* archers stood on the ramparts and drew their asymmetrical longbows to fire down on the attackers. The lord went up to the rampart and took a quick look. Bullets whined around him and he ducked behind the parapet.

As he came down from the rampart, the lord said, "We must hold the bridge at all costs. Couriers!" The lord gave the identical message to three of the yellow-uniformed riders. They would each take a different route and hope one of them lived to deliver the message. "Post Captain. You will hold the post station with your men. You are to give us cover fire as we make a sortie. I'll take fifty men with me. Chief Shuibai, follow me."

The Lord of the Highways led his troops to the postern gate on foot. It was a small door and had a path down to the river for drawing water and delivering supplies by boat. He gave them brief instructions, "When we leave, the soldiers on the opposite shore will see us and start firing. Everyone is to split up as soon as he leaves the gate and find cover if possible in the rough ground behind the station. We will work our way as quickly as possible to the top of the slope and travel behind the shops lining the Southern Highway. Our goal is to strike the flank or rear of the attackers and drive them into Low Marsh and away from the gate. Chief Shuibai, you will stick with me and be our guide through the neighborhood."

Shuibai turned very pale, but he nodded quickly. The postern door was thrown open and the first soldiers leaped out. They scattered and ran across the slope and among the shrubbery and willow trees bare of leaves. Lord Omel darted out, and then the rest of his troops. Shuibai's nerve almost failed him, but he didn't hear any shooting from the southern bank, so he darted out last and went scrambling up the hillside as fast as his legs could carry him. He searched for the brown of the Highway Lord's uniform, saw him sheltering behind a willow tree, and darted over to him. The lord saw him, and pulled him next to him behind the thick tree trunk.

The Iris Battalion didn't open fire. The rest of the warriors reached the top of the hill and took shelter amid the sheds and fences behind the buildings that faced the street. The soldiers leapfrogged in skirmish order, going from cover to cover, and glancing into the gaps as they passed. They could see the blossom uniforms of the mounted archers, but here and there amid them were the black uniforms of the pistol-toting soldiers of the Hooded Woman, the Lady Omo Sakoro.

The Lord of the Highways knelt behind a chicken coop and motioned for Shuibai. "Show us the way. Take us as far along their line as you can manage."

Shuibai's mouth was dry. He was far more frightened than when fighting a fire. Fire might very well kill him, but it held no personal malice towards him. He nodded, then jumped up and darted across the opening between the chicken coop and the brush fence that surrounded the yard behind the next building. The lord motioned his troops, and they followed Shuibai. Lord Omel darted across with them, and Shuibai kept going. In a few minutes he had reached the end of the cluster of shops. A wide open lot and a low boggy spot separated them from another cluster of half a dozen buildings.

The lord motioned, and the troops gathered themselves. Suddenly, fifty men burst out from behind the shops and charged into the mass of troops in the street. Surprise caused the Cherry Hill troops to waver, and the close quarters prevented the use of missile weapons. Lord Omel did not join his troops in the charge. He, his bodyguard, and Shuibai remained where they were.

Suddenly a mighty cheer went up from south of the bridge, and in a moment came the rumble of thousands of booted feet charging across the bridge to the gate. The Imperial Post Guards fell back with Cherry Hill in pursuit.

"The gate is open! The battle is lost, Noble Lord!" Of the soldiers who had made the sortie, only half returned.

"Fall back to the post station!" The Highway Lord leaped to his feet and drew his sword. He and his troops fought as they retreated back to whence they'd come.

Shuibai was no warrior. He ran like a rabbit and reached the postern gate well ahead of them. He pounded on the door. "Open up! Open up! The lord is retreating!"

The door opened. If he went inside, he'd be trapped. Instead, he darted down the hill turned to stumble and clamber over the uneven ground between the post station and the river. He feared Iris soldiers would shoot him, but nobody did. He gained the safety of the riverbank underneath the bridge. The stout timbers and stone piers of the foundation rose like a forest around him. He caught his breath while listening to the thunder of boots storming across the bridge. Much to his surprise, the Lord of the Highways and his bodyguard skidded through the mud beside him.

"Good thinking," grunted the lord. "I don't want to be trapped in the post station. Now where?"

CHAPTER 37 : THE BURNING OF LOW MARSH

Shuibai poked his head out, but the buildings on the west side of the highway were built so close together that there was barely any space between the bridge and the buildings. Being a firefighter, he had learned to look up and take note of everything around himself; he waited until the rearguard of the Iris Battalion had crossed the bridge, then motioned to the *taran* behind him. They slipped and scrambled along the face of the riverbank. Five to fifteen feet above them were the foundations of the buildings. Low Marsh had been a marsh, but the boggy terrain along the river had been filled with stone and dirt to create a steep drop off from the level of the street to the river. They splashed through freezing mud and their boots broke through the ice that rimmed the edge of the river. It stank. Privies emptied into the river at the end of every street. Much to Shuibai's surprise, the *taran* didn't complain.

Reaching the foot of his own street, Shuibai scrambled up the steep bank by grabbing onto rocks and weeds. He led them to his own back door and let them in. The sound of combat could be heard as a distant crack of pistol fire. The people of Low Marsh were either fleeing or hiding in their houses. Nobody saw the lord slip into Shuibai's back door.

Shuibai bowed to the *taran* as they entered. "Welcome to my humble home. I'm sorry it's so miserable. Kanko, make tea for the gentlemen!"

Kanko was completely astonished. He had no idea who the strangers were, but the sight of *taran* warriors made him leap to his feet, then bow like a bobbing marionette. He grabbed the tea kettle and put it under the spigot. They had a barrel of water delivered each week now; he didn't have to go to the well.

"We need to send a courier to the Capital to let them know the Lantern Gate is lost," the Lord of the Highways said, consulting Shuibai's map. "Tell the reinforcements—"

Suddenly Shuibai's head came up and he paid no attention to the lord's words. He ran to the front of the house, tore open the screen and shutter, and sniffed again.

"What is it?" the Highway Lord asked.

"Fire. I'm sorry, Noble Lord. I must leave you to fend for yourself. I have a fire to fight." He grabbed the hammer and tapped the assembly code on the bell. That done, he tested the wind and his face grew grim. "The wind is from the east."

Lord Omel didn't need an explanation. "They've fired the town. Very well. Send a message to your local garrison. I'm calling them up."

"We don't have a local garrison. We're a Free Town," Shuibai said apologetically.

"The next town then."

"That's Crane Marsh. They're a Free Town, too. The nearest *taran* town is Alla Far itself. Well, actually, the nearest is Cherry Hill, but that won't do you any good."

For the first time, Shuibai saw the Lord of the Highways express frustration as he clenched his fists. "Very well. Alla Far." He turned and gave instructions to his bodyguard.

Firemen swiftly assembled. Although the chaos at the eastern end of the town disturbed them all, they welcomed the fire alarm. Fire they understood. They had no idea what to do about a battle, but they knew how to battle fire.

Lord Omel spoke, "Chief Shuibai! If you go to fight that fire, you and your men could be killed."

Shuibai bowed. "That's no different from any other day, Noble Lord." Turning back to his men, he said, "Low Marsh Fire Company, form up!"

The men fell into position. Each man knew his job and brought his assigned equipment. At Shuibai's command, they marched along the Low Road and headed directly towards the smell of smoke and sound of battle.

They met townsfolk running away. Nobody carried anything with them; they were running for their lives. "Soldiers are fighting!" somebody warned them, but they already knew that. They kept marching.

Shuibai knew every block of his town. He and Zashi had walked it, mapped it, studied it, and laid their plans. He knew where the streets large enough to serve as fire breaks were and where all the wells, pumps, and cisterns were. He didn't know exactly where the fire was, but he laid out several contingency plans in his mind. Looking up at the sky, his heart fell as he saw five columns of smoke climbing above the town between

Broadway and the river. Three were heavy and showed that buildings were well engaged while two were fainter where fire had just taken hold. He halted the company and studied them.

"Runners! Call out Crane Marsh and Alla Far for support. Tell Alla Far we need the Fire Guards for protection from enemy troops." Two designated runners peeled away and took off at a sprint. To the rest he said, "We'll use East Street and Broadway as our firebreaks."

The men's faces turned white. "But Chief, we'll lose five blocks between East Street and the Southern Highway!" Axe protested.

"We're going to lose them anyway," Shuibai said, pointing at the sky. "There aren't enough of us to fight five fires at once. The first two blocks will be consumed before we even get there. We'll tear down the buildings on the east side of East Street. We'll need every hand we can get."

Turning, he trotted forward, shouting, "Every able-bodied man required for bucket brigade! Free beer afterwards!"

His recruiters took up his cry and banged on shutters and doors. "Turn out for the bucket brigade! Free beer! Turn out for the bucket brigade!"

They picked up thirty men who were willing to do anything for free beer. Shuibai parceled them out in squads with an experienced firefighter at the head of each. Turning up East Street, he dropped teams off at intervals. They met women and men hauling handcarts and lugging burdens on their back while their children cried and clung to their sleeves. They were following the Low Road, but as long as the wind was out of the east, the fire would pursue them. "Go north!" he told them. Nobody listened to him. The Low Road was broad and well maintained. It followed the river to Crane Marsh, then turned up into the southern part of the invincible Capital where nothing could hurt them, not even the Fire Dragon.

With a resounding crash the facade of a two story building toppled into the street. The Low Marsh Fire Company was at work. Whenever Shuibai saw a refugee without a burden run past, he shouted, "Hey you! Form bucket brigade!" Most of them ignored him.

They had been at work only a little while when black uniforms clattered past. The sound of horseshoes rang on the pavement and he whirled around. One of the black masked *taran* spoke to him, "Fall back. The town is burning."

"You run," Shuibai replied scornfully. "We're firefighters. We stand our ground."

"Fool," the warrior replied. He put spurs to his horse and galloped away.

Pink, white, and red uniforms with cherry blossom insignia retreated into the town on foot. They used their bows and arrows to shoot at whoever was pursuing them, but Shuibai couldn't see their attackers. Still, he heartened to see the rebels on the defensive. Shouting through his speaking trumpet, he called, "Runner!" A man appeared and he dispatched him with a message for the Lord of the Highways.

He could hear the fire now. The roar was unseen beyond the buildings his firefighters were busy tearing down. The smoke above his head was a thick black wall. He could taste the soot in the air and bits of ash floated down into the street. He looked hastily left and right, but only about half the buildings had come down that needed to come down. As he watched, another house collapsed under the assault of the firefighters. When it did, he could see the orange flames leaping above the house behind it. Judging it carefully, he thought the fire was still a block away. He could feel the breeze shifting—air was starting to flow into the base of the fire. The breeze continued to be from the east, but here on the west side of the fire, the air rushed into the base of the superheated column, creating the illusion of a western breeze. That frightened him. It was the sign of an impending firestorm. Low Marsh would burn like Cherry Hill had. He and his men were standing right in its path. It was time to fall back. Unfortunately, there was no broad north and south street for many blocks. Not even Narrow Way would serve because new construction was already in progress on the burned lots. Still, it was only partially rebuilt, so he would have less to tear down.

"Chief Shuibai!" shouted a familiar voice.

Shuibai whirled to see Zashi loping along at the head of a contingent of the Alla Far Fire Company. A troop of twenty men on foot was well ahead of their wagon. "We came at a run as soon as we got your message!"

The cherry blossom uniforms abandoned the street, penetrating deeper into Low Marsh. Hard on their heels came the green and purple uniforms of the Iris Battalion. Arrows whizzed and fell among the retreating pink and red uniforms. Some of the *taran* fell dead or wounded in the street. Whizzing arrows stuck into the wooden buildings and quivered when they missed their targets.

A squad of Iris soldiers pointed their bows at the firefighters. "Surrender or die!"

"We're firefighters!" Zashi shouted at them.

Shuibai raised his silver speaking trumpet in indication of his rank. "It's a criminal offense to interfere with firefighters doing their duty!"

The bows wavered and the firemen waited tensely. The *taran* weren't sure what to do, but they could see that the firefighters weren't armed with conventional weapons, although they had axes and grappling hooks for demolishing buildings.

"We have to tear down everything on this street to make a fire break! We don't have time to argue with you! Help or get out of the way!" Shuibai shouted through his speaking trumpet. Turning to Zashi he said, "Deploy your men. Take down that building and the one next to it. I'm going south to see what it's like further down the road. If you must fall back, the rendezvous is Broadway and Narrow Way. Narrow Way is our secondary firebreak. If you get there before I do, tear it down."

"Yes, Chief." Turning to his men, Zashi gave orders. Alla Far fanned out and ignored the soldiers, flinging their grappling hooks up over the ridgepoles of the houses to pull them down. The soldiers had to scamper to avoid collapsing houses. Making up their minds, they ran west in pursuit of the rebels.

Shuibai was too busy to worry about the revolt. He ran south along East Street to inspect the progress. The first teams he had put to work had made good headway, but still, he needed more men. Why didn't Crane Marsh come up? They were closer than Alla Far. He knew the answer, though. They weren't very well organized.

Embers dropped into the debris along East Street. All his men were busy tearing down the buildings; he had no bucket brigade and not enough men to form one. He decided it was better to let the debris burn than to take men away from the task of pulling down houses.

"Runner! Second alarm. Go to Crane Marsh, then up to Alla Far. Get me at least three more fire companies." The Capital was so big, it had more than a dozen fire companies of its own. The man took off at a sprint.

A different runner came up to Shuibai. "Deputy Fire Chief Mizaka says he's falling back. We can't hold it here. We don't have enough men."

"Acknowledged." Taking up his speaking trumpet, he cried, "Fall back! Tear down Narrow Way!"

His own home lay only a few blocks west of Narrow Way. If the fire didn't stop it there, his place would go, too. Not only that, but the fire would be in the densely built part of town with four story buildings and no space between them. He made sure all of his men retreated, then ran along behind them. He could feel the heat on his back and hear the fire roaring behind him.

Shuibai was the last one to arrive at the rendezvous. They hadn't waited for him; they knew what to do. The buildings between Strait Place and Narrow Way were coming down fast. Looking about, he was heartened to see more firefighters—another company from Alla Far had arrived. Women were screeching and trying to stop the firefighters from destroying their shops and homes.

Zashi shook off a woman impatiently. "Run. The fire is coming. We can't hold it at East Street."

"My shop!"

"Is already lost."

"No! You have to save it!"

Shuibai came up. "Reverend Mother, it can't be done. The wind is from the east. The fire will melt through the intervening blocks in less than half an hour."

Zashi said, "Less than that. Once it jumps East Street, we have twenty minutes at most."

"Where are the Fire Guards?" Shuibai asked.

"Fighting Cherry Hill troops on the Capital Highway," Zashi replied.

"All right. We have to do our own enforcement. You have permission to hit anyone who doesn't cooperate, including women. We must stop the fire here or we'll lose the whole town."

"Right, Chief," Zashi replied.

Shuibai made himself chief enforcer. He smacked several women before the rest got the message. The refugees worked as rapidly as they could to clear out their tools and clothes and other valuables. Ashes dropped down among them, then a live ember. The roaring crept nearer, but the buildings kept falling. Then a grappling hook pulled down a house and spilled a load of fire into the debris of demolition. Flames jumped up amid the ruins.

"Here it comes!" Zashi shouted.

"Hose!" Shuibai shouted. His hose team laid down a stream of water and doused the first flames in their firebreak.

"Zashi, finish those buildings, then tear down this side of Narrow Way. I'll command the hose teams."

"Right, Chief."

The heat rolled over them and soot coated their faces. Shuibai pulled his kerchief up over his face and donned his leather gauntlets. An ember rattled off his helmet, bounced on his shoulder, and fell to the ground. "Alla Far hose team! Wet us down!"

The Alla Far hosemen drenched Shuibai and all the other firefighters. They were now soaking wet on a winter day, but they weren't cold. The fire was a block away, but its hot breath covered them all.

CHAPTER 38 : THE FIRE DRAGON

Something cold and wet stung Shuibai's cheek. At first he thought it was a stray droplet from the hose, but he wasn't close enough to catch its spray. Then he thought it was a tear from his bleary, aching eyes, but it wasn't that, either. Another one hit his other cheek, then his nose. Something splatted onto his right shoulder. Staring stupidly around him, he saw the dark spots appear in the hard-packed dirt of the Narrow Way. He held out his gauntlet and more and more dark spots appeared on his glove, his sleeve, and his chest.

"It's raining!" he howled in delight.

The sprinkle turned into a shower which turned into a downpour. The temperature dropped noticeably and the flames in the debris smoked heavily. As he watched, a great grey serpent rose from the debris. He could see fire and half-toppled walls through its transparent body, but he wasn't even sure he saw the creature, so much did it resemble a column of smoke twisting and curling into the sky. Yet when he looked up, two orange eyes that flickered like fire were looking down—at Zashi.

The Deputy Fire Chief stood in the street with arms upraised to the sooty creature. The Fire Dragon hovered in the air a few feet above the debris, Its sinuous body rippling like the smoke It was made of. Silent communication passed between Spirit and Avatar. Suddenly, It shot into the sky and disappeared into the darkness of the streaming rain.

Everyone froze as the cold, cold rain soaked them. The flames dwindled, hissed, and in a quarter of an hour, died. Smoke continued to rise from the ruins, so they took their hooks and overhauled the debris. Flames flared up when the smoldering embers were exposed to air, but the play of the hose extinguished them. They could feel the banked heat beneath the soggy top, so kept overhauling the debris. Exposed embers hissed as the rain quenched them, and quenched the firefighters too, until they were as cold, black and dreary as the ashes they stirred.

Another company from Alla Far came up while they were overhauling the debris. They were glad to have the help. Zashi and Shuibai released the civilians they'd drafted, who immediately said, "Beer. You promised us beer."

"So I did. Zashi, send a detachment to find beer and bring it here."

Fifteen minutes later a keg was set on a foundation stone and the top broken in. Beer was ladled out with the tin cups that had come along with the beer, and the civilians got their drinks. Zashi and Shuibai started rotating the firefighters through breaks, starting with Low Marsh since they were on the scene first. One keg wasn't enough, so Zashi dispatched his scavengers to bring another.

Eventually Zashi and Shuibai got cups of their own. They were standing together chugging beer to wash the soot out of their throats when the clatter of hooves came up. The two of them turned around and were surprised to see the Golden Emperor mounted on a golden horse flanked by the Iris Lord and the Lord of the Highways. The rain soaked them as much as the firefighters, and their banners and surcotes were sodden. The Golden Emperor and His retainers reined up to survey the damage. All the firefighters quickly got down on their knees and kowtowed.

A swath ten blocks long between the Southern Highway and Narrow Way had burned. Nothing more than six feet high was left standing. The teahouse where Shuibai had been attacked by the gangsters was gone. So was the bath house where they gotten drunk after the Cherry Hill fire. The tannery across from where he had had his first shop was gone. A smoking black ruin lay between Broadway and the river. The Lantern Gate still stood, and so did the post station and bridge.

"Rise, Chief Shuibai, Deputy Chief Mizaka," the Golden Emperor said in His mellifluous voice.

Cautiously they looked up from where they crouched. Shuibai was astonished to see the Iris Lord in company with the Golden Emperor. He asked, "What happened?"

The Golden Emperor replied, "Lord Tellani sided with the government. He let the rebels think they had won him over, so they thought he was coming to reinforce them, and opened the Lantern Gate to him. His troops have crushed the rebellion. Tell me, Chief, is it safe for Our troops to occupy the Lantern Gate?" He gestured to the ruins, His box kite sleeve drooping like a sodden flag.

Zashi and Shuibai consulted, then Chief Shuibai spoke, "Yes, Your Grace, but go around the burned area. It's still hot in spite of the rain. Keep a lookout in case the wind shifts and carries sparks. We will continue to overhaul the debris around the edges, but it's too large to suppress. We have to let nature take its course. That will take several days."

"So long?" asked Lord Tellani.

"No, not long at all. Thanks to the rain, this should be cold in less than a week," Zashi replied.

"It's been a bad year for fires," the Golden Emperor replied.

"It was a very dry year. The drought dried out everything," Shuibai replied.

"So it did. And the Fire Dragon?" the Emperor continued.

"Pacified, Your Grace," Zashi said. He smiled up at the man. The Golden Emperor was one of the few people in the country who understood what he meant.

The Lord of the Highways said, "Thank you for your hard work, Chief. Tell your men, too."

"Thank you, Noble Lord." The new Lord of the Highways was very different from the previous one. Not that he knew either of them well, but this one didn't terrify him. "I wish you were the new Fire Lord," he couldn't help adding.

The Highway Lord gave him half a smile. "Why is that?"

Shuibai was abashed. How could he say what he was thinking? He hedged, "You didn't yell at me about the dirt when we were making our escape."

The lord shook his head. "I've had manure on my boots plenty of times, Chief. I know where to find soap when I want it."

That remark made Shuibai wish even more fervently that the man was the new Fire Lord. He transferred his gaze to the Iris Lord. "Are you going to be the new Fire Lord?"

The Iris Lord was taken aback. "No," he said shortly.

The Golden Emperor replied, "Lord Tellani is lord of one of the largest provinces in the country. He has done Us a great service. A minor position like Fire Lord is not an adequate reward."

The Lord of the Highways looked across to the Iris Lord and asked humorously, "How about Lord of the Highways? You saved the country, not me."

The green mask concealed the Iris Lord's expression, but he replied politely, "That office is already filled by a worthy gentleman."

The Highway Lord addressed himself to the Golden Emperor. "I think I might like to be Fire Lord. You know I'm not an ambitious man. I've been following Your improvements in the Capital with great interest. I think I could do some good if I were Fire Lord."

Shuibai and Zashi gaped at each other. Lord of the Highways was one of the most powerful offices in the country. It maintained the highway and post office, so controlled the movement of people, goods, and information.

The Golden Emperor smiled warmly at the Lord. "Omel-don, I love and admire you as one of the greatest men our country has ever known. If you sincerely wish it, I will grant it to you."

The Highway Lord turned to Shuibai and Zashi. He asked seriously, "I don't know anything about the fire service. What would my duties be?"

The two firefighters looked at each other, then Shuibai answered, "Enforce the fire code for the Capital District. Provide security at fires to prevent looting. Enforce cooperation with bucket brigades and demolition. Investigate arson. Administer justice. Our previous Fire Lord was effective at all but the last."

"You have some novel ideas about firefighting, I've heard. You've made pipes to carry water instead of buckets. Will you show me?"

"Of course, Noble Lord."

The *taran* watched curiously as Shuibai ordered the Low Marsh Fire Company back to duty.

"Hose company, charge the line!" A team of men ran up to Broadway to pump the well.

"Line charged!" the man at the nozzle called out.

"Hooks, overhaul debris!"

Men with hooks sprang forward, and wading carefully into the sodden ashes, raked through the debris until they found a hot spot. They stepped aside as a small flame flared up.

"Hose, quench!"

The brass nozzle was twisted and the two men managing the bamboo hose laid a stream of water directly at the base of the flame. It went out instantly.

"Cease pumping!"

The command was repeated from man to man so that those all the way at the well could hear it.

"Drain the line."

The men worked diligently to clear up their equipment and collect all the hose they'd laid. The wagon rattled as they pulled it by hand over the muddy lane. It got stuck and they worked together to push and pull it out. They picked up pipes and laid them in the wagon, then secured the pieces of bamboo with ropes to keep them from rolling around.

"They work like soldiers. Were any of them in the military?" the Iris Lord asked.

"No. Half of them are untouchable and most of them are illiterate," Shuibai replied.

"How much do you pay them?"

"They work for beer," Shuibai replied.

Both of the military men looked at him in astonishment, but the Golden Emperor merely smiled.

"They're proud of their work. That's why they do it. They're proud to wear the Low Marsh uniform. They know the work needs to be done, and they do it."

"Low Marsh, of all places," the Iris Lord marveled.

Lord Omel said, "Your Grace, I'd be very pleased to have the position of Fire Lord."

"So be it," replied the Golden Emperor. "You'll have to formally resign your position as Lord of the Highways."

"Done."

The Golden Emperor turned to the Iris Lord. "Lord Tellani. Would you consider assuming the burden of the position of Lord of the Highways? We must make certain the rebellion is entirely suppressed."

The Iris Lord bowed very deeply in his saddle, but not before they saw the look of satisfaction on his face that not even the green half mask could hide. "I would be honored to be of service, My Emperor."

"I shall count on your support," the Golden Emperor replied.

The Iris Lord, that is to say, the new Lord of the Highways, bowed again. "It will be my pleasure."

The new Fire Lord said, "If you will pardon me, Your Grace, I will assume the duties of Fire Lord immediately."

The Golden Emperor smiled. "I have no objection, but it will require a formal announcement before you can move into the Fire Court."

"No trouble. I'm staying with my brother anyhow."

When the Golden Emperor and the new Lord of the Highways and all their retainers rode away, the Fire Lord remained behind. He removed the yellow surcote, rolled it up in a neat bundle, and tucked it into a saddlebag. His first order was, "Tell me what I need to know."

"There is so much," Zashi replied.

"We'd better do it over beer then. My treat." He swung down from his horse and walked along with them.

They put away their equipment and followed Lord Omel into one of the better teahouses in Low Marsh (not Jozatha's). The new Fire Lord treated them to as much food, tobacco, and beer as they could handle, then sat smoking and drinking with them as if they were old comrades. This familiarity did not in anyway diminish their respect for him; on the contrary, it increased it. They were all as polite to him as their coarse manners could manage, and if he thought their language and accent uncouth, he showed no signs of it. By the time the evening was over, the firemen were all very drunk, and Shuibai and Zashi had poured as much information into the new Fire Lord's head as it would hold. The Chief and his Deputy staggered home to bed.

Snuggling together, Shuibai asked, "What happened with Lord Brice? Did you learn how to control the Fire Dragon? Is that why it rained?"

Zashi wrapped his tattooed leg over Shuibai's. "Ah, Lord Brice gave me some advice, but I haven't had a chance to practice it yet." He was blushing brightly.

"What sort of advice?"

"He recommended sex. He said orgasm is the only time humans voluntarily relinquish control of their bodies and minds and surrender to overwhelming sensation. He said that's what I have to do in order to survive being possessed by the Fire Dragon. He said it's quite pleasant if done with a partner who isn't frightened by the, um, 'special effects,' as he called them."

"I'm not afraid."

"Yessss . . . I know you're not. I think we ought to practice."

"I think so, too," Shuibai replied.

So they did. Kanko moved to the kitchen when things got loud, bright, and hot, but being a poor boy from a poor family, being able to fall asleep in a house that was warm enough made him happy.

A great many things happened in the country after that, but all that Shuibai cared about was that he got the funding he requested for his fire company, the new Fire Lord proved a diligent and humane master, and Zashi and the Fire Dragon made their peace. They worked hard and lived happily ever after.

THE END